If you want to know how to shoot a man crossing a narrow bridge, without being near the murder weapon when it is fired, the answer lies in this masterly novel of detection.

In *No Wind of Blame* Georgette Heyer once again shows her amazing talent for solving an ingeniously difficult problem.

'Georgette Heyer has strong claims to be considered the wittiest of detective story writers'
Daily Mail

'Georgette Heyer is second to none'
Sunday Times

By the same author

April Lady
Arabella
Bath Tangle
Beauvallet
Behold, Here's Poison
Black Moth
Black Sheep
A Blunt Instrument
Charity Girl
Civil Contract
The Conqueror
Convenient Marriage
The Corinthian
Cotillion
Cousin Kate
Death in the Stocks
Detection Unlimited
Devil's Club
Duplicate Death
Envious Casca
False Colours
Faro's Daughter
Footsteps in the Dark
The Foundling
They Found Him Dead
Frederica
Friday's Child
Grand Sophy
Infamous Army
Lady of Quality
The Masqueraders
The Nonesuch
Penhallow
Pistols For Two
Powder and Patch
Quiet Gentleman
Regency Buck
Reluctant Widow
Royal Escape
Spanish Bride
Sprig Muslin
Sylvester (The Wicked Uncle)
Talisman Ring
These Old Shades
Toll-gate
The Unfinished Clue
Unknown Ajax
Venetia
Why Shoot a Butler?

GEORGETTE HEYER

No Wind of Blame

GRAFTON BOOKS
A Division of the Collins Publishing Group

LONDON GLASGOW
TORONTO SYDNEY AUCKLAND

Grafton Books
A Division of the Collins Publishing Group
8 Grafton Street, London W1X 3LA

Published by Granada Publishing Limited
in Panther Books 1963
Reprinted 1964, 1965, 1967, 1969, 1971, 1973,
1977, 1981, 1983, 1988

First published in Great Britain by
William Heinemann Ltd 1939

ISBN 0-586-02766-1

Printed and bound in Great Britain by
Collins, Glasgow

Set in Times

1

'The Prince is coming by the one-forty-five. That means he'll be here in time for tea. Well, I do call that nice!'

No answer being made to this remark, the lady at the head of the table repeated it, adding: 'I'm sure you'll like him. He's such a gentleman, if you know what I mean.'

Miss Cliffe raised her eyes from her own correspondence. 'Sorry, Aunt Ermyntrude: I wasn't attending. The Prince – oh yes! Then the big car will be wanted to meet the train. I'll see to it.'

'Yes, do, dearie.' Mrs Carter restored the Prince's letter to its envelope, and stretched out a plump arm towards the toast-rack. She was a large woman, who had enjoyed, in youth, the advantages of golden hair and a pink-and-white complexion. Time had committed some ravages with both these adjuncts, but a lavish use of peroxide and the productions of a famous beauty specialist really worked wonders. If the gold of Ermyntrude's carefully waved hair was a trifle metallic, the colour in her cheeks was all and more than it had ever been. Artificial light was kinder to her than the daylight, but she never allowed this tiresome fact to worry her, applying her rouge each morning with a lavish yet skilled hand which recalled the days when she had adorned the front row of the chorus; and touching up her lashes with mascara, or (in her more dashing moments) with a species of vivid blue that was supposed to deepen the perfectly natural blue of her eyes.

The exigencies of this facial toilet apparently exhausted her matutinal energy, for she never put on her corsets until fortified by breakfast, and invariably appeared in the dining-room in a robe of silk and lace which she referred to as her *négligé*. Mary Cliffe, who had never been able to accustom herself to the sight of Ermyntrude's flowing sleeves trailing negligently across the butter-dishes, and occasionally, if Ermyntrude were more than usually careless, dipping into her coffee, had once suggested, with perfect tact, that she really ought to stay in bed for breakfast. But Ermyntrude was of a cheerful and a sociable disposition, and liked to preside over the breakfast-table, and to discover what were her family's plans for the day.

Mary Cliffe, who addressed her by the title of aunt, was not, in fact, her niece, but the cousin, and ward, of her husband, Willis Carter. She was a good-looking young woman in the early twenties, with a great deal of common sense, and a tidiness of mind which years of association with Wally Carter had only served to strengthen. She was fond of Wally, in a mild way, but she was not in the least blind to his faults, and had not suffered even a small pang of jealousy when, five years before, he had, rather surprisingly, married Ermyntrude Fanshawe. The possession of a small but securely tied-up income of her own had ensured her education at a respectable boarding-school, but her holidays, owing to Wally's nomadic tendencies and frequent insolvencies, had been spent in a succession of dingy boarding-houses, and enlivened only by the calls of creditors, and the recurrent dread that Wally would succumb to the attractions of one or other of his landladies. When, during a brief period of comparative affluence, he had patronized a large hotel at a fashionable watering-place, and had had the luck to captivate Ermyntrude Fanshawe, who was an extremely rich widow, Mary, with her customary good sense, had regarded his marriage as providential. Ermyntrude was undoubtedly flamboyant, and very often vulgar, but she was good-natured, and extremely generous, and so far from resenting the existence of her husband's young ward, behaved to her with the utmost kindness, and would not hear of her leaving Wally's roof to earn her own living. If Mary wanted to work, she said, she could act as her secretary at Palings, and perhaps help with the housekeeping. 'Besides, dearie, you'll be a real nice companion for my Vicky,' she added.

This had seemed to Mary to be a fair arrangement, although, when she met Vicky Fanshawe, a precocious schoolgirl, five years her junior, she could not feel that they were destined to become soul-mates.

Vicky, however, was being educated, at immense expense, first at a fashionable school on the south coast of England, and later at a still more fashionable finishing-school in Switzerland. During the last two years, she had spent her holidays abroad with Ermyntrude, so that Mary had hardly encountered her. Her education was now considered to be completed, and she was living at home, a source of pride and joy to her mother, but not precisely an ideal companion for Mary, who was alternately amused and exasperated by her.

She reflected, on this warm September morning, that the presence of a Russian prince in the house would be productive of all Vicky's most tiresome antics, and inquired in tones of foreboding whether the Prince were young.

'Well, I wouldn't say young,' replied Ermyntrude, helping herself to marmalade. 'He's at what I call the right age, if you know what I mean. You never saw anyone so distinguished – and then his manners! Well, you don't meet with such polish in England, not that I'm one to run down my own country, but there it is.'

'I don't like Russians much,' said Mary perversely. 'They always seem to talk so much and do so little.'

'You shouldn't be narrow-minded, dear. Besides, he

isn't actually a Russian, as I've told you a dozen times. He's a Georgian – he used to have a lovely estate in the Caucasus, which is somewhere near the Black Sea, I believe.'

At this moment the door opened, and Wally Carter came into the room. He was a medium-sized man, who had been good-looking in youth, but who had run rather badly to seed. His blue eyes were inclined to be bloodshot, and his mouth, under a drooping moustache, sagged a little. In the days when he had courted Ermyntrude, his fondness for strong liquor had not made him quite careless of appearances, but five years spent in opulent circumstances had caused him to deteriorate lamentably. He was naturally slovenly, and his clothes never seemed to fit him, nor his hair to be properly brushed. He was generally amiable, but grumbled a good deal, not in any bad-tempered spirit, but in a gently complaining way to which none of his family paid the slightest heed.

'Here you are, then!' said his wife, by way of greeting. 'Touch the bell, Mary, there's a love! We couldn't have had a better day, could we, Wally? Though, of course, as I always say, to see Palings at its best you ought to see it when the rhododendrons are out.'

'Who wants to see it?' inquired Wally, casting a lack-lustre glance towards the window.

'Now, Wally! As though you didn't know as well as I do that the Prince is coming today!'

This reminder seemed to set the seal to Wally's dissatisfaction. He lowered the newspaper behind which he had entrenched himself. 'Not that fellow you picked up at Antibes?' he said.

A spark of anger gleamed in Ermyntrude's eyes. 'I don't see that you've any call to be vulgar. I should hope I didn't go picking up men at my time of life! Alexis was introduced to me by Lady Fisher, I'll have you know.'

'Alexis!' ejaculated Wally. 'You needn't think I'm going to go about calling the fellow by a silly name like that, because I'm not.'

'You'll call him Prince Varasashvili, and that's all there is to it,' said Ermyntrude tartly.

'Well, I won't. For one thing, I don't like it, and for another, I couldn't remember it – not that I want to, because I don't. And if you take my advice, you'll be careful how *you* say it. If you start introducing this fellow as Prince Varasash – whatever-it-is, you'll have people saying you've been mixing your drinks.'

'I must say it's a bit of a tongue-twister,' remarked Mary. 'You'll have to write it down for me, Aunt Ermy.'

'It'll be quite all right if you just call him Prince,' said Ermyntrude kindly.

'Well, if that's your idea of quite all right it isn't mine,' said Wally. 'Nice fool you'll look when you say Prince, and find the poor old dog wagging his tail at you.'

This aspect of the situation struck Ermyntrude most forcibly. 'I hadn't thought of that,' she admitted. 'I must say, it does make things a bit awkward. I mean, you know what Prince is! It would be awful if I went and said, "Get off that chair, Prince," as I don't doubt I will do, thanks to the way you spoil that dog, Wally, and Alexis thought I was speaking to him. Oh well, Prince will have to be tied up, that's all.'

'Now, that's one thing I won't put up with,' said Wally. 'It's little enough I ever ask, but have my poor old dog tied up for the sake of a Russian prince I don't know and don't want to know, I won't. If you'd asked me before inviting the fellow, I should have said don't, because I don't like foreigners; but as usual, no one consulted me.'

Ermyntrude looked concerned. 'Well, I'm sorry you're so set against Alexis, Wally, but honestly he doesn't *speak* foreign.'

Wally paid not the slightest heed to this, but said: 'A set of wasters, that's what those White Russians are. I'm not surprised they had a revolution. Serves them right! What was this chap of yours doing at Antibes? You needn't tell me! Living on some rich woman, that's what he was doing!' He found that his ward had raised her eyes quickly to his face, and was flushing rather uncomfortably, and added: 'Yes, I know what you're thinking, but I shall be a wealthy man one of these days, so the cases aren't the same. When my Aunt Clara dies, I shall pay Ermyntrude back every penny.'

Mary made no remark. Wally's Aunt Clara, who had been an inmate for the past ten years of a Home for Mentally Deficients, was well known to her by repute, having served Wally as an excuse for his various extravagances ever since she could remember.

Ermyntrude gave a chuckle. 'Yes, we all know about this precious Aunt Clara of yours, dearie. All I can say is, I hope you may get her money, not that there's any question of paying back between us, because there isn't; and if you're trying to cast it up at me that I grudge you anything, you know I don't grudge a penny, except for what you squander on things which we won't mention.'

This sinister reference, accompanied as it was by a rising note in his wife's voice, quelled Wally. He hastily passed his cup to her for more coffee, and greeted, with frank relief, the sudden and tempestuous entrance of his stepdaughter.

This damsel came into the room on a wave of dogs. Two cocker spaniels, Ermyntrude's Pekinese, and an overgrown Borzoi cavorted about her, and since one of the cockers had apparently been in the river, a strong aroma of dog at once pervaded the room.

'The Sports Girl!' remarked Mary, casting an experienced eye over Vicky's costume.

This consisted of a pair of slacks, an Aertex shirt, and sandals which displayed two rows of reddened toe-nails.

'Oh, darling, not the spaniels! Oh, if Prince hasn't been in the water again!' exclaimed Ermyntrude distressfully.

'Poor sweets!' Vicky crooned, ejecting them from the room. 'Lovely, lovely pets, not now! Lie down, Roy! Good Roy, lie down!'

'What's this idea of bringing a pack of dogs in to breakfast?' demanded Wally, repulsing the advances of the Borzoi. 'Lie down, will you? You might as well try to eat in a damned menagerie!' He added, after a glance at Vicky's costume: 'What's more, it puts me off my food to see you in that get-up. I don't know why your mother allows it.'

'Oh, let her alone, Wally!' said Ermyntrude. 'I'm sure she looks as pretty as paint, whatever she wears. Not but what I don't care for trousers myself. Time and again when I've seen some fat creature waddling about in them, I've thought to myself, well, my girl, if you could see your own bottom you'd soon change into a skirt.'

'Darling! I practically haven't got a bottom!' protested Vicky, sliding into her place opposite to Mary.

'Nor you have, ducky. That's one way you *don't* take after me!'

Vicky smiled abstractedly, and began to read her letters, while her mother sat surveying her with fond admiration.

She was indeed a very pretty girl, with pale corn-coloured hair, which she wore rather long, and curled into a thick bush of ringlets at the base of her neck; and large blue eyes that gazed innocently forth from between darkened lashes. Even the ruthless plucking of her eye-brows, and the pencilling of improbable arches percepti-bly higher than the shadows of the original brows, failed to ruin her beauty. Her complexion varied in accordance with her mood, or her costume, but she had no need of powder to whiten a naturally fair skin.

'I suppose you know about this prince coming to stay?' said Wally, in a grumbling tone. 'What your mother wants with him I don't know, though I dare say you're as bad as she is, and think there's something fine about having a prince in the house.'

'Oh, I think it's lovely!' Vicky said.

This artless response disgusted Wally so much that he relapsed into silence.

Ermyntrude had slit open another letter, and suddenly exclaimed, 'Ah!' in an exultant tone. A triumphant smile curled her lips. 'There's nothing like a prince!' she said simply. 'The Derings have accepted!'

Even Wally seemed pleased by this announcement, but he said, with a glance in Mary's direction, that he didn't think the Prince had anything to do with it. 'I wouldn't mind betting young Dering's home,' he said.

Mary coloured, but replied calmly: 'I told you he was, yesterday.'

Vicky emerged from the clouds of some apparently beatific dream to inquire: 'Who is he?'

'He's an old friend of Mary's,' said Wally.

'The boy-friend?' asked Vicky, interested.

'No, *not* the boy-friend,' said Mary. 'His people live at the Manor, and I've known him ever since we came to live here. He's a Chancery barrister. You must remember him, surely!'

'No, but he sounds frightfully dull,' said Vicky.

'Well, he's a very nice young fellow,' said Wally. 'And if he wants to marry Mary I shall make no objection. No objection at all. What's more, I shall leave her all my money.'

'When you get it,' said Ermyntrude, with a chuckle. 'I'm sure I hope he will ask Mary to marry him, because it would be what I call a good match, and what's more, the man that gets you, my dear, will be very lucky, whatever his people may say.'

'Thank you!' said Mary. 'But as he hasn't asked me to marry him, I don't think we need worry about what his people would say, Aunt Ermy.' Conscious of her heightened colour, she made haste to change the subject, looking across the table at Vicky, and saying: 'By the way, what got you out of bed so bright and early this morning? I heard you carolling in the bath at an ungodly hour.'

'Oh, I went out to see if I could get a rabbit!'

Mary's lips twitched. 'I *thought* this was a Sports-Girl Day! Don't tell me you weren't wearing sandals and painted toe-nails, because it would spoil the whole picture for me!'

'But I was!' said Vicky, opening her eyes very wide.

'You must have looked a treat!'

'Yes, I do think I looked rather nice,' Vicky agreed wholeheartedly.

'Did you shoot anything?'

'Oh yes, very nearly!'

'That's where you take after your father, ducky,' said Ermyntrude. 'I never knew such a man for sport! Three times he went to Africa, big-game shooting. That was before he met me, of course.'

'Well, if you call missing rabbits taking after her father, I don't,' remarked Wally. 'As far as I can make out, her father never missed anything. It's a great pity he didn't, if you ask me, for if he had perhaps I shouldn't have had to live in a house full of bits of wild animals. I dare say there are people who like keeping their umbrellas in elephants' legs, and having gongs framed in hippo tusks, and tables made out of rhinoceros hides, and leopard skins chucked over their sofas, and heads stuck up all round the walls, but I'm not one of them, and I've never pretended that I was. You might as well live in the Natural History Museum, and be done with it.'

'And the Bawtrys are coming too!' said Ermyntrude, who had paid not the least attention to this speech. 'That'll make us ten, all told.'

'I think Alan would like to come to the party,' murmured Vicky.

Ermyntrude folded her lips for a moment. 'Well, he'll have to like,' she said. 'I don't mean that I've got anything against him, nor his sister either, if it comes to that, but have Harold White here with the Derings and the Bawtrys I won't, and that's flat!'

'Oh, I hate Mr White!' agreed Vicky.

'Well, ducky, I can't ask Alan and Janet without their father, now can I? I mean, you know what he is, and this being a dinner-party, and him a sort of connection of Wally's. It isn't like asking the young people over to tennis, when he wouldn't expect to be invited.'

'That's right!' said Wally. 'Crab poor old Harold! I thought it wouldn't be long before you started on him. I'd like to know what harm he's ever done you.'

'I don't like him,' said Ermyntrude. 'Some people might say he's done me plenty of harm leading you into ways we won't discuss at the breakfast-table, let alone planting himself down in the Dower House.'

'You never made any bones about letting it to him, did you?'

'No, I didn't, not with you asking me to let him rent the place, and saying he was a relation of yours. But if I'd known what sort of an influence he was going to be on you, and no more related to you than the man in the moon – '

'Well, that's where you're wrong, because he is related to me,' interrupted Wally. 'I forget just how it goes, but I know we've got the same great-great-grandfather. Or am I wrong? There may have been three greats, not that it matters.'

'Ancestors,' said Vicky.

Ermyntrude refused to allow a false trail she quite clearly perceived. 'It's no relationship at all to my way of thinking, and you know very well *that* isn't what I've got against Harold White, however hard you may try to turn the subject.'

'The Bawtrys are stuffy,' said Vicky suddenly.

'Well, they are a bit,' confessed her mother. 'But it's something to get the best people to come just for a friendly dinner-party, and I don't mind telling you, lovey, that they never have before.'

'And the Derings are stuffy.'

'Not Lady Dering. She's a good sort, and always was, and she's behaved to me more like a lady than a lot of others I could name.'

'And Hugh Dering is stuffy,' said Vicky obstinately. 'It's going to be a lousy party.'

'Not with the Prince,' said Ermyntrude.

'If anyone wants to know what I think, which I don't suppose they do,' interpoluted Wally, 'this Prince of yours will just about put the finishing touch to it. However, it's nothing to do with me, and all I say is, don't expect me to entertain him!'

Ermyntrude looked a little perturbed. 'But, Wally, you'll have to help entertain him! Now, don't be tiresome, there's a dear! You know we arranged it all weeks ago, and honestly I know you'll like Alexis. Besides, you won't have to do much, except take him out shooting, like we said.'

Wally rose from the table, tucking the newspaper under his arm. 'There you go again! If I've told you once, I've told you a dozen times that I don't like shooting. And now I come to think of it, I lent my gun to Harold, and he hasn't returned it yet, so I can't shoot even if I wanted to.'

This was too much, even for a woman of Ermyntrude's kindly disposition. She said hotly: 'Then you'll tell Harold White to return it, Wally, and if you don't, I will! The idea of your lending poor Geoffrey's gun without so much as by your leave!'

'I suppose I ought to have sat down with a planchette, or something,' said Wally.

Ermyntrude flushed, and said in a tearful voice: 'How dare you talk like that? Sometimes I think you don't care how much you hurt my feelings!'

'Oh, I do think you're quite too brutal and awful!' exclaimed Vicky.

'All right, all right!' Wally said, retreating to the door. 'There's no need for you to start! If a man can't make a perfectly innocent remark without creating a scene – now stop it, Ermy! There's nothing for you to cry about. Anyone would think Harold was going to hurt the gun!'

'*Do* get it back!' said Vicky. 'You're upsetting mother simply dreadfully!'

'Oh, all right!' replied Wally, goaded. 'Anything for a quiet life!'

As soon as he had left the room, Vicky abandoned the protective pose she had assumed, and went on eating her breakfast. Ermyntrude glanced apologetically at Mary, and said: 'I'm sorry, Mary, but what with that White, and him being so tiresome, and then my poor first husband's gun on top of everything, I just couldn't help bursting out.'

'No, he's in one of his annoying moods,' agreed Mary. 'I shouldn't worry, though. He'll get over it.'

'It's all that Harold White,' insisted Ermyntrude. 'He's been worse ever since he got under his influence.'

'I don't think he has, really,' said Mary, always fair-minded. 'I'm afraid it's just natural deterioration.'

'Well, all I can say is that I wish the Whites would go and live somewhere else. They've spoiled the place for me.'

'One does seem to *feel* White's influence,' said Vicky, with an artistic shiver.

Mary got up. 'Don't mix your roles!' she advised. 'That one doesn't go with the Sports-Girl outfit.'

'Oh, I'd forgotten I was wearing slacks!' said Vicky, quite unoffended. 'I think I've had enough of the Sports Girl. I'll change.'

Mary felt disinclined to enter into Vicky's vagaries at such an early hour of the morning, and, with a rather perfunctory smile, she gathered up her letters, and left the room.

It was part of her self-imposed duty to interview the very competent cook-housekeeper each morning, but before penetrating beyond the baize door to the servants' quarters, she collected a basket and some scissors, and went out into the gardens to cut fresh flowers for the house.

It was an extremely fine morning, and although Palings, as Ermyntrude had said, was best seen in springtime, when its rhododendrons and azaleas were in bloom, neither the sombre foliage of these shrubs, covering the long fall of ground to the stream at its foot, nor the glimpse of Harold White's house upon the opposite slope, detracted, in Mary's eyes, from its beauty. Ermyntrude employed a large staff of gardeners, and besides lawns where few weeds dared show their heads, and acres of kitchen-gardens and glass-houses, there was a sunk Italian garden, a rose-garden, a rock-garden, with a lily-pond in the centre, and broad herbaceous borders in which

Ermyntrude's own taste for set-effects had never been allowed to run riot.

Mary reflected, with a wry smile, that Ermyntrude was the best-natured woman imaginable. Even in her own house she allowed herself to be overruled on all matters of taste, and not only did she acquiesce in the decisions made for her, but she quite seriously endeavoured to school her eye to appreciate what she believed to be good taste. But although she felt a certain pride in her slopes of rhododendrons (which were, indeed, one of the sights of the county), Mary knew quite well that in her heart of hearts she thought this wild part of her garden rather untidy, and very much preferred the view of formal beds, and clipped yews, and impeccably raked carriage-drive, which was to be obtained from the front windows of the house. From these windows, moreover, no disturbing glimpse of the Dower House could be caught.

There was nothing intrinsically objectionable about the Dower House, but its temporary inmate, Harold White, had, during the course of two years, invested it, in Ermyntrude's eyes, with such disagreeable attributes, that she had not only been known to shudder at the sight of its grey roof, visible through the trees, but had lately carried her dislike of it to such a pitch that she would sometimes refuse even to stroll down the winding path that led through the rhododendron thickets to the rustic bridge that crossed the stream at the foot of the garden. It was a charming walk, but it was spoiled for Ermyntrude by the fact that from the little bridge an uninterrupted view of the Dower House, situated half-way up the farther slope, smote the eye. The bridge had been thrown across the stream to provide an easy way of communication between the two houses, a circumstance which, however convenient it might have been to the original owner of Palings, filled Ermyntrude with annoyance. She had more than once contemplated having the bridge removed, and had compromised, a few months previously, by erecting a wicket-gate on the Palings side of the stream. But although this might, as she confided to Mary, have seemed pointed enough, it had no apparent effect on Harold White, who continued to stroll across the bridge to call on Wally whenever he chose, or had opportunity to do so.

Fortunately, this was not often. Unlike Wally, White was not a gentleman of leisure, but the manager of a small group of collieries in the district. His daughter, Janet, kept house for him; and he had one son, a few years younger than Janet, who lived at home, and was articled to a solicitor in the neighbouring town of Fritton. Before Wally's marriage to the rich Mrs Fanshawe, White, whose salary never seemed to cover his expenses, had lived rather uncomfortably in a small villa in the town itself; but when Wally came to live at Palings, it had not taken Harold White long to discover that he was remotely related to him. The rest had been easy. Wally had found a kindred spirit in his connection, and had had very little difficulty in persuading Ermyntrude to lease the Dower House, which happened, providentially, to be unoccupied, to White, at a reduced rental. From this time, insisted Ermyntrude, Wally's increasing predilection for strong drink, and his flights into the realms of even less respectable pursuits, might fairly be said to date. Harold White encouraged him to drink more than was good for him, prompted him to back horses, and introduced him to undesirable acquaintances.

Mary, who disliked White, yet could not agree with Ermyntrude that he was Wally's *âme damnée*. Having lived with Wally for many more years than had Ermyntrude, she suffered from fewer illusions, and had long since realized that his character lacked moral fibre. He gravitated naturally into low society, and could be trusted upon all occasions to take the line of least resistance. While giving him due credit for having behaved to her with great kindness during the years of his guardianship, Mary knew him too well to allow herself to be blinded to the fact that the small income, advanced quarterly by her trustees to pay for her upkeep and education, had been extremely useful to Wally. Nor could she help regretting sometimes that her father, Wally's uncle, had not chosen to leave her a ward in Chancery rather than the ward of his one surviving relative.

This slightly shamefaced thought was in Mary's mind as she carried her basket of roses into the house. Wally had been a handicap to her during her schooldays; now that she was grown up, and marriageable, he was proving a still greater handicap.

She had denied that any understanding existed between herself and Mr Hugh Dering, but, although this was strictly true, she could not help feeling that Hugh's interest in her sprang from something more than long-standing acquaintance. There was a bond of very real sympathy between them, and although Dering's residence was in London, where he might be presumed to encounter girls prettier, more attractive, and certainly more eligible than Mary Cliffe, none of these unknown damsels seemed to have captivated his fancy, and whenever he came to stay with his parents, one of his first actions was to seek Mary out. What his mother, who was notoriously easy-going, thought about his predilection for her society, Mary did not know, but that Sir William Dering regarded Wally Carter with disfavour she was well aware. She had been surprised to hear of the Derings' acceptance of Ermyntrude's invitation, for although they were, like everyone else in the neighbourhood, on calling-terms with the Carters, they had never until now accepted nor extended invitations to dinner-parties. Mary wondered whether Hugh was indeed at the bottom of it, for she could not suppose that the presence of a Georgian prince would prove as tempting a bait as Ermyntrude so firmly believed. In this, she slightly misjudged Lady Dering.

2

Sir William Dering, whom no one had ever called Bill, was quite as astonished as Mary Cliffe when he discovered that he was to dine at Palings in the immediate future. He bent a stare upon his wife, which was rendered all the more alarming by his bushy eyebrows, and desired to know whether she had taken leave of her senses.

'Not only sane, but sober,' replied Lady Dering, quite unimpressed by the martial note in Sir William's voice. 'I wouldn't miss it for worlds! The amazing Ermyntrude has dug up a Russian prince!'

'Good God!' ejaculated Sir William. 'You're not going to tell me, I trust, that you accepted that invitation for the sake of meeting some wretched foreign prince?'

His wife considered this, a humorous gleam in her pleasant grey eyes. 'Well, not quite entirely. I mean, not for the Prince alone. But a Russian prince in that setting! You couldn't expect me to miss anything as rich as that!'

This response, so far from mollifying Sir William, made him look even more shocked than before. 'My dear Ruth, aren't you letting your sense of humour carry you too far? Dash it, you can't accept people's hospitality just to make fun of them!'

'Dear old silly!' said Lady Dering affectionately, 'I wasn't going to.'

'You said – '

'No, darling, far from it. I never make fun of anyone except you. I am just going to be gloriously entertained.'

'Well, I don't like it at all. I haven't anything against Mrs Carter, beyond the fact of her being a damned common woman, made up to the eyes, and reeking of scent, but that fellow, Carter, I bar. We've always kept them at arm's-length, and now heaven knows what you've let us in for!'

'An occasional invitation to them to dine.'

'But why?' demanded Sir William. 'Don't tell me it's because of a Russian prince! I never heard such nonsense!'

'Dear William, I like you so much when you're stupid! The amazing Ermyntrude is going to build the hospital for us.'

'*What?*'

'Not with her own fair hands, dearest. She's going to give us a really big cheque, though. I don't call a few dinner-parties much of a price to pay.'

'I call it disgusting!' said Sir William strongly.

'You may call it what you please, my dear, but you know as well as I do that that's how these things are done. Ermyntrude's a kind soul, but she's no fool, and she has a daughter to launch. I don't in the least mind being useful to her if she'll make our hospital possible.'

'Do you mean to tell me you're going to drive some sordid bargain with the woman?'

'Dear me, no! Nothing of the kind. I shall merely tell her how much we all want her to join the committee, and how we hope she and her husband will be free to dine with us next month, to meet Charles and Pussy, when they come to stay. Not a breath of sordidness, I promise you!'

'It makes me sick!' declared Sir William. 'You had better go a step further while you are about it, and tell Carter how delighted we should be to welcome his ward into our family.'

'That would be excessive,' replied Lady Dering calmly.

'Besides, I don't know that I should be altogether delighted.'

'You surprise me!' said her lord, with awful sarcasm.

The arrival upon the scene of their son and heir put an end to this particular topic of discussion. Hugh Dering, in grey flannel trousers, and an aged tweed coat, came strolling across the lawn towards them, and sat down beside his mother on the wooden garden seat.

He was a large, and sufficiently good-looking young man, not quite thirty years old, who was engaged in building up a practice at the Chancery Bar. He had his mother's eyes, but his father's stern mouth, and could look extremely pleasant, or equally forbidding, according to the mood of the moment.

Just now, he was looking pleasant. He began to fill a pipe, remarking cheerfully: 'Well, Ma? Secret conclave?'

'No, not a bit. Your father and I were just discussing tomorrow's party.'

Hugh grinned appreciatively. 'Ought to be pretty good value, I should think. Were you asked to shoot as well, sir?'

'No, I was not,' replied Sir William. 'And if I had been I should have refused!'

'I wasn't nearly so proud,' said Hugh, gently pressing the tobacco down into the bowl of his pipe.

'Are you telling me that you're going to shoot there tomorrow?'

'Rather! Why not?'

'If I'd known you wanted to shoot, you could have taken my place,' said Sir William, who belonged to a syndicate. 'You'd have had better company and better sport. The way the Palings' shoot has been allowed to deteriorate since Fanshawe's death is a scandal. You'll find the birds as wild as be – damned – if you see any birds at all.'

'Then I shan't shoot anything,' responded Hugh fatalistically. 'I'm not good enough for your crowd, in any case, sir. You're all so grand, with your loaders and your second guns. I can't cope at all.'

Sir William relapsed into silence. His wife, who knew him to be brooding over the changed times that had made it impossible for him any longer to run his own shoot, and thus see to it that his son was not flustered by two guns and a loader, diverted his attention by asking Hugh if he had yet met Vicky Fanshawe.

'No, that's a pleasure to come. Mary tells me she has to be seen to be believed.'

'I saw her in Fritton the other day,' said Lady Dering. 'Very pretty, rather what one imagines her mother might have been like at the same age. Why did Mary say she had to be seen to be believed?'

'I gather that she's a turn in herself. Full of histrionic talent.'

'She looked rather sweet. They tell me that all the young men in the neighbourhood are wild about her.'

'Gentlemen prefer blondes, in fact,' said Hugh, striking a match. 'Is the Russian prince one of the more eligible suitors?'

'Good gracious, I don't know! What an engaging idea, though! We *shall* have fun tomorrow!'

Sir William snorted audibly, but his son only laughed, and inquired who else was to be of the party.

'Well, I don't know the extent of the party, but the Bawtrys are going,' replied Lady Dering.

'The Bawtrys?' exclaimed Sir William, surprised out of his resolve to take no part in a conversation he found distasteful.

'Ermyntrude *is* getting on, isn't she?' said Hugh. 'I thought Connie Bawtry was stoutly Old Guard?'

'Ha!' said Sir William. 'Another of the hospital committe! Upon my soul, things have come to a pretty pass!'

'Oh, is *that* the racket?' said Hugh. 'I rather wondered.'

'That's my racket,' corrected his mother. 'Not Connie Bawtry's. At least, it is really, only she won't own it.'

'Then what the devil takes her to Palings?' demanded Sir William.

'God, apparently. It's all right, dear; I'm not being profane. Connie's been Changed. She's got under God-Control, or something, and she says what the world needs is God-guided citizens, and if you learn Absolute Love you don't mind about Ermyntrude's accent, or Wally Carter's habits.'

'Gone Groupy, has she?' said Hugh. 'How rotten for Tom!'

'Well, it is rather, because Connie's started forgiving him for all sorts of things he never knew he'd done. We're hoping that she'll get over it quickly, because she's president of the Women's Conservative Association, besides running the Mothers, and the Village Club, and now that she's a God-guided citizen she simply hasn't a moment to attend to Good Works. I don't know why it is, but when people get Changed they never seem to be as nice as they were before.'

'Tomfoolery!' said Sir William. 'I thought she had more sense!'

'It's since Elizabeth got married, and went to India,' explained his wife. 'Poor dear, I expect she suddenly felt rather aimless, and that's how it happened. Only I thought I'd better warn you both.'

'Good God!' said Sir William. 'She won't *talk* that stuff, will she?'

'Oh yes, she's bound to! As far as I can make out, you practically have to testify, if you're God-controlled.'

'At a dinner-party?' said Sir William awfully.

'Anywhere, dearest.'

'But you don't talk about God at dinner! Damme, it's not decent!'

'No, it does make it all seem rather cheap, doesn't it?' agreed Lady Dering. 'However, they seem to think that a good thing, and after all, it's nothing to do with us.'

'I wish more than ever that you had not been misguided enough to accept that woman's invitation!'

'Oh, I don't!' said Hugh. 'I'm definitely out to enjoy myself. What with a dizzy blonde, a Russian prince, and Connie Bawtry gone Groupy, I foresee a rare evening. Mary was rather dreading the Russian Prince when last I saw her, but she's bound to appreciate a really farcical situation. I hope the Prince turns out to be up to standard. I suppose he'll have arrived by now.'

The Prince had indeed arrived, and was at that moment bowing over his hostess's plump hand. He was very dark, and of uncertain age, but extremely handsome, blessed with the slimmest of figures, very gleaming teeth, and the most elegant address. In fact, when he raised Ermyntrude's hand to his lips, she could not refrain from casting a triumphant glance towards her husband and Mary.

'Dear lady!' murmured the Prince. 'As radiant as ever! I am enchanted! And the little Vicky! But no! This is not the little Vicky!'

He had turned to Mary, with his well-manicured hand held out. She put hers into it, saying rather inadequately: 'How do you do?' He continued to hold her hand, but looked towards Ermyntrude with a question in his smiling, dark eyes.

'No, this is my husband's ward, Miss Cliffe,' said Ermyntrude. 'And here is my husband. Wally, this is Prince Varasashvili.'

'Delighted!' the Prince said, releasing Mary's hand to clasp Wally's. 'Of you I have heard so much!'

Wally looked quite alarmed, but before he could demand to know who had been telling tales about him, Ermyntrude intervened with an offer to escort the Prince to his room.

Though perfectly well-meant, his remark had added considerably to Wally's prejudice against him, and he had no sooner gone away upstairs in Ermyntrude's wake, than Wally began to disparage his manners, tailoring, and general appearance. 'A gigolo, that's what he is,' he told Mary. 'Where does he get the money from to go about dressed up to the nines like that? Tell me that!'

Mary was quite unable to oblige him, but since she had not discovered from Ermyntrude that the Prince pursued any gainful occupation, she could not help feeling that there might be some truth in Wally's guess. Having been brought up exclusively in England, she was charitably inclined to ascribe the Prince's rather too smart attire to the fact of his being a foreigner. She thought that he looked out-of-place in the English countryside, and although willing to make every allowance for him, could not help hoping that his visit was not to be of long duration.

Ermyntrude, meanwhile, had led her guest upstairs to the best spare room, and had expressed an anxious hope that he would be comfortable there. As the apartment was extremely spacious, and furnished in the height of luxury, it seemed probable that he would be; but Ermyntrude, with purely British ideas about princes, could never see her Alexis without also perceiving an entirely apocryphal background of wealth, palaces, and royal purple.

He assured her that his comfort was a foregone conclusion, and she made haste to point out to him that a private bathroom led out of the apartment, and that if he wanted anything he had only to touch the bell.

He waved away the suggestion that he could want anything more than had been provided, and once more kissed her hand, saying, as he retained it in his clasp: 'Now, at last, I see you in your own setting! You must let me tell you that it is charming. And you! so beautiful! so gracious!'

No one had ever talked to Ermyntrude in this way, not even the late Geoffrey Fanshawe, in the first flush of his infatuation for her. She had, in fact, been more used to listen to strictures upon her lack of breeding; and, being a very humble-minded woman, had always accepted her neighbours' obvious valuation of her as the true one. It was, therefore, delightful to hear herself extolled, and by no less a person than a prince; and she made no attempt either to draw her hand away, or to discourage further flattery. She even blushed rather prettily under her rouge and her powder, and inquired artlessly whether Alexis thought that the setting became her.

'You are so many-sided: everything becomes you! You would be beautiful in a garret,' he replied earnestly. 'Yet – I may say it? – always since I have first seen you, I have felt that something there is lacking in your life. I think you are not understood. You have never been understood. On the surface you are so gay that everyone says: "She has everything to make her happy, the beautiful Mrs Carter: a husband, a lovely daughter, much money, much beauty!" It is perhaps only I who have seen behind the sparkle in those eyes, something – how shall I express it? – of loneliness, of a soul that is not guessed at, even by those who stand nearest to you.'

This was most gratifying, and although Ermyntrude had not previously suspected that she was misunderstood, she began to realize that it was so, and reflected that one of the more attractive attributes of foreign gentlemen was their subtle perception. She gave a faint sigh, and bestowed upon the Prince a very speaking glance. 'It's funny, isn't it?' she said. 'I seemed to know, right at the start, that you were what I call understanding.'

He pressed her hand. 'There is a bond of sympathy between us. You too are aware of it, for you are not like the rest of your country-women.'

Ermyntrude believed firmly that England was the best country in the world, and the English immeasurably superior to any other race, but she accepted this remark as a compliment, as indeed it was meant to be, and at once began to enumerate the characteristics that made her different from her compatriots. These were many, and varied from a hatred of tweeds and brogue shoes, to a sensitiveness of soul, which was hidden (as Alexis has so rightly supposed) under a cheerful demeanour, and a tolerance of foreigners rarely to be met with in other Englishwomen.

'You are a true cosmopolitan,' the Prince assured her.

Ermyntrude would have been perfectly happy to have continued this conversation indefinitely, but at that moment the Prince's suitcases were borne into the room, so she rather regretfully withdrew.

She rejoined Wally and Mary in a somewhat exalted mood. Her gait was queenly enough to attract Wally's attention, and he immediately demanded to be told why she was sailing about like a dying swan. She relaxed sufficiently to inform him pithily that if he wanted to be vulgar he could take his vulgarity to those that liked it; for in spite of having grace, beauty, and a lonely soul, she was also a woman of spirit, and saw no reason for putting up with rudeness from Wally, or from anyone else. But this was only a temporary emergence from the cloud of abstraction in which she had wrapped herself, and she sank into an armchair, with really very creditable grace for a woman of her size, and became so aloof from her surroundings that she failed to notice that the dog, Prince, was lying curled up under her husband's chair. Her discovery of his unwanted presence coincided rather unfortunately with the human-Prince's entry into the room, when the spaniel, who was of a friendly disposition, at once rushed forward to accord the stranger an effusive welcome.

Ermyntrude's air of pensiveness fell from her as soon as she saw the spaniel jumping up at her guest, and she exclaimed with strong indignation: 'If you haven't let that Prince come into the house, Wally! I told you the stable was the place for him!'

'There, I knew what it would be!' said Wally, not without satisfaction. He observed a slightly startled look upon the other Prince's face, and added: 'It's all right, she doesn't mean you. Down, Prince. Good old dog, lie down then!'

'Ah!' the Prince said, showing his gleaming teeth in a smile of perfect comprehension. 'There are two of us then, and this fine fellow is a prince also! It is very amusing! But you will not banish him on my account, I beg! I am very fond of dogs, I assure you.'

'He oughtn't to be in the drawing-room at all,' said Ermyntrude. 'He smells.'

'Ah, poor fellow!' said the Prince, sitting down, and stroking the spaniel. 'Look, Trudinka, what sad eyes he makes at you! But you are a lucky prince, and I shall not pity you, for you are more lucky than I am, do you see, with a fine home of your own, which no Bolsheviki will burn to the ground.'

'Is that what was done to your house?' asked Ermyntrude, shocked.

He made a gesture with his hands. 'Fortune of war, Trudinka. I am lucky that I have not also lost my life.'

'How dreadful for you!' said Mary, feeling that some remark was expected of her. 'I didn't know the Bolsheviks were as bad in Georgia.'

'Did you lose *everything*?' said Ermyntrude.

'Everything!' replied the Prince.

So comprehensive a statement, with the picture it conjured up of unspeakable privation, smote his audience into silence. Mary felt that it was prosaic to reflect that the Prince had exempted, in the largeness of his mind, his signet ring, and his gold cigarette-case, and perhaps some other trifles of the same nature.

Ermyntrude, easing the constraint of the moment, began to wonder, audibly, where Vicky could be. The Prince responded, with the effect of shaking off the dark thoughts his own words had evoked in his brain.

Vicky came in some little time after the tea-table had been spread before Ermyntrude. Mary had little patience with poses, but had too much humour not to appreciate the manner of this entrance.

The Sports Girl had vanished. Vicky was sinuous in a tea-gown that swathed her limbs in folds of chiffon, and trailed behind her over the floor. She came in with her hand resting lightly on the neck of the Borzoi, and paused for a moment, looking round with tragic vagueness. The Borzoi, lacking histrionic talent, escaped from the imperceptible restraint of her hand to investigate the Prince.

Ermyntrude found nothing to laugh at in the tea-gown, or the exotic air that hung about her daughter. Mentally she applauded a good entrance, and thought that Vicky looked lovely. She called her attention to the Prince, who had sprung to his feet.

Wally, in whom the sight of his stepdaughter outplaying his guest had engendered emotions that threatened to overcome him, very soon finished his tea, and withdrew, taking the dog – Prince, with him. Mary stayed on, a rather silent but interested spectator of the comedy being enacted before her. She had early written the Prince down as a fortune-hunter, and had wondered a little that he should waste his time on the married Ermyntrude. She now began to suspect that his designs were set on Vicky, for he devoted himself to her with the utmost gallantry, including Ermyntrude in the conversation merely to corroborate his various estimates of Vicky's unplumbed soul.

After a time, Mary grew tired of listening to absurdities, and went away. She did not see the Prince again until dinner-time, but went to Vicky's room, to remonstrate with her, as soon as she herself had changed her dress.

Vicky was engaged in rolling her fair locks into sophisticated curls upon the top of her head. She smiled happily at Mary, and said with disarming frankness: 'I say, isn't this grown-up, and rather repulsive? I feel frightfully *femme fatale.*'

'I do wish you wouldn't pose so much!' said Mary. 'Really, you're making a complete ass of yourself. You can't look like a *femme fatale* at nineteen.'

'With eye-black, I can,' replied Vicky optimistically.

'Well, don't. And if it's for the Prince's benefit, *I* think he's phoney.'

'Oh yes, so do I!' Vicky assented.

'Then why on earth bother to put on this sickening act?'

'It isn't a bother; I like it. I wish I were on the stage.'

'You're certainly wasted here. Why has the Prince come here, do you suppose?'

'Well, I think because Mummy's so rich.'

'Yes, but he knew she was married.'

'But she could divorce Wally, couldn't she? I think it's all frightfully subtle of Alexis, only Ermyntrude's very respectable, so perhaps he'll murder Wally in the end.'

'Oh, don't talk rot!' said Mary impatiently.

'Well, I do think he might, quite easily,' said Vicky, applying eye-black with a lavish hand. 'Oh, darling, don't I look grand and dangerous? I think Russians are sinister, particularly Alexis.'

'I don't see anything sinister about Alexis. And you look awful.'

'Ugly-awful, or fast-awful? I don't trust his smile. Like velvet, with something at the back of his eyes which makes me shiver a little.'

'Don't waste that stuff on me: I'm the worst audience you'll ever have.'

'I was rehearsing,' said Vicky, quite unabashed. 'Do you suppose secret agents have fun?'

'No. Why?'

'Oh, I don't know, except that I've made myself look like Sonia the Spy, and Robert Steel is dropping in after dinner.'

'I don't see what that's got to do with it.'

'Well, nothing really, except that I told him to, because it'll make a situation, and I think Robert and Alexis and Wally are the loveliest sort of triangle. Bottled passions, and things.'

'Vicky!' Mary sounded shocked.

Vicky was busy reddening her lips, and said with difficulty: 'Robert might murder Alexis. And anyway Mummy will know Solid Worth, and perhaps give up being thrilled by Alexis. Either way, it'll do.'

'Look here, Vicky, that isn't funny!' said Mary severely. 'You ought not to talk about your mother like that.'

'Oh, darling, I do think you're sweet!'

This response annoyed Mary so much that she walked out of the room, and went down to the drawing-room. Here she found the Prince in the smartest of dinner-jackets, and his *piqué* shirtfront embellished by pearl studs. He cast aside the newspaper he had been reading, and at once laid himself out to be agreeable. As though he was aware that the impression he had so far made on Mary was not good, he took pains to engage her liking, and succeeded fairly well. Yet the very fact of his adapting his conversation and manners to her taste had the effect of arousing a certain antagonism in her heart. She could not perceive any reason for his wanting her to like him.

Dinner passed without incident, but Wally did not keep the Prince long over his port, and led him presently into the drawing-room, his own face wearing an expression of sleepy resignation.

The question of what to do now began to trouble Ermyntrude, for although she would have enjoyed an evening spent *tête-à-tête* with the Prince, a party spent without the diversions of cards or dancing seemed to her not only dull, but a grave reflection upon the hostess.

Vicky, holding a cigarette-holder quite a foot long between her fingers, glided across the floor to turn on the radio. Ermyntrude was only saved from begging her to find something a bit more lively by the Prince's recognizing the music of Rimsky-Korsakoff, and hailing it with a kind of wistful delight.

At this moment, Vicky's invited guest was announced, a strong, square-looking man with crisp hair slightly grizzled at the temples, and rather hard grey eyes that looked directly out from under craggy brows.

Ermyntrude got up, looking surprised, but not displeased, and exclaimed: 'Well, I never! Who'd have thought of seeing you, Bob? Well, I do call this nice!'

Robert Steel took her hand in a firm clasp, reddening, and explaining somewhat self-consciously that Vicky had invited him. His gaze took in that damsel, as he spoke, and he blinked.

Ermyntrude had now to present him to the Prince.

They made a sufficiently odd contrast, the one so thin, and handsome, and smiling, the other stocky, and rugged, and a little grim. Mary, who knew, and was sorry for, Steel's silent adoration of Ermyntrude, was not surprised to see him look more uncompromising than usual, for Ermyntrude was hanging on the Prince's lips. To make matters worse, Wally, although he had not lingered over the port, had fortified himself with a good many drinks before dinner, and was now looking a little blear-eyed. Steel's lips had tightened when his glance had first fallen on him, and beyond giving him a curt good-evening he had not again addressed him.

If Vicky's aim had been to provoke an atmosphere of constraint, she had succeeded admirably, Mary reflected. Nor, having introduced Steel into the party, did she show the least disposition to try to ease the tension. She remained standing backed against the amber-silk curtains, beside the radio, which she had turned down until the music became a faint under-current, a murmur behind the voices. It was left to the Prince to set the party at its ease, which outwardly he did, to Ermyntrude's satisfaction, and Steel's silent annoyance.

'Well, Bob, how are the crops and things?' inquired Ermyntrude kindly. 'Mr Steel,' she added, turning to the Prince, 'farms his own land, you know.'

'I'm a farmer,' stated Steel, somewhat pugnaciously disclaiming the implied suggestion that he toiled for his pleasure.

'Ah, perfectly!' smiled the Prince. 'Alas, I find myself wholly ignorant of the art!'

'Precious little art about it,' said Steel. 'Hard work's more like it.'

From her stance beyond the group, Vicky spoke thoughtfully. 'I think there's something rather frightening about farming.'

'Frightening?' repeated Steel.

'Primordial,' murmured Vicky. 'The struggle against Nature, savagery of the soil.'

'What on earth are you talking about?' Steel demanded. 'I never heard such rot!'

'But no, one sees exactly what she means!' the Prince exclaimed.

'I'm afraid I don't,' replied Steel. 'Struggle against Nature! I assure you, I don't, young lady!'

'Oh yes! Rain. And weeds,' sighed Vicky.

'That's right,' said Wally, entering unexpectedly into the conversation. 'Getting earth under your nails, too. Oh, it's one long struggle!'

'It's a good life,' said Steel.

'It may be your idea of a good life. All I know is that it isn't mine. Fancy getting up in the middle of the night to help a sheep have a lamb! Well, I ask you!'

'That'll do!' said Ermyntrude. 'There's no need to get coarse.'

It was generally felt that the possibilities of farming as a topic for conversation had been exhausted. An uneasy silence fell. The Prince began to recall to Ermyntrude memories of Antibes. As Steel had not been there, he was unable to join in. He said that his own country was good enough for him, to which the Prince replied with suave courtesy that it might well be good enough for anyone.

A diversion was created by the sound of footsteps on the flagged terrace outside. The evening was so warm that the long windows had been left open behind the curtains. These parted suddenly, and a face looked in. 'Hallo! Anyone at home?' inquired Harold White with ill-timed playfulness.

Only Wally greeted this invasion with any semblance of delight. He got up and invited his friend to come in, and upon discovering that White was accompanied by his son and daughter, said the more the merrier.

Neither White nor his son had changed for dinner, a circumstance which still further prejudiced Ermyntrude against them. Janet White, a somewhat insignificant young woman, whose skirts had a way of dipping in the wrong places, was wearing a garment which she designated as semi-evening dress. It was she who first addressed Ermyntrude, saying with an anxious smile: 'I do hope you don't mind us dropping in like this, Mrs Carter? Father wanted to see Mr Carter, you see, so I thought probably you wouldn't mind if Alan and I came too. But if you do mind – I mean, if you'd rather we didn't – '

Ermyntrude broke in on this indeterminate speech, her natural kindliness prompting her to say with as much heartiness as she could assume: 'Now, you know I'm always pleased to see you and Alan, dear. This is Prince Alexis Varasashvili.'

Any fears that Ermyntrude might have nourished that Janet would try to monopolize her exalted guest were soon dispersed. Janet looked flustered, and retreated as soon as she could to Mary's side. Janet was engaged to be married to a tea-planter, living in Ceylon; and although she had so far been unable to reconcile it with her conscience to abandon her father and brother, she was a constant young woman, and found every other man than her tea-planter supremely uninteresting. The Prince alarmed her a little, for she was a simple creature, quite unused to cosmopolitan circles, and instead of listening to his conversation, she began to give Mary an account, in a tiresome undertone, of the tea-planter's adventures, as exemplified in his last letter to her.

Her brother, however, a willowy youth, who cultivated an errant lock of hair, took up a determined position on the sofa beside the Prince, and proclaimed himself to be a fervent admirer of the Russian School.

'And what school might that be?' asked Ermyntrude, bent on putting him in his place.

'My *dear* Mrs Carter!' said Alan with a superior smile. 'Literature!'

'Oh, *literature*!' said Ermyntrude. 'Is that all!'

'All! Yes, I am inclined to think that it is indeed all!'

White, who was waiting by a side-table while Wally mixed a drink for him, overheard this, and said, with a laugh: 'That young cub of mine getting astride his hobby-horse? You snub him, Mrs Carter, that's my advice to you! If he read less and worked more, he'd do well.'

'Oh well!' said Wally tolerantly. 'I'm very fond of reading myself. Not in the summer, of course.'

Alan apparently considered this remark beneath contempt, for he turned his shoulder to the rest of the room, and fixing the Prince with a stern and penetrating gaze, uttered one word: 'Tchekhov!'

Vicky, who thought she had been out of the limelight for long enough, and had once seen *The Cherry Orchard*, said thrillingly: 'The psychology of humanity! Too, too marvellous!'

'Oh, Vicky, you're doing your hair a new way!' exclaimed Janet, suddenly noticing it.

'Yes,' said Vicky, firmly putting the conversation back on to an elevated plane. 'It's an expression of mood. Tonight I felt as though some other, stranger soul had entered into me. I had to fit myself to it. *Had* to!'

'You look beautiful!' Alan said, in a low voice. 'I sometimes think there must be Russian blood in you. You're so sensitive, if you know what I mean.'

'Storm-tossed,' said Vicky unhappily.

'No, no, duchinka!' said the Prince, amused. 'I find instead that you are youth-tossed.'

'One must believe in youth,' said Alan intensely.

With the exception of Vicky, none of his audience showed much sign of agreeing with this dictum. White told him that he talked too much, and Steel said that, speaking for himself, he had no use for Tchekhov.

'Good God!' exclaimed Alan, profoundly disgusted. 'That mastery of under-statement! That fluid style! When I saw *The Three Sisters*, for instance, it absolutely shattered me!'

'Well, if it comes to that, it pretty well shattered me,' said Wally. 'In fact, had anyone told me what sort of a show it was, I wouldn't have gone.'

'I must say, that was a dreary piece,' admitted Ermyntrude. 'I dare say it was all very clever, but it wasn't my idea of a cheery evening.'

'To my mind, the *Seagull* was yet finer,' said Alan. 'There one had the crushing weight of cumulative gloom pressing on one until it became almost an agony!'

'When I go to the theatre,' said Ermyntrude flatly, 'I don't want to be crushed by gloom.'

It was plain that Alan thought such an attitude of mind contemptible, but the Prince threw Ermyntrude one of his brilliant smiles, and said: 'Always you are right, Trudinka. Indeed, you were made for light and laughter.'

'Take Gogol!' commanded Alan. 'Think of that subtle union of mysticism and realism, more especially in *Dead Souls*!'

'Well, what of it?' asked Wally. 'It's all very well for you to say take Gogol, but nobody wants to, and what's more we don't want to talk about dead souls either. You run along with Vicky and have a game of billiards, or something.'

'The panacea of the inevitable ball!' said Alan, with a bitter smile. 'Does it puzzle you, Prince, our obsession with Sport?'

'But I find that you are not obsessed with Sport, my friend, but on the contrary with the literature of my country. Yet I must tell you that in translation something is lost.'

The mention of sport put Ermyntrude in mind of the borrowed shot-gun, and she at once turned to catch Wally's eye. Failing, she was obliged to nudge Mary, and to whisper: 'Tell him to ask about the gun!'

Mary, who saw no reason for such stealth, at once said: 'Oh, Uncle Wally, don't forget you were going to ask Mr White for the shot-gun!'

Ermyntrude thought such a direct approach rather rude, and blushed; but White was at once profuse in apologies. 'It slipped my memory,' he said. 'If you'd only given me a ring I could have brought it over tonight! I'll tell you what, Mrs Carter, I'll pop across with it first thing in the morning.'

'Oh, I'm sure I didn't mean – That is, Wally's shooting tomorrow, you see!' said Ermyntrude, flustered. 'Naturally, you're very welcome, what with Wally using it so seldom, and that.'

Wally spoiled the effect of this generous speech by giving vent to his annoying snigger. 'Well, that's not what you said this morning. A nice slating I got for lending you the gun, I can tell you, Harold!'

Ready tears of mortification sprang to Ermyntrude's eyes. Mary saw Steel watching her steadily, a little angry pulse throbbing in his temple, and said quickly: 'I suggest we get up a game of snooker! You'll play, won't you, Janet?'

Janet, however, said that she was so bad at it that she would prefer to watch. Steel was more obliging, and the Prince announced that nothing could give him greater pleasure. After a good deal of argument, Janet was persuaded to overcome her diffidence, and everyone but

Ermyntrude, Vicky and Alan consented to play. Vicky volunteered to mark, and Alan, refusing to play on the score that the sides were even without him, attached himself to her, and tried to hold her attention with a description of the wealth of sordid misery to be found in the works of Maxim Gorky. The billiard-room was a very large room, one end of it being furnished to constitute what Ermyntrude called a smoking-lounge. Here Ermyntrude ensconced herself, in a deep armchair. Between shots, the Prince stood beside her, conversing in low tones, a circumstance which did not find favour in Steel's eyes.

The game was necessarily a light-hearted affair, for the Prince and White were the only really skilled players, and Janet insisted upon being told continually which ball to aim at, which pocket to put it in, and how to handle her cue. White took no part in the coaching of his daughter, but seized the opportunity afforded by the Prince's patiently instructing her, to draw Wally aside, and say to him in a confidential undertone: 'If you're looking for a good thing – mind you, when I say good I mean a regular snip! – I think I can put you on to it.'

Wally, who was imbibing his third whisky since dinner, was feeling slightly querulous, and replied in a complaining voice: 'What about that money I lent you?'

'That'll be all right, old man,' said White soothingly. 'No need for you to worry about that.'

'Oh, there isn't, isn't there? That's what you think, but I don't. Nice to-do there'd be if Ermy found out about it.'

'Well, she won't. I tell you it's all right!'

'No, she won't find out because now I come to think of it you've got to pay it back next week,' said Wally triumphantly.

These words, which were spoken in an unguarded tone, reached Mary's ears. At that moment, Janet, taking painstaking aim, miscued, and it became White's turn to play. As he walked over to the table, Mary caught Steel's eye, and realized, with a curious sinking of her spirits, that he also had overheard Wally's last speech. He was standing beside Mary, and asked in an abrupt undertone whether Wally had lent money to White.

'I don't know,' Mary replied repressively.

Steel's hard gaze travelled to Ermyntrude's unconscious profile. He muttered: 'Exploiting her! By God, I – ' He checked himself, remembering to whom he spoke, and said briefly: 'Sorry!'

Mary thought it wisest to disregard his outburst, and began to talk of something else, but she was privately a good deal perturbed by what she had heard, and contrived, soon after the departure of the Whites, to get a word with Wally alone. Knowing that evasive methods would not answer, she asked him bluntly whether he had lent money to White, and refused to be satisfied with his easy assurance that it was quite all right.

Questioned more strictly, Wally said bitterly that things were coming to a pretty pass now that his own ward spied upon him.

'You know I don't spy on you. I couldn't help hearing what you said to Mr White tonight. You spoke quite loudly. Robert Steel heard you as plainly as I did.'

Wally looked a little discomposed at this. 'I wish that fellow would stop poking his nose into my business! It's my belief he'd like nothing better than to see me knocked down by a tram, or something.'

'Nonsense!' said Mary.

'It isn't nonsense. Any fool can see with half an eye that he's after Ermy. He wants her money, you mark my words.'

'It's Aunt Ermy's money that I want to speak about,'

said Mary. 'You've no right to get money out of her to lend to Harold White.'

Wally looked offended. 'That's a nice way to talk to your guardian!'

'I know, but I must. I can't bear to see Aunt Ermy cheated. If she were mean I mightn't mind so much, but she gives you whatever you ask for without a murmur, and to be frank with you, Uncle, it makes me sick to hear the lies you tell her about what you want money for. What's more, she beginning to realize – things.'

'I must say, I didn't much like that crack of hers at breakfast today,' agreed Wally. 'Think she meant anything in particular?'

'I don't know, but I'll tell you this: if she finds out that you're lending her money to White, there'll be trouble. She'll stand a lot, but not that.'

'Well, all right, all right, don't make such a song and dance about it!' said Wally, irritated. 'As a matter of fact, I was a bit on at the time, or naturally I wouldn't have been such a fool. Lending money is a thing I never have believed in. However, there's nothing to worry about, because Harold's going to pay it back next week.'

'What if he doesn't?'

'Don't you fret, he's got to, because I've got his bill for it.'

Mary sighed. 'You're so hopeless, Uncle: if he tries to get out of it, you'll let him talk you over.'

'Well, that's where you're wrong. I may be easy-going, but if it comes to parting brass-rags with Harold, or getting under Ermy's skin, I'll part with Harold.'

'I wish you *would* part with him,' said Mary.

'Yes, I dare say you do, but the trouble with you is that you've got a down on poor old Harold. But as a matter of fact he can be very useful to me. You'll sing a different tune if you wake up one morning and find I've made a packet, all through Harold White.'

'I should still hate your having anything to do with him,' said Mary uncompromisingly.

3

Harold White redeemed his promise of returning the shot-gun early on the following morning by arriving with it in a hambone-case just as Ermyntrude was coming down-stairs to breakfast. Following his usual custom, he walked in at the front-door, which was kept on the latch, without the formality of ringing the bell, and bade Ermyntrude a cheerful good morning. Ermyntrude said pointedly that her butler could not have heard the bell, but White was quite impervious to hints, and said heartily: 'Oh, I didn't ring! I knew you wouldn't mind my just walking in. After all, we're practically relations, aren't we? You see, I've brought Wally's gun.'

'As a matter of fact,' said Ermyntrude, 'it's not Wally's gun. It belonged to my first husband.'

'Ah, sentimental value!' said White sympathetically. 'Still, I've taken every care of it. Wally won't find his barrels dirty, for I cleaned them myself, *and* oiled them.'

Ermyntrude thanked him frigidly. She was slightly mollified by the discovery that White had kept the gun in his hambone-case, but remarked with some bitterness that it was just like Wally not to have lent the gun in its own case. However, when White, who always made a point of agreeing with her, said that Wally was a careless chap, she remembered her loyalty, and remarking severely that Wally had more important things to think about, sailed into the breakfast-room, leaving White to restore the gun to its own case in the gun-room at the back of the house. 'For since he makes so free with my house, I'm sure I don't see why I should dance attendance on him,' she told Mary.

The entrance of the Prince into the room diverted her thoughts, and she at once asked solicitously how he had slept. It appeared that not only had he slept better than ever before in his life, but upon awakening he had been transported by the sound of a cock crowing in the distance. He knew then, perhaps for the first time, the magic of the English countryside. He gave Ermyntrude his word that he lay listening to cock answering cock in a sleepy trance of delight.

'Well, as long as the noise didn't *wake* you . . .' said Ermyntrude doubtfully.

Wally, when he put in a somewhat tardy appearance, was accompanied by the dog-Prince, and spent several minutes in explaining to the human-Prince that since the dog was necessary for the day's sport, he would be obliged to include him in the party.

'But of course!' the Prince said.

'I'm very glad you take it like that,' said Wally. 'In fact, I don't mind telling you that this dog question has been worrying us a good deal, because there's no denying it's very confusing to have a dog and a man both answering to the same name.'

'Ah, you fear that when you call "Heel, Prince!" I shall come running to you!' smiled the Prince. 'See, when you want me you should call "Varasashvili!" and then there will be no confusion.'

'Er – yes,' agreed Wally, 'but to tell you the truth I've a shocking memory for names. Runs in the family.'

Ermyntrude, who had tried several times to catch her husband's eye, interrupted him at this point, and began rather hastily to describe the rest of the shooting-party to the Prince. Besides himself and Wally, there would be Robert Steel, Hugh Dering, and Dr Chester.

'He's good,' said Mary, looking up. 'And Robert Steel's quite useful. Hugh says he's a rotten shot, but I dare say he isn't as bad as he makes out. I expect you're pretty good yourself, aren't you?'

He disclaimed, but not in such a way as to lead her to believe him. She said with a faint smile: 'I hope you're not speaking the truth, because if you are the gamekeeper won't be a bit pleased. However, Aunt Ermy told me that you shoot a good deal, so I'm not seriously alarmed.'

'But I find that you are a most unexpected lady!' he exclaimed. 'Have you then arranged the shoot, and do you perhaps accompany us?'

'No, I don't shoot myself, though I did arrange it. I've counted you and Maurice Chester as the good ones, Robert Steel as the medium one, and Uncle and Hugh as the definitely poor ones.'

Vicky, who had drifted in through the long, open window in time to overhear this speech, said: 'But I can shoot, and I think I might come too.'

'No, dearest, that you most certainly will not!' said Ermyntrude. 'I shouldn't have a quiet moment.'

Vicky became aware of the Prince, who had sprung up at her entrance, and smiled vaguely in his direction. 'Oh, hullo! Now I come to think of it, I can't shoot today. I'm going out with Alan.'

'Whatever for?' demanded Ermyntrude, not best pleased.

Vicky selected a peach from the dish on the sideboard, and sat down in the chair the Prince was gallantly holding for her. 'Well, I thought it would be a kind thing to do, because Janet's so very dim, and un-understanding about being miserable and squashed into a round hole.'

'Well, if you want to know what I think, Alan's very lucky these days to have got a job at all,' said Ermyntrude roundly.

'Lawyers are dusty,' murmured Vicky.

'It's a very respectable calling, and if you take my advice you'll tell Alan to stop talking a lot of nonsense, and get down to his work.'

'Yes, but I shouldn't like to be articled to a solicitor myself, so probably I won't,' replied Vicky with one of her pensive looks.

'That is the young man who came last night?' inquired the Prince. 'Such a very earnest young man! Do you like him so much, Vicky? For me, a little dull.'

'Oh no! he writes poetry,' said Vicky seriously. 'Not the rhyming sort, either. Can I have a picnic basket, Mummy?'

'But, dearie, aren't you going to join the shooting lunch?' said Ermyntrude, quite distressed. 'Mary and I are going.'

'No, I think definitely *not*,' replied Vicky. 'I thought I'd like to shoot, and now I've decided that after all I feel frightfully unhearty, besides rather loathing game-pie and steak-and-kidney pudding.'

'But, Vicky, this is cruel!' protested the Prince. 'You desert us for a poet!'

'Yes, but I hope you have a lovely time, and lots of sport,' she said kindly.

When Wally presently departed with his guest, Ermyntrude could not forbear to utter a few words of warning to her daughter. It seemed to her anxious eyes that Vicky was treating Alan White with quite unnecessary tolerance. 'You don't want to go putting ideas into his head,' she said. 'Not but what I've no doubt they're there already, but what I mean is there's no need for you to encourage him.'

'I think you're awfully right,' agreed Vicky, wrinkling her brow. 'Because, for one thing, I haven't made up my mind yet whether I'm the managing sort or the only-a-little-woman sort.'

'Did you ever?' Ermyntrude exclaimed, appealing to Mary.

'Vicky, you're a goop,' said Mary.

'Well, if I really am,' said Vicky hopefully, 'it quite solves the problem, because then I wouldn't be able to manage Alan at all.'

She drifted away, leaving Ermyntrude torn between diversion and doubt. Mary remarked soothingly that she thought there was no immediate need to worry over such a volatile damsel: 'In fact, if I were you, I'd let her go on the stage, Aunt Ermy,' she said. 'I believe that's what she'd really like best.'

'Don't you suggest such a thing!' said Ermyntrude, quite horrified. 'Why, her father would turn in his grave – well, as a matter of fact, he was cremated, but what I mean is, if he hadn't been he would have.'

'But why should he? You were on the stage, after all.'

'Yes, my dear, and you take it from me that my girl's not going to be. Not but what she's a proper little actress, bless her!'

'Well, anyway, don't worry about Alan!' begged Mary. 'I'm perfectly certain there's nothing in *that*!'

'I hope you're right, for I don't mind telling you nothing would make me consent. Nothing! As though I hadn't got enough to put up with without that being added!'

It transpired that Ermyntrude had more to put up with that morning than she had anticipated. Having noticed on the previous day that a button was missing from the sleeve of the coat Wally had been wearing, she went to his dressing-room to find the coat, and took it down to the morning-room for repair, and discovered, pushed carelessly into one of its pockets, a letter addressed to Wally in an illiterate and unknown hand. Ermyntrude, who had no scruples about inspecting her husband's correspondence, drew the letter from its envelope, remarking idly that it was just like Wally to stuff letters into his pocket and forget all about them.

Mary, to whom this observation was addressed, made a vague sound of agreement, and went on adding up the Household Expenses. Her attention was jerked away from such mundane matters by a sudden exclamation from Ermyntrude.

'Mary! Oh, my goodness! Oh, I never did in all my life!'

Mary turned in her chair, recognizing in Ermyntrude's voice a note of shock mingled with wrath. 'What is it?'

'Read it!' said Ermyntrude, dramatically. 'It's *too* much!' She held the letter out with a shaking hand, but as Mary took it she seemed to recollect herself, and said: 'Oh dear, whatever am I thinking about? Give it back, dearie: it isn't fit for you to read, and you his ward!'

Mary made no attempt to read the letter, but said in her sensible way: 'You know, Aunt Ermy, you really ought not to have looked at it. I don't know what it's about, but hadn't you better pretend you haven't seen it?'

The ready colour rose to Ermyntrude's cheeks. 'Pretend I haven't seen it? Pretend I don't know my husband's got some wretched little tart into trouble? I'll thank you to realize I'm made of flesh and blood, and not stone, my girl!'

Mary was accustomed to Wally's gyrations, but this piece of information startled her. 'You must be mistaken!'

'Oh, I must, must I? Well, if that's what you think, just you read that letter!'

'But, honestly, Aunt Ermy, one *doesn't* read other people's letters!'

'No, all one does it to be beholden to one's wife for

every penny one has, and then go round putting girls in the family way!' said Ermyntrude bitterly.

Vicky entered the room in time to hear this dictum, and inquired with interest: 'Who does?'

'Your precious stepfather!' snapped Ermyntrude.

Vicky opened her eyes very wide at this: 'Does he? Oh, I do think that's so wonderful of him! Poor sweet, I thought he was practically senile!'

'Don't be so disgusting!' said Mary sharply.

'Oh, I'm not! Darling Mummy, how did you find it out? Doesn't it give you an absolutely new *angle* on Wally?'

By this time Mary had decided to suppress her scruples, and had read the fatal letter. It was signed by one Percy Baker, who appeared to be the brother of the girl in question. Mary had no experience of such letters, but being a young woman of intelligence she was easily able to recognize it as an attempt at blackmail. The writer used illiterate but forceful threats, and ended by promising himself a visit to Palings if he did not hear from Wally immediately. Long association with Wally led her to assume that when he thrust the letter carelessly into his pocket he also thrust the memory of it from his mind. She looked up. 'This was written at the beginning of the week. Today's Saturday. He'll turn up.'

Vicky took the letter out of her hand. 'Angel-Mary, I do think you're dog-in-the-mangerish. Oh, I never knew anyone was actually called Gladys!'

'It's too much!' Ermyntrude said, kneading her hands together in her lap. 'It's too much! No one ever called me narrow-minded, but to get a local girl into trouble is more than I'll stand for. If it had been in London I wouldn't have said a word – well, what I mean is, anyone knows what men are, and what the eye doesn't see the heart won't grieve over – but to have Wally's by-blows absolutely under one's nose – well, I shall never be able to hold up my head again, and that's the truth!'

'Oh, darling, I do think you're so modern and marvellous!' said Vicky. 'If you were old-fashioned and feudal you wouldn't mind a bit, because it was awfully the done thing for the squire to have lots and lots of bastards.'

'I won't have you use that nasty, coarse word!' said Ermyntrude. 'The idea! Besides, Wally isn't the squire and never was.'

'It may not be true,' said Mary. She gave the letter back to Ermyntrude. 'I don't mean that Uncle hasn't had an affair with this Gladys person: I suppose he must have had; but we don't know that he's the one who got her into trouble. If you think it over, it looks as though the girl must be a pretty bad lot. You can't imagine a girl falling in love with Uncle, can you? Obviously, she thinks he's a rich man, and this brother of hers is going to try and get money out of him. Honestly, Aunt Ermy, I wouldn't let it upset you too much. It's no use blinking facts, after all, and you've known for ages that Uncle is simply hopeless about flirting with pretty girls.'

'It's never been as bad as this,' Ermyntrude said. 'I've borne all the rest, but I won't bear this. It's an insult, that's what you don't seem to see! Other people don't think I'm old and dull, and lost my looks, but not my own husband! Oh no! *He* has to get off with a girl from Fritton! On top of everything!'

'Darling, you're so rare and precious the poor sweet can't live on your plane,' said Vicky comfortingly. 'Really, it's all dreadfully sad, and rather like a Russian novel, and I wouldn't wonder a bit if you were one of those terribly *fated* women who go through life never being understood or appreciated.'

This speech seemed to Mary altogether too fulsome to be stomached, but Ermyntrude was visibly soothed by it, and volunteered the information that she had always been one of the deep ones.

'Oh, you are so awfully right, Ermyntrude, darling pet!' agreed Vicky. 'In fact, I think you're rather like one of those mysterious mountain tarns, and quite, quite wonderful!'

Ermyntrude was gratified by being thought to resemble a mountain tarn, but it was evident that Wally's latest misdemeanour had seriously upset her. Her colour remained alarmingly high, and her eyes very bright and sparkling. Nor was Mary reassured by her rising abruptly to her feet, and announcing with unaccustomed curtness that the subject would not bear further discussion. It was not Ermyntrude's way to bottle up her grievances, and the studied cheerfulness of her voice, when she began immediately to talk about the prospective dinner-party, had the effect of disturbing Mary more than a lively display of hysterics would have done.

Vicky seemed to feel this too, for, following Mary out of the room presently, she said rather unhappily that the atmosphere was thickening too fast. 'Volcanoes; sulphurous smoke,' she added, in somewhat vague explanation. 'I don't think it would be nice for her to have a divorce, do you?'

'It may not be true.'

'Oh, I feel sure it is! Poor sweet, I wish she could have got it off her chest to us, because now I think quite probably she'll tell Robert Steel.'

'She mustn't do that!' Mary said quickly.

'No, but I dare say she will,' said Vicky, accepting it with exasperating nonchalance.

When Mary rejoined Ermyntrude, it was with the intention of reopening the discussion, but Ermyntrude said, still in that unnaturally repressed voice, that the least said the soonest mended. Rather to Mary's surprise, she soon made it plain that she meant to join the shooting-party for a picnic lunch, just as she had originally planned.

Accordingly, they both set out, a little before one o'clock, in Ermyntrude's ponderous car, and were driven rather grandly to the appointed rendezvous. Here the men soon joined them, and Ermyntrude's bitter thoughts were a little distracted by the discovery that the morning's sport had been enlivened by a slight mishap.

'In fact, Trudinka, almost we have added our good host's hat to the bag!' the Prince said, with a gaiety that failed to lighten the scowl on Steel's brow, or the look of long-suffering on Wally's face.

'Yes, you can laugh,' Wally said. 'Very funny for you, I've no doubt. Ha-ha!'

'But what happened?' asked Mary.

Hugh, to whom her question seemed to be principally addressed, smiled, and shook his head. 'Not guilty!'

'Don't be absurd! There hasn't been an accident, has there?'

'Of course there hasn't been an accident!' said Steel testily.

'Oh no, of course there hasn't!' said Wally. 'I've only had a couple of barrels fired at me.'

'If a man's fool enough to move from his stand, he's asking to be shot!' said Steel.

'Yes, that's what you say, and I've no doubt you'll go on saying it however many times I tell you I didn't do any such thing.'

Dr Chester, a quiet-voiced man of about forty, interposed before Steel could reply. 'My dear Carter, you must have moved. Why go on arguing about it? Happily, there's no harm done.'

Wally was greatly offended by this, and demanded to be told whether he could have moved without having been aware of it.

'Obviously, if you are unaware of it,' said the doctor calmly. 'How are you, Mary? Where's that young baggage, Vicky? Not coming?'

'No, she's gone out with Alan White.' Mary drew him a little away from the group. 'What really happened, Maurice?'

'Nothing much. Without wishing to offend you, your cousin is about the most unsafe man on a shoot I've ever encountered. Instead of staying where he was posted, he seems to have wandered along the hedge, and nearly got shot.'

'Who by?' Mary asked, a vague, unacknowledged fear prompting the sharp question.

The level grey eyes scanned her face for one enigmatic moment. 'Probably by Steel, or Varasashvili. Why?'

'Oh, no reason!' Mary said. 'I only wondered. It sounds just like Wally to drift aimlessly about. He probably didn't know he was doing it. Is the Prince a good shot?'

'Yes. very.'

He seemed to be in a more than usually uncommunicative mood. Mary moved away from him to mingle with the rest of the party, and found Wally being voluble on the subject of what seemed, in his mind, to have become a deliberate attack upon him. He threw out so many dark hints about those who would be glad to see him underground that even the Prince's smile grew to be a little forced, while Steel could only control his rising anger by starting a determined conversation with his hostess.

'But this, in effect, is ridiculous!' the Prince said at last. 'Who should desire your death, my dear Carter?'

'Ah, that's the question!' said Wally mysteriously. 'Of course, I wouldn't know! Oh no!'

Hugh, who was frankly enjoying the scene, removed his pipe from his mouth to remark softly to Mary: 'I call this grand value. What's eating your impossible relative?'

'Oh, Hugh, isn't he dreadful?' said Mary, in rather despairing accents. 'I don't want to sound like Vicky, but things do seem to be getting a bit tense. I suppose he *did* move from his stand?'

'Can't say: I wasn't near enough to see. Steel and this superb Prince of yours say he did, and they ought to know. Why no Vicky?'

'She went off with Alan White. You'll see her tonight.'

'You sound a little below yourself,' remarked Hugh. 'What's gone wrong?'

'Nothing, really. Nerves, perhaps. Vicky's been talking about bottled passions and things, and I've caught the infection.'

'Good Lord! She must be a pretty good menace,' said Hugh, partly amused and partly scornful.

Ermyntrude, meanwhile, had been subjecting the rest of the party to a searching cross-examination. Wally's near escape put his misdemeanours temporarily out of her mind. She exclaimed a great deal over the misadventure, but disgusted Wally finally by giving it as her opinion that it had been all his own fault. He became very sarcastic over the affair, and Ermyntrude, who like most persons of limited education, was instantly antagonized by sarcasm, immediately recalled her discovery of Percy Baker's letter, and let fall some hints on her own account, which were broad enough to make Wally feel seriously alarmed, and the rest of the party extremely uncomfortable. Even Hugh, who was not ordinarily sensitive to atmosphere, suffered from an impression of sitting precariously on the edge of a volcano. The antagonism between Steel and Wally had never been more apparent; while behind the Prince's invincible smile lurked an expression hard to read, but oddly disquieting. The shooting lunch, to Hugh's growing comprehension, developed into a duel, not between Wally and his wife's admirers, but between those two men alone, Steel grimly possessive, the Prince flaunting his exotic charm, half in provocation of his rival, half to dazzle Ermyntrude.

Suddenly Hugh realized that Wally was outside this scene, thrust into the negligible background. Neither Steel nor the Prince had a look or a thought to spare for him; it was as though they considered him contemptible, or non-existent. Hugh had a lively sense of humour, but this situation, though verging upon farce, failed to amuse him. He felt uncomfortable, and recalled Mary's mention of bottled passions with a grimace of distaste. Nasty emotions about, he reflected, and let it go at that.

Mary was heartily glad when the luncheon-party broke up. Far more acutely than Hugh, she was aware of these emotions. She talked to Wally, for he seemed pathetic to her understanding, a puppet less than life-size, cruelly set up to provide a contrast to the animal vigour of Steel, and the glitter of the Prince. Ermyntrude became monstrous in her eyes, a great purring cat, sleeking herself between two males. For a distorted moment, Mary saw Steel as a figure of lust, and the Prince one of cold calculation. Ermyntrude, smiling and enjoying herself between them, seemed grotesque in her inability to see these men as they were. She dragged her eyes away from them with an effort, and encountered the doctor's level gaze. He said nothing then, but presently, when the party was over, and he strolled with Mary to where the car waited, he said in his measured way: 'You mustn't let your good sense get swamped by that kind of nonsense, Mary.'

Startled, she countered by saying defensively: 'I don't know what you mean!'

'Yes, I think you do. Don't be disgusted with Ermyntrude. People of intellect – that's you, my dear – are always inclined to be a little less than just to quite simple women.'

She gave a constrained laugh. 'I'm sorry if my face gave me away so badly. I don't like farmyard imitations.'

He smiled, but shook his head. She added contritely: 'That was abominably coarse of me. I didn't mean to be rude about Aunt Ermy. I'm really very fond of her. You are, too, aren't you?'

He looked a little surprised, but replied at once: 'Yes, I'm fond of her. She was very good to me once.'

'Oh! I didn't know,' said Mary, feeling that she had stepped on to thin ice.

They had reached the car by this time. Mary got in beside Ermyntrude, and they were driven slowly back to Palings. Ermyntrude, commenting on the sultriness of the weather, lost her resemblance to a purring cat; but when she began presently to discuss the circumstances of Wally's having been shot at, Mary was again conscious of a vague disquiet. She accused herself of distorting Ermyntrude's remarks until they seemed to express an unacknowledged sense of frustration, and made haste to introduce another topic of conversation.

She was surprised to find that Vicky had returned to Palings before them, and was lying in a hammock slung in the shade of a great elm-tree on the south lawn. Ermyntrude had gone up to her bedroom to rest before tea, and so did not encounter her daughter, but Mary saw her from the drawing-room window, and went out to ask what had brought the picnic to such an early end.

Vicky, who apparently considered the weather hot enough to make the wearing of a beach-suit desirable, crossed her arms under her honey coloured head, and said in an exhausted voice: 'Oh, darling, I found he was going to read to me, and it seemed to me as though there would probably be ants, or anyway thistles, because there always are whenever I lie on the ground. I do think all this healing-Mother-Earth racket is too utterly spurious, don't you? And it was definitely not one of my primeval days, so I said we'd go home.'

Mary was amused. 'Poor Alan! Was he fed up?'

'Yes, but I do feel that he ought to be rather crushed by adversity,' said Vicky seriously. 'I mean, major poets have to be, don't they? And it turned out that I'd done the proper thing, anyway, because you were quite right about that man.'

'What man?'

'Oh, Percy! The one who wrote Wally the funny letter.'

'What you found *funny* in it I fail to see. What are you talking about, anyway? How was I right?'

'About his calling here, darling, of course. I mean, he did.'

'Vicky! Good Lord, when?'

'Oh, about half an hour ago! Apparently he doesn't live at Fritton at all, but at Burntside, and so poor darling Ermyntrude was a frightful blow to him.'

'Do you mean to say he didn't know Uncle was married?'

'No, because Gladys didn't tell him that. He said it wasn't a thing he could mention to me, which I must say I thought was rather dear and old-world of him, and made me wish I'd gone all Early Victorian instead of River Girl. However, it didn't really matter, because by the time he'd absorbed Ermyntrude's rich-looking décor, he got rather fierce about plutocrats, and the Red Flag, and things, and I rather lost interest, because I've heard all about the lovely time everyone will have when we're all Communists from Alan; and though I do utterly agree that it's practically incumbent on one to go Red, I don't somehow think that I shall, because I don't feel as though I should enjoy it much.'

'Look here, Vicky, did you actually take it upon yourself to interview this young man?'

'Yes, of course, and I do think I may have done a lot of good, because I told him that Wally isn't rich at all, which made him talk about deceivers seducing innocent girls, though as a matter of fact I don't myself think that it makes it any better to seduce girls when you're rich, do you? Percy got more like Alan than ever when I said so, though, and I got bored, and gave it up.'

'Vicky, I wish you'd pull yourself together, and talk sense! It all sounds too garish to be believed so far. Of course, you oughtn't to have seen him at all, and I'm glad he had enough decency not to discuss it with you. But what's he going to do? Did you gather that he meant to make himself unpleasant?'

'Well, I wouldn't know,' replied Vicky, considering this. 'He said it was no good Wally's hiding himself, because he was going to see him sooner or later, but I shouldn't at all wonder if he cooled off. Because if Gladys really did tell him she thought Wally was a bachelor, he must see that she couldn't have thought anything of the kind, once he's thought it over, on account of her being the ticket-office girl at the Regal Cinema, and having seen Ermyntrude with Wally hundreds of times.'

'The cashier at the Regal!' ejaculated Mary. 'That nice girl with the freckles! Oh, I don't believe it!'

'Darling-sweet, you're thinking of the Odeon-girl. Gladys is the thin one with red finger-nails that click, and that sort of wobbly figure which looks pretty lewd in tight black satin.'

'O God!' said Mary blankly. 'And he's coming back?'

'I should think he probably will. He said so, anyway. It does rather look as though Ermyntrude will have to buy him off, which seems to me frightfully rotten for her, really, because though I quite like Percy, it's utterly common knowledge that Gladys is quite too phoney for words.'

'She won't do it,' Mary said. 'I know she won't do it. It's the wrong moment. Oh Lord, *what* a week-end!'

4

Neither Vicky nor Mary mentioned the circumstance of Mr Baker's visit to Ermyntrude when she came downstairs to tea; and although Vicky's sense of propriety would not have deterred her from giving her stepfather an account of it, the shooting-party returned to Palings too late to allow her the opportunity of seeking any private conversation with Wally.

The dinner guests began to assemble at a quarter-to-eight, the Bawtrys being the first people to arrive, and the Prince coming downstairs a few minutes later.

Ermyntrude, who had been persuaded by Mary's tactful flattery to wear black, was looking a good deal less startling than usual, though rather overloaded with jewellery. She knew, for she had been told, that it was not considered good form to wear rings upon her first and second fingers, but whenever she opened her jewel-box and saw the row of fat, sparkling gems she could not resist the temptation to push as many of the rings over her dimpled knuckles as was possible. 'After all,' she said reasonably, 'if I don't wear them, who's to know I've got them?'

So diamonds, emeralds and rubies jostled one another on her fingers; four or five expensive bangles clinked on each of her wrists; and a superb double row of pearls knocked against diamond clips, and a huge brooch, rather like a breastplate, on her bosom. A strong aroma of scent enveloped her like an ambrosial cloud; but these somewhat repelling features were in a great measure counteracted by the honesty of her smile, and the real kindliness that obviously underlay her extravagances.

She stood in awe of Mrs Bawtry, and was very ready to let Mary bear the burden of conversation with that brisk, bright-eyed, little matron. On the other hand, Tom Bawtry, a big bluff man of no great brain, but immense good nature, was a creature quite after her own heart. He laughed readily, and had often, in the past, annoyed his wife by describing Ermyntrude as a damned fine figure of a woman. Being a hunting-man, his strictures on any irregularities of dress in the field were sweeping and severe, but as Ermyntrude had never been on a horse in her life, and Tom was quite uncritical of female garb out of the saddle, he saw nothing very much amiss either with her *décolletage*, or her jewellery, and was a good deal flattered by the deferential way in which she listened to anything he had to say.

'My dear, what England wants at this moment is more God-guided citizens,' Connie Bawtry informed Mary energetically, as the Prince came into the room. 'You've no idea what a difference it makes to you, once you become God-controlled.'

Happily for Mary, Ermyntrude saved her from having to answer by introducing the Prince. Connie was not in the least interested in princes, whatever their nationality, but she saw in every new acquaintance a potential convert, and at once abandoned Mary for this fresh victim.

She was still telling him how Europe's troubles could be solved (without, apparently, any more human effort than was entailed by the subjugating of self to Divine Control), when the Derings were announced.

Lady Dering shook hands with her hostess in the friendly fashion that always soothed Ermyntrude's unhappy sense of inferiority, and passed on to Wally, who was still brooding over the morning's mishap. As she had heard all about it from Hugh, she at once congratulated him on his escape from death, and listened with assuaging sympathy to his own rambling account of the affair.

Sir William, who wore the parboiled look of a gentleman dragged out to dinner against his will, frightened Ermyntrude with the punctiliousness of his manners; and Hugh gravitated to where Mary was standing, and at once demanded to be told why the notorious Miss Fanshawe was not present.

'She's going to make an Entrance,' replied Mary gloomily. 'I had one or two things to see to after I'd changed, so I hadn't time to find out what her role is for tonight. She was a *femme fatale* last night, but I shouldn't think she'll repeat herself quite so soon.'

She was right. Vicky, entering the room five minutes later, was dressed in a wispy frock of startling design, and still more startling abbreviations. She displayed, without reserve, a remarkably pretty back, her frock being suspended round her neck by a plait of the material of which it was made. Her curls stood out in a bunch in the nape of her neck, but were swept severely off her brow and temples. A diamond bracelet, begged from Ermyntrude's collection, encircled one ankle under a filmy stocking, and her naturally long lashes were ruthlessly tinted with blue.

'One of the Younger Set,' said Mary knowledgeably.

'*So* sorry if I've kept anybody waiting!' said Vicky. 'Oh, how do you do, Lady Dering? How do you do, everybody? Oh, is that sherry? How filthy! No, I'll have a White Lady, thank you.'

'Good Lord!' murmured Hugh, taken aback.

Sir William was also startled, but when Vicky smiled at him, rather in the manner of an engaging street-urchin, his countenance relaxed slightly, and he asked her what she was doing with herself now that she had come home to live.

'Well, it all depends,' she replied seriously.

Sir William had no daughters, but only his memories of his sisters to guide him, so he said that he had no doubt she was a great help to her mother, arranging flowers, and that kind of thing.

'Oh no, only if it's that sort of a day!' said Vicky.

Sir William was still turning this remark over in his mind when the butler came in to announce that dinner was served. He found it so incomprehensible that presently, when he had taken a seat at Ermyntrude's right hand in the dining-room and found that Vicky had been placed on his other side, he inquired what she had meant by it.

'Well,' said Vicky confidingly, 'I don't always feel Edwardian: in fact, practically never.'

'Indeed! May I ask if helping one's mother is now thought to be an Edwardian habit?'

'Oh yes, definitely!' Vicky assured him.

'I am afraid I am sadly behind the times. Perhaps you are one of these young women who follow careers of their own?'

'It's so difficult to make up one's mind,' said Vicky, shaking sugar over her melon. 'Sometimes I think I should like to go on the stage, and then I think perhaps not, on account of boarding-houses, and travelling about in trains, which makes me sick. And I do rather feel that it might be awfully exhausting, living for one's art. It's a bit like having a Mission in Life, which sounds grand, but really isn't much fun, as far as I can make out.'

'All striving after art, and personal careers must go to the wall,' announced Mrs Bawtry, who happened to have been silent for long enough to have overheard some part of this interchange. 'The only things that count are Absolute Truth, and Absolute Love.'

'Dear Connie, not absolute truth, surely?' demurred Lady Dering. 'It wouldn't be at all comfortable, besides often becoming quite impossible.'

'If only you would become God-controlled you'd find how easy everything is!' said Mrs Bawtry earnestly.

'I saw a play once about speaking nothing but the truth,' remarked Wally. 'I remember I laughed a lot. It was very well done. Very funny indeed.'

'A great many people,' said Mrs Bawtry, who had her own way of forcing any conversation back to the channel of her choosing, 'think that if you belong to the Group you have to become deadly serious. But that's utterly false, and if ever you come to one of our House-Parties you'll see how jolly religion can be.'

Wally looked a good deal surprised by this, and said dubiously: 'Well, I dare say you know best, but all I can say is, it never seemed jolly to me.'

'That's because you haven't been Changed!' said Mrs Bawtry. 'Why don't you throw off all your foolish inhibitions, and join the march of the Christian revolution?'

Sir William had been trying to shut out the sound of this painful conversation by talking to his hostess, but these last words, uttered, as they were, in triumphant accents, made him break off what he was saying to demand: 'Christian *what*?'

'Christian revolution!' repeated Mrs Bawtry, unabashed. 'Our God-confident armies are marching to rout the troops of chaos, and moral-rot.'

'Here, I say, Connie!' protested her husband uncomfortably. 'Steady on!'

Hugh, who was seated between Connie Bawtry and Vicky, rather sacrificingly drew Connie's fire. 'I went to one of your meetings once,' he said.

'You did? I'm so glad!' Connie said enthusiastically. 'Now, tell me, what did you think of it?'

'Well,' said Hugh, 'I was rather disappointed.'

'Disappointed!'

'Yes,' he said, helping himself from the dish that was being offered to him. 'There seemed to me to be a depressing lack of spirituality about the whole proceeding. A lot of people got up one by one to address the meeting, but, without wanting to be offensive, Connie, I honestly couldn't see that they had any kind of message for us. What some of the members seemed to me to be suffering from was spiritual conceit in an aggravated form.'

This speech naturally made Connie feel extremely angry, and she had to pin the regulation smile rather firmly to her face. 'You are utterly wrong!' she said.

'What's more,' continued Hugh, 'I couldn't for the life of me see why the platform was draped with a Union Jack.'

'The rebirth of an Empire!'

'But, my dear Connie, what has the Empire got to do with a religious revival?'

'A lot of pernicious tomfoolery!' declared Sir William roundly.

'Oh, I wouldn't say that, sir! It was all quite innocuous as far as I could see.'

'You think you're annoying me, but I assure you you're not!' said Connie, not very convincingly. 'If ever you learn the three lessons of Absolute Truth, Absolute Honesty, and Absolute Love, you'll know how impossible it is for me to be annoyed by mere, silly, uninformed criticism.'

'That seems to dispose of me,' said Hugh, with a disarming grin.

The Prince, who considered that Connie Bawtry had held the stage for long enough, said that for himself he preferred ethics to religious creeds, and added that the narrow-mindedness of the Church had done much to bring Bolshevism into power. No one showed the smallest desire to argue the point, and Tom Bawtry, seizing the opportunity thus afforded of starting a less objectionable topic, leaned across Mary to ask the Prince whether he had been mixed up in the Russian Revolution. The Prince smiled somewhat cynically, and replied: 'Merely, I lost my all.'

Any sympathy that might have been expressed was nipped in the bud by Mrs Bawtry, who said that worldly possessions were only dross, and that she knew many people who had given up their all to the Group Movement. Naturally, the Prince was not going to stand this kind of thing, and he said, with just as firm a smile as hers, that making voluntary sacrifices was very different from being stripped bare of your every possession, and cast into prison into the bargain.

This was quite unanswerable, and had the effect of making the Prince at once the centre of attraction. Ermyntrude begged him, in a proprietary tone, to tell the rest of her guests about his dreadful experiences, and he at once began to do so, in a whimsical way which even Connie Bawtry thought very touching, and which made every man present feel a little unwell.

Hugh, who had the advantage of being acquainted with several distinguished Russians, had written the Prince down as spurious within twenty minutes of first setting eyes on him, and could not now resist the temptation of asking him one or two rather awkward questions. The Prince, however, proved to be most adroit in sliding out of uncomfortable corners, and had no difficulty in holding the interest of the female half of his audience. Tom Bawtry, too, who never expected any foreigner to be anything but grotesque, was considerably impressed, and exclaimed at intervals: 'By Jove!' and: 'Extraordinary fellers those Bolshies must be!'

The thought of the Prince's immeasurable losses had always the power to bring a little spring of tears to Ermyntrude's eyes, but Connie Bawtry's sympathy found a more practical expression. At the earliest opportunity, she told the Prince that if he would only put himself under God-control he would find that all his troubles would vanish. In proof of this statement, she cited the case of a certain business man, who (she said) was actually losing money when he got Changed. 'But *now*,' she said, 'he's absolutely God-controlled, and his whole business has taken a turn for the better, and he's actually doing very well indeed.'

Only two of her hearers appeared to be gratified by this uplifting reflection. Hugh said: 'Connie, I love you dearly; in fact, I regard you almost in the light of an aunt, but you do utter the most repellent remarks.'

'Well, I don't know,' said Wally facetiously. 'It sounds pretty good to me. You'd better try it, Prince.'

'Why, it's like a miracle, isn't it?' said Ermyntrude, looking round with a beaming smile. 'Fancy!'

For an almost imperceptible moment Hugh's eyes met Mary's across the table. Vicky's voice, holding an imperious note, recalled his attention. 'Crack these for me, please.'

He took the walnuts from her, and stretched out his hand for the nut-crackers. She said rather belligerently: 'I suppose you don't believe in miracles?'

'Not that kind of miracle. Do you?'

'Oh, I think it's lovely!'

He peeled one of the nuts, and gave it back to her. Feeling her last remark to be quite unworthy of being replied to, he said nothing.

Vicky put her elbows on the table, and began to nibble the nut. 'Lawyers never believe anything. You are a lawyer, aren't you?'

'Barrister.'

'Oh well, it's just the same. Fusty.'

He glanced down at her. 'Thanks a lot! Where did you learn your pretty manners?'

A sudden gurgle escaped her. '*Absolute* truth!'

He smiled, but said softly: 'Careful! What makes you think barristers are fusty?'

'Oh, they all are!'

'Of course, you know so many.' He saw her hunch one bare shoulder, and added: 'Come off it, Vicky! You're forgetting that I knew you when you were a skinny brat with a band round your teeth. It won't wash.'

'I must have been rather sweet,' she said reflectively.

'You weren't. You were a little pest.'

'I think it's *so* remembering and marvellous of you to know what I was like,' she said. 'I thought you were most frightfully grown-up and dull. In fact, I was rather hazy about you till I saw you tonight, and then, of course, it all came back to me. You haven't altered a bit.'

'You know, you have a real talent for small-talk,' said Hugh. 'Sorry I can't return your compliment!'

'Sorry?' repeated Vicky, raising a pair of startled eyes to his face. 'But don't you think I'm much, much prettier now? Everyone else does!'

'You wouldn't be so bad if you hadn't plastered so much make-up on your face,' he replied coolly.

'Ah, yes!' she said, recovering her balance in a flash. 'I thought you were rather the sort of man who'd prefer a violet by a mossy stone. Probably I shall be putting on that act one day.'

He regarded her from under brows lifted in faint

surprise. 'Is your incredible life a series of "acts"?' he inquired.

'Yes. Didn't you know?'

'I couldn't believe it. Don't you find it a pretty rotten way of living?'

'How silly! Of course not!' she said scornfully. 'Life seems to me a most frightfully overrated business, and practically always dull, if you stay the same person every day. On the other hand, you can't be dull if you're always somebody else.'

'Adventures in the spirit?'

Ermyntrude had risen to her feet. Vicky got up, remarking in a more friendly tone: 'I still think you're fusty, but not *so* fusty.'

In the drawing-room, Mrs Bawtry became guided to explain the Group Movement to Mary. Lady Dering seized the opportunity to seat herself beside her hostess, and, presently, to broach the subject of the proposed new hospital. Vicky powdered her nose, and deepened the scarlet of her lips, until her appearance was fairly certain to shock sober-minded persons.

Ermyntrude had had two card-tables set out, and had spent the greater part of the afternoon trying to arrange two Bridge fours. As she had once, at a Charity Bridge Afternoon, played with Connie Bawtry, who became very fierce over the game, and argued about the play of every hand, her task soon grew into an insoluble puzzle, for nothing, she had decided, would induce her to play at Connie's table, or with Sir William, of whom she stood in considerable awe; while it was clearly unthinkable that she should not have the Prince at her table, or should fail to separate husbands and wives.

However, when the men presently came into the drawing-room, it soon became apparent that the second table would have to be abandoned, for Hugh said firmly that he only took a hand if he was forced to do so, and Vicky developed a fit of contrariness, and said she hated Bridge. Ermyntrude was forced to fall back on Mary, an indifferent player, and on Wally, who had an unsuitable habit of cutting jokes all the time. But while she was trying to compose the two tables, the butler came into the room, and spoke in a disapproving undertone to Wally.

Ermyntrude was feeling flustered, and unfortunately demanded of Peake what was wanted. Peake, who despised both his employers, said primly, but not without a certain satisfaction: 'A person of the name of Baker wishes to see Mr Carter, madam.' He added fiendishly: 'Upon urgent business.'

Ermyntrude turned white, and then red. Wally looked as discomfited as anyone of his temperament could, and said that it was all right, and he would come. Ermyntrude was so much upset by this contretemps that she lost any grip over the Bridge-question that she may ever have had, and weakly jettisoned the second table. Finally, the Derings and the Bawtrys sat down to play, on the understanding that Ermyntrude and the Prince would cut in after the first rubber.

That the butler's announcement had been most unwelcome to Ermyntrude was apparent to all her guests, but the swift glance that passed between Mary and Vicky was noticed only by Hugh. As her elders moved towards the Bridge-table, fussed over solicitously by Ermyntrude, Vicky slid off the arm of the sofa, where she had perched herself, and strolled sinuously to the door. Mary said sharply: 'Vicky, where are you going? I was going to suggest billiards – or something.'

'All right,' said Vicky. 'I'll join you.'

She went out, and Mary, having the liveliest mistrust of

her discretion, said hurriedly to Hugh: 'Do go along to the billiard-room! I'll be with you in a minute. I must catch Vicky first.'

Considerably intrigued, Hugh docilely obeyed these instructions, and was discovered presently practising cannons. He straightened himself as Mary came in with Vicky at her heels, and after casting a look at two rather worried faces, said: 'Is anything the matter? Can I help, or do I pretend to be unconscious?'

'Oh, it's nothing!' replied Mary unconvincingly. 'At least, nothing of importance.'

'Well, I think it's awfully important that no one should be allowed to spoil Ermyntrude's party,' said Vicky. 'You may think it's lousy anyway, and as a matter of fact it is, but the point is she doesn't, and I'm perfectly certain she'd hate and loathe a scene.'

'For God's sake, Vicky, shut up!' implored Mary.

'Oh, don't make a stranger of me! Who's going to create a scene? The person of the name of Baker?' asked Hugh.

'Well, I'm not at all sure, but I shouldn't wonder if it seemed a pretty good sort of an act to him, on account of his being a Communist, and probably disapproving of parties,' said Vicky. She looked measuringly at Hugh, and her eyes brightened. 'Are you any good at chucking people out?' she demanded.

'I've never tried my hand at it. Do you want Baker chucked out?'

'I may,' said Vicky cautiously. 'But not if it would be a noisy business. Of course, I may be doing him a frightful injustice, or on the other hand, Wally may manage to get rid of him.' A fresh idea presented itself to her. She turned to Mary. 'I say, do you think he would be useful? On account of being a barrister, I mean?'

'No, certainly not,' said Mary. 'Nor do I think we need discuss the matter.'

'Yes, but, darling, I shouldn't be at all surprised if you turned out to be full of repressions, and inhibitions, and things, and in any case it's practically bound to be all over Fritton by this time, because things always are.'

'By all of which I deduce that your relative has got himself into some sort of a mess,' said Hugh, addressing himself to Mary. 'I shouldn't think I could be of any use, could I?'

'No, none at all, thank you,' said Mary. 'It's purely a family matter.'

'Oh, I thought you didn't want him to know!' exclaimed Vicky innocently.

Hugh looked quickly at Mary's indignant face, and said: 'Good Lord, you don't mean it? I don't believe it!'

'No, nor did we at first,' agreed Vicky. 'But I'm rather coming round to it, because I had a long talk with Percy this afternoon, and he utterly believes it. It's a sickening nuisance, isn't it?'

'Is Percy the person named Baker?' asked Hugh. 'Who and what is he?'

'He works in a garage. He's Gladys's brother,' explained Vicky.

'And is Gladys the lady involved?'

'Yes, of course. She's the box-office girl at the Regal. I dare say you know her.'

'Good God! But how do you two come into it? You know, really this is a bit thick! You've no business to be mixed up in it, either of you.'

'We aren't mixed up in it,' said Mary, in an annoyed voice. 'At least, we shouldn't be if Vicky hadn't taken it upon herself to interview the man when he came here this afternoon.'

Hugh looked Vicky over critically. 'Oh! Nice little

handful, aren't you? If you take my advice, you'll keep your nose out of it.'

'Yes, but I shouldn't think I would,' replied Vicky. 'I've been very modern and advanced all day, and I quite feel I may have done a lot of good, talking to Percy.'

'You're more likely to have made things much worse,' said Hugh unflatteringly. 'Leave your stepfather to settle his affairs for himself. He's probably quite capable of doing it without your assistance.'

'Oh dear, you do seem to me to be most frightfully fragrant and old-world!' said Vicky. 'Besides practically dumb. Poor darling Wally never settles things, and the more I think about it the more I'm definitely against Ermyntrude having to pay up.'

'You can't do any good,' persisted Hugh. 'You'd merely make a nuisance of yourself.'

Vicky's eyes glinted at him. 'Well, I think you're wrong. I often get very brilliant ideas, and I quite think I will over this, because I don't want Ermyntrude to have to put up with a scandal she doesn't like.'

With that she tossed the stump of her cigarette into the fireplace, and walked out of the room.

Hugh turned to Mary. 'But she's incredible!' he complained. 'She just isn't possible.'

'I warned you,' said Mary. 'I can't cope with her at all. I wish I could, because she's quite capable of doing something outrageous.'

'Little beast!' said Hugh wholeheartedly. 'Between friends, Mary, is this Baker fellow likely to make trouble?'

'I don't know, but if what Vicky told me was true I should think quite possibly. Oh dear, what a household we are!'

'Poor Mary! It's rotten for you.'

'It's worse for Aunt Ermy. I oughtn't to be talking about it, but just lately things seem to have got dreadfully tense. Ever since that ghastly Prince arrived it's been most uncomfortable – rather as though we were on the brink of something disastrous.'

'Do you mean that he's had something to do with it?'

'No, not really. Don't let's talk about it! I hope to heaven Vicky hasn't gone to barge in on Uncle and Percy Baker. That would just about tear things wide open.'

'Vicky,' said Hugh, 'wants suppressing.'

'You're telling me! I say, what on earth shall we do if Baker does start a row?'

'I haven't thought out the answer to that one,' Hugh confessed. 'What you might call a delicate situation.'

Happily, no sounds of strife in the library came to disturb the absorption of the Bridge-players in the drawing-room. Wally returned presently, not, apparently, much disturbed by his interview with Mr Baker, and was easily persuaded to cut into the game. He was mendaciously assuring his partner, Connie Bawtry, that he was conversant with the rules governing the Four-Five-No-Trump convention, when the butler made his second entrance, and informed him that Mr White wished to speak with him on the telephone.

This was too much for Ermyntrude. Before Wally had time to reply, she told Peake to inform Mr White that his master was engaged, and could not come to the telephone.

Bridge came to an end at eleven o'clock, and after everyone had added up his or her score, the errors had been traced to their sources, and a result arrived at which satisfied everyone, it was half an hour later, and the Derings' car had been announced quite twenty minutes earlier.

The initial strain of entertaining guests of whom she stood in awe, coupled with the alarming announcement of Mr Baker's arrival, and capped by Harold White's ill-timed telephone call, had proved to be too much for Ermyntrude. She felt quite unequal to the task (clearly incumbent on her) of demanding an explanation of his conduct from Wally, and after bidding the Prince good night in a failing voice, she went upstairs to bed, leaning heavily on the banisters.

The Prince did not long outstay her. He refilled his glass once, but as Wally, who had been replenishing his throughout the evening, showed an inclination to indulge in long, rambling reminiscences, he soon excused himself, and withdrew.

If Wally had hoped to have escaped questioning that night, he had reckoned without his stepdaughter. That damsel was lying in wait for him, and came out of her bedroom when he passed her door on his way to his own.

'What happened?' she demanded.

Wally eyed her uneasily. 'What are you talking about?'

'You might just as well come clean,' said Vicky. 'I know all about Gladys and Percy. In fact, we all know.'

Wally was pardonably affronted, and animadverted bitterly upon the licence permitted to the young in these unregenerate days. 'Nosing into my affairs!' he said. 'Nice behaviour for a girl just home from school, I must say!'

'Well, you're wrong. I didn't do any nosing. Ermyntrude found Percy's letter in your pocket, and was so upset that she told Mary and me.'

'Which pocket.' inquired Wally, with a kind of hazy interest.

'Oh, one of your coats! What on earth does it matter?'

'Well, it's nice to know, because as a matter of fact I couldn't for the life of me remember where I'd put the thing. However, I thought it would turn up sooner or later. Not that there's anything in it,' he added.

'You're pretty well bound to say that,' replied Vicky.

'The point is, we don't want Ermyntrude to be worried by a rancid scandal.'

'Nothing of the sort!' said Wally, with a lordly wave of one hand. 'It's just a slight mistake, that's all.'

'But what about Percy?' insisted Vicky. 'Is he going to make trouble?'

'Certainly not!' said Wally. 'The whole affair was absurd.'

'Oh!' said Vicky doubtfully. 'Did you get Percy to see that?'

'Naturally. Just a few minutes' plain talk, and I was able to put the whole thing straight.'

'That means that you've promised to pay,' said Vicky. 'Or else you've fobbed him off for the moment, and he'll come back.'

'It seems to me,' said Wally, with a good deal of asperity, 'that all you learned at that precious finishing-school of yours was to snoop round listening at keyholes. You may think that a smart thing to do, but let me tell you that it isn't at all the clean potato. In fact, it's very dishonourable, that's what it is.'

Upon which austere pronouncement he strayed away grandly, but a little uncertainly, in the direction of his bedroom.

5

If Wally hoped that his wife was going to turn a blind eye to his latest peccadillo, he was soon undeceived. Though the night might have brought little counsel and less repose to Ermyntrude, it did strengthen her determination to 'have it out' with Wally. Mary and Vicky, and probably the Prince too, knew that a highly dramatic scene had been staged in Ermyntrude's bedroom before breakfast on the following morning, for when Ermyntrude succumbed to her emotions she became not only hysterical, but extremely shrill. Anyone at Palings on that Sunday morning would have had to have been very deaf indeed not to have been disturbed by the sound of its mistress's voice, rising higher and higher, and finally breaking into gusty sobs.

When Ermyntrude did not appear to take her place behind the coffee-cups, Mary began to feel uneasy, for although Ermyntrude often indulged in hearty quarrels with Wally, they usually relieved her feelings so much that she was able to face her family, ten minutes later, with all her customary good-humour. When the sinister message was delivered to her that Ermyntrude would not be requiring any breakfast, her spirits sank to their lowest level. It was with an effort that she summoned up a smile to greet the Prince. She told him, in what she hoped was a careless tone, that Ermyntrude had a headache, and was breakfasting in her room. He accepted this information with all the polite concern of one who had not sipped his early tea to the accompaniment of an unleashed female voice reciting, in ruthless crescendo, every sin his host had committed since his marriage.

Mary could not but applaud the correctness of his attitude, and was just beginning to accuse herself of having been unjust to the Prince, when he once more alienated her sympathy by leading their conversation into a channel whither she refused to follow him. Gracefully, delicately, but none the less obviously, Prince Varasashvili was attempting to discover from Miss Cliffe the terms of the late Mr Fanshawe's will. The Prince, in fact, wanted to know whether Geoffrey Fanshawe's fortune had been left unconditionally to his relict, or whether it was tied up in his daughter.

Restraining an impulse to inform the Prince that the outlay of a small sum at Somerset House would place at his disposal the information that was so necessary to him, Mary returned no sort of reply to his adroit conversational feelers, but offered him instead a second cup of coffee. He spoke of what he must suppose to be Vicky's large expectations, adding with a smile which Mary thought brazen: 'She is at all times enchanting, but when it is known that she will have also a fortune when she comes of age – is it not so? – one is astonished that she is not already betrothed! It is very well, however: she should make what you call a good match, do you not agree?'

'Yes, Vicky's very attractive,' responded Mary woodenly.

'You also, Miss Cliffe, are one of the lucky ones, I understand,' he continued. 'I hear that you, too, are an heiress.'

For a startled moment, Mary wondered whether he were considering her as a possible bride, but came to the conclusion, after a glance at his face, that he was merely sliding by not too obvious stages away from a subject which he had been quick to see she disliked.

'An heiress!' she said. 'I'm afraid you've been listening to Uncle Wally, Prince.'

'Certainly, yes. It's not true? Alas, then! I understood that there is an aunt who leaves all her money to your guardian, and that you are his heiress.'

'You've got it wrong,' replied Mary. 'My guardian's Aunt Clara hasn't made a will at all, and isn't likely to, because, to tell you the truth, she's mad. Has been, for years and years.'

'Yes, and a good job too,' said Wally, who had just come into the room. 'I've no doubt if she were sane she'd go and leave every penny to a Home for Lost Cats, because that's just the sort of thing that happens to me. In fact, it would be just my luck if the old girl recovered, instead of kicking the bucket, which is what she ought to have done years ago.' He sat down, and shook out his napkin. 'And yet you'll hear people arguing that euthanasia's all wrong!' he added bitterly. 'The end of it'll be that I shall die first, and the only person who'll benefit will be Mary. Not that I don't want you to benefit, my dear, because I do, but it's a bit thick if I don't benefit first, if you see what I mean.'

Mary had finished her breakfast by this time, and now got up, adjuring Wally to look after his guest.

'As far as I can see, he doesn't need any looking after,' said Wally outrageously. 'Quite one of the family, aren't you?'

The Prince refused to take offence, but replied smilingly: 'Yes, indeed, you have made me feel so. It's very pleasant! I assure you, I enjoy my stay enormously.'

'Well, I'm glad someone's pleased,' retorted Wally, eyeing him with gloomy dislike.

Mary felt unequal to the task of coping with this situation, and left the room, preferring to perform another unpleasant duty. She went upstairs to visit Ermyntrude.

That afflicted lady was lying amorphously in the centre of a large rose-pink brocade bed. A strong aroma of scent filled the room, and the pink silk curtains were drawn to shut out the indiscreetly cheerful sunshine.

'Is that you, dearie?' she said faintly. 'Oh, my head!'

Mary was fond of Ermyntrude, and although she might deprecate her flights into hysteria, she thought that Wally treated her abominably, and so was able to reply with genuine sympathy: 'Poor Aunt Ermy! I'll bathe your forehead with eau-de-Cologne, and you'll soon feel more yourself.'

'I've come to the end!' announced Ermyntrude, in a voice that would have done credit to any tragedienne. 'God knows I've tried my best, but this is the parting of the ways!'

Mary opened the window at the bottom, and began to soak a handkerchief with eau-de-Cologne. 'Are you going to divorce Wally?' she asked bluntly.

This swift descent from the realms of drama to the practical was rather ill-timed. Ermyntrude gave a moan, and turned her face into one of the lace-edged pillows that sprawled all over the head of the bed.

Realizing that she had spoken out of turn, Mary said no more, but began to bathe Ermyntrude's brow. After a slight pause, Ermyntrude said: 'I oughtn't to speak of such things to you. You being his ward and all, and so young and innocent!'

'Never mind about that,' replied Mary, speaking as mechanically as she felt any actress must in the two hundred and fiftieth performance of a successful drama. 'What happened?'

'Oh, don't ask me!' besought Ermyntrude, with a shudder.

It was indeed unnecessary; the history of the morning's encounter with Wally came pouring out, a little garbled perhaps, and certainly incoherent, but graphic enough to present Mary with a comprehensive picture. Ermyntrude spoke in thrilling tones, working herself up to the moment when, starting up in bed, and flinging wide two plump arms, she demanded to be told why she should bear this humiliation, when a better and a nobler man asked nothing more of life than to be allowed to take her away from it all.

'The Prince?' asked Mary.

Ermyntrude sank back on to her pillows, and groped for the smelling-salts. 'He couldn't remain silent any longer,' she said simply. 'He has struggled, but when he saw – when he realized the life I lead, the way Wally treats me, flesh and blood wouldn't stand it! He spoke! Oh, Mary dear, when I think that if things had been different I might have been Princess Varasashvili, it seems as though I just can't bear it!'

Mary was silent for a moment, but presently she said: 'Well, why don't you divorce Wally, Aunt Ermy?'

Ermyntrude had cast an anguished arm across her eyes, but she lowered it at this, and replied with a note of sound common sense in her voice: 'Divorce Wally, on account of this Baker hussy? I'm not such a fool!'

'You needn't cite her as the co-respondent. It could be an unknown woman, couldn't it?'

'Catch Wally doing anything so obliging!' said Ermyntrude caustically. 'Of course he wouldn't! And what would I look like, cut out by a cheap little – Well, we'll leave it at that, for I'm sure I've no wish to soil my lips with what she is! Besides, look what harm it would do my Vicky, if I was to go and get a divorce!'

'I don't really see why it should.'

'I dare say you don't, but I wasn't born yesterday, and

I know what people are! Goodness knows the right people look down on me enough without my giving them something fresh to turn up their noses at!'

'Oh!' cried Mary, moved for the first time during this scene, 'you mustn't think that sort of thing, Aunt Ermy! If people look down on you, you can be sure they *aren't* the right people, and send them to the devil!'

'That's all very well for you, dearie: you've had education,' said Ermyntrude. 'I can't afford to send people to the devil, though I don't deny I've often been tempted to. Funny, isn't it, when you think how I could buy up the Derings and the Bawtrys, and all the rest of them, and never notice it? Oh well! there's no use repining, as they say. But there's one thing I'm determined on, and always have been, and that is that there's never going to be any sneering at my Vicky. She's been brought up a lady, and her father was a real gentleman, and whatever else I may have been, I've always been respectable, and no one can say different!'

'But no one would think you less respectable for having divorced Wally,' said Mary.

'That's all you know, dearie,' replied Ermyntrude tartly. 'There aren't any flies on me, thanks! What with my having been on the stage, and having the kind of looks I have, I can just hear all the dirty-minded Nosey-Parkers saying it was all a put-up job, and Wally doing it to oblige me, just so as I could marry a prince!' Mention of her exalted suitor, and the thoughts of splendour his title conjured up, proved too much for her. She abandoned herself to despair, moaning faintly that she would have to go on being a bird in a golden cage.

Mary could not help laughing at this. 'Dear Aunt Ermy, at least the gold is your own! Has the Prince actually asked you to divorce Wally, and marry him?'

'A woman,' proclaimed Ermyntrude in throbbing

accents, 'doesn't need to be told everything in black and white! The Prince is the soul of honour.'

'Quite,' said Mary dryly. 'Does he know that you don't approve of divorce?'

'I had to tell him! I couldn't let him waste his life on me, could I? The might-have-been! Oh, dear, my head feels as though it would split!'

Mary moistened the handkerchief again, and laid it across Ermyntrude's brow. 'If you don't mean to divorce Wally, what *are* you going to do?' she inquired.

'God knows!' responded Ermyntrude, letting her voice sink a tone. She added, more prosaically, but with quite as much feeling: 'I'm not going to spend my poor first husband's money buying that creature off, and that's flat!'

'It certainly seems most unfair that you should have to,' Mary agreed. 'At the same time, won't there be rather a nasty scandal if she isn't provided for?'

'Let him do the providing!' said Ermyntrude, her bosom heaving. 'The idea of his expecting his wife to pay off his mistress! Oh, I can't bear it, Mary! I can't go on! What – what, I ask you, does the future hold for me? Neglect and scandal, and me still in my prime, tied hand and foot to a man like Wally! I can see it all! He'll go from bad to worse, drinking himself into his grave, and behaving so that I won't be able to have a housemaid in the place that isn't over sixty and hare-lipped, just like that nasty old Williams, who led his poor wife such a dance when I first came to live here – before your time, that was, dearie, and personally I always did say and I always shall say that she drove him to it, going about with a face a mile long, and her hair scratched up on the top of her head, and her nose always shiny, and red at the tip, like she did!' She broke off, realizing that this reminiscence was not entirely felicitous, and retrieved the situation with a magnificent gesture indicating her own charms.

'You can't say Wally's goings-on are my fault!' she said. 'Look at me! Thrown away, Mary! Thrown away!'

'I don't want to sound unsympathetic, Aunt Ermy, but after all, you've known what Wally is for ages. Let me bring you up some tea, and some thin toast, and you'll feel better.'

'I couldn't touch a morsel!' said Ermyntrude. 'You know what I get like when Wally's upset me. Feel how burning hot I am! I shall probably be ill for a week. That's the worst of having an artist's temperament: one suffers for it.'

If Ermyntrude contemplated extending a nerve-crisis over a week, Mary could not help feeling that the other inmates of the house would suffer to an almost equal extent. She agreed that Ermyntrude was certainly in a high fever, and refrained from pointing out that the day was bidding fair to be a very hot one, and that a fat, satin-covered eiderdown might well be expected to make anyone burning hot. She offered to ring up Dr Chester's house, and to ask him to call.

This suggestion found favour. 'Tell him to bring me a sedative,' said Ermyntrude in a fading voice. 'I couldn't bear anyone else near me, but Maurice always understands. He's the kind of man I can *talk* to.'

Mary went away to perform this mission. While she would naturally have preferred Ermyntrude not to talk of her present difficulties to anybody, she was not a girl who expected impossibilities, and she considered that if Ermyntrude wished to unburden herself further it had better be to Maurice Chester, who had known her for many years, than to the Prince, or to Robert Steel.

She found Vicky hanging up the receiver of the telephone in the hall. Vicky had enlivened the Sabbath by coming down to breakfast in abbreviated tennis-shorts, and a sleeveless shirt. She said, when she saw Mary: 'Oh, hallo! That was that corrosive Harold White. I do think he's getting awfully redundant, don't you?'

'What does he want this time?'

'Wally. It's getting to be a habit with him. I say, would it be heartless, or anything, if I went and played tennis? Because I've told White to send Alan over. I quite meant to be a Comfort-to-Mother, in pale-blue organdie, but she turned her face to the wall.'

'No, much better leave her alone. I'm going to ask Maurice to come and see her. You might have invited Janet, too. 'Then you could have had a four, with the Prince.'

'Yes, I might, but I thought not. She's got such fuzzy edges. I think she's out of focus. Besides, she's going to church. I've asked Alexis to come and play, though, which is definitely a Sundayish sort of thing for me to have done, because as a matter of fact I've got frightfully tired of him.'

'Oh, so have I!' said Mary involuntarily. 'But he'll leave tomorrow, won't he?'

'Well, I'm not sure, but I've got a crushing suspicion that he means to linger. So I told him in the most utterly tactful way that Ermyntrude's one of those rather obsolete people who reckon nuts to divorce. It *may* shift him, but, of course, now that Wally's started this imbroglio, I do see that the stage is practically set for Alexis to do his big act. I suppose you wouldn't like to come and play tennis?'

'No, I can't. I must look after Aunt Ermy. What on earth are we going to do with the Prince this afternoon? We ought to have fixed up a proper tennis-party, of course. Well, it's too late now, and in any case, if Aunt Ermy doesn't pull herself together – ' She left the sentence unfinished, and picked up the telephone.

Dr Chester answered the call himself. He asked what was the matter with Ermyntrude, and when Mary replied guardedly that she was suffering from one of her nervous attacks, he said: 'I see. All right, I'll come along at once,' in his unemotional but reassuring way.

He had been on the point of setting out on his round, and he arrived at Palings ten minutes later, encountering in the hall Prince Varasashvili, who had changed into tennis-flannels, and was going out to join Vicky and Alan on the court.

Prostrate Ermyntrude might be, but she was not the woman to receive any gentleman (even her doctor) in a tumbled wrapper, with her hair in disorder, and her face not made-up. A message was brought down to Dr Chester that she would see him in ten minutes' time if he would be good enough to wait; and the Prince at once took it upon himself to conduct him into the morning-room, and to beguile the time for him with conversation. When Mary came, not ten, but twenty minutes later, to summon the doctor, she found that he had been cajoled into talking about prehistoric remains, the study of which was one of his hobbies. He had collected a certain amount of pottery and a number of flint weapons in the Dordogne, and in East Anglia, but the Prince claimed to have visited Anau, in South Turkistan, and was describing some fragments of pottery of geometric pattern in a way that made it seem probably that he really had seen these treasures.

Dr Chester remained with Ermyntrude for quite half an hour. When he at last left her, he found Mary waiting for him, in a large window embrasure half-way up the broad staircase. He smiled at her look of inquiry, and sat down beside her on the window-seat. 'All right,' he said briefly.

'I suppose she told you the whole sordid story?'

'Oh yes.'

'It's about the limit of Wally,' Mary said. 'I don't wonder Aunt Ermy's upset. I only wish I knew what I could do to help.'

'There's nothing that you can do,' he responded.

'I know, and I feel futile. I did suggest divorce to her, but it didn't go down very well.'

'No, she wouldn't like that.'

'Well, what have you advised her to do? You may just as well tell me, for she will.'

'Pay, and look pleasant.'

'Maurice, you haven't? But why should she? Really, that sticks in my throat!'

'My dear girl, either she must pay, or face the very scandal she dreads. There's nothing more to be said about that.'

'What's Baker demanding? Does anyone know?'

'Five hundred.'

'Maurice, it's blackmail!'

He shrugged.

'But, Maurice, it may not even be *true*!'

'Apparently, Carter knows that equally it may be true.'

'You can't seriously approve of Aunt Ermy's being made to pay a sum like that!'

'I think it's very hard luck on Ermyntrude, but I also think Gladys Baker has been grossly imposed upon.'

'Yes, if she'd been a sheltered plant, but as far as I can make out she's nothing of the sort, but perfectly able to take care of herself.'

'You're not in a position to judge of that,' he replied.

She said rather crossly: 'I never thought you'd give advice like that to Aunt Ermy. As a matter of fact, I was afraid you'd wish her to get rid of Wally, and do nothing about this mess of his.'

He looked at her in faint surprise. 'Why should I?'

'Well, I know you're fond of her, and you can't pretend that you think Wally's likely to improve with keeping.'

'You're quite right: I am fond of her, but I know very well that a divorce would only make her unhappy. As for your Cousin Wally, this episode may have taught him a lesson.'

'You know perfectly well that nothing will ever teach him anything,' sighed Mary.

He rose. 'Well, whatever I may think, there's nothing to be gained by discussing it,' he said. 'I've given Ermyntrude some cachets to take, but there's nothing much wrong with her. Keep her fairly quiet today: she'll be all right by tomorrow.'

'It would be a lot easier to keep her quiet if this wretched Russian weren't here,' said Mary. 'Vicky said an hour ago that the stage was all set for him to walk on and do his big act, and she's about right. I don't want Aunt Ermy to divorce Wally, though I think she has every right to, and I shall be very thankful if they agree to bury the hatchet. But he's in one of his impossible moods, and what chance can there be of Aunt Ermy's making it up with him while her precious Prince is beguiling her with his title and his flashing smile? What did he want with you just now?'

'I really don't know. Something that Bawtry said yesterday seems to have put him on the scent of my pet hobby-horse. I don't think he's really interested, though. He angled a little for an invitation to come over to my place and see my finds, but I'm afraid I wasn't very responsive. Do you want a respite from him? Shall I ask him to come over this afternoon?'

'Maurice, it would be an awfully Christian deed!' said Mary gratefully. 'But I don't quite see why he should want to.' Light dawned on her; the troubled crease vanished from between her brows; she gave a sudden ripple of laughter. 'Oh, what a fool I am! Of course I see! He's hoping to pump you about Aunt Ermy's money! He wants to know whether it's hers, or goes to Vicky when she comes of age! He tried me, but I snubbed him.'

'Let him hope!' said Chester, with rather a grim little smile.

Mary went with him downstairs, and out into the sunlit gardens. The tennis-court was within sight of the house, and they walked there together. Vicky was playing a single with Alan, while the Prince looked on from the side-line, but she left the court when she saw the doctor approaching, and ran to meet him, to know how her mother was. He returned a reassuring answer, and repeated it to the Prince, who came up a moment later to inquire solicitously after Ermyntrude. After that, he said easily that it had occurred to him that the Prince might be interested to see his small collection of prehistoric specimens, and invited him to call and take tea with him that afternoon.

The Prince was all smiles, but did not know whether perhaps his kind host and hostess had made other plans for him. However, Vicky promptly set that doubt to rest, by saying: 'Oh no, because poor darling Ermyntrude will be feeling frightfully motheaten, and I happen to know that Wally's going over to see Harold White at five. So do go! I'll lend you my car.'

'Then at about five, shall we say?' suggested the Prince.

Chester, trying to infuse some enthusiasm into his voice, replied that he would be delighted. He then glanced at his watch, and announced that as he had several patients to visit before lunch he must be going.

Mary walked across the lawn with him to the front drive. She said in an exasperated tone: 'How like Wally to trail his coat in front of Aunt Ermy like that! Why on earth he must choose this of all days to go and hob-nob with White, God alone knows!'

Chester did not make any reply to this outburst, and she said no more. As they reached the drive, Wally came out of the house. He stopped dead at the sight of the doctor, and said with strong indignation: 'Yes, I might have known you'd turn up. You needn't tell me you were sent for, because I'd have bet any money you would be. And don't start looking accusingly at me, as though it was my fault, because it wasn't! Anyone would think I was Bluebeard from the way Ermy's been behaving. And if you want my advice, don't you ever marry an actress, unless you're the kind of man that likes having a wife who carries on like Lady Macbeth and the second Mrs Tanqueray, and Mata Hari, all rolled into one! Before breakfast, too!' he added bitterly. 'If anyone's got the right to call you in, it's me! But if I took to my bed, and pulled down the blinds, and refused to eat any food, would I get any sympathy? Oh no! Oh dear me, no!'

'Certainly not from me,' said Chester, getting into his car, and switching on the engine. 'I've given your wife some cachets to take, and provided she's not agitated again, she should be all right in an hour or two. Goodbye!'

Wally watched the car move forward, and presently vanish from sight round a bend in the drive. 'Given her some cachets to take! Yes, I've no doubt! The wonder is he didn't give her a bottle of water with a bit of peppermint in it, and charge her three-and-sixpence for it! Cachets! Full of bread pellets, if we only knew!'

'Uncle Wally, is it true that Baker's trying to get five hundred out of you?' Mary demanded.

He looked rather suspiciously at her. 'What do you mean, is it true? You don't suppose I'd give him five hundred because I've got a kind heart, do you?'

'No, I don't. But it seems a sum out of all reason! In fact, it looks to me like blackmail.'

'You don't know anything about it. These things cost a lot of money. Besides, five hundred doesn't mean anything to Ermy.'

Mary struggled with herself. 'Uncle, can't you *see* how iniquitous it is that she should have to buy you out of this at all?'

'It's her own fault,' replied Wally. 'If she'd made a decent settlement on me at the outset, she wouldn't have had to stump up now, because naturally I'd have seen to it myself. You're very full of sympathy for her, but what do you suppose it's like for me to have to borrow money from my wife to provide for poor little Gladys? Humiliating, that's what it is, but I'm not lying in bed complaining of the way I've been treated.'

It was obviously hopeless to argue with him. Mary said coldly: 'You haven't a leg to stand on, and you know it. Is it true that you've arranged to go over to the Dower House this afternoon?'

'That's right! Now start to nag about that! Run up and tell Ermy! Then we can have another nice scene.'

'Look here, Uncle, if you want Ermyntrude to forgive you, don't annoy her again! It's sheer folly, for you know what she feels about Harold White! Surely you needn't go and see him today?'

'Well, that's where you're wrong, because I've got a bit of business to discuss with him. There's no need for Ermy to know anything about it, unless you go and give the show away to her.'

'She'll find out without any assistance from me,' replied Mary curtly, and left him.

Dr Chester's visit, or his cachets, seemed to have had a most beneficial effect upon Ermyntrude. Mary found her keeping body and soul together with a few delicate sandwiches and a glass of champagne, a diet which, however ill-advised it might have been for one in a high fever, apparently revived her considerably. She smiled sadly at Mary, and said: 'Maurice made me promise to try to eat something. I always think there's nothing like champagne if you're feeling wretched. But, Mary dear, I don't like this salt caviar. You oughtn't to have bought it, ducky: I know the Prince prefers it fresh.'

'It's a bit difficult to get the fresh out here,' explained Mary. 'And it doesn't keep.'

'Well, we don't want to keep it,' said Ermyntrude reasonably. She finished what was left of her champagne, and felt so much restored by it that after silently considering the disadvantages of a prolonged sojourn in bed, she said that little though she might be equal to it, she ought to make an effort to come down to lunch.

So at twelve o'clock, accompanied by her personal maid, who carried her smelling-salts, handkerchief, and eau-de-Cologne, and leaning artistically on Mary's arm, she came falteringly downstairs, and disposed herself on the sofa in the drawing-room. Though made quite faint by so much exertion, she was able to take an interest in the pleasing picture she presented, and to remark naïvely that the new tea-gown she was wearing might have been expressly designed for just an occasion.

It seemed at first as though the new tea-gown was going to be wasted, for Mary had neglected to inform the Prince that his hostess proposed to come downstairs to luncheon, so that instead of being at hand to lead Ermyntrude to her couch, he was playing an extremely competent game of tennis against both Vicky and Alan.

Happily, just as Ermyntrude was beginning to feel herself miserably neglected, Robert Steel dropped in on his way back from church, and showed so much concern over her condition that her depression fell away from her, and she forgot about the Prince. For, as she had more than once confided to Mary, there was something very attractive about a masterful man.

Mary left her basking in the care of this particular masterful man. She knew that in all probability Ermyntrude would pour out her woes to him, but it hardly seemed worth while to try to avert this indiscretion, since sooner or later Ermyntrude would be bound to tell him the whole story.

He left the house just after one o'clock, and when Mary, encountering him in the hall, asked him if he would not stay to luncheon, he declined so roughly that she knew that Ermyntrude had made the most of her wrongs to him.

He seemed to repent of his brusqueness, and said in his blunt way: 'Sorry, Mary, but if I had to sit down to table with Carter I'd choke! By God, I'd like to break his bloody neck!'

'Don't mind me, will you?' said Mary wearily

'I'm damned sorry for you!' retorted Steel. 'You needn't pretend you care tuppence about him, because I know you don't.'

'That doesn't mean that I like having to listen to your strictures on him!' said Mary, whose temper was wearing thin.

The muscles about his mouth seemed to stiffen. 'All right, I apologize!' he said in a carefully controlled voice. 'No business to have said that to you. I'd better go before I run into him.'

She felt a little stir of pity for him, and said: 'Robert, don't take it too seriously! I know it's pretty bad, but it isn't your affair, and honestly it's no use getting worked up about it.'

He looked down at her with an angry glow at the back of his eyes. 'Look here, my girl!' he said grimly, 'I've loved Ermy ever since I first laid eyes on her, and you know damned well what I've always felt about her, so you can stop handing out pap about what's my affair and what isn't, because I'm not interested in your views on the matter!'

He did not wait to hear what she might have to say in answer to this, but strode out of the house to his car, and drove off with a furious jarring of gears slammed home, and the scud of gravel slipping under wheels wrenched roughly round.

'An English Sunday at Home!' said Mary, apparently addressing a huge bowl filled with auratum lillies.

Ermyntrude's luncheon was carried into the drawing-room on a tray, an arrangement which met with Wally's undisguised approval, but although she was clearly too unwell to attempt to take her place in the dining-room, she felt just strong enough, after she had disposed of a nourishing and varied repast, to welcome the Prince to a chair beside her sofa, and to hold him in sad, low-voiced converse for over an hour.

'And I quite think that she's doing her Great Renunciation scene,' said Vicky, sprawling, all legs and arms, in the hammock. 'She definitely had that look on her face, hadn't she?'

'I don't know, and I think the way you talk about her is perfectly disgusting!' replied Mary.

'Oh, darling, do you? Are you feeling foul?'

'I'm feeling utterly fed-up with the whole situation!'

'Never mind, sweet! We're getting rid of Alexis for tea,' said Vicky.

'If your mother lets him go.'

'Well, if she does, it'll be a pretty sure sign that she's sacrificed him to Duty,' said Vicky cheerfully.

Whether Ermyntrude had indeed done this, or not, she put no obstacle in the way of the Prince's keeping his engagement with Dr Chester. When Mary interrupted her *tête-à-tête* with him, to suggest to her that she should rest on her bed until tea-time, she made no demur, but allowed herself to be supported upstairs to her room. She had had a disturbed night, an exhausting quarrel, and a large luncheon, and she felt extremely sleepy. She cherished no illusions about the appearance presented by middle-aged ladies overtaken by post-prandial slumber, and had no intention of sleeping anywhere but in the privacy of her bedroom. Moreoever, she wanted to take off her corsets.

Mary waited to see her comfortably bestowed, and retired to her own apartment. She felt that she was entitled to a respite, and she did not emerge until it was nearly time for tea.

Vicky was still in the hammock, and the Prince, very natty in a grey-flannel suit and wash-leather gloves, was inquiring the way to Dr Chester's house of his host.

'You can't miss it,' said Wally. 'It's in the village. Ivy-covered place standing right on the road, with a lot of white posts in front of it.'

'Ah, yes, I will remember. But the village, in effect, where is that?'

'Turn to the right when you come out of the garage entrance, and left when you get to the T road, past the Dower House,' said Wally, in the tone of one who found the subject tedious. 'And it's no good expecting anyone to drive you, because my wife's got a lot of silly ideas about giving the chauffeur the day off every Sunday. Of course, if I weren't going out myself I wouldn't mind running you there,' he added handsomely.

No amount of rudeness seemed to have the power of ruffling the Prince's temper. He replied with his inevitable smile: 'It is unnecessary, I assure you, for Vicky lends me her car. It is I who may perhaps drive you to this Dower House which you say I shall pass?'

'Very good of you, but you needn't bother. I always walk over by way of the bridge,' said Wally. 'Short cut through the garden,' he explained.

'Then I will say *au revoir,'* bowed the Prince.

'So long!' replied Wally, adding when his guest was out of earshot: 'And if you have a head-on collision with a steam-roller it'll be all right with me!'

6

Ermyntrude would have been extremely indignant had she known that her dislike of the intimacy prevailing between Wally and Harold White was shared by Janet White. Filial piety forbade Janet to ascribe her father's vagaries to any inherent weakness of character. She said sadly that Mr Carter had led him into bad ways, a pronouncement that enraged her brother, who did not suffer from filial piety, and who had never shown the slightest hesitation to proclaim his undeviating dislike of his parent. This shocked Janet very much, for she was a girl who believed firmly in doing one's duty, and what more certain duty could there be than that of loving one's father? As it was clearly very difficult to love a father who showed only the most infrequent signs of reciprocating her affection, but more often wondered aloud why he should have been cursed with an unsatisfactory son, and a damned fool of a daughter, Janet was forced to weave round him a veil of her own imagination. She decided that her mother's death had embittered him, conveniently forgetting the quarrels that had raged between the pair during the much-enduring Mrs White's lifetime. It was more difficult to find excuses to account for Harold White's predilection for low company, and Janet preferred not to think about this. When Alan spoke his mind on the subject of finding the house invaded by bookmakers and touts, she said that poor father had to mix with all sorts and conditions of men in the course of his duties at the colliery, and so had perhaps lost the power of discrimination. Her tea-planter, who privately considered that

Harold White was what he called, tersely, a wrong 'un, was anxious to remove her from the sphere of his influence; but Janet, though generally indeterminate, was firm on one point: until Alan was earning money, and could thus escape from the parental roof, her duty was to remain at home, and to keep the peace between father and son.

She was well aware that White had more than once managed to borrow money from Wally, and that the two men very often entered together into schemes for getting-rich-quick which were, she suspected, as dubious as they were unsuccessful. The information, therefore, that Wally Carter and Samuel Jones, of Fritton, were both coming to tea at five o'clock on Sunday, made her feel vaguely disquieted, since it drew from Alan a highly libellous estimate of Mr Jones's character and reputation.

'A man not fit to be in the same room with my sister!' he said dramatically.

His father was not unnaturally annoyed, and said angrily: 'Shut up, you young fool! You don't know what you're talking about, and if you think I'm going to put up with your bloody theatrical ways, you're wrong! What's more, Sam Jones is a Town Councillor, and goes to chapel regularly.'

'Yes,' sneered Alan. 'Votes against Sunday games in the park, too, not to mention Colonel Morrison's scheme for better housing for the poor devils in the Old Town. God, it makes me sick!'

'Perhaps it isn't true,' said Janet charitably.

'Perhaps it isn't! And perhaps it isn't true that he gets his own employees into trouble, and doesn't pay a brass cent in maintenance!'

'Oh dear!' said Janet. 'Not at the *dinner*-table, Alan, please!'

'I believe in facing facts unflinchingly,' said Alan superbly. 'If that greasy swine's coming here, I shall go out, that's all. I suppose, if the truth were told, he's got some shady scheme on foot, and you and Carter think you're going to benefit by it.'

'Alan dear, you oughtn't to talk to father like that.'

This mild reproof was endorsed by White in terms which finally drove Alan from the table, declaring that he would starve before he ate another morsel under the parental roof.

When he had slammed his way out of the room, Janet, in whom tact was not a predominant feature, said that she didn't know why it was, but she had never liked Samuel Jones.

'Well, you're not asked to like him,' snapped White. 'You needn't think he's coming for the pleasure of seeing you, because he's not. In fact, the scarcer you make yourself the better.'

'Oh dear, that means you're going to talk business! I do wish you wouldn't, father: I'm sure he's not a *good* man.'

'Never you mind what we're going to talk! And if I catch you blabbing all around the countryside any dam-fool rubbish about Jones and Carter, you'll be sorry!'

'Have you paid Mr Carter the money you owe him?' asked Janet. 'I know you don't like me to remind you, but it does worry me so.'

'Then it needn't worry you. Carter and I understand one another perfectly.'

'But I thought he was so cross about it? I'm sure the last time he came over here he was simply horrid, and I do so hate you to be beholden to him.'

'Oh, shut up!' said White. 'You talk like someone out of a cheap novel! What the devil do you suppose Wally's likely to do about it, even supposing he is annoyed?'

'But it's not right to borrow money, and not pay it back!' faltered Janet.

'Of course I'm going to pay it back! Good Lord, a

pretty opinion my own daughter has of me, I will say! Now, you get this, my girl! When I want you to poke your nose into my business, I'll tell you! Until then, keep it out!'

Janet was too well accustomed to this rough form of address to be hurt by it. She merely blinked at him, and said: 'Yes, father. Will they want tea? Because it's Florence's half-day.'

'I suppose you're just capable of making tea without assistance? God knows what other use you are!'

'Yes, only if you'd told me yesterday I could have made a cake. I'm afraid there isn't much.'

'No, there wouldn't be,' said her parent sardonically. 'Cut some sandwiches, or something.'

'We might have tea in the garden,' said Janet, as though this would compensate for the meagre nature of the repast.

Her father intimated that she might set the tea-table where she chose, and added that he had no desire to include his son in the party.

As Alan had expressed his intention of starving before he ate another meal at the Dower House, Janet did not think that he would appear again until suppertime. She went in search of him presently, but found that he had left the house. White went out into the garden, and peace once more descended, so that Janet was able to devote her attention to the writing of her weekly letter to her tea-planter.

She was one of those persons who could, without apparent effort, fill any number of sheets with harmless inanities, and she had not by any means come to the end of all she had to say, when the clock in the hall struck four, and recalled her to her duties. She put away her writing materials, and went into the kitchen to make scones for tea. She was still engaged on this task when

White shouted to know whether she was asleep, or meant to prepare for the coming of his guests. He did not show the least gratitude when she hurried out to tell him of her activities in the kitchen, but remarked, with perfect truth, that her hair was coming down, and that her nose was shining.

'It's so hot, bending over the stove on a day like this,' said poor Janet apologetically.

'Well, for the Lord's sake make yourself respectable before Jones and Carter turn up!' he replied. 'I've put some chairs out, but I don't know where you keep your tablecloths.'

'Oh, have you? Oh, thank you, father! I'll do the rest!' she said, feeling that she had been right in her judgement of him all along, and that a rough exterior hid a heart of gold.

The garden of the Dower House sloped down to the stream separating it from Palings, but a previous tenant had levelled part of the upper ground into a shallow terrace. Here White had dragged several chairs, and a weather-beaten garden table, disposing them in the shade cast by the house. Janet, who had a slightly depressing habit of making yards of crochet-lace in her spare time, spread a cloth, heavy with this evidence of her industry, over the table, and set the tea-tray down on top of it. Like Ermyntrude, she wished that the rhododendrons and the azaleas were in flower, for she was an indifferent gardener, and the prospect included only a few sickly-looking dahlias, some Michaelmas daisies, one or two late-flowering roses, and a thicket of funereal shrubs that ran from the corner of the house down to the stream. However, it seemed unlikely that either Mr Jones or Wally Carter was coming to admire the garden, so beyond casting a wistful glance at the blaze of colour on the southern slopes of the Palings garden, which she could see through a gap in the bushes, she wasted no time in idle repinings, but went indoors to take her scones out of the oven.

When she came out on to the terrace again, she had changed her workaday garb for a dress of a clear blue, startlingly unsuited to her rather sallow complexion, and had powdered her nose. She found that Mr Jones had already arrived, and was deep in conversation with her father. This conversation broke off abruptly upon her appearance, and Mr Jones hoisted himself out of his chair with a grunt, and shook hands with her.

He was a fat man, with a jowl, and a smile that was altogether too wide and guileless to be credible; and his notion of making himself agreeable to women was to talk to them with an air of patronage mixed with gallantry.

Janet's rigid standards of the civility due to a guest compelled her to receive Mr Jones's sallies with outward complaisance, but when, from her chair facing down the garden, she caught a glimpse of Wally descending the path to the bridge between the banks of rhododendrons on the opposite slope, she rose with rather obvious relief, and said that she could see Mr Carter coming, and would go and make the tea.

Her father, who had been treating her with the politeness he reserved for public use, forgot, in the irritation of finding his cigarette-case empty, that in the presence of strangers she was his indulged daughter, and got up, demanding to know why she had not put out a box of cigarettes.

'Oh dear, didn't I?' said Janet distressfully. 'I'll get it, shall I?'

'Not on my account, I beg!' said Mr Jones, holding up a plump hand.

'It's all right: you needn't bother!' said White hastily. 'My fault!'

This handsome admission, accompanied as it was by the smile of a fond parent, not unnaturally made Janet blink. As White moved towards the window of his study, and leaned in to reach the wooden cigarette-box that stood on his desk, Mr Jones said wisely that his guess was that Janet was one of the Marthas of this world.

Not even the most domesticated girl could be expected to relish this reading of her character, and Janet had just opened her mouth to deny it, when a diversion occurred which changed the words on her tongue to a small shriek of dismay.

From somewhere in the dense rhododendron thickets a shot had sounded, and Wally Carter, who had unlatched the gate on the farther side of the stream, and stepped on to the bridge, sagged suddenly at the knees, and crumpled up into an inanimate heap on the rough planks.

'Why – what – Good God, what's happened?' gasped Mr Jones, his eyes starting out of his head.

White, who had turned quickly at the sound of Janet's shriek, was not in a position to obtain a view of the bridge over the stream, and demanded testily to know the meaning of his daughter's scream.

'Mr Carter – the shot – !' whimpered Janet.

White strode up to her, and looked in the direction of her shaking finger. The sight of Wally's still form made him give an exclamation under his breath, but instead of joining Janet and Mr Jones in their stupefied immobility, he threw the cigarette-box into a chair, spilling its contents haphazard, and snapped out: 'Don't stand there like a stuck pig! Come on!'

His words jerked the other two out of their trance. Mr Jones heaved himself out of his chair, and set off down the slope in White's wake at a lumbering trot, while Janet followed, sobbing, 'Oh dear, oh dear!' in an ineffectual manner that would certainly have infuriated White had he lingered to hear it.

By the time she and Samuel Jones reached the bridge, White had raised Wally in his arms, and was feeling for his heart. He was looking rather pale, and when he drew his hand away it was reddened with blood.

'Oh, is he dead? Oh, whatever shall we do?' cried Janet distractedly.

'Stop that screeching, and get something to stanch the blood!' snapped White. 'Here, Sam, see what you can do! I don't know how far gone he is. I'll get hold of Chester at once. Thank God it's a Sunday, and he won't be out!'

Mr Jones, whose cheeks had assumed a yellow pallor, knelt clumsily down beside Wally's body, and told Janet in an unsteady voice to tear a piece off her petticoat, or something.

Janet, however, had had her father's handkerchief thrust into her hand, and with trembling fingers was unbuttoning Wally's shirt to lay bare a neat, red hole in his chest. The sight of blood made her feel sick, but after the first few moments of startled horror she had managed to pull herself together and even had the presence of mind to call after her father, who was running back to the house, that it was of no use for him to ring up Dr Chester.

'He's out!' she shouted. 'I saw his car pass the house from my bedroom window just before I came down! Going towards Palings!'

'Damn!' said White, checking for an instant. 'All right, I'll get his partner!'

He vanished from their sight round a clump of azaleas, and Janet, swallowing hard, turned back to Wally's body.

Samuel Jones had struggled out of his coat, and rolled it into a pillow for Wally's head. His gaily striped shirt seemed out of keeping with his blanched, horror-stricken countenance. He said in a hushed voice: 'It's no use, Miss Janet. He's gone.'

'Oh no, don't say that! He can't have!' quavered Janet, holding White's handkerchief pressed to the wound in Wally's chest. 'Oh, what an awful thing! Oughtn't we to try to give him brandy? Only, it says in my First-aid book that one should never – '

'He's gone,' repeated Jones, laying Wally's slack hand, which he had been holding by the wrist, down on the planks. 'You can't feel a pulse. Not a flicker. Clean through the heart, if you ask me. My God, if I'd known this was going to happen I'd never have come!'

Janet was too busy fussing over Wally's body to pay much heed to this somewhat egoistic remark. Under her sharp directions, Jones reluctantly undid Wally's collar and tie; but when neither this nor the chafing of his hands produced in him the smallest sign of life, Janet realized that he must indeed be dead, and broke into gulping sobs of nervous shock. Mr Jones, who was himself feeling, as he afterwards expressed it, a bit jumpy, with difficulty restrained himself from swearing at her, and tried, instead, to offer such comfort as lay in repeated assurances that it was not her fault, and she had done all that she could.

It seemed hours before White reappeared, and was, in actual fact, some seven minutes later. Neither Janet nor Mr Jones, though both now convinced that Wally was dead, had moved from the bridge, each feeling vaguely that to leave Wally's body would be a callous action; but when White came hurrying into sight, Jones rose with a good deal of puffing and groaning to his feet, and stepped forward to meet him.

'No use, old man. He's gone,' he said, for the third time that afternoon.

'God, what a ghastly thing!' muttered White, staring

down at Wally. 'I was afraid it was all up with him. But how the devil – Oh, shut up, Janet! Stop that bloody row!'

Janet tried, ineffectively, to muffle her sobs in her handkerchief. Mr Jones laid a hand on White's arm, saying in a deep voice: 'Steady on, old man! We stand in the presence of death, you know.'

'Oh, for God's sake don't give me any of that cant!' retorted White. 'As though it wasn't damnable enough for a thing like this to happen without your adding to it with the sort of talk that's enough to make a man sick!'

Mr Jones looked very much shocked by this explosion of temper, but excused it on the grounds that his host was naturally a little upset.

Janet struggled up from her knees, and leaned for support on the rustic rail of the bridge. 'Did you manage to get hold of Dr Hinchcliffe?' she asked, between sniffs. 'You were such ages!'

'Yes, of course I got hold of him, and the police, too,' said White savagely. 'They'll all be here before we know where we are, so don't try and move the body!'

Janet emerged from her handkerchief to show a startled face. 'The police?' she stammered. 'The *police*, father?'

'Yes, the police,' he said. 'You don't suppose poor old Wally died a natural death, do you?'

'An accident: it must have been an accident!'

'Pretty lucky sort of accident that gets a man clean through the heart!' replied White, with a short laugh.

'Come, come, Harold!' expostulated Jones uneasily, 'you oughtn't to talk like that! After all, accidents *do* happen, you know.'

'Yes, and one dam' nearly happened to Wally yesterday, from what I've been told!' said White.

'Oh dear, dear!' exclaimed Mr Jones, in accents of

profound distress. 'I don't like getting mixed up in a case like this. A man in my position – '

'No, and I don't like it either, so we can cut that bit!' replied White. A strangled cry from his daughter made him turn his head, saying angrily: '*Will* you stop making a fool of yourself? Anyone would think – ' He broke off, as the cause of this new disturbance became apparent to him. 'Go on! Quick! Head her off!' he said.

It was, however, too late for Janet to obey this command. Vicky's Borzoi had, an instant earlier, bounded up to the wicket-gate, followed at a little distance by Vicky herself, wending her way along one of the narrow paths through the shrubbery.

'Hullo!' said that damsel. 'What's all the noise about? Oh, Janet darling, was it you crying? Poor sweet, what's happened?'

Janet, who was really feeling extremely weak-limbed, stumbled towards the gate with her hands thrust out in a forbidding gesture. 'Go back, Vicky! You mustn't come any nearer! Please go back!'

Vicky made no movement to retreat, but regarded Janet with bright-eyed interest. 'Why? have you got smallpox or something?' she inquired.

'Blast the girl!' said White under his breath. 'Well, she's got to know sooner or later, and at least she isn't his daughter. Look here, Vicky, you run along up to the house, and tell your mother that Wally's met with an accident!'

'Oh no, has he? What kind of an accident?'

'Oh Vicky, I don't know how to tell you! We're afraid he's dead!' said Janet.

'Dead?' gasped Vicky. She looked from Janet's swollen face towards White, and then pushed Janet unceremoniously aside, and saw Wally lying in the middle of the bridge with Mr Jones's coat under his head, and a red stain on his shirt. She did not faint, and since she had decided after her lunch that she was tired of the Tennis Girl, and had reverted to one of the Younger Set, and had made up her face accordingly, she did not change colour either. Instead, she clutched at the top of the gate, and said, 'Oh gosh!' in rather a breathless voice. 'Someone's shot him! I heard it, too!'

'You heard it? Did you see anyone?' asked White sharply.

'Oh no, I thought it was someone potting rabbits.'

'Who, for instance? Got any idea who might have taken a gun out?'

Vicky shook her head. 'No, 'course not. I mean, I can't imagine, because everyone's out, now I come to think of it. Oh, I say, have I got to tell Ermyntrude? I haven't ever broken news to anyone, and I quite definitely don't want to.'

'It's your place to do it,' said White. 'Better go and get it over. There's nothing for you to do here. Janet, go up to the house, and bring Hinchcliffe down here: I thought I heard a car just now.'

'Oh hell, this is most frightfully disintegrating!' said Vicky, winking a sudden tear off the curling ends of her lashes. 'Poor sweet, I always thought he was a complete liability, and now I'm sorry!'

'Well!' said Mr Jones, looking after her retiring form with much disapproval, 'she took it pretty coolly, I *must* say!'

'No reason why she shouldn't,' replied White shortly. 'She's only his stepdaughter. If you want hysterics, hang around until his wife comes on the scene! She'll provide you with them – though, if you ask me, she'd have been glad enough to have got rid of him any time these past two years!'

Vicky, speeding up the path to the house, reached the

lawn where her hammock hung just as Hugh Dering came out of the drawing-room through the long open windows.

'Hullo!' said Hugh, taking in her bell-bottomed slacks, saffron straw sandals, and vermilion toe-nails in one awe-stricken glance. 'I called to see Mary. Your butler thought she might be in the garden. Is she?'

'Oh, I don't know, but I shouldn't think so, and anyway you can't start a necking-party now, because it would be too utterly anachronous!' said Vicky distractedly.

'Thanks, but surprising though it may seem to you I hadn't come to start a necking-party, as you so prettily put it!' said Hugh, a somewhat frosty gleam lighting his eyes.

'Oh well, I wouldn't know! The most disjointing thing has happened, and it's made me cry slightly, though why it should I can't imagine, because I'm not much given to weeping.'

'That accounts for it, then!' said Hugh, as one who was glad to have a mystery solved. 'That filthy stuff you put on your eye-lashes has run. The effect is even more peculiar than usual!'

Though Vicky could not appear to turn pale, she could flush quite unmistakably, and did so, stamping her foot, and darting so flashing a look at Hugh that he ought to have been withered on the spot. 'I now know that you're a beast, and practically reeking of moth-balls, or whatever it is you put with blankets, and winter coats, and everything else that's completely fusty! Also, you're as unfeeling as a cabbage, which is another thing you remind me of, and I suppose if you saw anyone stretched dead at your feet, you wouldn't shed a tear, but would just pass it off as a poor joke or something!'

'As I haven't yet seen anyone stretched dead at my feet, I can't say,' replied Hugh. 'And what that has got to do with your having black smudges on your face, I fail to grasp.'

'Well, that's exactly what I have seen!' said Vicky, trying to wipe away the smudges. 'You can be jolly thankful it's only a little eye-shadow gone astray, instead of me being sick in front of you, which, as a matter of fact, is a thing I might quite easily do, from the utterly eccentric feeling I've got in my tummy!'

Hugh stared at her suspiciously. 'Look here, are you putting on one of your acts?' he demanded. 'If not, what in the devil's name are you talking about?'

'You are an idiot, or you'd see I haven't had time to think up an act! It's caught me absolutely unawares, and I almost wish it hadn't happened, in spite of its probably being a blessing in disguise once we've got used to the idea.'

Hugh grasped her by the shoulders, and shook her. 'Stop talking in cypher, and pull yourself together! What's happened?'

'Someone's shot Wally right through the chest!' said Vicky. 'On the bridge, and Janet shedding the most apocryphal tears and a man in a striped shirt exactly like Brighton Rock, and that malignant Harold White telling me to break the news to Ermyntrude!'

'Good God in heaven!' ejaculated Hugh. 'Here, I say, don't throw a fit of hysterics, for the love of Pete! Is he dead?'

'Oh, he looked totally dead!' shuddered Vicky.

The same thought which Harold White had given utterance to, that Wally had very nearly been shot the day before, slid into Hugh's mind. He did not, however, speak of it, but turned his attention to the present task of soothing Vicky. She showed every sign of nervous collapse, and it was with a feeling of relief that he saw Mary come out of the house towards them.

'Thank the Lord you've come,' he said, thrusting Vicky into her arms. 'Look after this wretched wench, will you? There seems to have been some kind of an accident. In fact, your cousin's been shot. I'm going to find out what it's all about.'

He did not wait to observe the effect on Mary of this baldly delivered piece of news, but hurried off towards the path that wound down through the shrubbery to the bridge across the stream.

By the time he arrived on the scene of the accident, Dr Hinchcliffe, a bloodless-looking man some years older than his partner, Maurice Chester, had risen from his knees beside Wally's body, and had stated that there was nothing to be done, and that Wally had probably been killed instantaneously. Samuel Jones, still in his pink-striped shirt sleeves, was trying to explain to him, firstly how he himself came to be present, and secondly what he had been doing at the moment when the shot was heard. Harold White was standing beside Wally's body listening, with a sardonic expression on his face, to his friend's volubility, and Janet was hovering in the background, alternately sniffing, and blowing her nose.

Dr Hinchcliffe gave the impression of a man who disliked being called out on a Sunday afternoon, and, further, found such violent forms of death distasteful. He cut short Jones's explanations by saying testily: 'Yes, yes, my dear sir, but all that is a matter for the police, not for me!' He turned a cold grey eye upon White, and added: 'The police must be notified immediately. If you have not already done so, I will.'

'I notified them as soon as I'd got hold of you,' replied White. He caught sight of Hugh, and stared at him for a moment. 'What do you want?' he demanded. 'Oh! Dering, isn't it?'

'Yes, I'm Hugh Dering. I met Miss Fanshawe a few

minutes ago, and, frankly, what she told me sounded so incredible that I came along to find out just what has been happening.' His gaze flickered to Wally's body. 'Apparently,' he said, with the lightness of tone a man assumes when confronted by the macabre, 'her story was correct.'

'Wally Carter's been shot,' said White unnecessarily.

'So I see. Do you happen to know how, or by whom?'

'No, I don't. And since you seem to like questions, where, may I ask, did you spring from?'

'I,' said Hugh, quite pleasantly, but with a certain hardening of the jaw, 'sprang out of the drawing-room at Palings.'

'If you're Mr Dering,' said Jones, 'you're staying at the Manor. Had you been at Palings long?'

'No, I'd only just arrived there,' Hugh responded. 'Why?'

'Only that it struck me suddenly that you must have passed close by here on your way from the Manor,' explained Jones. 'What I mean is, you might have seen someone sneaking out of this blooming shrubbery on to the road.'

'Sorry,' said Hugh. 'I didn't.'

'Such questions, Mr – er – Jones,' interposed the doctor, with an air of disgust, 'would be better left to the police.' He nodded at Hugh. 'Good afternoon, Dering. Didn't know you were at home.'

'Just on a visit,' said Hugh. 'Nasty business, this.'

'Quite shocking,' replied the doctor repressively. 'Such a thing has never happened in all the years I've been in practice here. Not a patient of mine, I'm glad to say.'

'Well, I think I'll get back to the house,' said Hugh, unwilling to appear like an onlooker at a street accident. 'You don't want outsiders hanging about.'

'Hold on a bit!' said White. 'You were one of that shooting-party, yesterday, weren't you?'

'I was, yes. What's that got to do with it?'

'Only that I heard through the head gamekeeper that there was a funny sort of an accident in the morning. It seems to me the police will want to know a bit more about that, and as you were present you'll be able to tell them.'

'I should doubt whether that episode has the slightest bearing on the case,' Hugh answered. 'As far as I could make out – but I wasn't near enough to give any sort of an opinion – no one was to blame but Mr Carter himself.'

'Remember that we're speaking of the dead!' begged Mr Jones.

Hugh was prevented from uttering the retort that sprang to his lips by Janet's exclaiming suddenly that she heard a car. Her father at once hurried off up the slope to the house, and Hugh, thinking that a retreat now would present an odd appearance, remained to see what was going to happen next.

In a minute or two, White came back again, followed by a Police Inspector from Fritton, and several attendant satellites.

The Inspector, a foxy-haired man with a thin face and a very curt manner, cast a swift glance round the assembled company before turning his attention to Dr Hinchcliffe. This glance undoubtedly took in the body on the bridge, but did not dwell on it; and it seemed also to include Hugh. The Inspector, however, gave no sign of recognizing the son of a member of the local Bench. He nodded to Hinchcliffe, and said briskly: 'Well, doctor, what have you got to tell me about this?'

'The man's dead,' replied the doctor. 'Dead some time before I got here. Probably died almost immediately. Death was caused by a bullet passing either through or just above the heart – as far as I'm able to judge from a purely superficial examination.'

The Inspector stepped forward to Wally's body, and

looked at the wound. While the doctor called his attention to the absence of any burning of the clothes or powder-stains, and answered his various questions, Hugh watched the activities of his henchmen, and Mr Jones asked White, in an anxious undertone, if it would be permissible to ask to have his coat restored to him. He appeared to be unhappily conscious of his pink shirt sleeves.

The Inspector presently signified that he had finished questioning the doctor, who picked up his case, and departed, declining Janet's half-hearted offer to see him to his car.

'And now, sir, if you please!' said the Inspector, turning to White, and opening a small notebook. 'Your name?'

'I'm Harold White,' replied White. 'I live here, as you must know perfectly well.'

The Inspector paid no attention to this impatient rider. 'And where were you at the time of the occurrence?'

'Up there on the lawn, just outside the house,' said White, with a jerk of his head towards the Dower House.

'Anyone with you, sir?'

'Yes, Mr Jones here, and my daughter. We were waiting for Mr Carter to arrive. He was coming to tea at my place.'

The Inspector raised his eyes from his notebook to bestow a look on Jones. Jones seized the opportunity to ask for the return of his coat. The Inspector said: 'In just a moment, sir,' and directed his gaze towards White once more. 'An appointment, sir?'

'Yes, I rang up this morning to ask him if he'd drop in at about five o'clock.'

'I see, sir.' The Inspector looked meditatively up the slope at the chairs drawn round the deserted tea-table. 'Did you happen to see what took place here?'

'No, I didn't, but both my daughter and Mr Jones were sitting in full view of the bridge, and they saw Carter fall.'

'Not me,' interpolated Jones. 'I wasn't looking. I never thought anything till Miss White screamed, and then I couldn't believe my eyes.'

'Did you hear the sound of the shot, sir?'

'Yes, and then Miss White giving a scream.'

'Did you form any impression where it came from?'

'Well, I don't know,' said Jones hesitantly. 'You know what it is when you hear someone shooting, and don't pay much heed. Over there, I should have said.'

The Inspector watched him wave vaguely in the direction of the thickets on the Palings' side of the river, and demanded to know which way Wally had been facing when he was shot. Mr Jones at once disclaimed all knowledge, explaining that although he had glanced towards the stream upon Janet's first calling attention to Wally's approach down the path on the opposite slope, he had not looked that way again until after the shot had sounded.

Janet, who was still clutching a crumpled handkerchief with which she from time to time dabbed at her nose, interrupted to say in a lachrymose voice that she had seen the whole thing, and that Wally had been walking across the bridge towards the Dower House.

'If that's so,' said the Inspector, 'we can take it the shot didn't come from where you thought it did, sir. Else the gentleman would have got the bullet in his back, which you can see for yourself he didn't. Now, miss: you say you saw the whole thing. Would you be good enough to tell me just exactly what you did see?'

'Oh, I didn't see a thing!' said Janet earnestly. 'I mean, there was absolutely nothing. I saw poor Mr Carter coming down to the bridge, and I said, "Here comes Mr Carter," or something like that, but I don't exactly remember what; and then I said, "I'll go and make the tea," or words to that effect, because I'd been waiting till

Mr Carter arrived, you see, and left the kettle on the stove. O dear, and it's there still!' She added, in sharpened accents, as she recalled this circumstance: 'It must all have boiled away by this time, and probably burned a hole in the kettle! Oh, I can't think how I could have been so forgetful!'

'Never mind about the kettle!' said White. 'Answer the Inspector!'

'It's the *new* kettle!' said Janet, in very much the tone that Hugh felt convinced the Mad Hatter must have used in discussing the effect of the best butter upon his watch.

'Very unfortunate, miss, I'm sure, but hardly to be wondered at,' said the Inspector. 'And after you said you'd go and make the tea, what did you do?'

'Oh, I don't remember! I just got up out of my chair, and sort of stood, I think. And then my father spoke about the cigarettes. Or was that before?'

'Was Mr White with you at the tea-table at that moment, then?'

'Yes, he was sitting in the basket-chair, talking to Mr Jones. Then he said that about the cigarettes – '

'I beg pardon, miss, but I don't quite get this bit about the cigarettes,' said the Inspector, with unimpaired patience. 'You'll understand I don't want you to tell me what isn't relevant. Of course, if the cigarettes have got any sort of bearing on the case, or perhaps help you to remember just what happened, that's different.'

'Oh no, they haven't anything to do with it! I mean, how could they have? It was only that my father was annoyed at my having forgotten to bring out a box, and, of course, I said I'd run and fetch them at once, only he said not to bother, and he'd get them himself, or something like that. And he got up and went over to the study window, and leaned in to get the box on his desk, and I suppose Mr Jones was speaking to me, only I don't really remember, though if he hadn't been I should have gone in to make the tea, so I'm sure he must have been. And I was standing by the table, looking down here, not thinking a thing, except that I'd forgotten to oil the hinge of the gate – of course, it's really Mrs Carter's gate, but she can't hear it from her house, because it's further away than ours – '

'Good Lord, girl, can't you stick to the point?' exclaimed White. 'Get on with it, for heaven's sake!'

'Yes, father,' Janet said submissively. 'Only I'm so upset, and I don't want to keep anything back.'

'That's all right, miss,' said the Inspector. 'You were standing looking down here. Now, where would Mr Carter have been then?'

'Oh, he was coming across the bridge. I remember that distinctly, because he didn't bother to shut the gate after him. He never does. And then all of a sudden I heard a shot, and saw poor Mr Carter sort of collapse. It was awful!'

'You didn't see anyone, or notice any movement in all this shrubbery?' asked the Inspector, looking round with disfavour upon his leafy surroundings.

'Oh no, nothing like that! For a moment I simply didn't *realize* it. I mean, I hadn't an idea of anything like that happening.'

'No, miss. And did you notice where the shot seemed to come from?'

'Not at the time, because I was too shocked to think, only now I feel sure it must have come from somewhere there,' Janet said, indicating the shrubbery that stretched up to the Dower House.

The Inspector did not appear to be much gratified by this somewhat dubious testimony. White cast a look of withering contempt at his daughter, and said in an exasperated tone: 'You were asked what you noticed at the time, not what you feel sure of now. Sorry, Inspector: my daughter's a bit upset. Though, as a matter of fact, I believe she's right. I had a distinct impression of a shot being fired from somewhere in that direction.'

The Inspector transferred his attention to him. 'And you were standing just where, sir?'

'By my study window. You can't see it from here – it's behind that clump of azaleas – but I'll show you.'

The Inspector turned to stare at the sombre mass of rhododendron bushes. 'Those shrubs stretch as far as the road?' he asked.

'Yes, on both sides of the stream. Only it's a much bigger plantation on the Palings' side, of course. The road goes off to the right over the bridge across the stream, you know, skirting Mrs Carter's grounds. We're only about fifty yards from the road here.'

The Inspector nodded. 'We'll look into that presently, sir. Now, when Miss White screamed, what did you do?'

White gave a wry grin. 'As a matter of fact, I asked her what the devil was the matter. She gasped out something about Carter's being shot, and I naturally hurried up to see. Both she and Mr Jones were gaping – staring, down here. I told them both to pull themselves together, and ran down on to the bridge.'

'Just a moment, sir. I take it Mr Carter wasn't lying the way he is now?'

'No, of course he wasn't. I raised him in my arms, to see where he was hurt, and afterwards gave him to Mr Jones to support, while I dashed to the telephone. I suppose Mr Jones laid him down like that.'

'Yes, that's right,' said Jones, edging forward a little. 'And I put my coat under his head, just as you see, Inspector. And if it isn't needed any more, I'd be glad – '

'In a moment, sir,' said the Inspector severely. 'I shall

be coming to you presently. Can you describe to me, Mr White, how you found Mr Carter's body?'

'Well, I don't know that I can exactly. He was lying in a sort of heap, more or less across the bridge, facing towards the house – my house, I mean.'

'I see, sir. And when you realized Mr Carter had been shot, did either you, or Mr Jones, think to look in the thicket there?'

'I don't know what Mr Jones thought of: I certainly didn't,' replied White. 'All I thought of was to get a doctor as quickly as I could, in case Mr Carter was still alive.'

'Very proper, I'm sure, sir,' the Inspector said, and turned towards Hugh. 'And now, sir, if you'd tell me where you were at the time of Mr Carter's death?'

'I haven't any idea,' responded Hugh. 'You see, I don't know when he died, or, in fact, anything about it, other than what I've been told.'

'Then may I ask, sir, how you come to be here?'

'I came to discover just what had happened.'

'You knew something had happened?'

'Yes, certainly I did. I had gone to call at Palings, and I ran into Miss Fanshawe on the lawn outside the drawing-room windows. She had apparently come from here, and was on her way to break the news to her mother.'

'That's right,' said White. 'She turned up just after I'd got back here from ringing up the doctor, and the police station. We were too late to be able to head her off.'

'Miss Fanshawe being the deceased's stepdaughter?' said the Inspector. 'From what direction did the young lady come?'

'Down that path,' replied White, pointing to the thicket across the stream. She had her dog with her.'

'Indeed, sir!' said the Inspector, in an expressionless voice. 'Well, I think that's all we can do here, but if you gentlemen, and you, miss, will take me up to the house, my men can get on with what they've got to do before we have the body removed. There are one or two more questions I'd like to ask you, Mr White, and you too, Mr Jones.'

'I'm ready to answer anything,' offered Jones. 'But I would like to have my coat back, if it isn't wanted any longer.'

The Inspector said indulgently: 'No, sir, I'm sure we don't want your coat. You should have spoken about it before. Give the gentleman his coat, Sergeant.'

'Look here, do you want me?' asked Hugh.

Before the Inspector could answer, White said: 'Yes, we do want you. You can tell the Inspector just what happened at that shooting-party yesterday.'

Hugh sighed. 'You're barking up the wrong tree. My evidence is nothing but hearsay, and valueless.'

'Well, there's no reason why you should object to telling what you know, is there?' demanded White. 'Seems to me it might have a pretty important bearing on poor Wally's murder – a darned sight more than that kid Vicky's happening to be around!' he added scathingly.

The Inspector looked penetratingly at Hugh, and said: 'Yes, sir, I should be obliged if you would accompany us to the house.'

7

The Inspector, having been shown White's study window, and having verified the fact that from it no view of the bridge could be obtained, turned his attention to Hugh, and requested him to explain White's reference to the shooting-party of the day before. Hugh replied in a voice calculated to depress excitement that he supposed White to be referring to Wally Carter's carelessness in moving from his stand. 'Instead of remaining where he was posted,' he said, 'he apparently wandered some way along the hedgerow, with the result that he very nearly got himself shot. If you want to know any more about it, you should ask Mr Steel, or Prince Varasashvili, who were both in a position – which I was not – to see what happened.'

'Prince who, sir?' demanded the Inspector.

Hugh repeated the name, explaining the Prince's identity. It was evident that the Inspector thought the entrance into the case of a foreigner so exotically named at once invested it with immense possibilities. He said that he would have to see the gentleman himself. He next inquired of Hugh how long he had been at Palings before encountering Vicky, and as it appeared from Hugh's answer that, at the time of the murder, he had not arrived there, he asked him some searching questions about his journey from the Manor.

Hugh had driven himself to Palings in his own car, and admitted cheerfully that he had come through the village, and past the Dower House. But when urged to try to remember whether he had seen anyone in the neighbourhood of the Dower House, he shook his head. 'No, I don't think I saw anyone.'

'But you're not sure, sir?'

'No, not entirely. Let us say that I didn't notice anyone. But as I was driving, and not staring about me, that isn't very surprising.'

The Inspector accepted this, and announced that he had, at the moment, no further questions to put to him.

'Then I'll go back to Palings,' said Hugh.

The Inspector put his notebook into his pocket. 'I shall be calling there myself, sir,' he said. 'I'll run you there.'

It was plain that he did not want Hugh to reach Palings before himself, so Hugh made no demur, but meekly accompanied him to the police-car waiting in the drive. After conferring briefly with the Sergeant who had accompanied him, the Inspector got into the car beside Hugh, and they drove off.

The scene that awaited them at Palings was in the best traditions of the place. Ermyntrude, in a pink satin wrapper lavishly edged with ostrich feather trimming, was prostrate upon the couch in the hall, with a bottle of smelling-salts clasped in one plump hand, and a pink georgette handkerchief in the other. A glass and decanter on a low table beside her bore evidence that she had had to be revived with brandy. Vicky was not present, but Mary, looking rather white, was standing at the head of the couch, saturating a handkerchief with eau-de-Cologne. She glanced up quickly as Hugh walked in through the open front-door, and greeted him with a forced smile. 'Thank goodness you're back! Vicky told us – is it true?'

'Yes, I'm afraid it is,' Hugh replied. 'Inspector Cook's here. Can he come in?'

'Police!' moaned Ermyntrude. 'Oh, if my poor first husband were alive to see this day!'

The Inspector, pausing discreetly on the threshold, cast

a somewhat awed look at the widow. Ermyntrude seemed to be beyond human aid, but Mary stepped forward, saying: 'Yes, of course. Good afternoon, Inspector. This – this is an awful shock. I – I hardly know what . . . Please come in! We're rather upset, and Mrs Carter . . . But, of course, you must come in!'

'Very sorry to have to intrude on Mrs Carter at such a moment, miss,' said the Inspector. 'You'll understand that it's my duty to make certain inquiries.'

Ermyntrude lowered the handkerchief from her eyes. 'What have you done with his body?' she said tragically.

The Inspector glanced appealing towards Hugh, who took pity on his evident embarrassment, and tried to explain tactfully to Ermyntrude that Wally's body had been removed to the police mortuary.

'The mortuary!' Ermyntrude said in shuddering accents. 'Oh, my God!'

It was plain that the situation was fast getting out of the Inspector's control. Mary saw that it was her duty to pull herself together, and to assist the course of justice. She turned to the couch. 'Dear Aunt Ermy, what does it matter what becomes of his body? Don't think about that! The Inspector wants to ask you some questions.'

Ermyntrude found that her recumbent position made it impossible for her to fling wide her arms without hitting the sofa-back, so she sat up. 'Have you no mercy?' she demanded of the horrified Inspector. 'Haven't I borne enough without your coming here badgering and torturing me?'

'I'm sure, madam, I don't want to badger you!' expostulated the Inspector. 'If you'll just – '

'Ask me what you like!' said Ermyntrude, allowing her arms to fell, and bowing her golden head. 'What do I care? What is there left for me to care for?' She clutched suddenly at Mary's hand, and said in far more natural tones: 'Oh, Mary dear, the *disgrace* of it! Oh, I shall never get over it! Having the police in!'

The Inspector, who was beginning to feel like a leper, said defensively that he was sure there was no reason for her to take it that way, though he quite understood her feelings. 'What I want to know is, was there anyone who might have had any sort of grudge against your husband, madam? Anyone who'd quarrelled with him, for instance, or – '

He broke off, for the effect of this question was very alarming. Ermyntrude almost leaped to her feet, and confronted him in an attitude that would have done credit to a Duse. 'Are you accusing me of having done my husband to death?' she cried.

'Aunt Ermy, of course he isn't!' exclaimed Mary. 'What can you be thinking of? You must try and control yourself!'

'Am I to understand, madam, that you had quarrelled with Mr Carter?' asked the Inspector.

'Oh God!' said Ermyntrude. 'I parted from him in anger!' Once more she reverted to more ordinary accents. 'Oh, Mary dear, he was a bad husband to me, but I wish I hadn't told him off, for now I shall never see him again, and we can't all be perfect, can we?'

Mary gently pressed her down on to the couch again. 'It was nothing, Aunty Ermy; and I'm perfectly certain he didn't set any store by it.'

'Him set store by anything?' said Ermyntrude bitterly. 'Water off a duck's back!'

By this time, the Inspector was looking keenly interested. It seemed as though Ermyntrude had recovered from her histrionic fit, so he ventured to put a question to her. 'Had there been any unpleasantness between you and Mr Carter, madam?'

Mary could not resist giving Ermyntrude's hand, which

she was still holding, a squeeze of warning. Unfortunately, this acted upon Ermyntrude in a most disastrous way. She reared up her head, and declared that other people could wash their dirty linen in public if they liked, but she would not. 'What's past is done with!' she said. 'He may have been a waster – I'm not saying he wasn't – and heaven knows he treated me disgracefully, what with his goings-on, and encouraging that Harold White, and a lot of other things I could tell you if I wanted to; but he's dead now, and God forbid I should go taking his character away! You won't get a word out of me, and as for me telling him off; who had a better right, that's what I should like to know?'

Mary removed her hand, and said quietly to the Inspector: 'Mrs Carter is rather overwrought. Perhaps I can help you? What exactly do you wish to know?'

'Well, miss,' replied the Inspector, 'when a gentleman is shot dead practically in his own grounds, the police want to know everything. Mr Carter was related to you, I believe?'

'He was my cousin, and until I came of age, my guardian.'

'I take it you were on pretty intimate terms with him?'

'I think so – up to a point. I live here, you know.'

'Yes, miss. Now, did you ever have any reason to think he might have enemies?'

'No,' Mary replied. 'I know that many people – rather disliked him, but I can't imagine anyone having any cause to murder him.'

'Oh, Mary, what a shocking word to use!' gasped Ermyntrude. 'Oh, whatever have I done to deserve a thing like this coming upon me, and Lady Dering asking me to be Chairwoman of the Hospital Committee, and all!'

'Had he private means, miss?' asked the Inspector.

'Not a penny!' said Ermyntrude. 'And if he had he'd have gone through it inside of a week! The money I've squandered – well, I don't mean that exactly, but no one would believe the sums he's had out of me, and all spent on things I won't mention, let alone what found its way into White's pocket! Oh, you needn't look like that, Mary! I'm not such a fool but what I can see what's been under my nose since I don't know when! It was him led Wally to his ruin, not but what he didn't need much leading, but at least he wasn't ever so bad till he took up with White! Everything's been his fault, and if you ask me you'll find he's at the bottom of this, too!'

'What makes you say that, madam?' asked the Inspector.

Ermyntrude laid a hand on her breast. 'I feel it here! A woman's instinct is never wrong! I've always hated that man!'

'But, Aunt Ermy, really that isn't fair!' expostulated Mary. 'Why on earth should he murder Wally?'

'Don't ask me!' said Ermyntrude. 'I don't trust him, that's all I know.'

The Inspector said in a dry tone: 'I see, madam. You have, I understand, a foreign gentleman staying in the house?'

Ermyntrude gave a start. 'Alexis! If I hadn't forgotten him! That shows you the state my nerves are in!' Tears sprang to her eyes. 'And I wanted everything to be so nice – a real glimpse of English country-house life! Oh dear, Mary, you know the trouble I took over Alexis's coming, and Wally being as disagreeable as he knew how! And as though it wasn't enough for him to carry on like he did, spoiling everything, but he must needs go and get himself murdered! Whatever will Alexis think?'

'Ah!' said the Inspector. 'Mr Carter, then, didn't like the foreign gentleman?'

'Oh, I don't know what he liked, but if you ask me he'd have liked him well enough if it hadn't been for all that silly fuss about the dog. It sort of put him against poor Alexis.'

'Fuss about the dog?' repeated the Inspector, struggling to keep pace with Ermyntrude's erratic utterances.

Hugh, who had been listening entranced to these disclosures, met Mary's eye for a pregnant moment.

'Aunt Ermy, that can't possibly interest the Inspector,' said Mary. 'It has absolutely no bearing on the case!'

'I wouldn't be too sure of that, miss,' said the Inspector darkly. 'If there was some sort of a quarrel over the dog, foreign gentlemen not treating dumb animals the way we do, and Mr Carter took exception to it, as well he might, it may have a very important bearing on the case, for we all know that foreigners are hasty-tempered, and take offence where none's intended. Mind you, I don't say – '

'The man's mad!' exclaimed Ermyntrude, her tears arrested by astonishment. 'Whoever said there was a quarrel about the dog? The idea!'

'You misunderstood what Mrs Carter meant,' said Mary. 'Our guest is a Prince, and unfortunately my cousin's spaniel's called Prince. It was just that my cousin felt that it might be a little awkward.' She saw a look of bewilderment on the Inspector's face, and added desperately: 'On account of them both answering to the same name, I mean.'

Hugh gripped his underlip between his teeth, and gazed rigidly at the opposite wall.

The Inspector was obviously shaken. He stared very hard at Mary, and said severely: 'I'm bound to say, it doesn't make sense to me, miss.'

'No. No, it was very silly and trivial. I told you it had no bearing on the case.'

The Inspector turned back to Ermyntrude. 'This Prince, madam, is a friend of yours, I take it?'

'Well, of course he is!' replied Ermyntrude. 'He's a very dear friend of mine!'

'I should like to see him, if you please,' said the Inspector, feeling that he was nearing the centre of the labyrinth at last.

'You can't see him; he's gone out to tea with Dr Chester. Besides, what's the use of your seeing him? You don't suppose he killed my husband, do you?'

'I don't suppose anything, madam,' said the Inspector stiffly. 'But it's my duty to interrogate everyone staying in this house. If he's out, I'll wait for him to come back; and in the meantime I wish to ask Miss Fanshawe a few questions.'

'Don't you think you're going to drag my girl into this!' said Ermyntrude, a dangerous gleam in her eyes. 'I'll put up with a good deal, but I won't put up with that! My Vicky's an innocent child, just on the threshold of life, and if you imagine I'm going to stand by while you rub the bloom off her, you'll very soon find out where you get off, and so I warn you!'

The Inspector turned a dull red. 'There's no call for you to talk like that, madam. I'm sure I don't want to rub any bloom off anybody! But I've got my duty to do, and I'm bound to tell you that I can't have you trying to obstruct me the way you're trying to!'

A voice from above made him look quickly up the staircase. 'Oh, darling Ermyntrude, I do think that's so dear and quaint of you!' said Vicky. 'Only I simply haven't got any bloom left after what's happened, and anyway you can see what a nice man he probably is in his off-time.' She bestowed one of her more angelic smiles upon the Inspector, and said confidingly: 'I dare say you've got daughters of your own?'

The Inspector was not unnaturally put off his balance by the sudden and enchanting vision of a fragile beauty, ethereally fair in a frock of unrelieved black, and said that he was not a family man.

'Oh, aren't you? I quite thought you must be,' said Vicky. 'Do you want to talk to me? Shall I come down?'

'If you please, miss.'

Ermyntrude, whose wrath had given way to the fondest maternal admiration, watched her daughter float downstairs in a drift of black chiffon, and said involuntarily: 'Oh, Vicky, I am glad you've changed out of those trousers! Somehow they didn't seem right to me.'

'Oh no, they were utterly anomalous!' agreed Vicky. Her gaze fell upon Hugh. 'I can't imagine why you've come back. I think you're frightfully uncalled-for.'

'You ought to be grateful to me for swelling your audience,' replied Hugh.

'I must have people in sympathy with me,' said Vicky. '*All* great artists are like that.'

'What's that got to do with it?' inquired Hugh unkindly.

The Inspector interrupted this exchange without ceremony. 'You are Miss Victoria Fanshawe?' he said.

'Yes, didn't you know? Only *not* Victoria, if you don't mind, because I practically never feel like that.'

'My information,' pursued the Inspector relentlessly, 'is that at the time of your stepfather's death you were walking by the stream with your dog. Is that correct?'

'Yes, and I definitely heard the shot, only I quite thought it was someone potting rabbits.'

'Did you see anyone amongst the bushes, miss?'

'No, but I don't think I could have. They're awfully thick by the stream. Besides, I didn't look, and as a matter of fact I wasn't paying any attention at all, until I heard Mr White's voice, and Janet White sobbing. That's what made me go down to the bridge.'

'And this dog of yours, miss: he didn't bark, or anything, as though he knew there was a stranger prowling about?'

Vicky shook her head. 'No, he didn't, which makes it look rather as though it wasn't a stranger, now I come to think of it. Unless, of course, he kept jolly still, and Roy didn't get wind of him.'

Ermyntrude said uneasily: 'But, lovey, it can't have been other than a stranger. Not anyone belonging to us, I mean, and it isn't to be supposed any of our friends would go and do a thing like that.'

'No, I worked it all out while I was changing,' said Vicky. 'I think Percy must have done it.'

'Vicky, we don't want to go into that!' said Ermyntrude hurriedly. 'It'll be all over the country once anyone gets wind of it! Now, you hold your tongue, sweetie, like a good girl!'

'Oh, darling, did you want me not to mention Percy? I'm so sorry, but I haven't myself got any compunction, because he said he was the declared enemy of all our class, so that it seems awfully like he did it.'

'I must request you, miss, to give me a plain answer!' said the Inspector, regarding her with such an alert expression on his face that Mary's heart sank. 'Who is this person you refer to as Percy?'

'Well, he's a Communist,' said Vicky. 'He's Percy Baker, and he works at Gregg's, in Burntside.'

'What makes you suppose he might have had something to do with Mr Carter's death? Had he got a grudge against him?'

'Yes, but it's a very sordid story,' said Vicky softly. 'You wouldn't like to hear it from an innocent girl's lips.'

'I don't mind whose lips – look here, miss, are you trying to make game of me? Because, if so – '

'Oh no, no, no!' faltered Vicky, looking the picture of scared virginity.

Ermyntrude arose majestically from the couch. 'Is nothing sacred to you?' she demanded of the Inspector. 'Won't you be satisfied until you've crucified me?'

'No, I won't – I mean, there's no question of me doing anything of the sort!' said the exasperated Inspector. 'What I want, and what I'm going to have, is the truth! And I warn you, madam, you're doing yourself no good by carrying on in this unnatural way!'

'Don't think that you can bully me!' begged Ermyntrude. 'I may look to you like a defenceless woman, but you'll find your mistake if you try me too far!'

'Oh, Aunt Ermy, do, do control yourself!' said Mary wearily. 'Percy Baker, Inspector, is the brother of a girl whom my cousin, I'm sorry to say, had got into trouble. But as all he wanted from my cousin was money, I can't see why he should have killed him.'

'No, that's what I thought at first,' agreed Vicky, 'but I must say he did seem to me to be frightfully undecided about his racket, when I saw him. I wouldn't wonder at all if he suddenly made up his mind to go all out for revenge, because he rather approves of massacring people, and thinks the French Revolution was a pretty good act, 'specially while the Terror lasted.'

'The girl's name and address?' said the Inspector, holding his pencil poised above his notebook.

'Well, we're not, as a matter of fact, on calling-terms,' said Vicky. 'She works at the Regal Cinema, in Fritton.'

'That's right: brandish my shame over the whole countryside!' said Ermyntrude, tottering back to the couch. 'Pillory me as much as you like!'

'Darling Ermyntrude, it isn't your shame at all. You don't mind my brandishing Gladys's shame, do you?'

'I can assure you, madam, I shall, so far as I am able,

conduct my inquiries with the utmost discretion,' said the Inspector.

'Yes, I wish I may see you!' retorted Ermyntrude tartly. 'And if you're going to interview that – that – well, never mind what, but if you're going to see that girl, you can tell her that she can sing for her five hundred pounds, for she won't get it out of me, not after this!'

'Is that the sum that was demanded from Mr Carter, madam?'

'Yes, you may well look surprised!' said Ermyntrude. 'And the young man coming up here, as bold as brass, to blackmail my husband in the middle of a dinner-party, and him having the face to tell me as cool as you please that he'd have to ask me for five hundred to get rid of this Gladys with!'

'Mr Carter told you what he wanted this sum for?' said the Inspector incredulously.

'Well, he had to, or I wouldn't have given it to him.'

The Inspector coughed. 'No doubt that was the cause of your disagreement with Mr Carter, madam?'

'Of course it was!' replied Ermyntrude. 'Well, I ask you, wouldn't you be a bit upset if you found that your husband was carrying on like a Mormon all over the town, and expecting you to provide for a pack of – well, I don't want to be coarse, so we'll leave it at that!'

The Inspector was staring at her. 'Yes, madam, I'm bound to say I would. But – but – did you tell Mr Carter you would give him this money?'

'Well, what else was I to do?' demanded Ermyntrude. 'Faults I may have, and I don't deny it, but thank God no one's ever said I was mean!'

A new train of thought had been set up in the Inspector's mind. He said in a suspiciously mild voice: 'I don't think I need to ask you any more questions at present, madam, except what you were doing at the time of Mr

Carter's death – just a matter of routine!' he added, perceiving a spark in Ermyntrude's eye.

'How do I know when he died? What are you trying to get at?'

'Judging from the evidence I've heard so far, madam, and the time of Mr White's phone call to the police station, Mr Carter was shot at about five minutes to five.'

'It makes no difference to me when he was shot,' said Ermyntrude. 'I've been lying down the whole afternoon on my bed.'

'And you, miss?' said the Inspector, turning suddenly towards Mary.

'I came downstairs just before my cousin set out to go to the Dower House. When he left, I went out to get some tomatoes from one of the hot-houses.'

'Where is this hot-house, miss?'

'By the kitchen-garden, on the other side of the house.'

'I take it you heard nothing?'

'No, nothing at all.'

'I see, miss.' The Inspector shut his note book. 'I should like to interview the servants, if you please.'

'Certainly,' Mary replied. 'But only the butler and his wife, and the under-housemaid are in. The rest of them went out immediately after luncheon. If you'll come into the morning-room, I'll send the butler to you at once.'

The Inspector thanked her, and followed her to the morning-room. Ermyntrude, after commenting acridly on the effrontery of policemen who behaved as though the place belonged to them, allowed herself to be persuaded to go into the drawing-room.

When Mary came back to the hall she found Hugh alone there. 'I think I ought to clear out,' he said. 'But if there's anything I can do, you know you've only to tell me.'

'Oh, don't go!' said Mary, who was feeling a good deal

shaken. 'I can't cope with them! It's like being in a madhouse, and when that awful Prince gets back, it'll be worse. Wasn't Aunt Ermy ghastly? And as for that little beast, Vicky, I'd like to wring her neck! She deliberately dragged Wally's affair with Gladys Baker into it! The one thing we wanted to keep quiet about!'

'I don't think you could have done that, though I admit I was a trifle startled when Vicky flung the bomb into our midst. She seems to have recovered from her first shock.'

'Of course she's recovered! She's probably enjoying all the sensation. But, Hugh, what are we going to do? Who did kill Wally? And how am I to stop Aunt Ermy making foolish admissions?'

'I shouldn't think you could do that,' said Hugh frankly. 'You might have a shot at quelling Vicky, though. As for who killed Wally, I haven't the faintest idea, unless Vicky was right, and it was Baker.'

'Oh, I hope it was!' Mary said, pressing her hands to her temples.

Hugh lifted his brows. 'Like that, is it? Not keeping anything back from the police, are you, Mary? Because, if so, don't.'

'No, no, of course I'm not! Only we've been living in a sort of atmosphere of drama, and repressions, and I expect I've let it get on my nerves. Hugh, couldn't it have been an accident?'

'Hardly,' he replied. 'The only persons who could conceivably have been shooting at rabbits in the Dower House grounds – five o'clock on a Sunday afternoon, too! – are White, or his son. Well, it wasn't White, and I don't see why it should have been his son.'

'Where was Alan?'

'I don't know. Not present.'

'Anyway, there isn't the slightest reason why he should want to kill Wally,' said Mary, with a sigh.

Vicky came out of the drawing-room just then, with a large box of chocolates, which she offered both to Mary and Hugh. When they declined this form of refreshment, she perched herself on the back of the sofa, with her feet on the cushioned seat, and laid the box across her knees. 'Poor darling Ermyntrude is a bit exhausted,' she remarked, selecting a truffle from the box. 'Myself, I thought the scene was too long for her, and *much* too heavy.'

'Need you talk as though we were taking part in theatricals?' snapped Mary.

'Yes, because we're bound to be, with Ermyntrude and me in the thick of it. We simply can't help it, darling. Particularly Ermyntrude, because she always wanted to play in heavy tragedy, and no one ever gave her the chance, so you can't blame her for letting herself go now.'

'It's so false!' Mary exclaimed. 'You know as well as I do that she didn't care tuppence about Wally!'

'No, I do think she had got awfully sick of him,' agreed Vicky, choosing another chocolate from the box.

'Very well then, all this pretence of tragedy is in the worst of bad taste!'

'Don't be silly, darling: if she still cared about Wally I don't think she'd do it. I'm not *sure*, mind you, but I rather believe not. And after all, you can't very well expect her to go all hard-boiled, and let everyone know she doesn't care a bit.'

'I don't expect it, but a little reticence, and dignity – '

Vicky raised her eyes from the chocolates. 'Oh, Mary, you must be completely addled! Why on earth should poor Ermyntrude suddenly become reticent and dignified, when that isn't her line at all? She couldn't put over an act like that, which is why I think it's so right of her just to play herself, if you know what I mean.'

'Leaving your mother out of the discussion,' said Hugh, 'what part are you proposing to play?'

'It depends,' replied Vicky. 'How hellish! I've struck a hard chocolate which is wholly inedible. What on earth will I do with it?'

'I wish you'd stop eating chocolates!' said Mary crossly. '*Is* this quite the moment?'

Vicky wrinkled her brow. 'Well, I didn't have any tea, and quite truthfully I don't see anything particularly irreverent about it. In fact, darling, you're being fairly fraudulent yourself, when you come to consider it. What's more, the whole situation seems to me so awful that if you're going to make it worse, by putting over a pious act of your own, life will become definitely unbearable.'

'I'm sorry if I sounded artificially pious,' replied Mary. 'I suppose you feel that you helped to make things more bearable by telling that policeman all about Baker?'

'I wouldn't wonder. I get very brilliant in my bath, and I had a bath before I came down, and I decided that if you've got a dissolute secret which is practically bound to come to light, you'd much better be the first person to mention it. Moreover,' she added, eyeing the chocolates with her head on one side, 'it took the Inspector's mind off me for the moment, which I particularly wanted to do.'

'Particularly wanted to do?'

'Well, I've got to think up a convincing excuse for being practically on the scene of the crime, haven't I?'

'You little fool,' interrupted Hugh, 'are you seriously proposing to fake an alibi for yourself?'

'Oh yes, I was a Girl Guide once, for about a fortnight, and they say you should always Be Prepared. Which reminds me of what I actually came to talk to you about, Mary. Do you think, considering everything, it might do good if we directed the Inspector's attention to Alexis?'

'Do good?' gasped Mary. 'Do you mean, try and cast suspicion on the unfortunate man?'

'Yes, but in an utterly lady-like way.'

'No, I do not! I never heard of anything so – so conscienceless!'

'But, darling, don't be one of those irksome people who can't look at a thing from more than one angle! Because this is probably going to be very momentous. You can't pretend it would be a cherishing sort of thing to do to let Ermyntrude marry Alexis. The more I consort with him, the more I feel convinced he's exactly like somebody or other in Shakespeare, who smiled and smiled and was a villain. And, unless we gum up the works, there isn't a thing to stop him marrying Ermyntrude, and then abandoning the poor sweet as soon as he's hypnotized her into making a colossal settlement on him.'

Mary looked appealingly towards Hugh. He said judicially: 'I quite agree that it would be a mistake for your mother to marry Varasashvili, but it would be a damned dirty trick to try and cast suspicion on him, and you mustn't do it. Not that the police are likely to pay much heed to you once they've been privileged to see a little more of you.'

'You never know,' Vicky murmured.

'In any case, it won't be necessary for you to shove your oar in,' said Hugh. 'The police are naturally suspicious of everyone who was in any way connected with your stepfather.'

'Yes,' said Mary. 'And what the Inspector won't know of the cross-currents in this house after his heart-to-heart talk with Peake, won't be worth knowing!'

8

Inspector Cook, who had had no very wide experience of murder cases, and who had been thrown badly out of his stride by his interview with the members of Wally Carter's family, was discovering in Peake, the butler, the first witness who gave his evidence fully, and to the point. Mrs Peake and the young housemaid he had soon dismissed, for the housemaid was too frightened to stop sobbing, and Mrs Peake, a comfortably shaped woman who had, she informed him, been in the best service all her life, declined knowing anything beyond the realm of her kitchen.

But Peake gave the Inspector no trouble at all. He had been in his pantry, he said, at the time of Wally's death, but he admitted without any hesitation that he could produce no proof of this statement. When he was asked if he knew of anyone having a grudge against Wally, he looked down his thin nose, and replied primly that he believed a young man calling himself Baker had considerable cause to bear Wally a grudge.

'Yes, I want to know more about that young fellow,' said the Inspector. 'I understand he came up to the house to see Mr Carter?'

'He came twice,' said Peake. 'Upon the first occasion, which was early yesterday afternoon, Miss Vicky interviewed him. I could not say what took place between them, I'm sure. He returned about half past nine in the evening, and although I informed him that Mr Carter was engaged with guests, he refused to withdraw. He came upon a motor bicycle on both occasions. He appeared to me to be a very violent young man.'

'Ah, violent, was he? What makes you think that?'

'He uttered threats of a mysterious nature, and when I told him to be off he put his foot down so that I was unable to shut the door.'

'What sort of threats?'

'I should not like to say,' replied Peake. 'I paid very little heed to him, seeing that he was quite a common person, and wearing one of those red ties. I recall that he said Mr Carter would be sorry if he refused to see him, besides ranting a great deal about his sister's honour, in a very vulgar way.'

'Oh! Did Mr Carter see him?'

'Mr Carter was with him in the library for about half an hour.'

'Did you happen to hear what was said?' asked the Inspector.

'Certainly not,' replied Peake frigidly.

'Any sounds of altercation?'

'Upon my way through the hall, I noticed that Baker's voice was unbecomingly raised,' admitted Peake.

'What about today? Has he been here again?'

'He has not been here to my knowledge.'

'And is he the only person you know of who might have wanted to murder Mr Carter?'

'Oh no, Inspector!' said Peake calmly.

The Inspector looked narrowly at him. 'Come on, then: out with it! What other enemies had he got?'

'There is Mr Steel, for one,' answered Peake.

'Do you mean Mr Steel of Oaklands Farm?'

'That's right, Inspector.'

'What had he got against Mr Carter?'

'It is common knowledge that Mr Steel is greatly attached to Mrs Carter.'

'Do you mean he's in love with her?'

'That is the general opinion, Inspector. Mr Steel is not one to hide his feelings, and I have more than once seen him look at Mr Carter in a way which gave me quite a turn.' He coughed behind his hand. 'I wouldn't want to conceal anything from you, Inspector, and I am bound to say that Mr Carter did not behave to Mrs Carter as he should. There have been some very regrettable incidents. One could not altogether blame Mr Steel for feeling as he did. We have thought lately in the servants' hall, that matters were approaching what one might call a crisis. Mr Steel called to see Mrs Carter this morning, at a time when she was greatly upset by a quarrel with Mr Carter. When Mr Steel left, I chanced to be within earshot, and I could not but hear what he said to Miss Cliffe in the hall.'

'What was that?'

'I'm sure I don't wish to say anything that might give you a wrong impression, Inspector. Mr Steel was in a black rage, and he told Miss Cliffe he would like to break Mr Carter's neck.'

'Did he see Mr Carter this morning?'

'No, Inspector. He left the house saying he could not bring himself to sit at table with Mr Carter. He told Miss Cliffe he had been in love with Mrs Carter ever since he had first known her.'

'Nice goings-on in this house!' muttered the Inspector. 'What about this Prince? What's he doing here?'

'Prince Varasashvili,' replied Peake, 'is a friend of Mrs Carter. She met him at Antibes.'

'Oh, one of those, is he?' said the Inspector knowingly.

'An impoverished foreign nobleman, I understand, Inspector. Very much the ladies' man. We have noticed that Mrs Carter seems to be greatly taken with him.'

'What about Mr Carter?'

'Mr Carter was not in favour of the Prince's visit. Mr

Carter went so far as to say to me, when he was slightly intoxicated, that it was his belief the Prince was after his wife's money.'

'He did, did he? What about Mrs Carter's daughter? It wouldn't by any chance be her he's after?'

'I fancy not, Inspector.'

'What kind of a girl is this Miss Fanshawe?'

'Miss Vicky, Inspector, is a very unexpected young lady. One never knows what she will be at next, in a manner of speaking. She is devoted to Mrs Carter.'

'And the other one?'

'Miss Cliffe is a nice young lady. She was Mr Carter's ward, and Mr Carter did tell me that he should leave all his money to her.'

'Well, that wasn't much, by all accounts.'

'Mr Carter, Inspector, was expecting to come into a great deal of money. He never made any secret of that. He had a rich aunt, a very old lady, I understand, who has been confined in a private lunatic asylum for many years.'

'From what I've seen of this house, that's one thing that doesn't surprise me!' said the Inspector.

He put one or two more questions to the butler, but soon found that Peake had told him all he knew. He requested him to summon Miss Cliffe to the morning-room, and sat digesting the information he had acquired until Mary came in.

'You want to speak to me, Inspector?'

'If you please, miss,' said the Inspector, indicating a chair.

She sat down on it. She was looking a little pale, and there was an anxious expression in her eyes which did not escape the Inspector.

'Now, miss! I understand that Mr Robert Steel called here this morning to see Mrs Carter. Is that a fact?'

'Yes.'

'You didn't mention it to me before. How was that?'

'I didn't think it was important. Mr Steel is a close friend, and often drops in to see us.'

'Was Mr Steel a close friend of Mr Carter's, miss?'

She hesitated. 'I should call him a friend of the house.'

'Is it not a fact that he is Mrs Carter's friend?'

'He is more her friend than Mr Carter's. But he is also a friend of mine.'

'We'll let that pass, miss. Had you no reason to suppose that Mr Steel might feel more than friendly towards Mrs Carter?'

'You had better ask him,' said Mary stiffly.

'I shall do so, miss, make no mistake about that! But I'm asking you now: when he was here this morning did Mr Steel give you any reason to suppose that he was feeling very *un*-friendly towards Mr Carter?'

'Mr Steel and Mr Carter never hit it off very well,' she replied evasively.

'No, miss? Why was that?'

'I don't know. They are very different types.'

'I put it to you, miss, that you know very well that Mr Steel is in love with Mrs Carter.'

'Perhaps,' Mary said. 'It wouldn't be surprising if he were.'

'My information is that Mr Steel told you this morning that he had been in love with Mrs Carter ever since he first knew her. Is that correct?'

Though she had mistrusted Peake, she had not suspected that he had overheard her conversation with Steel. Colour rushed into her cheeks; she felt the ground sliding from under her feet; and could only answer: 'Yes. He did say so.'

'Did he also tell you that he would like to break Mr Carter's neck?'

'I don't know. I can't remember.'

'Come, come, miss! Don't you think you would remember if anyone had made a threat like that?'

'Oh, it wasn't a threat!' Mary said unguardedly. 'Mr Steel was very angry with Mr Carter for upsetting his wife, and people *do* say stupid things when they're angry.'

'And it didn't seem important to you, in view of what has happened?'

'No, not in the least.'

'You weren't surprised that Mr Steel should say such a thing?'

'No. He has rather a quick temper – ' She broke off, aghast at her own disclosures.

'He has rather a quick temper, has he? Perhaps he has said very much the same sort of thing before about what he'd like to do to Mr Carter?'

'No, indeed he hasn't!'

'Oh? And yet you weren't surprised when he said it today?'

'No. I can't explain, but surely you know how one says extravagant things one doesn't really mean when one is angry?'

The Inspector ignored this, and as he seemed to have no more questions to ask, Mary rose to her feet. 'If that's all – ? You wanted to see Prince Varasashvili. He came back about ten minutes ago. Shall I ask him to come in here?'

'Thank you, miss, if you'll be so good.'

The Inspector's first view of the Prince did not predispose him in his favour. The Prince's sleek black hair, with its ordered waves, his brilliant smile, and his accentuated waist-line, filled the Inspector, a plain man, with vague repulsion. He thought that the Prince looked just the type of good-for-nothing lizard whom you would expect to find hanging round a rich woman like Ermyntrude Carter.

The Prince came in without hesitation, and made a

gesture with his expressive hands. 'You are the Inspector of Police? You desire to interrogate me? I understand perfectly. This terrible affair! You will forgive me that I find myself so startled, so very much shocked, I can find no words! Ah, my poor hostess!'

'Yes, indeed, sir,' said the Inspector woodenly. 'Very bad business. May I have your full name and address, please?'

'My address!' said the Prince, with one of his mournful smiles. 'Alas, I have no longer an address to call my own since my country has been in the hands of my enemies. My name is Alexis Feodor Gregorovitch Varasashvili. I am absolutely at your service.'

The Inspector drew a breath, and requested him to spell it. When he had succeeded in transcribing the name correctly in his notebook, he said that he understood that the Prince was a friend of Mrs Carter.

'She does me the honour of saying so,' bowed the Prince.

'Have you been acquainted with her for long?'

'No, for I met her a few months ago only, at Antibes.'

'And Mr Carter, too?'

'Ah no, Mr Carter did not accompany his wife! I met Mr Carter for the first time on Friday, when I arrived to spend the week-end here. Little did I think then it would end in such tragedy!'

'No, sir. I understand that you were one of the last people to see Mr Carter before he set out for the Dower House this afternoon?'

'Is it so indeed? That I did not know, for I myself was gone from the house before he left it. I asked of him the way to Dr Chester's house. Miss Cliffe, I think, was present. Yes, I am sure. I left her with him.'

'At what time would that have been, sir?'

The Prince shook his head. 'I am sorry. I cannot tell

you. It was certainly more than half past four, but I cannot be precise, for I had not the occasion to look at my watch.'

'What did you do when you left the house, sir?'

'But naturally I walked to the garage. I should explain, perhaps, that Miss Fanshawe was so very kind as to lend me her car. I drove myself, therefore, to the doctor's house.'

'Did you happen to notice what the time was when you arrived there?'

The smile flashed out again. 'It is, I see, very fortunate for me that I can say yes, Inspector. Mr Carter told me it was impossible that I should mistake the house, and this I found was entirely true. I did, in fact, arrive at five minutes to five. The doctor was not in: he had been called out, his housekeeper told me. But in perhaps ten minutes he came back, and we had tea together, and he showed me his relics, until it was time for him to go to his surgery. Then I motored back here, to find – what horror!'

'Yes, indeed, sir, I'm sure. I take it you can prove what you've just told me? That you reached the doctor's house at five minutes to five?'

The Prince wrinkled his brow. 'Of course it is most necessary. Surely the good woman, Dr Chester's housekeeper, would know? Yes, for we spoke of the time, since I had arrived a little before I was expected.'

The Inspector nodded. 'Very good, sir. Were you a member of the shooting-party Mr Carter went on yesterday?'

'Certainly, yes.'

'I understand there was some sort of an accident, sir?'

The Prince flung up his hands. 'Oh no, no, no! That is to exaggerate, I assure you! There was no accident, but only a great piece of folly, I am persuaded.'

'On whose part, sir?'

'I must not conceal from you that it was the carelessness of Mr Carter that so nearly made an accident. You have heard, perhaps, that Mr Carter spoke of being fired at, in particular pointing to Mr Steel in a manner not at all polite, and quite absurd also! I do not know whether there was some misunderstanding about Mr Carter's post: it is certain that I, and Mr Steel, and Dr Chester, thought he was to have stood in a certain place. It is possible that Mr Carter mistook, though Mr Steel, and indeed the good doctor too, declared it was not so, but merely that he had moved from his original stand. I do not know, but that Mr Steel should shoot with deliberation at his host I find not at all probable.'

'So Mr Carter thought it was Mr Steel who shot at him, sir? What made him pick on him rather than you, or the doctor, who, I understand, might as easily have done it?'

'Ah no, not as easily!' protested the Prince. 'For both of us, it would have been a more difficult shot. But it is a piece of nonsense! It is not worth discussing.'

'That's as may be, sir, and for me to judge. What exactly did Mr Carter say about this incident?'

'You ask me to recall absurdities, Inspector. Mr Carter was one who talked a great deal, without much sense. I did not concern myself, for when a man talks in the style of the theatre about those who desire his death, it is not important, but on the contrary, quite tiresome. For me, I did not find that Mr Carter's dislike of Mr Steel was at all sensible.'

'Did you form any opinion why Mr Carter should have thought Mr Steel wanted him put away?'

The Prince studied his polished finger-nails for a moment in silence. Then he looked up rather deprecatingly. 'Inspector, you ask of me a very delicate question. I must tell you that I am not familiar with these people. I speak as an onlooker: I am nothing but a week-end guest here. But it is plain to me that Mr Steel admires excessively Mrs Carter. One understands in part the jealousy of Mr Carter. I have perhaps said too much. You will not regard it. Is there more that you would ask of me?'

'That'll be all for the present, sir. Were you meaning to go back to London tomorrow? Because if so, I must trouble you – '

'Ah, not now!' the Prince said. 'If I can be of use to Mrs Carter, who is left without a protector, be assured that I shall remain! She asks me, in fact.'

'No doubt that would be best, sir,' agreed the Inspector.

He left the house, shortly after his interview with the Prince, feeling that he had amassed sufficient evidence to keep him busy for some time. Returning to the Dower House, he was met in the drive by the Sergeant he had left in charge of investigations there. The Sergeant greeted him with an air of considerable satisfaction. 'We've got the gun, sir!' he said.

'Got the gun, have you? Where did you find it?'

'Down there in the shrubbery,' replied the Sergeant, jerking his thumb over his shoulder. 'Wright's been over it for fingerprints, but there aren't any. That makes it murder all right, I reckon. Not a doubt but that the bloke who did this took his shot, dropped the gun, and slipped off through them bushes to the road. Nice, neat job, if you ask me.'

'Find any footprints?'

'No, sir. Ground's baked hard, you know. I'll show you.'

He led the Inspector to the lawn that ran down to the stream, but instead of going to the bridge, he plunged into the thicket at a point where a clump of azaleas jutted out beyond the dark mass of rhododendrons. Worming his way between the bushes, and holding back stray branches so that his superior's face should not be scratched by them, he conducted him to a place in the centre of the shrubbery where the bushes grew less thickly. 'This is where I found the rifle,' he said. 'Now, you take a look, sir! Beautiful, easy shot, wouldn't it be?'

The Inspector dropped on to his knee, and found that he was looking down at the bridge some twenty yards away, and clearly visible between an azalea and a towering rhododendron. 'Yes,' he said slowly. 'Easy enough. He must have stayed quiet, though, till Mr White, and the other two, had run down to the bridge, or they'd have heard him.'

'That's all right,' replied the Sergeant. 'Plenty of time for him to make his getaway while they was on the bridge. I reckon this is the way he went.' He pushed on through the thicket, demonstrating to his chief, as he went, why the unknown murderer must, in his opinion, have struck up towards the carriage-drive, which was at the side of the house. 'The stream bends right round, as you know, sir. There's a bit of a pool on the other side of that bank, so it stands to reason he didn't go that way. No, the way I look at it is, he fired his shot, waited till the people by the house had run down to the bridge, dropped the rifle, and slunk off the way he came, either taking a chance of being seen from the house, and coming out on the drive just by the gate, or, more likely, climbing over the wall and walking off down the road. Anyone could get over that wall, as you'll see for yourself in a minute, sir.'

'Hold on a moment! I'll take a look at the lie of the land,' said the Inspector, surmounting the slight, sandy bank which the Sergeant had pointed out to him.

The stream, taking a bend to the south, widened, below the bank, into a pool, narrowed again, and meandered on until it ran under a bridge in the highway not far from one of the drive-gates. The Inspector gazed at the pool in ruminative silence until the Sergeant, unable to discover what was holding his interest, ventured to ask him.

'I was thinking,' said the Inspector, 'that no one could jump over that pool.'

'Well, they wouldn't want to, would they?' said the Sergeant, a little impatiently. 'The getaway must have been the way I told you, sir. Stands to reason!'

'Nor,' said the Inspector, 'could they jump the stream above it without being seen by anyone standing on the bridge between the two houses.'

'But sir – '

'Just a moment, if you please!' said the Inspector, moving along the bank. 'Didn't happen to notice that below the pool the stream's a sight narrower, did you?'

'Well, I'm bound to say I don't get what you're after, sir!' protested the Sergeant. 'Are you telling me the murderer got away through the Palings' grounds?'

'I'm not telling you anything as yet,' replied the Inspector. 'I'm not leaving a possibility out of my calculations, either.'

The Sergeant looked at the stream running below him, and then glanced across at the opposite bank. 'I suppose it would be easy enough to jump,' he said. 'I'd expect to find a footmark or so, though. Ground's bound to be soft, not to say boggy, down by the water.'

'Take a look,' said the Inspector briefly, and went off to explore the other way of escape.

The Sergeant rejoined him later by the police-car in the drive. There was mud on his boots, and he was looking rather sulky. 'I didn't find any trace of footmarks,' he said.

'Ah well!' replied the Inspector. 'Maybe I'm wrong. Nothing more to be done here: we'll get back to the station.'

As the police-car reached the gate, it had to wait to

allow another car, on the road, to go past. The Sergeant remarked that it was Dr Chester's Rover. 'Dashing off to Palings, I wouldn't wonder. By all accounts, Mrs Carter sends for him to hold her hand every time her little finger aches. I don't envy him his job today.'

'No,' agreed the Inspector. 'Nor me.'

'It wasn't him called in when Carter was shot, was it?'

'No. Hinchcliffe. Chester was out on a case.'

'I'll bet he's thanking his stars for it!' said the Sergeant. 'Fancy having to tell Mrs C. how he found her husband!'

The Sergeant was quite right in thinking that the car was the doctor's, and that the doctor was bound for Palings. A few minutes later he drew up outside the porch, and got out, stripping off the gloves he wore for driving, and tossing them into the car. The front-door was still standing open, and he walked into the hall, encountering there Mary, who had just come down the stairs. She was looking pale, and worried, but her eyes lit up when she saw Chester, and she went quickly towards him, holding out her hands.

'Oh, Maurice, I'm so glad you've come!'

He took her hands, holding them firmly in his for a moment. 'I couldn't come sooner. I was in the middle of my surgery when Hinchcliffe rang up to tell me. How's Ermyntrude?'

'Awful!' said Mary, with a shudder. 'Lyceum stage. It's no use frowning at me. You'll see.'

He looked critically at her. 'You look as though you're in need of my professional services yourself. I prescribe a stiff whisky-and-soda. See you take it!'

'It's not such a bad idea,' she admitted. 'I don't seem to have had time to collect myself. I can't even quite grasp what's happened. It doesn't seem possible!'

'What did happen?' he asked. 'Hinchcliffe merely told

me that White sent for him, and that he found Carter dead – shot on the bridge. Is anything known?'

'No, nothing. There are only the most nightmarish possibilities. We had a Police Inspector here until a short time ago. It was – pretty ghastly. I always thought I was a level-headed sort of person, but I didn't seem able to think things out a bit, and I'm afraid I made a perfect fool of myself. Hugh keeps on drumming it into me that I must tell the truth, the whole truth, and nothing but the truth, but you know what a hopelessly wrong impression one can give by telling some truths!'

'Hugh Dering? Is he here?'

'No, not now. He was here when it happened, and he stayed, like the angel he is, until the Inspector left. Do you want to see Ermyntrude?'

'Yes, where is she?'

'Receiving consolation from the Prince in the drawing-room,' she replied.

'That fellow!' Chester said, in a tone of disgust. 'All right, show me in!'

Ermyntrude was once more reclining on a couch, but by this time she had put on her corsets again, and, following her daughter's example, a black tea-gown. A shaded lamp stood behind the couch, and beside her the Prince sat, upon a low chair, holding one of her hands in his, and talking to her in his soft, caressing way. When Mary opened the door, Ermyntrude sighed: 'Oh, can't I be left in peace ever?' But when she saw Chester walk in, she exclaimed in a much more robust tone: 'Oh, Maurice, if it's not you! Oh, come in, come in! You're the very person I want!'

The Prince got up. If he was annoyed, he did not show it, but smiled and bowed, and said that he gladly relinquished his place to the doctor.

Ermyntrude sat up, extending her hand towards

Chester. 'Oh, Maurice, I wish it had been you!' she said. 'Somehow it seems to make it worse, Hinchcliffe being sent for, for you know I've never liked him, nor poor Wally either!'

Chester took her hand, but glanced over his shoulder, addressing himself impartially both to Mary and to the Prince. 'Too many people in this room,' he said. 'Prince, take Miss Cliffe into the dining-room, and give her a whisky-and-soda, will you? See she drinks it, too.'

'But with the greatest pleasure on earth!' the Prince said. 'We have indeed neglected Miss Cliffe, who is all the time so thoughtful for the welfare of others!'

He held open the door for Mary, but instead of permitting her to go with him to the dining-room, he insisted on her sitting down in one of the big leather armchairs that stood in the hall, while he went to mix a drink for her.

He had just brought it to her when Vicky wandered downstairs. 'Oh, hallo! Bottle party?' she inquired.

'Poor Miss Cliffe is exhausted,' explained the Prince. 'I am commanded by Dr Chester to give her whisky, and to be sure she drinks it. I warn you, I shall obey my orders, Miss Cliffe, so do not make a face at your whisky! I am here to make myself useful, and this is my first task.'

Mary pressed her hand to her forehead. 'Vicky, what about dinner?' she asked. 'It must be nearly time. I hope Mrs Peake hasn't taken it into her head that it won't be wanted.'

'Ah no, for Peake is even now setting the table!' the Prince assured her. He smiled at Vicky. 'Sit down, duchinka: you have had so great a shock! You are pale, my little one; you, too, need Alexis to take care of you, I think.'

'Not if it means whisky,' replied Vicky. 'I've already

had three cocktails, so I shouldn't think whisky would agree with me much. Is Maurice here, Mary?'

'Yes, with your mother.'

'Oh, good! Perhaps he'll make her go to bed.' She turned to the Prince, and said prettily: 'We're so sorry this should have happened during your visit, Alexis. I'm afraid you'll take a perfectly ghoulish memory of Palings away with you tomorrow.'

'I do not go tomorrow,' he replied. 'You do not suppose that I would run from you when you are in such trouble! No, no, while that poor Trudinka has need of me, I stay!'

'Oh, Alexis, I do think that's so sweet and sacrificing of you!' said Vicky. 'Only, do you feel it's wise of you?'

'Wise of me? I do not understand!'

'I *rather* suspect that the police will think it's a bit odd of you. That Inspector asked the most unnerving questions about you, and he's *so* dumb that I wouldn't be at all surprised if he's cast you for the part of the murderer.'

'But it is ridiculous!' exclaimed the Prince. 'You are joking, surely!'

'Oh, Alexis, joking at such a time! Oh, how could you think I'd be so frightful?'

'You are overwrought, then. As for your Police Inspector, I snap my fingers at him, so! Do not trouble your so lovely little head on my account, my Vicky!'

A telephone-bell had rung in the distance a minute or two before, and Peake now came into the hall to tell Mary that Mr Steel wished to speak to her.

She pulled herself out of her chair. 'All right, Peake; I'll take it in the library,' she said.

Steel's voice, at the other end of the wire, sounded deeper even than usual. He said: 'That you, Mary? I've just heard the most incredible – It isn't true, is it?'

'If you mean Wally's death, yes, it's true.'

There was a slight pause. 'Mary, you don't mean he was actually murdered, do you?'

'I'm afraid so. How did you hear of it?'

'One of my men's just come in with the news. He says it's all over the village. Good God, I couldn't believe it! Mary, how's Ermyntrude?'

'She's upset, naturally. We hope to get her to bed.'

'I'll come over at once. We can't talk on the telephone.'

'Oh no, you will not come over!' said Mary. 'Dr Chester's with her now, and she doesn't want any visitors tonight. Besides, the more you stay out of this the better it'll be, Robert. Peake heard what you said to me this morning, and he told the police.'

'Hell, what do you think I care for that?'

'I don't know, and I'm past minding, but if you come over here you won't see Aunty Ermy, I promise you.'

There was another pause. 'All right. I'll wait till the morning. Tell her I rang up, won't you?'

'Oh, yes, I'll tell her!' said Mary, glancing round as the door opened, and Vicky came into the room. 'Sorry, I can't stay any longer. Good-bye!' She put the receiver down. 'What have you done with the Prince, Vicky? He hasn't gone back into the drawing-room, has he?'

'No, upstairs. That was one time I didn't strike on the box, wasn't it?'

'Did you think you were going to?'

'Well, I thought there was just a chance. Did Robert ring up to condole?'

'He rang up to know if it was true. He wanted to come round, but I stopped him.'

Vicky lit a cigarette, and flicked the match into the hearth. 'Oh, I think you were frightfully right! I shouldn't be at all taken aback if we discovered he did it, would you?'

'Don't!' implored Mary. 'Yes, of course I should. It isn't possible!'

'Darling, I'm simply dripping with sympathy for you, but don't suddenly be a dewy innocent, because I don't feel I can bear it. If Percy didn't do it, Alexis or Robert must have. There isn't anybody else.'

'Vicky, don't say things like that! You don't know: there may have been others we've never heard of. What would you think if Robert or the Prince said it must be you, because you happened to be in the shrubbery at the time?'

Vicky blew a cloud of smoke. 'But, Mary, dear pet, how could I possibly? I practically never hit anything when I take a gun out.'

'That isn't the impression you generally try to put across,' said Mary dryly. 'Anyone listening to you would imagine you were a pretty good shot.'

'Yes, but when I give *that* impression, I'm just putting on an act,' explained Vicky. 'Actually, I'm rather a lousy shot, I think.'

'I'll remember to tell the Inspector so, if he asks me,' promised Mary.

9

By the next morning, nearly everyone connected with the case, instead of having been soothed by a night's repose, was in a state either of exasperation or of foreboding. The Inspector found himself bogged in a quagmire of evidence; Mary foresaw endless days of strain; the Prince had, apparently, realized his own position, and was feeling it acutely; and Ermyntrude had discovered a fresh grievance against Harold White. Only Vicky came down to breakfast with her usual serenity.

Ermyntrude had been persuaded to breakfast in her room, but not in solitude. She held a sort of court, sitting up in bed against such a background of silk, and lace-edged pillows, and in such an exotic wrapper, that she reminded her visitors irresistibly of a sultan's favourite wife. The morning's post had brought her a certain measure of comfort, for the news of Wally's death had spread quickly over the countryside, and she was able to say with mournful pride that all the best people had written to her. Letters strewed the coverlet of her bed, and whenever she opened one that particularly gratified her, she summoned Mary or Vicky to her side to hear about it. In the intervals of reading the letters of condolence, and absentmindedly consuming a quantity of toast and marmalade, she issued general orders for the day, directed her maid what clothes to lay out for her, and discussed exhaustively the mourning raiment that must instantly be bought for her. Breakfast for those in the dining-room became an unquiet meal, disturbed continuously by the ringing of Ermyntrude's bell, and the constant appearances of housemaids bearing urgent, and very often contradictory, messages from the widow.

It had occurred to Ermyntrude, in the night watches, that not only had her husband met his death on his way to keep an assignation which she had known nothing about, but that no one had so far explained to her why he had gone over to see that Harold White. A note from Lady Dering, delivered by hand, took her mind off this problem for a little while, but she remembered it again when she rang for her breakfast, and at once sent for Mary and commanded her instantly to ring up the Dower House, and to summon White to her presence.

'You mark my words, dearie, whatever it was that took poor Wally there, that White wasn't up to any good!' she said. 'And considering my position, and Wally being shot practically in his garden, I should have thought the least he could do would be to have come right over to apologize – well, no, I don't mean that exactly, but, anyway, he ought to have come.'

By this time, Mary had been connected with the Dower House. Janet's voice hurried into distressful speech, and for quite a few moments Mary had no opportunity of delivering Ermyntrude's message. However, when she saw Ermyntrude stretch out a hand to wrest the pink enamel receiver away from her, she broke in on the flood of Janet's condolences, and said that Ermyntrude was anxious to see White, and would be grateful if he could spare the time to call on her on his way to the colliery offices.

'Grateful!' ejaculated Ermyntrude. 'Don't talk so silly to her, Mary! Tell her I say he is to come!'

Mary did not pass on this peremptory message, because Janet was explaining that her father had left for the collieries.

Mary covered the mouthpiece with her hand. 'He's

gone to work. Janet wants to know if you'd like him to look in this evening.'

'Oh, he's gone to work, has he?' said Ermyntrude wrathfully. 'And no more thought for me lying here in the dark than that bed-post! Not so much as a note, or a message, either!'

'Janet says he told her she was to call this morning, and leave cards.'

'What's the good of cards?' demanded Ermyntrude. 'I don't want her cards! I don't want her either, if it comes to that, for though I'm sure I've nothing against the girl, she frets me to death, and if there *is* a time when I might expect to have my nerves considered, it's now!'

Mary made frantic signs to her to be quiet, and tried to tell Janet that Ermyntrude was not up to receiving visitors. Janet said: 'I thought as I was the last person who saw him alive, she'd like me to come and tell her just how he died.'

'No, I don't think that would be very desirable,' said Mary.

'I thought it might be a comfort to her,' said Janet. 'I'm certain he didn't suffer at all. It was over in an instant. One moment I was standing looking at him – '

'Look here, Janet, not over the telephone!' begged Mary.

'No, of course not. I'll come over and tell you all about it, and it'll sort of set your mind at rest.'

'Thank you,' said Mary faintly.

She hung up the receiver, and turned her attention to Ermyntrude, who had succeeded in working herself up into a state of indignation against White, for having callously gone to work as though nothing had happened; against Janet, for pushing herself in where she was not wanted, and no doubt thinking Wally's death had made her very important, and against Alan, for no very intelligible reason, except that he was the son of his father.

When she was in the middle of a really impassioned diatribe against the Whites, Vicky walked into the room with her table-napkin under her arm, and a slice of toast and butter in one hand, and announced that two reporters were seeking to gain admittance to the house.

Ermyntrude first exclaimed, 'The Press!' in a throbbing voice of anguish, and clasped her head in her hands; but this gesture was merely mechanical, and an instant later she let her hands fall, and sat up, thrusting her breakfast-tray to one side of the bed. 'Whatever happens you're not to talk to them, nor see them either, Vicky!' she said briskly.

'Oh, darling, can't I? I've never had my picture in the papers, and I quite think they might take one of me.'

'That's just what they're not going to get a chance of doing. Now, don't argue, there's a love! God knows I want you to have your photograph in the papers, ducky, and so you shall, but this is the wrong kind of publicity for you, you take my word for it! Mary, run quick, and tell Peake they're not to be let in! Good gracious, it would ruin Vicky's chances – absolutely ruin them! Mary, wait a minute! Let me think! We shall have to give them some kind of a statement, and I was just thinking if Alexis doesn't mind he might have a talk with them; and if they choose to take a picture of him, and say how he's a guest here I'm sure I've no objection to that. Ask him, Mary dear, but tell him to be careful what he says to them!'

The Prince did not at first take very kindly to the suggestion that he should interview the representatives of the Press, but Mary, remembering with what ease Inspector Cook had induced her to disclose far more than she had meant to, was determined that she was not going to allow herself to be interrogated by eager reporters, and made it plain to the Prince that if his object in staying at Palings was to be of use, here was his chance.

It was not long before Janet arrived, carrying a bunch of dahlias, which she begged Mary to give to Ermyntrude with her love.

'I couldn't go into Fritton, because my bicycle's got a puncture, so I had to pick what I could out of the garden,' she explained. 'I'm sorry they aren't nicer, but I felt I must bring something. I wish they could have been lilies.'

Mary took the flowers, and thanked her, and went away to put them in water, leaving Janet to wait in the morning-room. When Ermyntrude, who happened to be on her way downstairs as Mary crossed the hall, saw the offering, she was not at all grateful, but, on the contrary, inclined to be affronted. She said that a lot of dahlias ranging in colour from rich scarlet to flaming yellow looked more like a harvest festival than a funeral, and told Mary to put them where they wouldn't be noticed.

So Mary put them in the garden-hall, and went back to give Janet a mendacious message from Ermyntrude.

Janet presented an even more untidy appearance than usual, and showed a tendency to cry. Though she had not herself liked Wally Carter, and knew very well that he had been a most unsatisfactory husband, stepfather and guardian, she apparently expected Mary to be heartbroken at his death, and asked her anxiously if she had been able to cry.

'No,' said Mary. 'I mean, I don't want to cry.'

'It's the shock,' said Janet. 'I expect you're numbed. I know so well what you're feeling, and if only you could break down and cry you'd be better!'

It was clearly impossible to tell Janet that though shock might be present, grief was not, so Mary merely murmured something unintelligible, and tried not to look as uncomfortable as she felt.

Janet gave her hand a squeeze that conveyed both sympathy and understanding, and stated: 'You want me to tell you exactly what happened.'

Mary agreed, and Janet at once launched into her story, decorating it with such a wealth of detail that the main thread was more than once in danger of being lost in the tangle. The information that Samuel Jones had been asked to tea to meet Wally brought a frown to Mary's brow, and she interrupted to say: 'Do you mean the man who owns the store in Fritton?'

'Yes, that's the man. Somehow I can't like him, but he can't be as bad as Alan says, because after all he's a Town Councillor, and I mean to say, he wouldn't be, would he? Oh dear, I can't bear to think of it! You just don't know how awful it was, all day, Mary! Because Alan quarrelled with Father at lunch, and rushed out of the house without finishing his pudding, simply because Mr Jones was coming to tea. And I made some scones, but of course we didn't eat them, and a brand new kettle was ruined, and naturally I couldn't replace it on a Sunday, and Florence had a dreadful time trying to make tea for breakfast in a saucepan, because I need hardly tell you, my dear, that I discovered that the other kettle had a hole in it, and she'd never told me! I'm afraid Father had to wait for his breakfast, and he particularly wanted it at a quarter to eight, so that he could be at the office early. And Alan never came home to supper last night, and when I asked him this morning what he'd been doing, he simply bit my head off! So what with Father being cross, and Alan worse, I've had an awful time. And, you know, when one has seen Death for the first time, it does upset one, only neither Father nor Alan seem to realize what I've been through in the least!'

She burst into tears, and Mary had considerable difficulty in soothing her. When she had at last succeeded, and had also managed to persuade her to go home by the garden-way, in order to escape any reporter who might be lurking by the front gates, she discovered that Robert Steel had arrived, and was waiting to speak to her before presenting himself to Ermyntrude.

She took him at once into the library, and shut the door. 'There's something I've got to tell you, Robert,' she said.

'You told me last night, he replied. 'That butler of yours heard what I said to you yesterday. I've already had a visit from the police.'

'Robert, I'm awfully sorry! What I didn't tell you yesterday, was that I'm afraid I rather gave it away too. When the Inspector asked me point-blank about it, I didn't know what to say, and probably made it all sound much worse than it really was.'

'You needn't worry,' he said calmly. 'I'm not making any secret of the fact that I'm damned glad Carter's dead. But how I can be supposed to have had a hand in it I fail to see.'

'Where were you when it happened?'

'On the farm.'

'Can you prove it? Was anyone with you?'

'Old Jefferson was somewhere around. He wasn't actually with me, but it doesn't matter a tinker's curse, anyway. I'm in no danger of being arrested.'

'But, Robert, are you sure? Everyone knows how you feel about Aunt Ermy, and I'm positive the Inspector's awfully suspicious.'

'He can be as suspicious as he likes, but it'll puzzle him to pin Carter's murder on to me. How the devil am I supposed to have known that Carter would be on that bridge at five minutes to five? I didn't even know he was going to tea at White's place. Look here, I didn't come here to discuss that: I want to know how Ermyntrude is.'

'She's all right. Did the Inspector seem satisfied?'

'Can't say; I didn't ask him. Has that fellow gone yet?'

'No,' replied Mary, correctly guessing the identity of that fellow. 'He isn't going till all this has been cleared up.'

'Do you mean the police have refused to let him go?'

'I don't think so. Aunt Ermy asked him if he would stay.'

The muscles about his jaw seemed to harden. 'I get it. Can I see Ermyntrude?'

'Yes, I expect she'll be very glad to see you,' replied Mary. 'Only, if it's all the same to you, I'd rather you didn't pick a quarrel with the Prince. We've got enough to contend with already.'

'Don't be a fool!' said Steel shortly. He looked frowningly down at her. 'What was this precious Prince doing when Carter was shot?'

'He was at Dr Chester's house.'

'Seems to me the police might look into his movements before badgering me. I suppose the truth is that the case is beyond their capabilities.'

This, though merely a remark occasioned by annoyance, was the conclusion Inspector Cook had rather despairingly reached. He had come away from Palings with enough evidence to make him feel hopeful of a speedy result to his investigations, but a quiet study of this evidence, coupled with several conflicting circumstan ces, had shaken his confidence.

He was a zealous officer, and he had lost no time in interrogating Percy Baker. He guessed that Baker would leave Fritton on Sunday evening, or very early on Monday morning, since he worked at the larger, manufacturing town of Burntside, some twenty miles from Fritton; and he forwent his supper in order to catch this important witness.

Miss Gladys Baker was easily located. She lived with her widowed mother, in one of the back streets of Fritton. When the Inspector arrived at the house, she, and her mother and brother, were sitting down to supper, in company with Mrs Baker's lodger, an earnest young man who worked in Jones's store. Mrs Baker opened the door to the Inspector, which was perhaps unfortunate, since she was a lady of extremely delicate sensibility, and the information that he wanted to see her son at once brought on her palpitations. However, when she had been supported into the kitchen, and left there in the care of her daughter and the lodger, Percy Baker took the Inspector into the front room, a neat apartment, smelling strongly of must, and decorated with red plush, aspidistras, and pampas grass, and asked him belligerently what he wanted.

He was a good-looking young man, but rather spoiled by the pugnacious expression he habitually wore; and it soon became apparent to the Inspector that in his different way he was quite as dramatically inclined as Ermyntrude Carter. When asked what he had been doing that afternoon, he countered by demanding what his movements had got to do with the police; and when told never to mind about that, he plunged into a dark, and somewhat involved diatribe against the police, whom he called minions of the *bourgeoisie*. Finally, the Inspector managed to elicit from him the admission that he had been out on his motor bicycle.

'Out on your motor-bike, were you? Take anyone with you?'

Baker looked suspiciously at him. 'What are you getting at?'

'You answer my question, and never mind what I'm getting at. Come on, now! Took your young lady, I dare say, pillion-riding?'

Baker sneered horribly at him. 'I've got no time for young ladies. Think I'd get married, with the world the way it is? Marriage is for the rich, and a man who – '

'All right, I don't want to hear about that. Had you got anyone with you, or hadn't you?'

'No,' said Baker sulkily.

'Where did you go?'

'What's that got to do with you?'

'You take it from me, my lad, it's got a lot to do with me. What's more, you're doing yourself no good by refusing to answer my questions.'

'Don't think you can come here brow-beating me!' said Baker. 'The day will come when your kind will be in the gutter, where you'd like to trample the Workers of the World under your feet!'

'One of that sort, are you?' said the Inspector. 'Now you answer me quick, or I'll ask you to come along to the police station!'

'One law for the rich and another for the poor!' said Baker bitterly. 'I went for a run to try out a new bike, since you want to know. I took her to Kershaw, and back. So what?'

'Kershaw, eh? Went through Stilhurst village, didn't you?'

'Suppose I did?' countered Baker, watching him.

'What time would that have been?'

'I don't know. Think I go along looking at my watch?'

'Must have passed by Mrs Carter's place, Palings,' said the Inspector conversationally.

Baker's lean cheeks flamed suddenly. He took a step towards the Inspector, his fists clenched. 'What are you getting at?'

'Now, what is there for you to be all hot-up over in that?' wondered the Inspector.

'Come on, out with it! What are you nosing round

after? Supposing I did pass Palings? What the bloody hell's it got to do with you?'

'Don't you take that tone with me, my lad!' said the Inspector. 'I know how you went out to Palings twice yesterday, to see Mr Carter. What did you want with him, eh?'

'If you know I went twice to see the dirty bastard, you ought to know that too! Go and ask him, if you don't!'

'Very clever, but it won't wash,' said the Inspector. 'You'd better come clean! Trying to put the black on him, weren't you?'

The flush returned. 'I'll knock the teeth down the throat of the lying swine who says so!'

'Oh, lay off that stuff!' the Inspector said roughly. 'You went out to Palings, ranting about Mr Carter having put your sister in the family way – '

'Damn you, keep your ugly trap shut! So that's the game, is it? Well, you can tell Mr Lousy Carter that my sister's got her rights, and he needn't think he can scare me out of bringing him to book! When the Red Flag's raised in this country, it'll be him and them like him that – '

'Stow it! You went to Palings to blackmail Mr Carter for five hundred pounds, didn't you?'

The effect of this accusation was not quite what Cook had expected. Baker's jaw dropped; he repeated in a dazed voice: 'Five hundred pounds?'

'Well? Didn't you?'

'Five hundred – pounds?' said Baker again. 'What the hell do you take me for? Here, I've had enough of your insults! You clear out of this! Five hundred pounds, my foot! I suppose that's what the stinking swine told you? Well, you can damned well tell him from me that he's a bloody liar! And if you think I'd make capital out of my sister's shame, you're as big a bastard as he is!'

'Careful, now! Are you denying you went to Palings to get money out of Mr Carter?'

'I never mentioned five hundred pounds, nor nothing like it! But when a man in his position, fair reeking of money, and old enough to be the girl's father, God damn his soul, gets a poor girl into trouble, he's got to help her, or I'll know the reason why! Oh, it's all very nice and easy for them as has money to burn, but what about them as hasn't? Who's going to support Carter's brat, that's what I'm asking you? Isn't it only justice he should pay for what he done to my sister? What would five bob a week mean to the likes of him? You answer me that, and then say I've been blackmailing the swine!'

'Leaving alone, for the moment, how much you tried to get out of him,' said the Inspector, looking very hard at him, 'you didn't find him willing to pay, did you?'

'No one,' said Baker, somewhat obscurely, 'is going to make out my sister's no better than a common street-walker!'

'Oh! So Mr Carter had his doubts, had he? He didn't see why he should pay for what he suspected wasn't his? Now we're getting at it, aren't we?'

'I'll make him provide for Gladys, if it's the last thing I do!' retorted Baker.

'*But*,' said the Inspector, 'he refused to pay, didn't he?'

'Fobbing me off with excuses!' muttered Baker. 'If I had my way, I'd blow his brains out, the mealy scoundrel! That 'ud learn him to seduce innocent girls! But that's not going to help my sister, that's the way I've got to look at it!'

'Would it surprise you to learn that Mr Carter was shot dead at five minutes to five this afternoon?' asked the Inspector.

'Shot dead?' Baker said numbly. 'I didn't do it. I don't know a thing about it, as God's my witness!'

That was all the Inspector had managed to get out of Percy Baker, and it left him profoundly dissatisfied, for he could not quite bring himself to believe that the young man was acting a part. Nor did he believe that Baker had been acting when he so hotly denied having demanded five hundred pounds from Carter. It began to seem to the Inspector as though the murdered man's relations were playing some deep game, and had not scrupled to entangle Baker in its meshes. It might, he reflected, prove to be a difficult task for Baker to refute the accusation of blackmail.

When he reached the police station, it was to be met with the news that the rifle found in the shrubbery at the Dower House had been identified. It had been registered ten years previously by the late Mr Fanshawe, and was the property of his relict, in whose name the licence had been kept up.

The Inspector drew a breath. 'Someone living in the house,' he said. 'Well! I thought that from the start. And the whole lot of them combining to shift the blame on to young Baker, by spinning this yarn about him putting the black on Carter! It's that woman at the back of it, Superintendent: that screeching blonde, wanting to get rid of Carter, so that she can marry a foreign prince!'

'Go easy!' advised his superior. 'If that was what she wanted, she could have divorced him, couldn't she? By all accounts, he gave her plenty of cause. The Chief Constable thinks this is a case for Scotland Yard.'

The Inspector did not agree with him, but by the time he had interviewed Robert Steel next morning, and Dr Chester's housekeeper, he was forced to admit that he could not see his way through the maze. Robert Steel's scornful demand to be told how he could have known that Carter would be on the bridge at five minutes to five, seemed unanswerable. Steel stated that he had not known that Carter had meant to visit White, and if that were true, it did not seem possible that he could be the murderer. Whether it was true, remained, of course, to be proved; but the Inspector realized that it was not going to be an easy task to prove it.

Dr Chester's housekeeper was a little flustered, but she perfectly recalled the foreign gentleman's visit, and said without an instant's hesitation that he had arrived at a few minutes to five o'clock, before the doctor had got back from the call he had had to make.

The Inspector went next to Palings. He found Lady Dering sitting with Ermyntrude, having been brought over by Hugh, who was talking to Mary in the garden. When Peake announced the Inspector, Lady Dering at once got up to take her leave, and went out through the French window to join her son. She had exercised a most beneficial effect on Ermyntrude, who was both touched and gratified by her visit, and had unburdened her soul without much reserve. Ruth Dering's sympathetic good sense had done much to calm her agitated nerves, and she was even able to greet the Inspector without any display of dramatic horror.

He came to the point without preamble, asking her whether she was the owner of a Mannlicher-Schönauer .275 rifle, registered as No. 668942.

'I'm sure I don't know!' replied Ermyntrude. 'Though, now you come to mention it, I believe one of my first husband's rifles was a Mannlicher – whatever-it-is. Mind you, it wasn't his best gun! A Rigby, that's what he used to swear by, and he had another gun, too, but that was only for elephants. My first husband was a big game shooter.'

'When he died, madam, you kept his guns?'

'Of course I kept his guns! Not that they were any use to me, but I'd as soon have sold his hairbrushes!' said

Ermyntrude, becoming a little intense. 'Everything in the gun-room's kept just as he used to have it. Or rather,' she added, 'it *was* till I married Mr Carter, and he started messing about with things.'

'Are the late Mr Fanshawe's guns kept under lock and key, madam?'

'The gun-room isn't locked, if that's what you mean. Of course, I know very well it ought to be, but that was Mr Carter all over! He never locked anything, without he went and lost the key, and it was a miracle when he put anything away, what's more!'

'Then anyone could have had access to your first husband's rifles?'

She stared at him. 'They're in a glass case. The key's generally in the lock. What would anyone want with them? Look here, what are you driving at?'

'A Mannlicher-Schönauer .275 rifle, No. 668942, was found yesterday in the shrubbery across the stream, madam.'

Ermyntrude gave a gasp, and rose from her chair with quite surprising agility, and stalked to the door. 'Come along!' she said over her shoulder, and led the Inspector to the gun-room.

In a baize-lined mahogany case with glass panels, two rifles stood in a rack which was designed to take four.

'My gracious goodness me!' exclaimed Ermyntrude.

The key was in the lock, the Inspector turned it, and opened the case. 'A Holland & Holland, and a Rigby,' he said, after examining the two rifles.

'That's what I told you,' said Ermyntrude mechanically.

'Are there any cartridges for any of the three rifles, or did you turn them in when Mr Fanshawe died?'

'Oh, I don't know! I can't remember. There used to be cartridges in that drawer.'

The Inspector pulled it open, disclosing various gun

accessories, and a broken box containing a handful of cartridges. 'I'll take these, if you please,' he said.

'Take what you like,' said Ermyntrude. 'Oh dear, whatever does this mean?'

'It means, madam, that your husband was shot by someone who had access to these guns.'

Ermyntrude flung out her hands in a wide gesture. 'But that's anyone!'

'It can't be quite anyone,' said the Inspector. 'It must have been someone who knew the house pretty well.'

'Lots of people know it well enough to find their way to the gun-room. Any of Mr Carter's friends, for instance. Oh dear, it seems to make it worse, somehow, knowing he was shot with one of my first husband's guns! I don't know what to think!'

The Inspector followed her back to the drawing-room, where she sank on to the sofa, looking as though she were on the verge of bursting into tears. This danger was averted by her suddenly becoming aware of his presence. It seemed to annoy her; she said sharply: 'Well, what more do you want? I should have thought you'd done enough for one morning!'

'Not quite,' replied the Inspector. 'I want to ask you a few questions about Mr Carter's dealings with Percy Baker.'

Ermyntrude's sagging shoulders straightened. 'I'm not going to discuss it! It's painful enough for me without you dragging it all up and insulting me with it.'

'You informed me, madam, that Baker demanded five hundred pounds from Mr Carter.'

'Yes, and if you ask me it was nothing but a try-on! Blackmail, that's my name for it!'

'I think I'd better tell you, madam, to save misunderstanding, that Baker denies that he ever asked for such a sum.'

Ermyntrude was quite unimpressed. 'You don't say so! I suppose you expected him to admit he'd been blackmailing my husband?'

'I've reason to believe he may have been speaking the truth,' said the Inspector slowly.

Ermyntrude's eyes began to kindle wrathfully. 'Oh, you have, have you?'

'Are you quite sure that five hundred was the sum your husband told you?'

'Yes, I am quite sure. Do you suppose I'd make a mistake about a thing like that?' She got up, and went to the window. 'Mary! Mary! Oh, there you are! Come in here, will you, dearie?'

Mary, who was sitting under the elm-tree with Hugh and Vicky, came at once. Ermyntrude drew her into the drawing-room, and pointed to the Inspector. 'That man has given me the lie!' she declared. 'It's not enough for me to have my husband murdered, I've got to be bullied and brow-beaten by the police!'

'That's not fair, madam. All I'm doing is to ask you if you're sure the evidence you've given is correct. There's no need – '

'Silence!' said Ermyntrude, rather magnificently. 'Mary tell that creature how much money Wally wanted to pay off the Bakers!'

'Five hundred pounds,' said Mary.

'Thank you, dearie. *Now* perhaps you'll be satisfied, Inspector Cook?'

Mary glanced quickly towards the Inspector. 'Is there some doubt about that? Five hundred was certainly the sum my cousin told me. I can't have been mistaken, for I thought it was out of all reason, and I said so.'

'Very well, miss,' said the Inspector. 'I won't need to trouble you further at present. Good day, madam!'

After he had gone, Ermyntrude continued to fume until

she was struck by the thoughtful expression on Mary's face. She demanded to know its cause.

Mary said worriedly: 'Aunt Ermy, why did he put that question?'

'Don't ask me, love! Well, I never did like policemen, and it just shows you, doesn't it? As though I'd make up a thing like that! Why, whatever would I do it for, when the one thing I dread is everyone finding out about Wally's goings-on with that girl?'

'Not you,' Mary said. 'There's no doubt Wally did say five hundred. He said it to you, and he said it to me. But was it true?'

'But heavens alive, ducky, even Wally wouldn't ask me for five hundred for his mistress, unless he couldn't get out of it! I mean to say!'

'You knew already about Gladys Baker. It wasn't like making a confession to you. Supposing he wanted five hundred?'

'Mary, what's come over you? I never grudged Wally a penny! He could have had five hundred any day!'

'Not for something you disapproved of.'

Ermyntrude blinked at her uncomprehendingly. 'I don't get what you're after, dear. I don't know what I could have disapproved of more than his getting that Baker girl into trouble, I'm sure!'

'Aunt Ermy, do you mind if we have Hugh in? I've got an idea in my head, and I don't know whether I ought to tell the police, or – or whether it's all too vague. But if they're suspicious of Baker, because of this five hundred pound business, and all the time he didn't ask Wally for it, surely I ought to – Hugh would know!'

'Well, I don't mind his hearing about it. But what about Lady Dering? We can't leave her all alone out there, can we?'

'She's gone.' Mary went to the window and called to Hugh.

He came, but not unaccompanied. Vicky stepped into the room ahead of him, and inquired what the Inspector had wanted.

'Oh, Vicky, you could have knocked me down with a feather! They've found one of your poor father's rifles in the shrubbery! It's quite true; it isn't in the case.'

'Good Lord!' said Hugh. 'Then – who could have got hold of it, Mrs Carter?'

'Anybody!' said Ermyntrude.

'Not Baker,' said Mary. 'Surely not Baker! How could he have known about it? That makes me feel more than ever that he didn't ask Wally for that money!'

Hugh said frowningly: 'What's all this?'

'Mary darling, you aren't coming unstuck or anything, are you?' asked Vicky.

'No. But I – I rather think I know something the rest of you don't. And I can't help feeling it may have something to do with Wally's going to the Dower House yesterday, though what it has to do with his being shot, I can't quite see.'

'Do you mind being a little more explicit?' said Hugh. 'What is it you think you know?'

'I believe Wally and Harold White had some scheme on hand for making money. He said something to me – oh, more than once! – about making his fortune, all through White. As a matter of fact, it was when I rather went for him about lending money to White. He had lent him money, you know, Aunt Ermy, and I told him he'd no right to. And then he said that about making his fortune, and White putting him on to a good thing. I didn't pay much heed at the time, but now I can't help wondering. It would be so *like* him!'

'I'm afraid I haven't grasped the gist of this, Mary,' said Hugh. 'What's the connection between this, and Baker?'

'Wally knew Aunty Ermy wouldn't give him money to invest in any scheme of Harold White's making. Then Aunt Ermy found out about Gladys Baker. Do you think – do you think he could possibly have made up that story of being blackmailed for five hundred, to get money for whatever scheme it was White had put up to him?'

Hugh, who had listened in blank amazement, said: 'Frankly, no, I don't. Good Lord, Mary, think it over for yourself! It's preposterous! Dash it, it's indecent!'

'She's very likely right!' said Ermyntrude, in tones of swelling indignation. 'That would just be Wally all over! Oh, I see it now! The idea of it! Getting money out of me to save a scandal, as he knew very well he would, and then blueing the lot on some rubbishy plan of White's!'

'Do you mean to tell me you seriously believe that to get money for an investment, he would have told you he was being blackmailed by the brother of a girl he'd seduced?' said Hugh. 'Look here, Mrs Carter, surely that's too steep!'

'Oh no, it isn't! I can see him doing it!' said Ermyntrude. 'There never was such a man for turning things to good account. Oh, it fairly makes my blood boil!'

'I – I should think it might,' said Hugh, awed.

10

Hugh, although he was becoming inured to the vagaries of Ermyntrude and her daughter, was not prepared to find them accepting Mary's theory with enthusiasm. But, within five minutes of her having explained it to them, nothing could have shaken their belief in its truth. Ermyntrude, indeed, seemed to feel that such duplicity on Wally's part was unpardonable; but Vicky accorded it her frank admiration.

'It's rather sad, really, the way one never appreciates a person till he's dead,' she said. 'Oh, I do think it was truly adroit of him, don't you, Ermyntrude darling? Do you suppose it had anything to do with his being murdered?'

'Even if it were true, why should it have?' asked Hugh.

'Oh, I don't know, but I wouldn't be at all surprised if we discovered it was all part of some colossal plot, and wholly tortuous and incredible.'

'Then the sooner you get rid of that idea the better!'

She looked at him through the sweep of her lashes. 'Fusty!' she said gently.

Hugh was annoyed. 'I'm not in the least fusty, but – '

'And dusty, and rolled up with those disgusting mothballs.'

'Ducky, don't be *rude*!' said Ermyntrude, quite shocked.

'Well, he reminds me of greenfly, and blight, and frost in May, and old clothes, and – '

'Anything else?' inquired Hugh, with an edge to his voice.

'Yes, lots of things. Cabbages, and fire-extinguishers, and – '

'Would you by any chance like to know what you remind me of?' said Hugh, descending ignobly to a *tu quoque*! form of argument.

'No, thank you,' said Vicky sweetly.

Hugh could not help grinning at this simple method of spiking his guns, but Ermyntrude, who thought him a very nice young man, was for once almost cross with her daughter, and commanded her to remember her manners. 'One thing's certain,' she said, reverting to the original topic of discussion, 'I shall ask that Harold White just what he wanted with Wally yesterday!'

'Yes, but ought I to say anything to the Inspector?' said Mary.

'I don't think I would,' said Hugh. 'Unless, of course, you find that your theory is correct. Frankly, I doubt whether he'd believe such a tale.'

'No, I don't think he would,' agreed Vicky. 'He's got a petrified kind of mind which reminds me frightfully of someone, only I can't remember who it is, for the moment.'

'Me,' said Hugh cheerfully.

'Oh, I wouldn't be at all surprised if you're right!' said Vicky.

'I'm ashamed of you, Vicky!' said Ermyntrude.

Mary echoed this statement a few minutes later, when she accompanied Hugh to his car, but he only laughed and said he rather enjoyed Vicky's antics.

'You don't have to live with her,' said Mary.

'No, I admit it's tough on you. Seriously, Mary, do you believe that your extraordinary cousin really did make up that blackmailing story?'

'It's a dreadful thing to say, but I can't help seeing that it would be just like him,' replied Mary.

Harold White, to whom Janet faithfully delivered Ermyntrude's message, walked over to Palings after dinner. The party he disturbed was not an entirely happy one, for the Prince, who did not believe in letting grass grow under his feet, had been interrupted at the beginning of a promising *tête-à-tête* with his hostess, by the entrance into the room of Vicky and Mary. This naturally put an end to his projected tender passages, and he was annoyed when he discovered that neither lady seemed to have the least intention of leaving him alone with Ermyntrude. Mary sat down with a tea-cloth which she was embroidering, an occupation, which, however meritorious in itself, the Prince found depressing; and Vicky (in a demure black taffeta frock with puff sleeves) chose to enact the role of innocent little daughter, sinking down on to a floor cushion at her mother's feet, and leaning her head confidingly against Ermyntrude's knees. As she had previously told Mary that she thought it was time she awoke the mother-complex in Ermyntrude, Mary had no difficulty in recognizing the tactics underlying this touching pose. The Prince, of course, could not be expected to realize that this display of daughterly affection was part of a plot to undo him, but he very soon became aware of a change in an atmosphere which had been extremely propitious. He made the best of it, for it was part of his stock-in-trade to adapt himself gracefully to existing conditions, but Mary surprised a very unamiable look on his face when she happened to glance up once, and saw him watching Vicky.

When Harold White came in, maternal love gave place to palpable hostility. Ermyntrude cut short his speech of condolence, by saying: 'I'm sure it's very kind of you to spare the time to come and see me, Mr White. I hope it wasn't asking too much of you!'

'Oh, not a bit of it! Only too glad!' responded White,

drawing up a chair. 'Poor old Wally! Dreadful business, isn't it? The house doesn't seem the same without him.'

'I dare say it doesn't,' said Ermyntrude. 'But what I want to know, Mr White, is what Wally was doing at your place yesterday.'

He looked slightly taken aback. 'Doing there? What do you mean? He wasn't doing anything.'

'What did he go for?' demanded Ermyntrude.

'Look here, Mrs Carter, I asked poor old Wally to come over and have tea, if he'd nothing better to do, and that's all there was to it.'

'Well, I've got a strong notion it wasn't all,' said Ermyntrude. 'What's more, I'd like to know what that Jones person had got to do with it.'

'Really, if I can't invite a couple of friends to tea without being asked why – '

'That's not so, Mr White, and heaven forbid I should go prying into what doesn't concern me, but it seems a funny thing to me that you should be so anxious to get Wally over to your place – which you won't deny you were, ringing him up no less than three times – if it was only to see him drink a cup of tea. Besides, he was murdered.'

'Well, you don't think I murdered him, do you?' retorted White.

The Prince rose, begging his hostess to excuse him. 'You wish to speak privately to Mr White, Trudinka. You will permit me to vanish.'

'You needn't vanish on my account,' said White. 'I've no secrets to talk about.'

The Prince, however, bowed himself out of the room; and Ermyntrude announced that she did not believe in beating about the bush. 'What I'm asking you, Mr White, is, had you and Wally got some deal on which I wasn't supposed to know about?'

'Who's been telling you anything about a deal?' asked White suspiciously. 'It's news to me!'

'That's as may be, but I hope you aren't going to tell me you haven't gone into a whole lot of deals with Wally in the past, because I wasn't born yesterday!'

'I suppose,' said White, his colour darkening, 'you're hinting that I happen to owe Wally a bit of money. You needn't be afraid, Mrs Carter: naturally I shall pay it back to you. As a matter of fact, it isn't due till Wednesday, but of course if you're anxious about it you can have it before. It was just a loan to help me over a temporary embarrassment. That's what I liked about Wally. He was open-handed.'

'Yes, it's very easy to be open-handed with other people's money!' said Ermyntrude. 'Not that anyone's ever called me mean, and as for my hinting about it, such a notion never entered my head, and I'm sure I'm not worrying about being paid back, so don't think it!'

Matters seemed to be becoming a trifle strained. Mary said: 'Perhaps you wonder at Mrs Carter's asking you that question, Mr White, but the fact is that my cousin said something that led us to believe that he was contemplating some sort of a business deal.'

'He may have been, for all I know. I suppose I'm not the only person he could do business with?'

'There's no need for you to be offended,' said Ermyntrude, incensed by the sneering note in his voice. 'Considering you've time and again led poor Wally into investing money in schemes which never turned out to be a bit of good – '

'Look here, Mrs Carter, you've never liked me, and you needn't think I haven't known it. I'm sure I don't blame you; it's a free world, and you can like whom you damned well please. I don't know what you think you're getting at with all this talk about my having a secret deal on with Wally, but if you've got some notion of dragging me into the poor chap's murder, and making out it was in some way connected with a business deal which I was leading him into, you can drop it, because you're a long way off the mark. And if that's all you wanted to see me about, I'll say, good night! You needn't trouble to show me out!'

Ermyntrude took him at his word, but Mary rose to her feet, and accompanied him to the front-door. When she came back into the drawing-room, Vicky said: 'I thought he was awfully fallacious, didn't you?'

'No, I don't think I did, really. After all, you were rather impossible, Aunt Ermy!'

'If you ask me,' said Ermyntrude darkly, 'he was up to something. Ten to one, if Wally hadn't been shot, he'd have been up to his neck in a plan to lose a lot of money by this time.'

'Five hundred pounds,' said Vicky. '*Do* let's tell the Inspector, Mary!'

'I'm not going to. In fact, I'm beginning to wish I hadn't said anything about it. Moreover, Hugh doesn't think the Inspector would believe a word of it.'

'Well, I think we ought to broaden his mind,' said Vicky. 'Or do you feel that this is really a case for Scotland Yard?'

'Oh, my goodness, don't suggest such a thing!' exclaimed Ermyntrude. 'I mean, what's the use? Scotland Yard can't bring Wally to life again, and when you think that I've got to face an inquest, it's too much to expect me to put up with detectives as well. Because you know, dearie, once they start, heaven alone knows what they won't dig up!'

Unfortunately, this point of view was not shared by the police. On the afternoon of the following day a brisk and bright-eyed Inspector from the Criminal Investigation

Department arrived in Fritton, accompanied by an earnest young Sergeant, and several less distinguished assistants.

Neither Inspector Cook nor Superintendent Small viewed with much pleasure the prospect of handing over their case to the Inspector from London, but Inspector Hemingway, when he arrived, disarmed hostility by a certain engaging breeziness of manner, which had long been the despair of his superiors.

'Nice goings-on in the country!' said Inspector Hemingway, who had beguiled the tedium of his journey from town with a careful perusal of the account of the case, submitted to his Department. 'Mind you, I don't say I'm not going to like the case. It looks to me a very high-class bit of work, what with rich wives, and Russian princes, and I don't know what besides.'

'Properly speaking, this Prince isn't a Russian, but a Georgian,' said the Superintendent. 'At least, that's what he says.'

'My mistake,' apologized Hemingway. 'Matter of fact, I knew it all along. My chief tells me that if he's a Georgian, he ought by rights to be a dark chap, with an aquiline kind of face, and not over-tall. He tells me he's got a Georgian name all right, so no doubt he was speaking the truth.'

'He's dark and aquiline right enough,' said Cook. 'And I don't mind telling you that I don't take to him, not by a long chalk.'

'That's insular prejudice,' said Hemingway cheerfully. He opened the folder he had brought with him, and ran his eye over the first type-written sheet. 'Well, let's get down to it. What I want is a bit of local colour. By what I can make out, the murdered man's no loss to his family.'

'I'll say he's not!' said Cook, and without further encouragement regaled Hemingway with a description of

Wally Carter which, though crude, would have been sworn to by any member of Wally's family.

Inspector Hemingway nodded. 'That's what I thought. Now let's go over the *dramatis personnae*. We'll take the widow first. Anything on her?'

'I can't say as I have,' replied Cook reluctantly. 'She's one of those flashy blondes, but apart from her silly way of carrying on, I've nothing against her. Mind you, if you was to ask anybody hereabouts, they'd tell you that Carter's death just suits her plans. It's common knowledge Mr Steel's been hanging round her for the past three years. He only came to live in the district a few years ago. Grim sort of chap, not given to talking much. Until this Prince turned up, the general opinion was that it was a wonder Mrs Carter didn't divorce Carter, and hitch up with Steel. But from what I can make out, the Prince has changed all that. He's staying at Palings now, and if you was to ask me, he means to marry Mrs Carter. It was him told me about Carter suspecting that it was Steel took a pot-shot at him on that shooting-party.'

'It was, was it? Didn't hear him hiss, did you?'

'Hiss?' repeated Cook.

'Let it go,' said Hemingway. 'Sounds a bit on the snakeish side to me, that's all.'

'Well, I don't know,' said Cook. 'It's possible, of course, but there's no doubt there wasn't any love lost between Carter and Steel.'

Hemingway consulted the typescript under his hand. 'No proper alibi, I see. Out on the farm, but can't bring anyone forward to corroborate. Well, it's my experience that that kind of alibi is the hardest of all to upset. Give me what looks like a water-tight alibi every time!'

'Seems plausible to me,' said Cook doubtfully. 'You'll see that he says he didn't even know Carter was going to the Dower House that afternoon. Well, why should he?

Stands to reason he wouldn't hide himself in the shrubbery on the off-chance.'

'I'm bound to say I don't fancy him for the chief part,' replied Hemingway. 'All the same, that statement of his will bear looking into. As far as I can make out, you've only got his word for it he didn't know about this assignation.'

'I'd say he was speaking the truth. Didn't turn a hair when I questioned him. No, nor he didn't deny he'd no use for Carter.'

'Well, that's put a query against his name all right,' said Hemingway. 'There's something about strong, silent men who don't keep anything back, that makes me highly suspicious. Now, what about this Prince? I see he states he arrived at the doctor's house more or less at the time the murder was being committed. Statement corroborated by the doctor's housekeeper. Well, that's very nice, I'm sure. What made her so certain of the time?'

'She hadn't any doubt. When I asked her, she said at once the Prince arrived before five o'clock.'

'How did she know?'

Inspector Cook looked a little taken aback. 'She didn't hesitate. She said the Prince arrived before the doctor had got back from a case he'd been called out to, and it was a few minutes before five.'

'That's the kind of airy statement I like to see checked up on,' said Hemingway. 'Now, I see you've got a query against this Miss Fanshawe. Properly speaking, I don't hold with women in shooting cases, but you never know with some of these modern girls.'

'You wouldn't know with her, that's a certainty,' said Cook. 'She was in the shrubbery at the time the murder was committed, and she had her dog with her. It's one of those Borzois, and a young one, and from what I can make out it's the sort of noisy brute that 'ud bark its head off if it got wind of a stranger being about the place. But the point is the dog didn't bark, nor yet give any sign that he knew anyone was near. Seems to me we've got something there.'

'What you might call a highly significant feature of the case,' agreed Hemingway. 'Could this Fanshawe-dame have got across the stream other than by way of the bridge?'

'Yes, she could,' said Cook. 'Though I'm bound to say my Sergeant couldn't find any footmarks, which you'd expect to. You see, Inspector, the stream takes a bend to the south about thirty yards beyond that bridge. Anyone crossing it beyond the bend couldn't be seen from the bridge. Get the idea? Well, there's a bit of a pool just round the bend, but it isn't any size, and the stream narrows beyond it, so that I reckon it would be an easy job to jump it. What's more, the young lady wasn't hampered by skirts, because I've discovered that she was wearing slacks at the time. The butler tells me she's devoted to her mother, so that it seems to me it won't do to rule her out of the case.'

Hemingway pursed his lips. 'If it comes to that, it won't do to rule anyone out, but if you were to think that every girl who's devoted to her mother will up and shoot her stepfather as soon as look at him, you'd soon land yourself in a mess. What about this young fellow, Baker?'

Inspector Cook's account of Percy Baker made Hemingway open his eyes. 'You do see life in these parts, don't you?' he remarked. 'Talk about the great, wicked city! Well, well, I think I'll go and take a look at the scene of the crime.'

'I'll send one of my young chaps with you, shall I?' offered the Superintendent. 'Not that you'll find anything there. Nothing to find. The murderer dropped the rifle, and bunked, and the ground's too hard after this drought to show any footmarks.'

'You never know,' said Hemingway.

Waiting with his own Sergeant for the promised guide, he remarked that the conduct of this case was a very good object lesson for the student of crime.

'Yes?' said Sergeant Wake incredulously. 'How's that, sir?'

'Police faults analysed,' replied Hemingway. 'What with Mr Silent Steel and his nice, open admissions, and the doctor's housekeeper, you've got a couple of bits of unchecked evidence that aren't doing us any good at all.'

A young constable joined them at this moment, and they set out for Palings, arriving at the Dower House shortly before five o'clock. Janet was in the garden, and looked rather frightened when Inspector Hemingway's identity was revealed to her. The Inspector, who had a genius for inspiring people with confidence, soon put her at ease, and drew her into a description of what had happened on the Sunday. His Sergeant waited patiently in the background, and the local constable betrayed signs of boredom, but Hemingway listened to Janet's spate of talk with keen interest. He learned about Alan White's quarrel with his father, and his hasty departure from the house; he learned of White's debt to Carter; of Janet's dislike of Carter; of Alan's opinion of Mr Sam Jones; of Vicky Fanshaw's cool way of greeting the news of Carter's death; he even learned of the ruining of a new kettle, and the waste of a batch of scones. By the time he parted from Janet, even Sergeant Wake, who had a great respect for him, felt that he had allowed himself to be drawn into a singularly unprofitable conversation.

'I wonder Inspector Cook didn't warn you about Miss White,' the constable ventured to say. 'A regular talker, that's what she is. Doesn't know anything, either.'

'I like talkers,' replied Hemingway. 'You never know what you may pick up from them. Now, I've found out a lot from Miss White that you people never told me. Is that the bridge?'

'That's it, sir, and if you'll follow me, I'll show you the spot where the rifle was found.'

The Inspector plunged into the shrubbery in his wake, and the zealous constable pointed out to him not only where the rifle was found, which was close to a slim sapling, but also the view to be obtained of the bridge. Hemingway grunted, and asked if anything else had been found near the spot. The constable shook his head, and offered to show him next the way by which the murderer had probably made his escape. The ground was strewn with fallen leaves, which in some places made a thick bed, and the Inspector, tripping over a little mound, kicked some of these out of place, disclosing a small object which instantly caught his eye. He bent, and picked up a horn hair-slide.

'Didn't search very closely, did you?' he said. 'Supposing you were to have another search? You never know: we might find some more little things of this nature.'

The Sergeant joined in the search, but the result, though surprising, was not very helpful.

'In fact,' said Hemingway, regarding the collection of objects which the shrubbery had yielded, 'you might call it a bit confusing. It beats me how things get into places like this. Where did you find that old boot?'

'That was just by the wall by the road,' said the constable.

'Thrown over by some tramp. It's been there for months, from the looks of it. You can take it away, and that broken bit of saucer with it. And if that rusty thing's the lid of a kettle, I shan't want that either. Now, what have we got left?'

"One broken nail-file, one toy magnet, and a pocket-knife,' said the Sergeant, as one checking an inventory.

Hemingway scratched his chin. 'I'm bound to admit it's a mixed bag,' he said. 'Still, you never know. I don't myself carry nail-files in my pocket, nor magnets either, but that isn't to say others mayn't. Mind you, the nail-file, being broken, may have been chucked away, same as the kettle-lid, and that bit of china.'

'Seems a funny place to use as a rubbish heap,' demurred the Sergeant. 'I know a chap that used to carry a nail-file about with him. Sissy sort of fellow, with waved hair.'

'He would be,' said Hemingway. 'We'll keep that file, in case it turns out to be relevant.'

'What about the magnet?' asked Wake. 'Who'd go dropping a thing like that around? Looks to me like it could only have been some kid, playing around in the shrubbery.'

'Trespassing, do you mean?' inquired the constable. 'Well, they could, easy, because the wall's only a low one, as you'll see, sir.'

'Know of anyone, other than a kid, who'd be likely to carry a small magnet in his pocket?' asked Hemingway.

'Can't say I do, sir. Sort of engineer, it would have to be, wouldn't it?'

'I'm bothered if I know,' replied Hemingway frankly.

'Well, the pocket-knife seems the likeliest find to me,' said Wake. 'Nothing the matter with it; both blades intact, so we can take it it wasn't chucked away. I don't know what you think about it, sir, but I don't set much store by that hair-slide. Sort of thing that might easily get lost. I was thinking it might be Miss White's.'

'It might,' agreed Hemingway. 'If it is, she can identify it. But what strikes me is that it hasn't, from the looks of it, been lying out here long. Tell me what you make of this.'

He drew the Sergeant towards the sapling which stood a few paces from where the rifle had been found, and pointed out to him some grazes on the smooth bark, about eighteen inches from the ground.

Wake inspected the marks rather dubiously. 'Well, I don't know that I make anything of it, sir. Not immediately, that is. Someone might have scraped the tree, I suppose.'

'What for?' inquired Hemingway.

The Sergeant shook his head. 'You have me there, sir. Still, trees do get bruised, don't they? Does it mean anything to you?'

'I can't say it does,' confessed Hemingway. 'All the same, something did scrape that tree, and not so long ago either, from the looks of it; and as it's only a couple of steps from where the rifle was found, it may turn out to be highly relevant. You never know. All right, what's-your-name, I've finished here. I'll take a look at the stream now.'

The stream, however, did not hold his interest for long. Having visually measured the width between the opposite banks, the Inspector sighed, and passed on to look at the wall separating the Dower House grounds from the road. Finally he went back to the lawn where he had left Janet, and asked her if she recognized the hair-slide.

'It's not mine,' Janet said. 'I'm absolutely certain of that, because I never wear them.'

'Do you know anyone who does, Miss White?'

'Oh, I couldn't say! I mean, I've never thought. Lots of people do, I expect. As a matter of fact, I think Florence does. She's our maid, and if you found it in the shrubbery it just shows I was right all along, and she does slip out to meet her young man when it isn't her half-day at all!'

Florence, however, when confronted with the hair-slide, promptly disowned it, and denied strenuously, if not altogether convincingly, that she had ever set foot in the shrubbery, or had ever entertained her young man within the gates of the Dower House.

'Well, that was a lie, anyway,' said the constable, as they left the Dower House. 'I know Florrie Benson's young man, and he comes out here pretty well every evening.'

'She's one of those who'd sooner tell a lie than not,' said Hemingway. 'She'll keep. Where does this Dr Chester live? I'll see that housekeeper of his next.'

The doctor was out when they presently reached his house in the village. A manservant opened the door to them, and ushered the Inspector and his Sergeant into a room in the front of the house. Here, the housekeeper, an elderly woman with kindly, short-sighted blue eyes, soon joined them. She looked rather alarmed, but assured Hemingway that, although she knew nothing about Mr Carter's death, she would be only too glad to tell him anything that could be of use to him.

'I'm just checking up on the evidence,' explained Hemingway. 'By what I hear, the doctor had a visit on Sunday from this Prince that's staying with Mrs Carter, didn't he?'

'Oh yes, that's right! He's foreign, and ever such a pleasant-spoken gentleman! He was expected, you know. The doctor told me to make tea for two, because the Prince was coming to look at his bits of stuff that he dug up. Remains, that's what they are, and very valuable, I understand, though they look to me like a lot of rubbishy trash.'

'Do you happen to remember when the Prince arrived?' asked Hemingway.

'Well, now, that's something I can answer!' said Mrs

Phelps, beaming at him. 'Not that I'm generally much of a one for taking notice of the time, but I do remember *that*! It was just on five-to-five.'

'It's queer how some things will stick in one's head, while others won't,' said Hemingway conversationally. 'I wonder what made you remember that?'

'I'll tell you just how it was,' said Mrs Phelps. 'You see, it was Thompson's day off, and I was alone in the kitchen. So when the doctor was called out to a case, he shouted to me that he had to go out, but that he'd be back in time to receive the Prince.'

'What time was the doctor called out?'

'Now, that I can't tell you, not happening to notice, but it can't have been much after half past four, if as late, I shouldn't think, because it didn't seem long before I heard the front-door bell, and when I went to answer it, there was a foreign-looking gentleman. Of course, I guessed it was the Prince, for he had Miss Vicky's car, besides speaking in a foreign way. Well, naturally, I asked him to come in, and I told him about the doctor's being sent for. "He must have been kept," I said, "for he told me distinctly he'd be back before you arrived." Well, I was quite flustered, because it isn't every day you have a Prince coming to tea, and I don't pretend to know the way to behave towards people like that. "Oh, I am sorry the doctor's not back!" I said, because I thought he'd very likely take offence. "He'll be very put out," I said, "but your Highness knows how it is with doctors. I do hope you won't be offended," I said. Well, really, I'd no idea a prince would be as easy to explain anything to! "There's nothing in the world to worry about," he said, or something of the sort, for I wouldn't swear to his exact words. "It is I who am at fault," he said, with ever such a lovely smile. "I have made the journey more quickly than I expected, and I am before my time. I see that it is not yet five o'clock," he said. And he showed me his wrist-watch, just like anyone might, and it was five-to-five. It isn't likely I'd forget a thing like that! It was a lovely watch, too.'

'And did you happen to compare his watch with one of the clocks in the house?' inquired the Inspector.

'Why, whatever should I do that for?' said Mrs Phelps. 'I'm sure I'd no reason to doubt the Prince's word! I just showed him into the doctor's sitting-room, and begged him to take a chair, and it can't have been more than ten minutes, or perhaps a quarter of an hour, before the doctor got back, though that I won't swear to.'

'That's all I wanted to know,' said the Inspector, and took his leave of her.

'Well,' said Sergeant Wake, when they reached the street again, 'that certainly makes the Prince's alibi look a bit funny.'

'Yes, and it makes the local police-work here look a bit funny, too,' said Hemingway. 'Nice way to take evidence! If you ask me, the Prince hasn't got an alibi at all – to put it no stronger! Very fishy it looks, him calling attention to the time, *as* registered, by his own watch! Now we'll make a few inquiries, my lad, and see what's what!'

11

The inquiries made by Inspector Hemingway in Stilhurst village were fruitless. The only person who seemed to have seen Vicky's sports-car draw up outside the doctor's house had such hazy ideas of the time that Hemingway gave him up in disgust. He was about to get into the police-car again when the constable nodded towards a car which had drawn up outside the post office. 'That's the doctor,' he said.

Hemingway did not follow Chester into the post office, which was also the grocery, but waited by his car until he returned to it. When he presently made himself known to Chester, the doctor showed no surprise, but merely asked in what way he could be of use.

'Well, sir, I'm checking up on certain times,' Hemingway explained. 'If you can tell me when you got back to your house on Sunday afternoon, it might help me a lot.'

'I'm sorry, I don't think I can. It was some time after five – possibly nearly half past five, for I was kept longer than I had foreseen.'

'Thank you,' said the Inspector, with a comical look that drew a smile from Chester.

'I'm really very sorry. Hullo, Hugh!'

The Inspector turned, as Hugh Dering came strolling across the street. Dr Chester said: 'You seem to have constituted yourself legal adviser up at Palings, so perhaps you'd like to be introduced to Inspector Hemingway, from Scotland Yard. This is Mr Dering, Inspector.'

The Inspector had an excellent memory, and he said at

once: 'Are you the gentleman who arrived at Palings shortly after the murder?'

'Me,' said Hugh cheerfully. 'Don't ask me if I'm sure I didn't see a suspicious stranger, because I don't think I can bear it! Are you on your way to Palings now? Can I give you a lift? My car's just down the street.'

'Well, that's very kind of you, sir. I'll be glad to go along with you. I'll just have a word with my Sergeant, if you'll wait a minute.'

Hugh nodded, and watched him walk over to the police-car. 'I hoped this wasn't going to happen,' he remarked.

'It was bound to. The gentleman from Scotland Yard seems a decent chap, however. How are they, up at Palings?'

'I haven't been there today. They were all right last night. I suppose you've heard that one of the late Fanshawe's rifles was found in the shrubbery?'

'Yes, I'd heard, but I don't know that I set much store by it.'

The Inspector, having given his Sergeant certain instructions, came walking back to them, and went off down the street with Hugh to where Hugh's car was parked.

'Nasty case, Inspector,' said Hugh, opening the door for him.

'Oh, I don't know about that, sir!' Hemingway replied. 'It's got some very classy features, besides showing me a bit of real high life. Foreign princes,' he added, as Hugh looked a trifle mystified.

Hugh laughed, and got into the car beside him. 'I hope you'll find him up to standard. Have you got a sense of humour?'

An intelligent eye was cocked at him. 'Will I need one?'

'Absolutely essential. Your predecessor suffered from a total lack of it.'

'I can see it's a fortunate thing I met you,' said the Inspector. 'I'm not like some detectives: I'm grateful for a bit of help. 'Matter of fact, I came with you because there's something I shouldn't be at all surprised if you could put me right on.'

'What is it?' asked Hugh, letting in his clutch.

'How do you pronounce this Prince's unnatural name?'

Hugh grinned appreciatively. 'It's a privilege to know you, Inspector. Varasashvili.'

The Inspector sighed. 'Wonderful what foreigners can get their tongues round, isn't it? Now, don't you drive too fast, sir, because I'm a very nervous man. Besides, it isn't often I get a free ride, and I'm enjoying myself.'

'Also you want to take in the features of the countryside,' said Hugh, slowing to a sedate pace.

'That's right, I do,' replied the Inspector. 'Décor and scenery are my specialities. Where would this road lead to, supposing we were to follow it?'

'To Kershaw, eventually. But we turn off to the right.'

'I remember that. How long do you reckon it takes you to drive from Palings to Stilhurst?'

'Ten minutes, possibly a little less.'

'You're very helpful,' said the Inspector. 'Whereabouts is Oaklands Farm?'

'Towards Kershaw. Do you want me to take you there?'

'No, but it's put me in mind of another thing I want to ask you. They tell me you were at that shoot on Saturday. What do you reckon were the rights of that little mix-up?'

'Oh, lord, are you on to that?' said Hugh. 'I don't believe it has the least bearing on the case. Carter was just the sort of vague ass who would stray about and get himself shot.'

'Is that so? Well, it's a wonder to me there aren't more accidents at shoots. Where does that lane lead to?'

'A farm. It's a dead end.'

'Oh! Not much traffic down it?'

'None at all on a Sunday.' Hugh cast him a flickering smile. 'Quite safe to park a car there.'

The Inspector shook his head admiringly. 'It's wonderful the way you read what's in my mind, sir.'

The gates of the Dower House came into sight upon the left-hand side of the road, and beyond them the little humpbacked bridge over the stream. The lane curved away to the right, and the Inspector inquired whether they were running beside the grounds of Palings. Hugh nodded, and presently pointed out the entrance to the garage. Fifty yards on, he turned the car in at the main gate, and drove up the neat avenue to the front-door.

'Well, here we are,' Hugh said. He got out of the car, and was just about to ring the bell when Vicky came round the corner of the house. 'You can prepare yourself for the first shock, Inspector,' he said. 'Hullo, Vicky! Gone into half-mourning?'

Vicky, who was wearing a frock of white organdie with an artless sash of black velvet ribbon with immensely long ends, replied: 'Oh, I think white is *so* suitable for a young girl, don't you? I began to feel like Anna Karenina, so I changed, because it was all very exhausting.'

The Inspector had climbed out of the car, and was regarding Vicky with frank approbation. Hugh said: 'Let me introduce Inspector Hemingway, of Scotland Yard, Miss Fanshawe.'

'From Scotland Yard?' repeated Vicky, turning a face of the deepest reproach towards Hugh. 'What a viperous thing to do! Oh, I think you're the most repellent creature I've ever met! in fact, not merely sub-human, but a snake and a traitor as well!'

'One of your dramatic days, I see,' said Hugh, quite unmoved. 'Don't mind the Inspector, will you? And get it out of your head that I sent for him: all I did was to give him a lift from the village.'

'*Just* when Ermyntrude's been upset again!' Vicky said. She looked critically at Hemingway, and suddenly bestowed an unexpectedly beguiling smile upon him. 'Oh, I like you more than Inspector Cook! Has he told you about my being practically on the scene of the crime? Isn't it ghoulish?'

'He told me that you didn't hear or see anything unusual,' replied Hemingway diplomatically. 'Nor yet your dog either.' He glanced at the black ribbon which she had tied round her head to keep the feathery curls in position. 'What I'm wondering is whether you happened to lose a hair-slide in the shrubbery at any time?'

'No, I don't wear them. I think they're definitely unlovely. Do you want to see my mother?'

'Yes, please. But are you quite sure this isn't yours?'

Vicky looked at the hair-slide he was holding in the palm of his hand. 'How touching! Absolutely Mother's Good Girl, isn't it? *Not* one of my acts.'

She evidently had no further interest in the slide, so the Inspector put it back in his pocket, and followed her into the house.

Ermyntrude was sitting in the drawing-room with Mary. A number of daily periodicals were piled untidily on a low table beside her, and as soon as she saw Hugh, she exclaimed: 'Well, if you're not the very person I was hoping would look in on us! To my mind, it's practically libel, and if I can't sue them there's no justice in England. Look at that!'

Hugh took the newspaper that was being thrust at him. A most unflattering portrait of Prince Varasashvili met his eye, and nearly surprised a laugh out of him.

'"Mrs Carter's distinguished Russian guest"!' quoted Ermyntrude bitterly. 'If they'd said it was Mrs Carter's boot-boy, it would have been more likely, except that I wouldn't have a boot-boy that looked like a cross between an organ-grinder and a gangster! No, really, Hugh, I *am* put out! What's more, Alexis particularly told them he was a Georgian, not that it makes a bit of difference to my mind, but you know how touchy foreigners are!' She broke off, perceiving Hemingway, and demanded suspiciously: 'Who's that?'

'Darling Ermyntrude, it's an Inspector from Scotland Yard,' said Vicky. 'His name is Hemingway, and he's rather a lamb, except for nourishing degrading suspicions about me.'

The Inspector was startled. 'I never!' he said. 'Now, that's not fair, miss!'

'Hair-slides,' said Vicky reproachfully. 'I call that utterly degrading.'

'Scotland Yard!' ejaculated Ermyntrude, letting fall the second newspaper, which she had been holding out to Hugh. 'Am I never to be left in peace? Haven't I had enough to worry me? I wish to God Wally had never been shot!'

Inspector Hemingway at once won Hugh's respect by his instant grasp of the situation. He responded promptly: 'I'm sure I'm not surprised. But don't you get thinking I've come to badger you, madam, because I'm a feeling man myself, and I know just how you feel. You've had reporters pestering you, have you? Regular body-snatchers, that's what they are. So this is the Prince! Well, I must say I wouldn't have thought it!'

Ermyntrude wrested the paper from his grasp. 'It's nothing like him! What's all this about your suspecting my girl? I never heard of such a thing!'

'That was just Miss Fanshawe trying to have a little game with me,' replied the Inspector. 'As a matter of fact, it wasn't Miss Fanshawe I came to see. It wasn't, strictly speaking, you either, madam, but I'm sure it's a pleasure. Ever see that before?' He held out the hair-slide as he spoke.

'Nasty, cheap thing!' said Ermyntrude, after a cursory glance at it.

'Can I see it?' asked Mary. 'I sometimes wear one.'

The Inspector held it out to her. She looked at it, and shook her head. 'No, it's not one of mine. Who is it you wish to see, Inspector?'

'The Prince, miss, if you please.'

'Well, I suppose, it's no good my trying to stop you,' said Ermyntrude. 'The way you policemen behave, anyone would think the house belonged to you! Oh Hugh, you know all about the law! Have they got to go worrying Alexis? I can't bear it if on top of everything else they get him all upset, which is what they very likely will do, for he's very sensitive, and what with that photograph, and the papers getting his name wrong, and one of them calling him a Baron instead of a Prince, he's very put-out already.'

'I'm afraid,' began Hugh, but broke off short, as the object of this discussion stepped in through the French window. 'Here is the Prince, Inspector.'

The Prince's smile faded; he threw up his hands, exclaiming: 'Ah, not more police! It becomes too much! My poor Trudinka, you are distressed: they have been worrying you again! You should have sent for me immediately!'

'I'm sure that's just like you, Alexis, always so thoughtful and sweet to me!' said Ermyntrude warmly. 'I was going to send for you, too, because it's you the Inspector wants to see.'

The Prince raised his brows. 'Yes? I am at your disposal, Inspector, though what more I can say I do not know. I have told all I know. I must confess I do not understand these English methods. What do you want with me?'

'Well, I'd like a little chat with you alone, sir,' said Hemingway.

'I'm sure you needn't be so anxious to keep me in the dark!' said Ermyntrude. 'I'd like to know who had a bigger right to know what's going on! What's more, I dare say I can answer your questions a lot better than the Prince can. It stands to reason!'

'Yes, but I'm funny like that,' returned Hemingway, quite unruffled. 'When I ask one person a question I get muddled in my head if half a dozen other people start answering.'

'But naturally I will go apart with you, my dear Inspector!' said the Prince, recovering his smile. 'Come! I am at your service!'

He bowed the Inspector out of the room, and took him across the hall to the library. As he closed the door, he said: 'You do not wish me to repeat my evidence, that is certain. You wish to question me about the affair at the shoot on Saturday. But it is absurd! I must tell you at once that for myself I do not believe that it was anything but a foolish accident. That Mr Steel would fire with deliberation upon Mr Carter I find ridiculous. It is not possible. I cannot discuss such a piece of nonsense.'

'That's right, sir, and very handsomely spoken, I'm sure,' said the Inspector. 'I won't ask you anything at all about it.'

'Ah!' said the Prince, rather taken aback. 'You are a sensible man, I perceive. You do not set any store by the strange suspicions of poor Mr Carter. I can speak openly to you, in effect.'

'That's just what I hope you will do, sir. I can see we shall get along fine. All I want you to tell me is what time it was when you arrived at the doctor's house on Sunday?'

'But, my friend, I have told already once! It was at five minutes to five.'

'And how did you happen to know that, sir?'

The Prince shrugged. 'I was too early. The doctor was not in, and when I looked at the time I found it was not then five o'clock. It is very simple! The housekeeper will uphold me, for we spoke of the time together.'

'Yes,' said the Inspector mildly. 'She said she remembered it distinctly, on account of your showing her your watch.'

'Did I? It may well have been so.'

'I wonder if I might have a look at that watch of yours, sir?'

'But certainly!' The Prince extended his wrist.

The Inspector glanced at his own watch. 'Thank you, sir. Do you find it keeps good time? They tell me those fancy ones very often don't.'

'Excellent time. You would say that I was not at Dr Chester's house before five? Is that it, may I ask?'

'Oh no! I wouldn't say that at all, sir! Not unless I was sure of my facts, that is,' he added thoughtfully. 'Still, watches do lose sometimes, and we have to be so careful in the Department, you know. So I've set a couple of my people on to see if they can't find someone to corroborate your statement.'

The Prince said in rather a high-pitched voice: 'This is to insult me! Am I then suspected of having murdered my host? It is iniquitous! It is, in fact, quite laughable, when one considers that it is not I who have the motive for killing that unfortunate! I do not pretend to know anything, but I find it strange that the poor foreigner must be suspected rather than a man who has been detested by Carter; or than Miss Cliffe, who inherits Carter's fortune; or than – for one must be frank – Miss Fanshawe, who was on the spot, and knows well how to handle a gun!'

'You've got me quite wrong, sir,' said the Inspector. 'I've got a natural mistrust of watches, that's all. Yes, what do you want?'

This question was addressed to the butler, who had come into the room. Peake said stiffly that Sergeant Wake wished to speak to him.

'You can send him in here,' replied the Inspector, adding kindly to the Prince: 'I dare say he's found someone to corroborate your evidence, sir. He's a very able young fellow, my Sergeant.'

Sergeant Wake, however, had not found any such person. He had found instead the son of the local publican, who had informed him that he had been out walking with his young lady on Sunday afternoon, along the road from Stilhurst to Kershaw, and had seen Miss Fanshawe's car, with a strange gentleman at the wheel, travelling towards the village just after five o'clock.

'It's a lie! I denounce it!' exclaimed the Prince, grasping the back of a chair.

'Well, and what makes him so sure it was after five?' inquired the Inspector.

'He states that both him and his young lady had heard the village church clock strike the hour about ten minutes before,' replied Wake. 'Very positive, he is.'

Inspector Hemingway looked at the Prince. 'I had a notion all along that watch of yours wasn't to be trusted,' he remarked. 'What you might call a hunch. We shall have to rub it all out and start again. Suppose, sir, you were to talk to me openly, just like you said you would?'

'It is not true. I dispute it! If my watch can lose so, why then is it now correct?'

'Would it be because you've set it right?' suggested the Inspector helpfully.

The Prince glared at him. 'You take the word of an

ignorant country fellow before mine? You are insolent, my friend, and I resent it!'

'Yes, well, we'll get along a sight better, sir, if you don't waste my time with that kind of talk. What I want to know is just what you were doing in between the time you left this house, which, by all accounts, can't have been later than a quarter-to-five, and the time you arrived at the doctor's house.'

'I should be accustomed to persecution!' the Prince said, with a dramatic gesture. 'My God, have I not been persecuted enough already by the Bolsheviki?'

'Not knowing, I can't say, sir, but you won't get persecuted by Bolsheviks in this country, that I do know; though if you refuse to answer my questions you stand a very good chance of ending up inside a police cell.'

'I did not know that my watch was slow!' the Prince cried. 'It was in innocence that I showed it to that woman! What would you? Do I know this place? Was I conducted to the doctor's house? It is not easy to remember exactly what is told one! Of the murder I know nothing! But nothing!'

'Oh! So you admit that your watch was slow, sir?'

'It was slow, yes, but I did not then know it! Listen, for I will tell you all! It is true that I left this house at a quarter-to-five. I asked of Mr Carter the way to the doctor's house, and he told me, but I forget. I remember that I shall come to a T-road, but there is no sign-post, and I do not recall which way I must turn. I turn to the right, but there is no village. I go slowly, but when in two – three – miles there is still no village, I am sure that I have taken the wrong turning. I come to a cross-road, and I see at last a sign-post, which tells me I have come away from Stilhurst. I turn the auto, therefore, and I go back. That is all!'

'That's all very well, sir, but when you fetched up at the

doctor's house after all this joy-riding, weren't you a bit surprised to find it was only five-to-five by your watch?'

'It didn't signify. I did not take count of the time. Perhaps I was a little surprised, but what matter?'

'When did you discover that your watch was wrong?'

'Later. When I came back to this house.'

'Oh you did, did you, sir? Then why did you tell Inspector Cook nothing about it? Why didn't you tell him what you've just told me?'

The Prince flung out his hand. 'But put yourself in my place! What a situation! What horror did I find here! I have done nothing, I am innocent! Must I say then that when Mr Carter was murdered I have no alibi? It is not reasonable! It is folly! I see that it will be better not to divulge the truth.'

'Well, that may be your idea of what's best, but it's not mine!' said the Inspector.

'Ah, you do not understand! You do not appreciate the predicament in which I find myself! Of what use to tell the police of the truth? It is not helpful; it will only confuse them, for I know nothing of the murder. It is clear to me, moreover, that it will lead to much unpleasantness if I speak the truth. It is more comfortable, much wiser, to tell a little lie. You cannot blame me for that!'

'Well, that's where you're mistaken, sir, because if this story of yours is true, you've acted very wrongly.'

'Ah, you are blind, stupid! You have no imagination, no understanding! What does it matter where I may be at the time of this murder? Ask, instead, where was Mr Steel? Where was Miss Cliffe? Did I not say you would become confused if it was known that I have not an alibi? Or is it because I am not English that you desire to make a case against me? Yes, I perceive what is in your mind! You say to yourself, "This man is a foreigner, therefore I do not trust him."'

The Inspector strove with himself. 'Of all the – ! Look here, sir, on your own showing you've told me a lot of lies, not to mention what you told Inspector Cook, and now you turn round and say I don't believe you because you're a foreigner! Whatever next!'

'I have shown you that it is of no account that I have concealed from you the truth. It is, in fact, for the best. You have made a mistake to drag from me the fact that I have lied to you, and you will regret it, for you think now that it is I who have killed Carter, and that is not so. Ah, but it is folly! Why, I demand of you, should I kill him?'

'By all I can hear, sir, you're very friendly with Mrs Carter,' said Hemingway significantly.

'You think that I killed Carter that I might marry Mrs Carter?'

'Well,' said Hemingway, 'that's why you'd like me to think Mr Steel did it, isn't it?'

'Oh, my friend, you are quite mistaken! No, no, it was not necessary that I should kill Carter, I assure you! You must know that he was not an estimable man, not a good husband, not any longer attractive, you understand. The affair would have arranged itself better, for Mrs Carter might so easily have divorced him. You perceive? You are a man of the world; I can speak frankly to you. I desire to marry Mrs Carter: I do not make a secret of it. But I do not like that Carter should be murdered; I prefer infinitely a divorce. It is reasonable that, is it not? Consider!'

The unexpected candour of this speech quite took the Inspector's breath away. The Prince's face had cleared; in his voice was a note of unmistakable sincerity.

'Am I to understand, sir, that Mrs Carter was intending to divorce her husband?'

The Prince's eyelids drooped; his sidelong look, and the gleam of a smile, seemed to take the Inspector into his confidence. He spread out his well-manicured hands. 'Gently, gently, if you please! You wish me to tell you that it was arranged already, but you must know that these things do not arrange themselves in the flash of an eye. I am entirely honest with you, and I say that all was in good train. I do not flatter myself when I say that I am a more desirable *parti* than this poor Carter. What would you? He is already growing old; he drinks; he spends the money that is his wife's on other women; he is not even amusing! Above all, she does not love him. Consider again! I am not old; I do not become a little fuddled every night; I do not forget to accord to Mrs Carter that admiration which is her due. I am poor, yes, but I am a prince, and to be, instead of Mrs Carter, the Princess Varasashvili, would be a great thing, would it not? Ah, yes, one may say that the divorce was sure! You will see that I am perfectly frank with you, Inspector.'

'You certainly are!' said Hemingway, almost bereft of speech.

'It is best. Between men of the world these little affairs are easily understood. The matter is now made plain, I think? You have no more to ask me?'

'At the moment, I haven't,' said Hemingway. 'But I wouldn't like you to run away with the idea that telling me these highly remarkable plans of yours has cleared you, sir, because it hasn't. Do you use a nail-file?'

The suddenness of the question startled the Prince. He replied evasively: 'I do not know why you should ask!'

'No, nor I don't know why you shouldn't answer,' said the Inspector.

The Prince flushed. 'Let me tell you, I do not like your manner!'

'Well, since we're being so nice and open,' retorted the Inspector, 'I don't mind telling you that I don't like your story, sir. You'd better consider your position.'

The Prince said uneasily: 'You ask me what I do not understand. Certainly I use a nail-file! Why should I not tell you, since you are so curious?'

'Don't happen to have lost one lately, do you, sir?'

'No!'

'Ah, well!' said the Inspector. 'Then I won't detain you any longer.'

He waited until the door had closed behind the Prince before turning an expressive gaze upon his Sergeant. That grave-eyed man shook his head. 'I wouldn't have believed it!' he said.

'Yes, I reckon we're seeing life,' agreed Hemingway. 'Wonderful how frank and above-board he got as soon as he found he wasn't going over big with me!'

'Do you think he did it, sir?'

'I wouldn't put it above him. All the same, this is a highly intricate case, and it won't do for you and me to go jumping to conclusions.'

'He's a real nasty piece of work,' said the Sergeant sternly. 'He fairly made my gorge rise!'

'Yes, I never have thought that new way they have at the zoo of keeping snakes was safe,' said Hemingway. 'If I weren't a very conscientious man, I'd arrest his Highness right now, and go off and get a bit of supper, which is what I need.'

The Sergeant frowned. 'I wouldn't say, myself, we'd got quite enough on him, sir,' he suggested diffidently.

'That's another reason why I'm not arresting him,' said the Inspector.

He went out into the hall. The door into the drawing-room stood open, and he could see Vicky Fanshawe, perched on the arm of a chair. He walked across the hall, and went into the drawing-room. Only the two girls and Hugh Dering were there, for Ermyntrude had gone upstairs to dress for dinner, and the Prince seemed to have followed her example.

'I do hope I'm not intruding,' said Hemingway cheerfully. 'Of course, if I am, you've only got to tell me.'

'And then I suppose you'd go away?' said Vicky.

'I'd be in a very awkward position,' confessed the Inspector. 'Because, as it happens, I want to ask both you young ladies one or two questions.'

'Right, then I'll clear out,' said Hugh, knocking out his pipe, and putting it in his pocket.

Vicky flung out a hand. 'Don't leave us!' she said throbbingly. 'Can't you see that we may need you?'

'Can it, Vicky!' said Hugh, unimpressed.

'I wish you would stay,' said Mary nervously.

'I'm sure I've no objection,' said the Inspector. 'There's no need for anyone to get the shudders yet. What I want to know first, is whether it's true that you, miss, are Mr Carter's heiress?'

Mary stared at him in dawning dismay. 'Who's been telling you that nonsense?'

'Alexis!' said Vicky tensely.

'Well, that's what I want to know, miss. Is it nonsense, or had Mr Carter got a fortune to leave?'

'No. At least, he himself was heir to a lot of money. It's quite true that it comes to me. He always said he should leave it to me, and, as a matter of fact, I believe he made out some kind of a will, which two of the servants witnessed. I don't know whether it was legal, of course.'

'Just a moment!' interposed Hugh. 'What is all this about Carter's expectations? Something was said about them the other day, but where are you supposed to come into it?'

'It's Wally's Aunt Clara,' explained Mary. 'She's been in a lunatic asylum for years, but she's frightfully rich, and Wally was her next-of-kin. I believe she's going on for eighty, so she must die fairly soon. Not that I ever set much store by it. I mean, Wally's expectations were practically a family joke.'

'But it's you who'll come into the money now that Mr Carter's dead?' said the Inspector.

'Yes, I suppose so. I hadn't really thought about it,' replied Mary, looking rather scared.

'Do you mind if we get this straightened out?' said Hugh. 'I frankly haven't got the hang of it. What relation to you is this aunt of Carter's?'

'Oh, she isn't *my* aunt!'

'No, that I'd grasped. How does the relationship work?'

'Well, I don't think it does really. She's a Carter, you see. I suppose, in a way, I'm connected with her through Wally, but she isn't actually a relation. She wasn't actually Wally's aunt either, though he always called her aunt. She was a cousin.'

Hugh said patiently: 'What exactly was your relationship to Carter?'

'I was his first cousin. My father's elder sister married Wally's father.'

'Then you've no Carter blood at all?'

'Oh no, none!'

'In that case,' said Hugh, 'it's just as well that you never set much store by Aunt Clara's money. You won't get it.'

'Won't I? Are you sure?' said Mary, bewildered.

'*How* you must be enjoying yourself!' said Vicky, addressing herself to Hugh. 'You practically *couldn't* be more blighting! Poor Mary, do you mind frightfully?'

'No. I don't think so. It never really entered into my calculations.'

'I'm bound to say this is all very surprising,' said the Inspector. 'I suppose you're sure of your facts, sir?'

'Of course I'm sure! A man can't bequeath property which he doesn't possess.'

'Well, but who will get it?' asked Mary. 'After all, I was Wally's nearest surviving relative!'

'That has nothing to do with it. When the old lady dies, the money will go to her next-of-kin. You don't come into it at all.'

'But, Hugh, she hasn't *got* any next-of-kin now that Wally's dead! I know Wally told me she was an only child, and she certainly never got married.'

'My dear girl, it doesn't make the least difference to you. You're out of it altogether. Sorry, but there it is!'

'Is that the law?' said Vicky incredulously.

'That, my fair one, is the law,' replied Hugh.

'Well, I think it's *all* for the best,' said Vicky, 'and a complete sell for Alexis, because the Inspector now sees that Mary hadn't got a motive. Don't you, Inspector?'

'No,' said Mary. 'No, it doesn't clear me, because I didn't know about this next-of-kin business. Oh dear, what a nightmare it's beginning to be! But surely you *can't* think I'd shoot my cousin!'

'Darling Mary, no one who'd ever seen you with a gun could possibly think you'd fired a shot in your life,' said Vicky, with lovely frankness.

'It's a funny thing, but it's not often you'll find a lady who won't behave as though she thought a gun would bite her,' remarked the Inspector. 'But I understand you're not like that, miss?'

Vicky's seraphic blue eyes surveyed him for a moment. 'Did the Prince tell you that?' she asked softly.

'It doesn't matter who told me, miss. Do you shoot?'

'No! I mean, yes, in a way I do,' said Vicky, becoming flustered all at once. 'But I practically never hit anything! *Do* I, Mary? Mary, you know it was only one of my acts, and I'm not really a good shot at all! If I hit anything, it's quite by accident. Mary, why are you looking at me like that?'

Mary, who had been taken by surprise by the sudden loss of poise in Vicky, stammered: 'I wasn't! I mean, I don't know what you're talking about!'

'You think I did it!' Vicky cried, springing to her feet. 'You've always thought so! Well, you can't prove it, any of you! You'll never be able to prove it!'

'Vicky!' gasped Mary, quite horrified.

Vicky brushed her aside, and rounded tempestuously upon the Inspector. 'The dog isn't evidence. He often doesn't bark at people. I don't wear hair-slides. I'd nothing to gain, nothing! Oh, leave me alone, leave me alone!'

The Inspector's bright, quick-glancing eyes, which had been fixed on her with a kind of bird-like interest, moved towards Mary, saw on her face a look of the blankest astonishment, and finally came to rest on Hugh, who seemed to be torn between anger and amusement.

Vicky, who had cast herself down on the sofa, raised her face from her hands, and demanded: 'Why don't you say something?'

'I haven't had time to learn my part, miss,' replied the Inspector promptly.

'Inspector, it's a privilege to know you!' said Hugh.

Vicky said fiercely, between her teeth: 'If you ruin my act, I'll murder you!'

'Look here, miss, I haven't come to play at amateur theatricals!' protested the Inspector. 'Nor this isn't the moment to be larking about!'

Vicky flew up off the sofa. 'Answer me, answer me! I was on the scene of the crime, wasn't I?'

'So I've been told, but if you were to ask me – '

'My dog didn't bark. That's important. That other Inspector saw that, and you do too. Don't you?'

'I don't deny it's a point. It's a very interesting point, what's more, but it doesn't necessarily mean – '

'I can shoot. Anyone will tell you that! I'm not afraid of guns.'

'You don't seem to me to be afraid of anything,' said Hemingway with some asperity. 'In fact, it's a great pity you're not, because the way you're carrying on, trying to convict yourself of murder, is highly confusing, and will very likely land you in trouble!'

'There is a case against me, isn't there? You didn't think so at first, but the Prince told you that I could shoot, and you began to wonder. Didn't you?'

'All right, we'll say I did, and there is a case against you. Anything for a quiet life!'

Vicky stamped her foot. 'Don't laugh! If I'm not a suspect, you must be mad! Quick, I can hear my mother coming! Am I a suspect or am I not?'

'Very well, miss, since you will have it! You are a suspect!'

'*Angel!*' breathed Vicky, with the most melting look through her lashes, and turned towards the door.

Ermyntrude came in. Before anyone could speak, Vicky had cast herself upon the maternal bosom. 'Oh, mother, mother, don't let them!'

The Inspector opened his mouth, and shut it again. Mary said indignantly: 'Vicky, it's not fair! Stop it!'

Ermyntrude clasped her daughter in her arms. Over Vicky's golden head, she cast a flaming look at Hemingway. 'What have you been saying to her?' she demanded, in a voice that would have made a braver man than Hemingway quail. 'Tell me this instant!'

'It isn't his fault!' sobbed Vicky. 'Alexis has told him about my shooting, and being on the scene! Oh mother, I knew all along Alexis thought I'd done it, but I never, never thought he'd set the police on to me!'

'*Oh!*' said Mary, in a choking voice.

'*Alexis* told you?' Ermyntrude said terribly.

'Look here, madam – '

'You called to me, Trudinka?' said the Prince, appearing suddenly in the doorway. 'Ah, but what is this? What has distressed the little Vicky?'

He encountered a look from the widow which made him take an involuntary step backwards.

'Answer me this!' commanded Ermyntrude. 'What have you been saying to that man about my child?'

'But, Trudinka – '

'Don't you call me Trudinka! What did you say to that man?'

'I said nothing! But nothing!' declared the Prince, the smile quite vanished from his face. 'If he has told you that I said a word about Vicky, it is a lie!'

Inspector Hemingway, whose senses were reeling, discovered the breaking-point of his admirable temper. 'I've had more than enough of you!' he said. 'Not say a word about her! Oh, didn't you, indeed!'

Ermyntrude extended an arm towards the Prince in the most superb gesture of her life. 'Out of my sight!' she said. 'You viper!'

12

From that moment, the situation developed with such rapidity, and rose to such heights of dramatic fervour, that Mary, and Hugh, and the Inspector could do nothing but retire into the background. Ermyntrude certainly dominated the stage, but the Prince, no mean performer, very nearly stole the scene from her, once he had recovered from his first stupefaction.

'Above all else, I am a Mother!' Ermyntrude declared. She then said that she felt herself to be seeing Alexis for the first time, and announced in tragic accents that she had been a blind fool.

The Prince countered by assuring her that he had been grossly misunderstood by the Inspector, who was a dunderhead; but any mollifying effect that this might have had was at once ruined by Vicky, who accused him of wanting to get her out of the way. This made the Prince lose his temper, and he found himself in the middle of a violent quarrel with his persecutor before he had time to reflect that to call heaven to witness that she was a liar, a mischief-maker, and an unprincipled baggage was scarcely likely to assuage her mother's wrath. He clapped a hand to his brow, and cried out: 'Ah, my God, what am I saying? No, no, I do not mean it! But when you try to come between me and this dear Ermyntrude, I grow mad, I do not know what I say! For I love her, do you see? I love her!'

'A fine way to show me you love me!' said Ermyntrude. 'Standing there insulting my baby! Oh, my eyes are opened at last! Don't touch me!'

'Duchinka, be calm!' implored the Prince. 'It is a plot to undo me! Do not heed this foolish Vicky! She is jealous, but that I understand, and I forgive. You cannot think that I would seek to harm one who is dear to you!'

'Don't you talk to me!' said Ermyntrude. 'You who try to fling my Vicky to the wolves!'

'Yes, I thought it wouldn't be long before I got cast for a part in this,' said the Inspector, in a gloomy undertone.

'But I did not fling her to the wolves! It is false, quite false! Merely, when the police would have accused me, I said, to laugh to scorn the idea, "As well accuse Miss Fanshawe, or Miss Cliffe!" You see? To show the folly of it!'

Unfortunately Ermyntrude seized on only one point of this explanation, and exclaimed indignantly: 'You dare to tell me you tried to drag Mary into it too? Well, never did I think to live to see the day when a Prince would behave like a cad! The idea of trying to put the blame on to two innocent girls, when for all we know, it was you who shot poor Wally all along, just because I told you I didn't hold with divorce! And if you think I'd marry a man who comes to me with his hands red with my husband's blood, you've got a very funny idea of me in your head, because I wouldn't marry you, not if you had fifty titles! I dare say that's the way you carry on in Russia, but you needn't think you can bring your heathenish ways into this country, because you can't!'

The Prince showed signs of being about to tear his hair. 'But I did not kill your husband! I defy you to say such a thing!'

'Then don't you let me hear you insinuating that my girl had anything to do with it! No, nor Mary either, for if anyone's behaved like a daughter to me I'm sure she has, and not a word will I hear against her!'

'Yet it is this quiet, good Mary who benefits by Carter's

death!' said the Prince, nettled into taking another false step.

'It's not true! Mary won't inherit Clara Carter's fortune!' said Vicky. 'Hugh says so!'

'She won't?' said Ermyntrude, momentarily diverted. 'Well, I do call that a shame! Not that I ever believed in Wally's precious Aunt Clara, because, if you ask me, there isn't any such person. And whatever the rights of it, I call it a real ungentlemanly thing to try to put the blame of Wally's death on to a couple of girls!'

Nothing that the Prince could say had the power to move her from this standpoint, and as he had, in fact, tried to do exactly what she accused him of, and was hampered in his denials by the Inspector's presence, he soon found himself in a very awkward position, and ended by losing his head, and recommending the Inspector to ask himself why the murdered man's relatives desired so palpably to discredit him.

It was not necessary for Vicky to fan the flames kindled by this unwary hand. The scene rocketed into the realms of melodrama, with Ermyntrude holding the centre of the stage, and the Prince trying to deliver an impassioned speech which was invariably interruped at the third word.

Mary made one attempt to intervene, for she recognized the signs of rising hysteria in Ermyntrude, and guessed that this unleashed rage was to a great extent the outcome of overstrained nerves. Neither of the combatants paid the least attention to her soothing remarks, so she retired again into the background, and told Vicky that she ought to be ashamed of herself.

The Inspector glanced towards the door, measuring his chances of escape, but before he had made up his mind to risk the attempt, a fresh actor appeared upon the scene. Dr Chester stood upon the threshold, surveying the room.

'What in the name of all that's wonderful is the matter?' he asked.

'Oh, Maurice, thank God you've come!' cried Mary, hurring across the room towards him. 'Oh, for heaven's sake, *do* something!'

He took her hand, but looked towards Ermyntrude. 'What is it?' he asked.

Her wrath had exhausted Ermyntrude. She collapsed suddenly on to the sofa, and burst into tears. 'Ask him! Ask him what he said about my Vicky!' she sobbed. 'Oh, I've never been so deceived in anyone in my life!'

The Prince at once burst into speech, but as his agitation had made him forget his English, no one, least of all the doctor, could understand much of what he said. It was Mary who gave the doctor a hurried account of the quarrel. He betrayed neither surprise nor indignation, but merely said that since the situation was clearly impossible, he thought the Prince had better come and stay at his house until after the inquest.

Ermyntrude, who was weeping on Vicky's shoulder, lifted her head to say in a broken voice that she was sure she didn't want to hurry the Prince's departure, but Mary threw the doctor a look of heartfelt gratitude, and took the Prince aside to explain to him that Ermyntrude's nerves were in such a precarious condition that she feared a breakdown, and thought he would be better out of the house.

Finally, the Prince went upstairs to superintend the packing of his suitcases; Ermyntrude was resuscitated with brandy, and smelling-salts; and the rest of the party, with the exception of Vicky, who stayed to hold her mother's hand, withdrew into the hall.

Mary said: 'I'll never forget this, Maurice, never! You are the truest friend anyone ever had!'

'Well, I think I'd better be getting along,' said Hugh. 'Can I give you a lift, Inspector?'

'No, thank you, sir: the police-car's waiting for me. Now, I don't want to worry you, miss, but just tell me one thing! Was Mrs Carter thinking of divorcing her husband, or was she not?'

'No, no, of course she wasn't!' replied Mary. 'She told me quite definitely that nothing would induce her to.'

'Thank you, that's all I wanted to know,' said Hemingway, and left the house in Hugh Dering's wake.

In the porch he drew a long breath, and said: 'Talk about the old Lyceum! Why, it was nothing to it! Don't you run away, sir! I want you to tell me just what that young terror was playing at! I don't mind owning I didn't see my way at all.'

'I warned you that you were in for a shock,' grinned Hugh.

'Seems to me you'd better have warned me to bring along my trick cycle,' retorted the Inspector. 'Quite out of the picture, I was. Well, I've met some queer people in my time, but this little lot fairly takes my breath away. Don't tell me the Duchess of Malfi isn't on the stage, because I wouldn't believe you!'

Hugh laughed. 'Was, not is. Are you interested in the Drama?'

'I am, but I never had a bit of use for Family Charades. What was it all about, that's what I'd like to know?'

'Miss Fanshawe,' said Hugh carefully, 'does not wish her mother to marry Prince Varasashvili.'

'Well, I'm bound to say she shows sense,' remarked the Inspector. 'All the same, you'd think the girl could think of some way of getting rid of him without putting on a three-reel drama, wouldn't you? The nerve of her dragging me into her antics! Not but what it was a highly talented performance. She's got more brain that I gave her credit for.'

At this moment, Vicky came out of the house. 'Oh, good, you haven't gone!' she said, addressing Hugh. 'It's suddenly dawned on me that it's very nearly eight o'clock. You'd better stay to dinner, because you'll be frightfully late if you go back to the Manor. Besides, we may as well think out a good plan of campaign while we have the chance.' She noticed the Inspector, half hidden in the shadows beyond the shaft of light coming through the open door. 'Oh, you weren't meant to hear that! I dare say it doesn't actually matter, but I do rather feel that it's time you went home.'

'Thanks to you, miss, I'm feeling very much the same myself. I suppose you didn't happen to think when you were carrying on like that, that there might be two ways of looking at that big act of yours?'

'There aren't two ways of looking at the Prince,' said Vicky positively. 'Anyone can see that he's utterly apocryphal, besides being a complete adder.'

'We won't go into that,' said the Inspector. 'What I meant was, that you were so anxious to get me to say I'd a case against you to suit your own ends, that perhaps you didn't stop to think whether I might really have a case against you?'

'That's nonsense!' Hugh said quickly.

The Inspector looked at him. 'Oh, is it? What makes you so sure of that, sir?'

'I saw Miss Fanshawe when she came up from the bridge. If she had just shot her stepfather, she's a better actress than she's yet given me any reason to suppose.'

'Well, you needn't spoil it!' said Vicky indignantly. 'What about the act I've just put on? *I* thought it went awfully well, and though you may not know it, it isn't everyone who can cry real tears in an act. *I* did!'

'Why didn't your dog bark, miss?'

'I can't think, and it's bothered me a lot,' replied Vicky frankly. 'Does that look as though I must have done it? Shall you arrest me?'

'Go inside, you impossible brat!' said Hugh, grasping her by the arm, and twisting her round. 'You don't want her, do you, Inspector?'

'No, sir, you're more than welcome,' replied Hemingway.

Hugh pushed Vicky into the house, and shook her. 'You ought to have been drowned at birth! Do you imagine all this is some kind of a parlour game?

'Oh no, I think it's quite ghoulish, and as a matter of fact, it gives me nightmares. Oh, I can hear Alexis! Come quickly into the library! It would be most frightfully *gauche* and tactless of me to run into him after all that lovely sabotage! Besides, I'm going to ring Robert up.'

'What the devil for?' demanded Hugh, following her into the library.

Vicky picked up the receiver and began to dial a number. 'Oh, don't be silly! It's his cue, of course. You've no idea how cherishing he is, which is just what Ermyntrude needs. *Darling* Robert! *He* wouldn't try and set the police on to little Vicky! . . . Oh, is that you, Robert? This is Vicky. Would you like to come and see Ermyntrude after dinner? I thought it would be a goodish sort of a move if you were just to drift in too utterly casually, because everything is most dislocated here, and I'm practically imprisoned already, which is naturally very upsetting for Ermyntrude . . . Oh no, truly, I'm not joking! It's only that I *do* so believe in wearing a brave smile, like Invictus . . . No, I don't think I could explain over the telephone, on account of people listening in . . . Oh no! that's all part of it; he's gone – at least he's going . . . Yes, I thought you would. Good-bye, and come at about nine!' She put the receiver down, and turned towards Hugh, who was standing with his shoulders against the door, somewhat grimly regarding her. 'The great thing is to strike while the iron's hot,' she said earnestly.

'Does it occur to you,' said Hugh, 'that this matchmaking of yours is a trifle premature?'

'No, because Ermyntrude simply must have a protector. Poor sweet, she's not very sensible, you know, and she might quite easily let her kind heart get the better of her, and forgive Alexis, which would be fatal. Even you must see that he's the most appalling menace!'

Hugh could not deny this, but said: 'You're a bit of a menace yourself, if I may say so, Vicky.'

'Yes, but I have the most beautiful intentions,' Vicky assured him.

But Mary, when they joined her in the dining-room a quarter of an hour later, seemed unable to perceive the beauty of Vicky's intentions. She had done what she could do to soothe the Prince's injured feelings, and had bidden him a most civil farewell upon the doorstep; and she had then been called to Ermyntrude's side, so that she had a good deal of excuse for being out of temper.

Although Ermyntrude had chosen to have her dinner sent into the drawing-room on a tray, conversation between Hugh and the two girls was necessarily of a spasmodic nature, since the butler was continually coming in and out of the room. This helped to add to Mary's exasperation, and by the time the dessert was on the table, and they were finally rid of Peake, she was cross enough, and tired enough, to say angrily to Vicky: 'Well, I hope you're satisfied with your work!'

'Artists are never wholly satisfied, but I must say I thought it went with quite a swing,' replied Vicky sunnily.

'It may interest you to know that I think you behaved disgustingly! I was absolutely ashamed of you!'

'But, darling, be fair!' begged Vicky. 'You said only yesterday that you didn't know how on earth to get rid of Alexis.'

'I never dreamed you meant to do anything so ill-bred, and – and atrocious!'

'No, but I do rather feel that we couldn't have got rid of Alexis in a well-bred way. As a matter of fact, I've been frightfully bothered about it the whole afternoon, because I found him making the most subtle love to Ermyntrude, and I couldn't see my way at all. Only he very kindly played right into my hands, setting the police on to me.'

'I don't believe he did any such thing!'

'Oh, I'm pretty sure you're wrong there, Mary!' Hugh interposed. 'Every time I've had the privilege of meeting him, he's managed to cast suspicion on to someone or other.'

'Next you'll say that you enjoyed that vulgar exhibition!' snapped Mary.

'Well, I did, rather,' Hugh confessed. 'You must admit it was epic!'

'I don't admit anything of the kind. I feel hot with shame whenever I think of it.'

'Poor sweet, that isn't shame: this room's awfully stuffy. I'll open a window, shall I?' suggested Vicky.

'No! I'm only sorry that you can't see how badly you've behaved. Hugh may think it was very funny, and egg you on, but Maurice didn't. He said you ought to be smacked!'

'How dear and mild of him! He's rather precious, isn't he? Hugh said I ought to have been drowned at birth.'

'You can try to turn it into a joke as much as you like, but you won't succeed in getting me to see the humour of it. You pitchforked us into a perfectly ghastly scene – in front of that Inspector, too! – and though I don't expect you to care about my feelings, I should have thought you'd have had more consideration for your mother than to have upset her like that.'

'Darling, you simply can't imagine how resilient the poor lamb is! Besides, I've told Robert to look in this evening. To catch her first bounce, you know, because I *quite* agree it would be fatal for her just to trickle away to some frightful person on the boundary.'

'Vicky, how can you talk like that?'

Vicky stretched out a hand towards a dish of grapes. 'But, dearest pet, I don't see that it would be a bit helpful of me to pretend that Ermyntrude isn't the sort of darling idiot who'll make the most unparalleled muck of things, if not cherished by a Good Man. Well, I mean to say, just look at the way she fell for Wally, who was an utter loss! Naturally, you don't see it as I do, because she isn't your mother; but it's no good expecting me to sit back in a well-bred way while she lets a boa-constrictor like Alexis coil himself all round her.'

'You're impossible,' said Mary hopelessly. 'Did it occur to you, when you deliberately played on her feelings, that the one thing she's been dreading, ever since Sunday, was that you'd be accused of having had something to do with Wally's death?'

'Oh, then that was why she reacted so superbly! I must say, I didn't expect her to turn on Alexis quite so fiercely. Now you come to mention it, though, I did think something was weighing on her mind. Did she tell you about it?'

'Just now. Perhaps you'll soothe her yourself the next time you elect to drive her into hysterics!'

'I don't suppose I will,' said Vicky, considering it. 'You're so much better at it than I am. Are you going to the inquest tomorrow?'

'No, and I hope you're not either!'

'Well, I am, because it seems to me I'm a very

interested party, and I want to see what's likely to happen next.'

'I shouldn't go, if I were you,' said Hugh. 'I'll let you know if anything startling comes out. Not that it's likely to. The police are sure to ask for an adjournment.'

'I should like,' said Vicky, dipping her fingers in the cut-glass bowl before her, 'to find out why Harold White wanted to see Wally on Sunday, and what they were going to do with that five hundred pounds.'

'Oh, it's got to that now, has it?' said Hugh. 'Any good my reminding you that that idea is nothing more than a suspicion of Mary's?'

'Well, not much,' Vicky said, with one of her enchanting smiles.

'In any case, you're not likely to hear anything about it at the inquest.'

'I expect I'll go all the same,' said Vicky tranquilly.

'Then I suppose I shall have to take you,' said Hugh.

'Oh, no! Not a bit necessary.'

'You'll only get into mischief if I don't keep an eye on you.'

'I wouldn't wonder,' Vicky murmured. 'Oh, I've just been smitten with the most awesome reflection! How do you suppose Maurice is managing to entertain Alexis?'

'Vicky, you little beast!' said Mary. 'That's the worst part of it all, that Maurice should be stuck with that awful man!'

'Well, I don't know,' said Vicky. 'After all, we've had him ever since Friday, so it's time somebody else had a turn.'

This was too much for Mary, and she got up from the table, bringing the party to an end. Hugh declined going into the drawing-room with the two girls, but instead took his leave of them, and drove back to the Manor, having promised to meet Vicky outside the Coroner's Court on the following morning.

'Not long after his departure, Steel arrived, and was ushered into the drawing-room. Ermyntrude, still reclining upon the sofa, greeted him with unaffected pleasure; and Mary could not help feeling, as she watched him take Ermyntrude's little plump hand in his own strong one, that he must undoubtedly represent a pillar of strength to clinging womanhood. The story was poured into his ears, and his reactions to it were all that Vicky had hoped they might be. Nothing could have formed a greater contrast to the Prince's excitable display than Steel's rugged calm. He indulged in no aspersions upon his late rival's character; he merely said that it was a good thing the fellow had gone, and that he had never taken to him much. He even refused to join Ermyntrude in attributing the Prince's oblique attack on Vicky to his having murdered Wally himself, remarking that he didn't think the fellow would have the guts to do it. When he was alone with Ermyntrude, he held her hand in an uncomfortably strong grasp, and told her that whatever happened she could rely on him.

Ermyntrude wept a little, and confided to him the fear that was gnawing at her nerves. 'Oh, Bob, they won't think it was my Vicky, will they?'

'No,' he replied.

The simple negative was wonderfully reassuring, but she could not be quite satisfied. 'Bob, it keeps nagging at me day and night! I ought never to have told her about Wally and that girl, only I was so upset at the time, it just slipped out. And I keep thinking about it, wondering, because she's not like most girls, my Vicky. You never know what she'll get up to next! Bob, she – she *couldn't* have done a thing like that! She couldn't!'

'She didn't do it. You can put that clean out of your head.'

'I know, I know! But I can't help its coming back to me. For there's no denying she was there, and it's in the blood, Bob. You can't get away from that!'

'That's a lot of rot,' said Steel. 'Your first husband wasn't a murderer!'

'No, but look at the animals he killed in his time! I mean, he had a regular passion for it, but he took it out on lions and tigers and things; and I can't help thinking of a book I read once, all about impulses, and what you inherit from your parents, and things that happen to you in the cradle that go and give you fixtures, or some such nonsense, and I ask myself if perhaps there is something in it after all, and I ought to have seen to it my Vicky had a chance to shoot bigger things than just a few rabbits here and there.'

The suggestion that Vicky, finding rabbits poor sport, had added her stepfather to the bag, did not draw even a smile from Steel. He was rather shocked and extremely scornful of such far-fetched ideas; and he told Ermyntrude that she was not to worry her head over it any more.

She dabbed cautiously at her eyes. 'You won't let that dreadful policeman take her away, Bob, will you? He's been at her already.'

'Then he's a fool. But nothing's going to happen to Vicky, I give you my word.'

'Oh, Bob, you are a comfort to me!' Ermyntrude said gratefully. 'I feel better just for having seen you. Only you know what the law is, and if the Inspector was to get it into his head Vicky's done it, there isn't one of us could stop him taking her up for it!'

'Listen to me, Ermyntrude!' Steel said, looking very steadily at her. 'You've got my word for it no harm's coming to Vicky. I told you you could depend on me, and

I'm not a chap who says what he doesn't mean. Whatever happens, I won't let your girl get mixed up in this. Now, you trust me, and don't think another thing about it!' He gave her hand a final squeeze, and released it, rising to his feet. 'I'm going home now, and you're going to get to bed, and have a good night's rest. That's what you need, and that's what I'm going to tell Mary.'

Mary, when this piece of information was delivered to her, said that she had tried to put Ermyntrude to bed before dinner.

'She'll go now,' Steel said. He turned to Vicky, and said abruptly: 'So the police are on to you, are they?'

'Yes, I'm having a very crowded life all at once,' replied Vicky. 'Do you suppose I'll be arrested?'

'No. I've just set your mother's mind at rest about that. Don't you worry either! See?'

Vicky was quite entranced by this masterful speech, and no sooner had Steel left the house than she turned to Mary, and said: 'Oh, I do think I've created a grand situation! Do you suppose he's going to give himself up in my stead?'

'I hope he wouldn't be such a fool!'

'So do I, but I can't help seeing that it would be a very Nordic act. Really, darling, you must admit I was quite right to send for him. He's even soothed Ermyntrude!'

'You know, Vicky,' said Mary, 'I'm absolutely horrified by the way you talk about your mother! It's positively indecent,'

'Dearest pet, the way I talk truly isn't as indecent as the way you think,' Vicky replied. 'Because you've got the most degrading suspicions, and you disapprove of the poor sweet so much that you daren't put it into words. I don't disapprove of her at all; in fact, she has my vote.'

Mary was silenced, and turned away, merely remarking

over her shoulder that she hoped Vicky was not really going to the inquest.

The hope, however, was without foundation, and she was not surprised when Vicky left the house next morning at half past ten, and drove off in the direction of Fritton.

Hugh Dering had already arrived at the King's Head Hotel, where the Coroner's Court was to sit, but he was not alone. He had brought his father to the inquest, in spite of Sir William's strongly-worded announcement that he wished to have nothing to do with the affair. 'I wish you would come, sir,' Hugh had said. 'I'd like you to take a look at some of the protagonists, and tell me what you make of them.'

'Why?' demanded Sir William.

'I want your opinion. It's got me guessing, and I'd very much like to know how it strikes you.'

After this, Sir William's protests had been merely a matter of form, for although he would have hotly denied such an idea, he was secretly much flattered to think that Hugh wanted his opinion. Whenever anyone asked him questions about Hugh, he naturally disparaged him, and said that he was an idle young hound, and that he didn't think he was at all clever (though, as a matter of fact, he took a first in Greats, for what that was worth), or particularly good at games (although actually he got his Rugger Blue, and had entered for the Amateur Golf Championship last year; not that that was anything to make a fuss about); but if Sir William had ever been obliged to enter a confessional, and to state his true opinion of his son, he would have said, with the utmost reluctance, that Hugh's equal for character, brains, physique, athletic prowess, and general virtue did not exist. So when this paragon expressed a desire to hear his opinion on the Carter case, Sir William swelled with inward gratification, and allowed himself to be persuaded to give up his own plans for the morning, and to accompany his young fool of a son to a stuffy room at the King's Head, all to listen to an inquest which he had no interest in, and which Hugh wouldn't have had any interest in either if he had had a grain of sense, which, however, he knew from long experience he hadn't, and probably never would have.

Having made quite clear his extreme reluctance to accompany Hugh, he got happily into the car beside him; wished he could drive as well as the boy could; said that Hugh took his corners too fast; was sorry for an acquaintance whom they passed on the road. whose son was a very poor specimen compared with Hugh, and never wanted to take his father anywhere.

When Hugh drew up outside the King's Head behind Vicky's sports-car, and Sir William saw Vicky sitting pensively at the wheel, and looking very young and fragile in a black hat and frock, he exclaimed: 'Surely it's not necessary for that child to be present!'

'She thinks it is,' responded Hugh, opening the door for him to get out. 'She's a suspected party.'

'Preposterous!' said Sir William. 'As though a girl of her age could have had anything to do with it!'

'I wouldn't put it beyond her,' said Hugh. 'Hallo, Vicky! Congratulations on the ensemble!'

'Hush, I'm feeling frightfully holy, because black has that effect on me, I find. Oh, how do you do, Sir William! I'm glad you've come, because so far the most scruffy-looking people have turned up, and I thought it was going to be utterly drab.'

'My dear child, you ought not to be here,' said Sir William, shaking hands with her. 'There's no need at all: I can't think what that boy of mine was about to let you come.'

'You *don't* think he could stop me, do you?' asked

Vicky, quite shocked. 'Besides, I've rather fallen for the Inspector from Scotland Yard, on account of his reminding me awfully of a robin that got so tame it used to hop into the dining-room. Oh, Hugh, *all* the Whites have turned up, and Janet was terribly sweet to me, and said she'd stay with me, only I thought not, because she's wearing the kind of hat that makes you feel perhaps after all you're frittering your life away, and ought to be telling people how to look after their babies, or drilling Girl Guides, or something just as dispiriting. And the Prince hasn't turned up, which seems to me pretty callous, really.'

Sir William rather blinked at these confidences, but though he did not approve of the younger generation, he was easily won over by a pretty face. Vicky made him feel fatherly, so he smiled tolerantly at the extravagances of her speech, and took her into the King's Head, telling her that he was glad she did not think he was scruffy-looking.

Quite a number of people had come to attend the inquest. Robert Steel was present, Dr Hinchcliffe, the three Whites, Mrs Jones, and, as Vicky immediately pointed out to Hugh, Gladys Baker, who was sitting beside her mother at the back of the room. In addition to these interested persons there was a large sprinkling of strangers, who appeared to have come in the hope of hearing startling revelations.

In this they were disappointed, for, as Hugh had warned Vicky, nothing exciting happened. Inspector Cook gave his evidence in a monotone; Dr Hinchcliffe followed him; and a man, who, Vicky said, looked like a haddock, got up, and announced that he was a gunsmith, and that he was prepared to swear that the bullet lodged in Wally Carter's chest had been fired from the rifle found in the shrubbery. No one, except, perhaps, the Coroner and the police, was at all interested in his evidence, for it was very dull, quite lacking in human interest. He said that the rifle was a Mannlicher-Schönauer .275, standard in all respects, except that it had a hair-trigger pull; and that it had the appearance of not having been kept in very good order, since the barrels were slightly rusty. He then displayed photographs, taken through a comparing microscope, of test bullets in juxtaposition with the bullet found in Wally Carter's body, and sat down.

After that, Harold White gave his evidence, and was followed by his friend Samuel Jones, and his daughter Janet. Sir William Dering muttered into his son's ear an uncharitable estimate of Mr Jones's character, which differed hardly at all from that given by Alan White to his sister, and said that in his opinion there was not a penny to choose between him and Harold White.

Janet's way of giving her evidence made the optimists in the room feel that they had not wasted their time in coming, after all, but no sooner had she sat down, than Inspector Hemingway rose, and disappointed everyone by asking for an adjournment. This was granted, and there was nothing for the interested to do but to disperse.

'Well, sir?' said Hugh. 'What do you make of it?'

'Not enough evidence. I don't make anything of it,' answered Sir William. 'I should like to know what those three were up to.'

'Carter, Jones, and White? You think they were up to something?'

'All birds of a feather,' said Sir William, with a snort.

'That's what Mary suspects, that there was some deal on, probably shady.'

'I shouldn't be surprised. Who's that child got hold of?'

Hugh looked round. 'The Scotland Yard man. Heaven grant she isn't putting on some disastrous act! I think I'd better go and keep an eye on her.'

By the time he reached Vicky's side, Janet and Alan

White had also joined her, and Robert Steel was making his way towards the group. Janet at once began to describe her sensations at finding herself giving evidence in a murder case, and Hugh, feeling that there was no reason why he should listen to this recital, said good morning to the Inspector, and asked him, with a twinkle, whether he had recovered from the shocks of the previous day.

'I have,' responded Hemingway. 'I'm told you hold a watching brief for Miss Fanshawe, sir.'

'By Miss Fanshawe, I should think,' said Hugh. 'I wish you'd put her under lock and key till all this is over.'

'The trouble is, I'm hampered,' explained the Inspector. 'Who's the gentleman with the jaw, sir?'

'Steel.'

Robert Steel had broken into the flood of Janet's conversation to address Vicky, in rather a rough voice. 'Vicky, what are you doing here? You'd no business to come!'

'Oh, but I had, Robert! I told you I'd been entangled in the meshes.'

'And I told you you were a little idiot! You've nothing to do with the case at all.'

'But, darling Robert, I've got far more to do with it than you have, because I was there, and you weren't,' Vicky pointed out.

'Oh, how *thankful* you must be that you weren't there!' said Janet earnestly. 'It was dreadful! And you might have been, only, of course, I'm very glad you weren't, because it would have made it worse for me. I mean, inviting you, and then *that* happening!'

'What on earth are you talking about?' said Steel. 'You didn't invite me!'

'Yes, I did. Don't you remember, when we came out of

church, and I was asking you about King Edward raspberries?'

'No, I don't,' said Steel shortly.

'Oh, but you must!' insisted Janet. 'Because I always think it must be so lonely for you, living all by yourself, and I asked you if you wouldn't drop in at about five, only Father said he'd asked Mr Carter, and you probably wouldn't want to come, which I'm afraid you must have thought was awfully rude of him, but it's only his *way*, you know, and he doesn't *mean* anything.'

'Oh!' said Steel, looking rather annoyed. 'Yes, I do remember now that you said something about dropping in to tea.'

Hugh cast a covert glance at the Inspector. That gentleman's bird-like gaze was fixed with an expression of the deepest interest on Steel's frowning countenance.

13

Alan White, never one to pay much heed to other people's utterances, was not interested either in his sister's artless disclosure, or in Steel's obvious annoyance. He plucked at Vicky's sleeve, and said in a portentous undertone that he wanted to talk to her.

'Oh, not now!' Vicky replied, not looking at him but at the Inspector. 'I can't think of anything but this afflictive murder!'

'Well, it's about that. I think you ought to know. I may say that I'm absolutely horrified!'

This was arresting enough to drag Vicky's attention from the Inspector. She bent an inquiring gaze upon Alan. 'About Wally's murder?'

'In a way. I mean, it's something I've found out, only I can't tell you here.'

Vicky saw that the Inspector had made himself known to Steel, and that both he and Steel had moved out of earshot. She said: 'Well, all right, but let's go into the lounge, if there is one, only I must tell Hugh, because he thinks he's looking after me.'

'I can't see what you can possibly have to say to Vicky!' exclaimed Janet, when Alan informed her that she would have to leave the King's Head without him.

'It's just as well that you can't,' said Alan darkly.

'Oh, Alan, I do wish you wouldn't be so theatrical!' Janet said. 'You know how Father hates it!'

'Father!' he said, with a crack of bitter laughter.

'Well, I'm sure I don't want to pry into any secrets. I've got some shopping to do anyway,' said Janet.

Vicky found Hugh talking to his father in the hall of the hotel. He was not much impressed by the news that Alan had important tidings to disclose, for he held a poor opinion of that young gentleman, but he agreed to await the outcome of the interview.

'Because if he really has discovered a clue, or something, I shall immediately tell you,' said Vicky. 'And if it's anything incriminating about Robert, we must suppress it, because it will upset all my plans if he's arrested. Oh, I do think Janet is a calamitous female, don't you?'

'What was that she said?' asked Sir William, looking after Vicky's retreating form in some bewilderment. 'Extraordinary girl! Times have certainly changed since I was a young man!'

Vicky, meanwhile, had led Alan into a leather-upholstered room leading out of the hall. It smelled of stale smoke, and was such a gloomy apartment that it was not surprising that no one ever sat in it. The discovery that the few weary flowers in a vase on the mantelpiece were made of paper pleased Vicky so much that she seemed to be in danger of forgetting the serious nature of Alan's business. He recalled her to it by saying in a sepulchral tone that he knew why Wally Carter had visited his father on Sunday.

This at once claimed Vicky's attention. 'Alan, do you really? Tell me instantly!'

Alan, however, did not mean to be baulked of his dramatic effects. He said: 'God knows what I've done to deserve such a father! If it weren't for Janet, of course, I'd sooner starve than live under his roof. I mean, when one has ideals – '

'I know about them,' interrupted Vicky. 'Go on about your father!'

'I only heard of it in the most roundabout way,' said Alan. 'Though, I need hardly say I had my suspicions, and as a matter of fact I told Father that nothing would induce me to meet Samuel Jones. I'm afraid I let him have it from the shoulder, which shocked Janet, but you know how I feel about that kind of worn-out shibboleth, Vicky. Why one should be expected to respect a man simply because he happens to be one's father – '

'Oh, Alan, do get on!' begged Vicky. 'Wally and your father had got a deal on, hadn't they?'

'Of course, if you already know about it – '

'No, I don't, but Mary guessed it. And if you don't stop reciting this voluminous prologue, and tell me what you've discovered, I shall go into a screaming fit! *Do* be more congruous, Alan darling!'

'Well, you've heard about the new building scheme, haven't you?' said Alan, rather sulkily.

'Here, in Fritton? Yes, they're going to build a sort of ghastly garden-city all over Valley Reach, or something.'

'That's just where you're wrong, because they're not going to build over Valley Reach at all. I happen to know the Council has chosen quite a different site. Mind you, it's absolutely secret so far!'

'Well, I don't care,' said Vicky impatiently. 'Is there any point to it? Because Hugh's waiting for me.'

'The point is that that swine Jones is a member of the Council. Also, he's as thick as thieves with my father. Mind you, I can't actually swear to this, but from what I know of Father I don't think there's a doubt I'm right. Do you know Frith Field?'

'Yes, of course I do.'

'Well, a friend of mine, whose name I can't tell you, happens to know that that's the site they've chosen for the new building scheme. It isn't publicly known yet, but naturally Jones knows. And I happen to have discovered that Father's negotiating to buy some of the land!'

Vicky frowned. 'Why? Oh, I see! I suppose it'll suddenly be much more valuable! How on earth did you find out about it?'

'Actually, through a chap I know who's Andrews's clerk. I dare say you don't know whom I mean, but Andrews is my boss's rival. Get it?'

'Well, not utterly,' confessed Vicky.

'How was Father going to pay for that plot of land?' demanded Alan. 'He had to borrow a hundred from Carter only a couple of months ago, so I'd just like to know where the price of this land is supposed to be coming from! Why, it's as plain as a pikestaff! Obviously he'd put the scheme up to Carter, and they were going into some kind of a partnership over it, Carter putting up the cash, and Father and Jones getting a fat rake-off for having let him in on it, I dare say.'

'Oh!' said Vicky, digesting it. 'I wouldn't wonder if you're right, only I don't immediately see that it's going to help. I rather hoped there was something frightfully tortuous on, which would bring on an utterly undreamed-of suspect, and solve everything.'

'You don't seem to see how damnable it is!' said Alan. 'It's absolutely disgusting, and when I think of my father going in for that kind of dirty work it makes me feel like cutting away from him altogether.'

'Oh, is it dirty?' said Vicky innocently. 'Would you mind frightfully if I told Hugh Dering? Because at the moment the police think Percy Baker was blackmailing Wally, and this seems to show that he wasn't at all. You don't know Percy, and I don't really feel I can explain him to you, but he's a garage-hand, and I do rather feel that it's bad luck on him to be suspected of something he didn't do.'

'With me,' said Alan grandly, 'the State comes above every other tie. Naturally I shall confront Father with my suspicions, and if some unfortunate devil is being ruined through his filthy dealings I shall go to the police myself, and tell them all I know. Of course, it won't be very pleasant for me – in fact, it's practically crucifying myself but – '

'Darling Alan, I should hate you to crucify yourself, besides it isn't in the least necessary, and I don't think it's the done thing to sneak about your father to the police. So I shall just tell Hugh, and see what he thinks we ought to do about it.'

'I don't see what it's got to do with him,' said Alan discontentedly. 'As a matter of fact, I haven't got much use for him. He's one of those hearty, old school-tie fellows who make me rather sick.'

'Well, I dare say you make him feel a bit squeamish, if he's noticed you, which I rather doubt,' retorted Vicky.

This unexpected championing of Hugh had the effect of putting Alan so much on his dignity that he needed no urging to go away, but said in an offended voice that it was obvious he was not wanted, and he only hoped that Vicky would not regret having succumbed to the glamour of an Old Etonian tie.

So when Vicky joined Hugh at one of the little tables which were dotted about the hall of the hotel, she naturally had a good look at the tie he was wearing, and said in a tone of considerable astonishment: 'Is that an old Etonian tie?'

'No,' said Hugh, pulling forward a chair for her. 'Sit down, and I'll give you a drink. What would you like?'

'I'll have a Side-car, please. Weren't you at Eton?'

'I was. Why?'

'Well, I wondered, because Alan said that was an old Etonian tie. I though he must be wrong. What sort of a tie is it?'

Hugh had moved away to ring the bell for a waiter, but he turned at this, and regarded Vicky with a mixture of amusement and surprise. 'It's just a tie. Did Alan take you aside to give you erroneous information about my neck-wear?'

'Oh no, that was merely by the way! Actually, he's found out a sordid story about Wally and his father, and fat Mr Jones, which proves that Mary was right all along. So that ought to be a lesson to you not to be fusty and dusty again.'

'What sort of a sordid story?' asked Hugh. 'Do you mean that he really did ask your mother for that five hundred from some business deal?'

'Yes, I'm now definitely sure he did. I say, what's become of your father?'

'Gone to buy some tobacco.'

A waiter came into the hall at that moment, and while Hugh gave his order, Vicky had time to take stock of her surroundings, and to discover that at the far end of the hall, in a dim inglenook by the empty fireplace, Robert Steel and Inspector Hemingway were seated in close conversation. As soon as the waiter had departed, she called Hugh's attention to this circumstance. 'Oh, I do think Janet is a menace!' she said. 'I don't *want* Robert to be the guilty man!'

'Don't be silly,' replied Hugh calmly. 'And don't forget, in your anxiety to provide your mother with a husband, that you would hardly want her to marry Carter's murderer. I suggest that you wait until he's been cleared of all suspicion before you start match-making. Are you going to tell me about Alan's revelations?'

'Yes, because I quite think it's time I told the police that Percy wasn't blackmailing Wally. Because, though he said he was the enemy of my class, he was rather pathetic in a way, and I don't at all mind clearing his fair name.'

'A beautiful thought,' said Hugh. 'The only flaw being that if you dispose of the blackmailing charge you at once pin a motive on to him.'

'Oh dear, how tiresome! Yes, I see. The police will think he did it for revenge. Now I don't know what to do!'

The waiter came back with two cocktails on a tray. Hugh paid for them, and lifted his glass. 'Here's to you, Vicky. Tell me the whole story.'

'Well, I will, only I expect you'll cast a blight on it, and refuse to believe a word,' said Vicky gloomily.

But when Hugh had heard the tale, he gratified Vicky by taking it quite seriously, and admitting that it seemed probable that he had been mistaken in his first disbelief in Mary's theory.

'Yes, but it isn't really in the least helpful,' said Vicky. 'Except that it shows Percy wasn't blackmailing Wally, and even that doesn't seem to be altogether a good thing.'

'It doesn't help to explain the murder,' said Hugh, 'but I certainly think the police ought to be told about it – for what it's worth.' He glanced over his shoulder, and saw that Steel and Hemingway had got up, and that Steel was moving towards the door. He caught the Inspector's eye, and made a sign to him.

Hemingway came across the hall. 'Want me, sir?' he inquired.

'Yes, Miss Fanshawe's got something to tell you, which I think you ought to know. Sit down, won't you? What's yours?'

The Inspector declined refreshment, but turned an interested eye upon Vicky. 'Now, is this going to be on the level?' he asked. 'Because if it's just one of your variety turns, miss, there's nothing doing. I'm a busy man.'

'Oh, it's absolutely on the level!' Vicky assured him. 'And if you're busy trying to convict Mr Steel, just because of what Miss White said, it's the most utter waste of time. I don't say she didn't ask him to tea on Sunday, because she probably did, but she talks so much that I don't suppose he was paying the least attention to her. No one ever does.'

The Inspector made no reply to this, but as Vicky's was precisely the explanation which Steel had already given him, her words carried more weight than even she had expected.

He listened to Alan White's story, as recounted by Hugh, in attentive silence, remarking at the end that he was sorry he had never had the privilege of meeting Wally Carter. He did not seem inclined to comment further upon the story, so Vicky, who felt that it had fallen flat, said hopefully that it was probably the cluc to the crime. But even this failed to draw the Inspector. He shook his head, and said that he wouldn't be at all surprised if she were right.

To his Sergeant, twenty minutes later, he said that the case had now reached a highly promising stage. Wake scratched his chin, and said: 'It beats me why you should say that, sir. What I was thinking myself is that whichever way we turn there doesn't seem to be anything to grasp hold of. You keep thinking you're on to something, and though you can't say definitely that you're not, yet it don't seem to lead far enough, if you take my meaning.'

'That's what I like about it,' replied Hemingway cheerfully. 'In my experience, once a case gets so tangled up that it's like the Hampton Court maze, it's a very good sign. Something's going to break. Now, I've just discovered two things which don't seem to me to help much, but I've got a very open kind of mind, and I'm prepared to find that they're a lot more important than I think. We've got to add Mr Silent Steel to the list of suspects, my lad.'

'How's that?' inquired the Sergeant. 'Not but what we always have had an eye on him, haven't we?'

'We'll have two eyes on him now, because according to

Miss White, that story of his about not knowing that Carter was going to the Dower House on Sunday won't hold water. It transpires that she asked him to tea when they came out of church, and her father put him off by saying he'd got Carter coming.'

'Is that so!' exclaimed the Sergeant. 'That doesn't look too good, I will say!'

'It doesn't, but it doesn't look too bad either, Steel's explanation being that Miss White was talking nineteen to the dozen all the time he was trying to have a word with a friend of his, and he didn't pay much heed to her. I'm bound to say I don't altogether disbelieve him.'

The Sergeant thought it over. 'She does talk,' he admitted reluctantly. 'What was the second thing you discovered, sir?'

'The second thing, if true, bears out friend Baker's story that he never had a notion of asking Carter for five hundred pounds. Jones, White and Carter wanted it for their own nefarious doings. You certainly have to hand it to Carter: regular turn in himself!'

The Sergeant, when the story was told him, said severely that there was too much of that sort of thing going on, but he didn't see that it had much bearing on the case.

'Not at first glance,' agreed Hemingway. 'But if young Baker wasn't blackmailing Carter, then we've got to consider whether he shot him out of revenge, and if so, how he knew where to lay his hands on that rifle.'

The Sergeant frowned. 'It's my belief he's too much of a wind-bag.'

'You may be right, and I'm not denying I don't fancy him much myself. The trouble is I've got something on the whole gang of them, and not enough to hang any one of them. You take the Prince: he's got no alibi; he fakes one, which naturally makes me very suspicious. At the same time, I'm not surprised he wasn't so keen on coming clean before he was forced to, supposing he didn't shoot Carter; and I wouldn't like to say that what he finally told us wasn't true. It might have been. In fact, it's quite plausible. Then there's Steel. He's in love with the widow, and it's common knowledge that he hated Carter, and got remarkably hot under the collar at the way he treated the fair Ermyntrude. He's not the sort of man I take to, and he's just about as anxious to make me think that the Prince did it as the Prince is to make me think he did it. After him, we have to consider the Glamour-girl.'

'Miss Fanshawe? Why, she's only a kid, sir!'

'Well, if she's a kid she's a shocking precocious one, that's all I have to say!' replied Hemingway. 'She was in the shrubbery; she could have got the rifle any time she wanted; and she knew how to handle it.'

'Pretty heavy gun for a little bit of a thing like her,' objected the Sergeant.

'I wouldn't put it beyond her to fire it, not with that hair-trigger pull. If it had had a five-pound pull, which I'm told is the usual, she might have found it a bit too much for her. However, I don't fancy her any more than I fancy the other girl. If she did it, it was to do her mother a good turn, which I grant you would seem to me a lot too far-fetched, if she weren't such a caution. As it is, I wouldn't like to say what she'd take it into her head to do. But if the other girl did it, she did it for the reason that nine people out of ten would: money. She thought she'd come into Aunt Clara's fortune; and from what I can make out, it would have been sound sense to see to it that Carter didn't get the chance to splurge around with it first.'

'She doesn't give *me* the impression of being that kind of a girl,' said Wake.

'Nor me either, but that's not to say I'm right. Finally,

we've got that young Bolshie, Baker. And I say finally, because he's the one I fancy least of all. I'm a psychologist.'

'Are you ruling out the widow, sir? Seems to me she had as much cause to shoot Carter as anyone, and we've only got her word for it she was lying down in her room at the time.'

'You go and take another look at her, my lad,' recommended the Inspector. 'If she or either of the girls did it, they had to jump across the stream. Well, if you see her doing that you've got more imagination that what I have.'

Upon reflection the Sergeant apologized and said that he had spoken without thinking. He added: 'We've got to remember that funny business at the shoot on Saturday, haven't we?'

'You're right; we have. By all accounts, the Prince or Steel was responsible for that affair. Everyone seems to be agreed it couldn't have been the doctor, nor yet young Dering.'

'Well, that puts it on to one of the other two,' said the Sergeant. 'The murder, I mean.'

'Funny,' mused Hemingway. 'I was thinking just the opposite.'

'Why, sir?'

'Psychology,' replied Hemingway. 'You're jumping to conclusions, and that's a very dangerous thing to do. I grant you it wouldn't be a bad way of getting rid of anyone, to stage an accident at a shoot. But to my way of thinking the man that misses his victim one day and has a second shot at him the next must be plain crazy. And no question of accident about the second shot, either! The more I look at this case, the more I feel I want someone who wasn't mixed up in Saturday's little affair.'

'Yes, I see,' said Wake slowly. 'That's assuming the first affair was an accident. Gave the murderer the idea, so to speak, or at least made him feel it would be a good moment to bump off Carter, because we'd be bound to connect the two shootings.'

'Yes, you speak for yourself!' said the Inspector tartly.

The Sergeant pondered a while, a frown creasing his brow. 'You know, sir, I don't like it,' he pronounced at last. 'When I get to thinking about the people who are mixed up in the case, I can't but come to the conclusion there isn't one of them has what you could call a real motive. That Prince said he could have got Mrs Carter to divorce Carter. I don't say he could, and I'm not forgetting what Miss Cliffe told us, that Mrs Carter didn't hold with divorce; but the way he talked you could see he thought himself such a one with the ladies he could get them to do anything he wanted. Well, then there's Mr Steel. Of course, I'm not saying he mightn't have got all worked up to murder Carter, but what I ask myself is, why didn't he do it any time these last two years?'

'There's an answer to that one,' interposed the Inspector. 'If Steel did it, it was the Baker business set him off. We know the widow pitched in a tale to him that made him see red.'

'That's so,' Wake admitted. 'But would you say, from all we've been able to pick up, that it was the first time she'd complained to him about Carter?'

'I wouldn't, of course, but have you ever heard of the straw that broke the camel's back?'

'All right, sir: have it that it's Steel we're after. He's more likely than either of those two girls to my mind.'

'Yes, you've got a lot of old-fashioned ideas,' said the Inspector. 'They're a handicap to you.'

'Well, what's in your mind, sir?' demanded Wake. 'What are we going to do next?'

'You're going to do a bit of nosing around,' replied Hemingway. 'You can put young Jupp on to it, too. I've noticed he's got quite a gift for getting people to open their hearts to him. Reminds me of what I was at his age, except that he isn't as bright. Find out all you can about Carter. It strikes me he was the sort of chap that might have made a whole lot more enemies than we've yet seen. Meanwhile, I'm going to go into the question of this rifle, and who could have pinched it. I'll see you later.'

When he reached Palings, the Inspector found that Dr Chester was with Ermyntrude, and that Vicky had not returned from Fritton. Mary received him, and upon his disclosing his errand to her, said frankly: 'I've been thinking over that question, and going over in my mind who could have taken the rifle out of the case, and walked off with it. And I do think that I ought, in fairness, to tell you that when the Prince left for Dr Chester's house on Sunday, I saw him go, and he had nothing at all in his hands. Of course, I quite see that he might have taken the rifle earlier in the day, and hidden it somewhere on the way to the garage, but I don't honestly see when he got the chance. I mean, it would surely have been taking the most frightful risk to have removed it from the gun-room during the morning, with all the servants about, not to speak of ourselves.'

'Can you remember, miss, when you last saw the rifle in the gun-case?'

'No, that's the trouble: I can't! I doubt if any of us could, because naturally we none of us have ever used Mr Fanshawe's rifles. One just doesn't notice things one isn't interested in.'

The Inspector nodded. 'Well, casting your mind over young Baker's visits to the house, could he have had the oppportunity to take the rifle?'

'No, I don't think so. Certainly not, when he called the second time. I wasn't here when he called earlier in the day, but could he have carried off a rifle on his motor-cycle?'

'Not without its being noticed, he couldn't. I'm not setting much store by that first visit of his, I don't mind telling you, miss. Stands to reason he wouldn't have come up to the house again to see Mr Carter if he'd already made up his mind to shoot him, and pinched the weapon he meant to use. The question is, could he have known that there were rifles in the house?'

Mary wrinkled her brow. 'I shouldn't think so. According to Miss Fanshawe, he didn't even know that my cousin was married, so it doesn't look as though he could have had any knowledge of the house, does it?' She looked the Inspector in the eyes, 'I could have taken the gun at any time; so could Miss Fanshawe. I shan't say we didn't, because you wouldn't believe me. But I can tell you one thing: Mr Steel didn't take the gun when he was here on Sunday, because I saw him when he came out of the drawing-room, where he'd been talking to Mrs Carter, and I was with him until he left the house, and drove off.'

'For the sake of argument, miss, he could have come back while you were all at lunch, couldn't he?'

'I don't think so. Mrs Carter had her lunch in the drawing-room, so that the butler was continually passing through the hall, to wait on her.'

'No other way he could have got into the house than by the front-door?'

'Well, yes, he could have entered through the garden-hall, or the morning-room, or the library. They both have French windows. But he'd still have run the risk of walking into one of the servants.'

'Then it boils down to this, miss: you can't think of anyone other than yourself or Miss Fanshawe who could have taken the rifle.'

'Not on Sunday,' Mary said. 'And there's no point in going back farther than that, is there?'

'Have you got something in your mind, miss?' said Hemingway, watching her.

'No, not really. Only that I do know of one person who was in the gun-room on Saturday morning. But it isn't helpful, I'm afraid.'

'You never know. Who was it, miss?'

'Mr White. My cousin had lent him a shot-gun, and he brought it back on his way to work on Saturday. I didn't see him myself, but Mrs Carter told me about it.'

'Did Mr White go into the gun-room, then?'

'Yes, he did.'

'Alone, miss?'

'Yes. Mrs Carter said she didn't see why she should bother to put the gun back in its place for him.'

'And you don't know of anyone else who went to the gun-room?'

'No, but I quite see that almost anyone could have. The front-door is always open during the summer, and any number of people must know that Mrs Carter kept all her first husband's rifles.' She turned, for the morning-room door had opened, and Dr Chester had come out into the hall.

Chester glanced from her to Hemingway. 'Good morning, Inspector,' he said. 'I hope you haven't come to upset my patient again?'

'Oh no, I don't think so, sir!' replied Hemingway. 'Very sorry Mrs Carter was upset yesteday, but if you don't mind my saying so, you'd better speak to Miss Fanshawe about that. That was her little show, not mine. Any objection to my seeing Mrs Carter?'

'No,' Chester said, re-opening the morning-room door. 'None at all.'

The Inspector passed into the room. Chester shut the

door behind him, and looked across at Mary with the enigmatical expression in his eyes which always made her feel that he saw a great deal more than one wanted him to. 'Tired, Mary?'

She smiled, but with an effort. 'A little. Rather bothered. How do you find Aunt Ermy?'

'She'll be all right. Nothing for you to worry about.'

'I thought last night she was going to have a thorough breakdown. It's absurd, Maurice, but she's worrying herself sick over Vicky.'

'Yes. I've assured her that there's no need. I'd like to have a word with that young lady.'

'You can't; she's gone to the inquest, with Hugh.'

Again he looked at her in that considering way of his. 'Has she, indeed? Why?'

'Oh, heaven knows! In search of a thrill, I dare say. She will have it that she's closely concerned. She'll probably treat us all to another act – Innocent girl suspected of Murder, or Mystery Woman, or something of that nature. I'm sorry to say Hugh rather encourages her. I suppose I must be lacking in a sense of humour, for I don't find it amusing.'

'No, nor I. Especially when she saddles me with Ermyntrude's exalted foreign guests,' said Chester dryly.

'I feel terribly remorseful about that,' confessed Mary. 'Only you were so like the god in the car, that I jumped at your offer.'

He smiled. 'It's all right, my dear.'

'Is he a frightful scourge to you?'

'Oh no! I don't see much of him. He had some idea of coming round to explain himself to Ermyntrude, but I headed him off. I trust that the police will soon arrive at some conclusion about him.'

She could not help laughing. 'Maurice, you've no idea

how cold-blooded that sounds! Between ourselves, do you think he did it?'

'I've no idea,' he replied shortly.

'I can't make up my mind about it. Somehow, it doesn't seem possible that any one of the people suspected can have done such a thing.'

'Nevertheless, it's obvious that one of them must have.'

'Couldn't it have been someone quite different? Perhaps someone we don't even know about?'

'My dear, I'm not a detective. It doesn't seem very likely to me.'

'It sounds ridiculous, but I do rather wish you hadn't been out on a case at the time. I feel you might have been more use than Dr Hinchcliffe.'

'Rubbish! Your cousin was dead before Hinchcliffe got there.'

'I didn't mean that. Something might have struck you. You're much cleverer than Dr Hinchcliffe. Everyone says so.'

'Very gratifying, but if you're imagining that I could have done anything more than he did, you're quite wrong, Mary.'

They were interrupted at this moment by Ermyntrude, who bounced out of the morning-room, with Inspector Hemingway on her heels. 'Oh, there you are, love!' she exclaimed. 'Look, Mary, isn't it a fact that Harold White was in the gun-room on Saturday, all by himself?'

'Yes, I've already told the Inspector so.'

'And what's more hadn't Wally lent him a hundred pounds, which he hadn't paid back?'

'I don't know how much it was, but certainly Wally did – '

'Well, I do know, because I've been through the counterfoils of Wally's old cheque-books,' said Ermyntrude. 'It's as plain as a pikestaff he walked off with that rifle. I always said he was at the bottom of it!'

'Yes, I know,' said Mary patiently, 'but you're forgetting that Mr White can't possibly have had anything to do with it, Aunt Ermy.'

'Oh, don't talk to me!' said Ermyntrude, brushing this trifling objection aside. 'If he didn't actually do it himself, I dare say he got Alan to. Yes, and now I come to think of it, what was Alan doing when Wally was shot? All we've been told is that he was out. Out where, that's what I should like to know?'

'But, Aunt, why on earth should Alan shoot Wally? It isn't even as though he's on good terms with his father!'

'I'm sure I don't know, but I've always hated those Whites, and don't anyone tell me that my instinct's wrong, because a woman's instinct never lies!'

She threw a challenging glance at the Inspector, who replied promptly that he wouldn't dream of telling her anything of the sort. 'At the same time,' he added, 'if the story your daughter's got hold of is true, madam, I'm bound to say Mr White should be the last person in the world to want Mr Carter dead.'

'What's this about my daughter?' demanded Ermyntrude. 'Have you been persecuting her again with your wicked, false suspicions?'

'Aunt Ermy!' began Mary in an imploring tone.

'Don't Aunt Ermy me!' snapped Ermyntrude. 'No one's going to badger my girl, so understand that, once and for all. Over my dead body you may, but not while I'm alive to protect her!'

The Inspector was not in the least ruffled by this unjust attack. He said cordially: 'And I'm sure I don't blame you! But as for my badgering her, she's more likely to get me running round in circles, from all I've seen of her. Of course, it's easy to see where she gets her spirit from.

Same place as where she got her looks if you'll pardon my saying so, madam.'

Ermyntrude was naturally a little mollified by this speech, but she said sternly: 'Well, what business had you with her today?'

'I hadn't,' replied the Inspector. 'It was she who had business with me, and since you're bound to hear about it from her, I don't mind telling you that she thinks she's discovered the reason why your husband went to see Mr White on Sunday.'

'She has?' Mary exclaimed. 'Are you sure she wasn't – well, pulling you leg?'

'I wouldn't be sure, only that Mr Dering was there, fairly egging her on to tell me all,' replied Hemingway candidly.

'Oh! Was I right, then? Had my cousin got some deal on with White and Jones?'

'According to Miss Fanshawe, he had. Which, if true, doesn't make it look as though he'd have shot your husband, now does it, madam?'

Mary pushed back a lock of hair from her brow. 'But surely there isn't any question of that?' she said. 'I understood that he wasn't even in sight of the bridge when my cousin was shot! He couldn't have had anything to do with it!'

'As a matter of fact, he couldn't,' admitted the Inspector. 'However, I'm not one to set myself up against a woman's instinct. Broad-minded, that's what I am.'

Ermyntrude looked suspiciously at him, but he met her gaze so unblushingly that she decided that he was not being sarcastic at her expense. 'I don't know anything about where he was standing when Wally was shot,' she said. 'Ten to one, it's a pack of lies, for though I've nothing against the girl I wouldn't trust Janet White further than I could see her, while as for Sam Jones, if ever there was a wrong 'un, he's one! All I do know is that White brought my poor first husband's shot-gun back on Saturday morning, and what's more no one went with him into the gun-room! I'm sure I don't know who else had as good an opportunity to make off with that rifle, unless it was that young man that came blackmailing Wally. I suppose you aren't going to accuse the Bawtrys or the Derings of having stolen it!'

'But, Aunt Ermy, they aren't the only people who could have taken it! There's all Sunday to be reckoned with, remember.'

'The only people we had here on Sunday were Bob Steel and you, Maurice. And if you're going to tell me Bob took the gun you can spare your breath, for it's a lie.' She broke off, frowning, and then said triumphantly: 'Now I come to think of it, didn't Alan White come over on Sunday morning to play tennis? There you are, then! Not but what I still say it was White himself took the rifle, and nothing will ever make me alter my opinion.'

The Inspector regarded her with visible awe. At that moment Peake came into the hall from the servants' wing. Hemingway lifted an imperative finger. 'Just you come here a minute, will you?' he said. 'Did you happen to see Mr White on Saturday morning, when he brought back the shot-gun he'd borrowed off Mr Carter?'

'I did not see Mr White arrive, Inspector.'

'Did you see him at all, that's what I want to know?'

'I encountered Mr White coming out of the gun-room. I was momentarily taken aback, but Mr White explained that he had madam's leave to replace the gun.'

'Did you notice whether he was carrying anything?'

'Yes, Inspector, Mr White had his case in his hand.'

'What case?' demanded the Inspector.

'That's right,' corroborated Ermyntrude. 'He brought

the gun back in a case of his own, and I said at the time it was just like my husband to lend the gun out of its case.'

'An ordinary shot-gun case?' said the Inspector.

'No, a nasty, cheap-looking thing,' replied Ermyntrude.

Peake coughed behind his hand. 'If I might be allowed to explain to the Inspector, madam? Mr White was carrying what is known as a hambone-case.'

'He was, was he? Was he carrying anything else?'

'No, Inspector, nothing else.'

'Did you see him out of the house?'

'Certainly I did,' answered Peake, slightly affronted.

'All right, that's all.' He waited until the butler had departed, and then said with all the air of one whose most cherished illusion has been shattered: 'There, now, we shall have to give up thinking about White after all. Seems a pity, but there it is.'

'I don't see why,' said Ermyntrude. 'Something tells me he did it!'

'Yes, but the trouble is that something tells me that you can't get a three-foot rifle into a thirty-inch case,' replied Hemingway. 'It does seem a shame, doesn't it? But, there, that's a detective's life all over! Full of disappointements.'

14

Since Ermyntrude was extremely loth to abandon what by this time amounted to a conviction that her *bête noire* had murdered Wally, the Inspector's last remark annoyed her considerably. She said that to carp and to criticize and to raise niggling objections was men all over; and when the Inspector patiently asked her to explain how White could have packed a rifle into a case designed to carry, separately, the barrels and stock of a shot-gun, she replied that it was not her business to solve such problems, but rather his.

The Inspector swallowed twice before he could trust himself to answer. 'Well, if he did it, all I can say is that he must be a highly talented conjurer, which, if true, is a piece of very important information which has been concealed from me.'

'Of course he's not a conjurer!' said Ermyntrude crossly. 'And don't think you can laugh at me, because I won't put up with it!'

At this point, Dr Chester intervened, saying with authority that Ermyntrude had talked enough, and must on no account allow herself to become agitated. He ordered her to rest quietly until luncheon was served, and, at a sign from him, Mary coaxed her to retire to the sofa in the drawing-room.

The Inspector threw Chester a look of gratitude, and said, when Mary had taken Ermyntrude away: 'It beats me how you medical gentlemen get away with it, sir! If I'd so much as hinted to her that what she wanted was to cool-off, she'd have turned me out of the house, or had a fit of hysterics, which would have come to the same thing.'

'You're not her doctor, Inspector,' answered Chester with a faint smile. 'You mustn't forget that I've attended Mrs Carter for many years.'

'Know her very well, I dare say?'

'A doctor always knows his patients well.'

'Yes, but I'm not talking about her bronchial tubes,' said the Inspector. 'To tell you the truth, I'm not over and above fond of people's insides. Not that I'm squeamish, mind you, but once you start thinking about how many yards of intestines, and I don't know what besides, you've got, it's enough to give you the horrors. Was Mr Carter a patient of yours too?'

'Yes, but he didn't often have occasion to call me in on his own account.'

'Still, you probably knew him pretty well, I dare say?'

'Fairly. If you want to know whether he was an intimate friend of mine, no: he wasn't.'

The Inspector's penetrating gaze held a question. 'I take it you didn't like him any more than anyone else seems to have done?'

'No, I didn't like him much,' Chester replied calmly. 'He was a tiresome sort of a man – no moral sense whatsoever, and as weak as water.'

'Did it surprise you, when you heard he'd been shot, sir?'

'Naturally it did.'

'You didn't know of anybody who might have wanted him out of the way?'

'Certainly not. I know of many people who have thought for years that it was a pity Mrs Carter ever married him, of course.'

His tone was uncommunicative. The Inspector said:

'It's a funny thing, doctor, but I get the impression that you're not being as open with me as I'd like.'

'Sorry, I'm afraid there's nothing I can tell you,' Chester answered. 'I wasn't in Carter's confidence.'

He turned to pick up his attaché-case from the table, but before he could leave the house, Vicky had entered it, with Hugh Dering behind her.

'Oh, hallo!' Vicky said, mildly surprised to see the Inspector. 'Hallo, Maurice! How's Ermyntrude?'

'Not very well. You ought to know that,' Chester said, rather sternly.

'Poor sweet, I'm afraid she won't be until this is all over. Why didn't you come to the inquest? I quite thought you'd be there, though as a matter of fact it turned out to be frightfully stagnant.'

'I couldn't see that it concerned me,' replied Chester. He nodded to the Inspector, told Vicky briefly not to agitate her mother, and left the house.

'But why is Maurice so curt and unloving?' wondered Vicky. 'Did you annoy him, Inspector? And, I say, what are you doing here? Or can't you tell me?'

'Oh, there's no secret about what I'm doing,' responded Hemingway. 'I'm trying to discover who could have taken that rifle out of the house, and not getting much help either.'

'*I'll* help you!' offered Vicky. 'Practically anyone could, I should think.'

'Yes, that's a lot of use,' said the Inspector.

'Well, I could have,' she suggested. 'Easily! The only thing is that I've never shot with it, so I shouldn't think I'd have managed to kill my stepfather.'

'Tell me this, miss!' said the Inspector suddenly. 'When you heard that shot, just exactly where were you?'

'Oh, I was round the bend in the stream! And I *didn't*

hear or see anyone, and my dog *didn't* bark, or cock his ears, or anything, and *have* I got to say it all over again?'

'Didn't you think it was a bit odd, anyone shooting in the shrubbery?'

'No, because actually I didn't think about it. You often hear shots in the country, you know, and it might easily have been Mr White, or someone, shooting a rabbit.'

'You weren't within sight of the bridge?'

'No, round the bend. I told you. And then I wandered up one of the paths, climbing the hill, and it wasn't till I heard Janet crying, that it dawned on me that something had gone wrong. But why on earth you worry about me when you've got the Prince right under your nose, absolutely asking to be arrested, I can't imagine. He could have taken the rifle as easily as I could.'

'Not on Sunday afternoon,' said Mary, who had just come out of the drawing-room.

'Darling Mary, are you trying to send me to the gallows?' asked Vicky reproachfully.

'Of course I'm not, but one must be fair, and I saw the Prince leave the house on Sunday afternoon.'

'If he did it,' said Vicky, 'he'd laid his plans long before Sunday. Probably on Saturday.'

'Did he go into the gun-room on Saturday?' asked Hugh.

'Yes, of course he did. I shouldn't be at all surprised if he took the rifle at dead of night, and hid it somewhere. In fact, it would be a good thing to assume that he did, and then work it out from that point.'

'If you don't mind my putting in a word, miss, before you take the gentleman's character clean away,' said the Inspector mildly, 'I would like to point out that according to all the evidence I've heard so far, Mr White didn't invite your stepfather until Sunday morning.'

'Oh well, we can easily get round that!' replied Vicky.

'I expect Alexis just hid the rifle in case it should come in handy. After all, my stepfather was bound to go out for a stroll sometime or other, and I do definitely feel that Alexis is a very thoughtful person and would have had everthing ready just on the off-chance.'

This was too much, even for the Inspector, and he looked round for his hat. Mary said: 'I wish you wouldn't talk in that irresponsible way, Vicky! It's absolutely actionable!'

'Oh, is it? Could I be had up for libel, or something?' asked Vicky, her eyes brightening.

'Now look what you've done!' said Hugh, addressing Mary. 'No, Vicky, no! Don't start seeing yourself in the witness-box, causing strong jurymen to shed tears of pity for you!'

'Yes, it strikes me that you're just about as bad as she is, sir,' said Hemingway severely, and left them.

Mary found herself to be so much in agreement with this pronouncement, that instead of inviting Hugh to stay to lunch, she asked somewhat crossly if he had come to Palings for any particular purpose.

'Only to return Sarah Bernhardt to the bosom of her family,' he replied. 'The lady's car died on her.'

'Yes, and I quite think I went over rather well with your father,' said Vicky, 'which is a thing I didn't expect, because he didn't take to me in the least when I was being a Girl of the Century. Mary, you were too utterly right not to go to the inquest! It was wholly spurious.'

'Where's Maurice?' Mary demanded, unheeding.

'Oh, he went away! He didn't seem to me to have the party spirit at all. Probably Alexis had trodden him down, like Keats, or someone.'

Mary sighed. 'I suppose you mean by that that he saw how serious the whole situation is.'

'We all see that,' said Hugh.

'Well, you seem to be getting a good deal of amusement out of it.'

'Sorry! You shouldn't have loosed Vicky on to me.'

'I'm glad you find her so funny. I don't,' said Mary, walking to the staircase.

Hugh watched her till she was out of sight, and then took Vicky by the elbow, and gave her an admonitory shake. 'Look here, my little ray of sunshine, you're getting on Mary's nerves! I know you think Carter's death a blessing imperfectly disguised, but it's just conceivable that Mary doesn't. After all, he was her cousin. You've got to behave yourself.'

'I am behaving myself!' said Vicky indignantly. 'Why, I even gave up the idea of being mysterious with the Inspector, just because I thought Mary mightn't like it! I've been polite to you, too, which takes a lot of doing, I can tell you!'

'Vicky, you little beast, if I see much more of you I shall end by wringing your neck!' said Hugh.

'If Peake's listening, you'll be sorry you said that,' remarked Vicky. ''Specially if my body is found lying about the place tomorrow. Are you staying to lunch?'

'No, I must get back. Don't spread that story of Alan White's about by the way!'

When he had left the house, Vicky went upstairs, and presently wandered into Mary's bedroom. 'Are you feeling jaded, darling Mary?'

'Extremely jaded.'

'Poor sweet! All the same, I do truly think you make yourself worse through not looking on the bright side. Quite honestly, do you mind Wally's being dead?'

'Of course I – ' Mary stopped short, under the clear gaze bent upon her. 'That is, I suppose I don't. Yes, I do, a bit, though. Anyway, I can't bear the thought of his having been murdered.'

'No, I'm not frightfully partial to it myself,' agreed Vicky. 'That's why I don't dwell on it.'

'Yes, you do. You keep on wondering who could have killed him, and it seems to me dreadful!'

'Well, so do you,' said Vicky. 'Which reminds me that something rather disgruntling happened after that mouldy inquest. Janet went and queered Robert's pitch, by divulging that he knew all along Wally was going to tea at the Dower House, so I'm rather afraid the Inspector may try to pin the murder on to him.'

'No!' Mary exclaimed, startled. 'Robert *did* know?'

'So Janet said. Of course, I always did think he might have done it, only if so I'd rather he got away with it, on account of Ermyntrude. That was why I tried to put the Inspector on to Alexis.'

'But you can't! You mustn't! If Robert – but I won't believe it! If he *did*, it would be absolutely wicked to try to make the police suspect the Prince instead!'

'Oh no, really it wouldn't! Because Robert's much nicer than Alexis, who was after poor Ermyntrude's money, and I dare say has a perfectly revolting past, which Robert hasn't in the least. And if Robert did murder Wally, he probably thought it was the right thing to do. Why was Maurice so peevish?'

'He wasn't. Naturally, he must be rather worried about all this, for Aunt Ermy's sake.'

Vicky opened her eyes at that. 'But she isn't ill, is she?'

'No, but I've always fancied that he was very fond of her,' Mary said.

'Darling, you don't suppose he's in love with her, do you?'

'No, no, of course I don't! Only he did say that she'd been very good to him once, or something.'

'Oh, that must have been on account of his sister! He used to have one, only she died, and I believe Ermyntrude did rather succour her; only it all happened in the Dark Ages, when I was small, so I don't really know. I wouldn't wonder if Maurice thinks Robert did it.'

'Why? Surely he hasn't said anything to you about it?'

'No, but Robert's a friend of his, and you must admit that he's taking it all frightfully seriously, so that it looks rather as though he feared the worst.'

'He can't think that! In any case, I didn't find him any different from his usual self. He certainly wasn't with me.'

'Oh well! then it was probably Hugh who made him so glum. I've noticed that he doesn't seem to like Hugh much.'

Mary stared at her. 'But what could he possibly find to dislike in Hugh?'

'Old school tie. Alan does. Besides, there's plenty to dislike in him. Moth-balls, and being dictatorial, and – oh, lots of things!'

'Hallo!' said Mary, suddenly making a discovery. 'Have you fallen for Hugh?'

'No, I think he's noisome, and I do *not* fall for other people's boy-friends!'

'If that means me, don't worry! I told you he wasn't, when you asked me.'

'But isn't he?' asked Vicky anxiously.

'Definitely not. If you want the truth, I did rather wonder if he was going to be, at one time, because I like him tremendously. Only, since all this happened – I can't explain, but I know he isn't. We don't think on the same lines, You probably think I'm very dull and serious-minded, and I dare say I am, for I can't see any humour in the present situation, and, frankly, it annoys me when I hear Hugh being thoroughly flippant about it.'

'Well, it means nothing to me,' said Vicky. 'He's fusty, and dusty, and he doesn't think I'm a great actress. In fact, I practically abominate him, and I shouldn't in the least mind if the Inspector suddenly started to suspect him of being the murderer.'

Fortunately for Mr Hugh Dering, the Inspector had not yet started to suspect him of anything worse than a pronouced partiality for his chief tormentor. The Inspector's suspicions were still equally divided between the only five people who appeared to have any motive for having killed Wally Carter. Of these, young Baker, whom he interviewed at Burntside after leaving Palings, seemed to be the least likely, and Robert Steel the most probable suspect.

The Inspector, returning to Fritton a little while after five o'clock, said that he knew Baker's type well, and that his knowledge of psychology informed him that loud-voiced young men who stood upon soap-boxes and inveighed against the existing rules of society were not potential murderers. Sergeant Wake, who had a prosaic mind, said: 'To my way of thinking, the fact of its having been Carter's own rifle pretty well rules him out. It doesn't seem to me that he could have got hold of it, let alone have carried it off on his motor-bike, which is what you'd think he must have done, if he stole it on the Saturday evening.'

But a day spent by the Sergeant and his underlings in searching for circumstances or witnesses either to disprove or to corroborate the stories told by Prince Varasashvili and Robert Steel, had been unsuccessful enough to cast him into a mood of pessimism. 'The case looked straightforward enough when we started on it, but the conclusion I've come to is that the man who did this murder laid his plans a sight more carefully than we gave him credit for.'

'Yes,' said the Inspector cheerfully, 'he certainly knew his onions. It's a pleasure to deal with him. You keep right on pursuing investigations into Steel and the Prince. You'll maybe get something sooner or later.' He looked at Superintendent Small, who had joined the conference. 'Am I right in thinking Mr Silent Steel's well-liked in these parts?'

'I never heard anyone speak ill of him,' replied Small. 'He's not one to throw his weight about, mind you, and he doesn't belong to the real gentry, but they all seem to like him well enough.'

'That's what I thought. Everyone likes him, and everyone knows he's been hanging round the fair Ermyntrude these two years, and nobody means to give him away if he can help it.'

'Why, what makes you say that?'

'Arithmetic,' replied the Inspector. 'Habit of putting two and two together. I've been like it from a child.'

'That's right,' said Wake slowly. 'You can get any of the folk here to talk about the Prince; and the way Percy Baker's talked of in this town you'd think people would like to see him convicted, and his sister, too. Not at all popular, they aren't. But the instant you start making inquiries into Steel you're up against a lot of deaf mutes. No one knows anything about his movements, and no one's ever had any idea of his being in love with Mrs Carter.'

'Well, he may be the whitest man they know in these parts, but he's too cool a customer for my taste,' said Hemingway. 'Nothing rattles him, not even having his story of not knowing Carter was going to the Whites blown up by Miss White. He has a nice quiet think, too, before he answers a question. Of course, his mother may have told him always to think before he spoke, but it isn't a habit which makes me take to him much. Is he a friend of the doctor?'

'Chester?' said Small. 'Yes, I'd say they were pretty friendly. Why?'

'Oh, nothing!' said Hemingway airily. 'Only that I had

a bit of a chat with the doctor up at Palings this morning, and it struck me that he wasn't what you might call bursting with information. The way I look at it is, if anyone knows the ins and outs of that household, it's the doctor, for if you were to tell me the fair Ermyntrude doesn't treat him like a confession-box I wouldn't believe you.'

'Well, I don't know,' said Small. 'You wouldn't hardly expect him to give away anything she may have said to him, would you?'

'No, nor I wouldn't expect him to be so much on his guard that he leaves the house sooner than let me ask him a few questions,' retorted Hemingway

'You think he knows something against Steel?'

'I wouldn't go as far as to say that, but I've a strong notion that he's got his suspicions. Of course, he may know something highly incriminating about one of those two girls. On the face of it, though, I'd say it's Steel he's shielding.'

'Or the Prince,' interpolated Wake.

'No,' replied the Inspector positively. 'Not since he's had him staying in his house. It wouldn't be human nature for him to want to protect that chap.'

'Do you think he saw something?' asked the Superintendent. 'According to what he told Cook, he was called out to a case on Sunday afternoon, and must have driven past the Dower House. Did you happen to ask him?'

'No,' replied Hemingway. 'I didn't, because I knew what answer I'd get.' He looked at his watch. 'Well, I'm off to have a heart-to-heart with Mr Harold White. He ought to be back from his work by now.'

'You're going to question him about that tale you had from Mr Dering and Miss Fanshawe?' said Wake. 'Myself, I can't see that it's got anything to do with the murder.'

'I've been told it's probably the clue to the whole mystery,' responded Hemingway.

Wake blinked. 'You have, sir? Who told you that?'

'Miss Fanshawe did,' said Hemingway.

The Superintendent was so astonished by this answer that for some time after Hemingway had left the room he sat turning it over in his mind. Finally he said in somewhat severe accents: 'What does Miss Fanshawe know about it? Seems a funny thing to me to act on what a kid like that says!'

'That's all right, sir: it's only his way of talking,' said Wake indulgently. 'Sharp as a needle, he is, I give you my word.'

The Inspector, meanwhile, made his way out of Fritton to the Dower House, where he found Harold White, who had just returned from the collieries.

White received him in his study, an uninteresting apartment with an outlook on to a clump of tall evergreens. He seemed rather surprised to see the Inspector, but asked at once what he might have the pleasure of doing for him. 'I suppose you've got a lot more tucked up your sleeve than we heard at the inquest this morning,' he remarked. 'Queer business, isn't it? I'd have said Carter was the last man in the world anyone would want to put out of the way, but don't anyone tell me he was shot by accident! There was no accident about that.' He picked up a box of cigarettes from his desk, and offered it to Hemingway. 'Have you come about what my daughter seems to have told you after I'd gone this morning? She's a bit worried about that. Poured it all out to me as soon as I got home. Well – ' He hesitated, and struck a match, and held it for the Inspector – 'It isn't for me to give you advice, but the fact of the matter is my daughter's a bit of a talker. I wouldn't set too much store by what she told you.'

'How's that?' inquired Hemingway. 'Didn't she invite Mr Steel here on Sunday?'

'Oh yes, I didn't mean that! She's always trying to get him to come over. Thinks he must be lonely, living by himself. You know what women are. What I meant was, that it didn't strike me that Steel was listening to her with more than half an ear.'

'I see,' said Hemingway. 'Was he listening when you warned him that you'd got Carter coming?'

'Warned him I'd got Carter coming!' repeated White derisively. 'Trust my daughter to make mountain out of a molehill! What I actually did was to say to her, not to him, that as I'd asked Carter over I didn't think Steel would want to come.'

'Like that, was it?' said Hemingway. 'Would he have been listening to that, by any chance?'

'Lord, I don't know! He might have been.'

'Well, that's very interesting,' said Hemingway. 'What's more, it brings me to what I came to talk to you about.'

'Shoot!' invited White, waving him to an armchair, and himself sitting down by his desk.

'The first thing I should like to know,' said Hemingway, 'is whether you'd got any particular reason for asking Mr Carter here on Sunday.'

'Oh!' said White, the smile leaving his face. 'You needn't tell me who put you up to asking me that question. And while I'm about it, I may as well tell you that there's no love lost between me and Ermyntrude Carter, and never has been. Give her time, and she'll go around saying I killed Carter, though what on earth I should want to do such a dam'-fool thing for it would puzzle even her to say!'

'Now what makes you call it a dam'-fool thing, sir?' inquired the Inspector.

'Seems obvious to me. Wouldn't you say it was a dam'-fool thing to murder a man for no shadow of reason?'

'I'd be more likely to say it if there was a reason why it mightn't suit your book for Mr Carter to be murdered,' responded Hemingway.

'Oh, come off it!' said White. 'I know just what you're at, and a pack of rubbish it is!'

The Inspector rose, and stubbed out his cigarette in an ashtray. 'I wouldn't like you to get me wrong,' he said. 'When I get on to a delicate matter, you'd be surprised how discreet I can be. You're quite sure that you and Mr Jones and Mr Carter weren't out to make a bit of money over this new building scheme they've got in Fritton?'

White looked a little discomfited by this direct method of attack, and shifted the blotter on his desk. 'There's no reason why I should answer that sort of question.'

'Oh, I wouldn't say that, sir! You're bound to assist me all you can, you know.'

'You can't expect me to admit anything like that. Besides – '

'There, now, if you haven't got me wrong after all! Properly speaking, I'm not interested in building schemes.'

'Well, supposing I say I had got a little scheme on? Nothing illegal in that, is there?'

'I don't know, and what's more I shan't inquire,' said Hemingway encouragingly.

'All right, then, I had.'

'Just as a matter of interest, was Mr Carter to put up the cash?'

'Considering we – I – never had the chance to tell him about it, I can't say. I thought he might be glad of the chance to make a bit of money.'

'And you and Mr Jones were going to get a rake-off, I take it?'

'I'm not going to answer for Jones. Naturally, there would have been some sort of a commission.'

'My mistake!' apologized the Inspector. 'Seems to have been a fair pleasure to handle, Mr Carter.'

White gave a short laugh. 'Poor devil, he was anxious to make some money of his own, which he hadn't got to account for to that wife of his!'

'How did he account to her for the hundred pounds he lent you a couple of months ago?' asked the Inspector.

'I don't suppose he did. She made him an allowance. No reason for her ever to have found out about it if he hadn't been shot. I only wanted a loan to tide me over to the quarter. Don't get any wrong idea into your head about that! I could sit down and write a cheque for the amount right now. I don't say it's convenient, but my bank will meet it all right.' He glanced up rather shamefacedly, and added: 'If you want the truth, it's damned inconvenient that Carter's dead! Of course, we weren't going to make a fortune out of that little deal, but anything's welcome in these hard times.'

The Inspector nodded. 'Anyone but Jones and Carter know of this scheme of yours?

'Well, of course not!' said White impatiently.'A nice stink there'd have been if they had! I can't see what you want to know about it for. It can't have any bearing on the case.' A thought struck him; he said sharply: 'Who put you on to it, anyway?'

'I needn't worry you with that,' replied Hemingway. He thrust a hand into his pocket, and drew out certain objects, which he laid on the desk before White. 'Now, if you could identify any of these, you might help me a lot,' he said. 'One lady's hair-slide; one broken nail-file; one small magnet; and one gent's pocket-knife in good condition. Seen any of them before?'

White took a moment to answer. 'What's this? Starting an ironmongery business? Where did you find them?'

'In your shrubbery.'

'I've never seen any of them before in my life.'

'Funny. I thought for a moment you had,' said the Inspector blandly.

'Well, I haven't.' White flicked the hair-slide with a contemptuous finger. 'Probably the maid's. I don't wear them myself. I don't amuse myself picking up needles with magnets either; and I've never used a nail-file in my life.'

'What about the knife?' inquired the Inspector.

'It might belong to anyone. I've seen dozens like it. I used to have one myself, if it comes to that. Anyone could have dropped it.'

'No idea who, sir?'

'No, none at all,' said White, looking him in the eye.

'Well, that's very disappointing. Mind if I ask your son if he happens to know anything about it?'

'Good Lord, you don't suppose my son had anything to do with Carter's death, do you? You're wasting your time! He'd got no interest in Carter whatsoever.'

'Still, I don't know why you should object to my asking him if he's seen the knife before,' said the Inspector.

White got up. 'Object! I don't care a damn how you choose to waste your time. I'll call my son.'

Alan, stridently summoned, lounged into the study a moment or two later. From the defensive expression on his face, the Inspector judged that he expected to be violently taxed with having betrayed his parent. He made haste to dispel this fear by holding out the pocket-knife. 'Good afternoon, sir. Ever seen that before?'

Alan looked rather relieved, and took the knife. 'Where did you find it?'

'Do you recognize it, sir?'

'Yes, it's mine. At least, I think it is. I lost one just like it only the other day, anyway.'

'That doesn't prove it's yours,' said White. 'It's common enough pattern.'

'I didn't say it did prove it. All I said was that it looks as though it might be mine. What's the mystery about? Where was the thing found?'

'In the shrubbery,' replied the Inspector.

Alan put the knife down rather hastily. 'Oh, I see! Well, what of it? I often go there, and I dare say it dropped out of my pocket.'

'Exactly what I was thinking myself,' said the Inspector. 'I wonder if you know anything about the rest of my little collection?'

Alan glanced at the desk. 'Good Lord, did you find them all in the shrubbery? No, I don't know whose they are. They certainly don't belong to me. What's that thing? A nail-file? Oh well, it probably belonged to the last maid we had. She used to file her nails into points, and paint them red into the bargain. That's why she got the push.'

'Yes, that's very interesting to the Inspector,' said White sarcastically. 'If that's all you can tell him, you may as well make yourself scarce.'

'Not on my account,' said Hemingway. 'I'm just off myself.'

'Sorry I couldn't be of more assistance to you,' said White, accompanying him out into the hall. 'As for that other little affair – you'll keep it under your hat, won't you?'

The Inspector said briefly that there was no need for him to worry about that, and left the house, a thoughtful man. When he told his Sergeant the result of his visit, Wake knit his brows, and said after profound consideration: 'Well, I suppose one might get something out of it, sir, though it doesn't seem very likely to me. If young

White got wind of that scheme of his father's, others might have done likewise.'

'So they might,' said Hemingway, somewhat acidly. 'And then have shot Carter just to upset the scheme. I've come across people like that, of course. In books.'

Sergeant Wake flushed, and said in a mortified voice that he was only trying to use his imagination, as his chief had frequently advised him to do.

'Forget it!' said Hemingway.

Silence fell. Hemingway, sitting at his desk, drew an intricate mosaic of cubes and squares on the blotting-paper, apparently absorbed in this childish occupation. Sergeant Wake watched him hopefully. Suddenly the Inspector threw his pencil down. 'What's the most common motive for murder, Wake?' he demanded.

'Passion,' replied the Sergeant promptly.

'Not by a long chalk it isn't. Money, my lad; that's why five out of seven murders are committed.'

'Yes, but Carter hadn't got any money,' objected Wake.

'He'd got something just as important, if only I'd had the sense to see it sooner,' said Hemingway. 'He'd got an aunt.'

The Sergeant frowned disapproval. 'That brings us back to the young lady: Miss Cliffe. I must say, I don't like it, sir.'

'Oh no, it doesn't!' replied Hemingway. 'Miss Cliffe doesn't get Aunt Clara's fortune, by what Mr Dering tells me, and as he's a Chancery barrister I wouldn't be surprised if he knew what he was talking about.'

'Well, I know that, sir, but she didn't, did she?'

'No, she didn't, but that isn't to say that others were as ignorant. What I want to know is who the old lady's heir is, now that Carter's been disposed of. Get me Miss Cliffe on the phone, will you?'

The Sergeant found the number in the directory, and picked up the receiver. 'But, good Lord, sir, that's very likely bringing in someone we've never even heard of!' he said.

'Well, why not?' demanded Hemingway. 'I don't know about you, but I'm sick and tired of this lot, for there isn't a penny to choose between any of them!'

The Sergeant told the Telephone Exchange the number he wanted, and tried to put his jostling thoughts into words. 'Yes, sir, I know; but if we go and dig out some stranger I don't see how he could have known what Carter's movements were, or – Hallo, is that Mrs Carter's residence? Inspector Hemingway would like to speak to Miss Cliffe, please.'

15

Mary, rather bewildered at the other end of the wire, was unable to tell the Inspector very much, but although she had no idea of the exact locality of the Home which housed Clara Carter, she did remember that it was situated in an opulent suburb of London. The Inspector noted down this somewhat vague address, and asked her if she happened to know who managed Miss Carter's affairs. No, she had never heard, but she thought the old lady must have some trustees – if she actually existed.

'What, is there any doubt about that?' demanded Hemingway.

'I don't know. I mean, I've never set eyes on her, and I never heard of my cousin's going to see her, or anything. He only talked about inheriting her money, and being rich one day, whenever he got into debt, or wanted to get money out of Mrs Carter, so he may have made her up.'

The Inspector said in a shaken voice: 'May have made her up. Yes, I see, miss. Thank you very much indeed . . . No, I don't think there's anything more I want to ask you.' He laid down the receiver, and said to his Sergeant: 'I'll have to be taken off this case soon, I can see that. Did you get that? Carter's rich aunt probably never existed outside of his imagination. I'll bet he floated a whole lot of phoney companies in his time! Now you get the Department for me, and find out if the Chief's there.'

In a few minutes' time the Sergeant handed him the receiver, and the deep, calm, voice of Superintendent Hannasyde hailed him. 'Hallo, Hemingway! How's it going?'

'Fine!' replied the Inspector. 'Lovely décor, very classy cast, right out of Ibsen.'

A chuckle reached him. 'What's the matter?'

'Oh, nothing, only that I'm beginning to hear noises in my head,' said the Inspector.

'Oh! Like that, is it? Is that what you rang up to say?'

'No, sir, I rang up to ask for a bit of research to be done by the Department.'

'All right, what is it?'

'You know Chipston?' said Hemingway. 'Well, I want someone to find out if there's a Home for Mentally Deficients there. If there is, I want an old lady of the name of Clara Carter. She's a spinster, she's very rich, and she's been in residence a good many years. I want to know who looks after her affairs, and where he lives; and I want someone to find out from him who, after Wallis Carter, is the heir to her property.'

'Very well. It doesn't sound very difficult. It that all?'

'Except for booking a nice quiet room for me, it is,' replied the Inspector. 'But I wouldn't like to keep anything back, Chief, and I'm bound to tell you that I'm not absolutely sure that there's any such person as Clara Carter.'

Hannasyde's voice sounded a little puzzled. 'I thought you said she was a rich spinster?'

'That's right,' responded the Inspector. 'She's a rich spinster, gone cuckoo, if she exists. Of course, if she doesn't exist, we shall just have to forget about her, and start all over again from the beginning. That's what I want to discover.'

'I suppose you know what you're about,' said Hannasyde. 'Clara Carter, Chipston, present heir to property. Right?'

'Right it is, Chief,' replied the Inspector, and rang off. 'And that's about finished me for today,' he announced.

'If I'm on to what I think I am, there's nothing more I can do till I hear from the Department. And if I'm not on to it, I'm still packing up for the night, because my brain's addled.'

'You certainly have been hard at it today, sir,' said the Sergeant. 'You want to get a good night's rest.'

Apparently, the Inspector enjoyed a very good night's rest, for when his subordinate saw him next morning he was his usual brisk and bright-eyed self. He went off to Stilhurst Village to pursue inquiries into Robert Steel's possible movements on the afternoon of the murder, and was coming out of the general shop there when he walked into Hugh Dering.

'Hallo!' Hugh said. 'I rather wanted to see you.'

'That's funny,' said the Inspector. 'I could do with a few minutes' chat with you myself.'

'Hold on while I buy some stamps, and I'll be with you.' Hugh vanished into the shop, reappearing presently to find that the Inspector had strolled on down the street to where Hugh had left his car. He soon overtook him. 'Miss Cliffe tells me that you rang her up last night to make inquiries about the mythical aunt. I see what you're after, of course, but do you really believe in the aunt?'

'I've got an open mind, sir. What's your feeling on the subject?'

'I haven't an idea. My instinct always prompted me to disbelieve any statement Carter made, but in this case I've nothing to go on, beyond the fact that Mrs Carter doesn't seem ever to have set much store by the aunt. A rich aunt, conveniently mad, and hidden from sight in an asylum, sounds suspiciously unlikely to me.'

'Yes, it does,' agreed Hemingway. 'All the same, he went so far as to say that she lived in Chipston.'

'H'm! Giving a local habitation and a name to an airy nothing, perhaps.'

'Look here, sir, I don't want a Job's comforter, if it's all the same to you!' protested Hemingway. 'What I do want, on the other hand, is a bit of expert information. You told Miss Cliffe in my presence, the day before yesterday, that there was no question of her inheriting this aunt's money.'

'I did.'

'I take it you're sure of your facts, sir?'

'Quite sure. According to what Carter let fall from time to time, she became insane before she had made a will. The law regarding intestacy is perfectly clear.'

'Would it be bothering you if I were to ask you to tell me this law, sir?'

'Not at all. When an intestate dies, leaving no issue, and his parents having predeceased him, the relations who can inherit his fortune are first, brothers and sisters of the whole blood, or their issue; second, brothers and sisters of the half-blood, or their issue; third, the grandparents, in equal shares; fourth, uncles and aunts of the whole blood of the intestate's parents, or their issue; and fifth, uncles and aunts of the half-blood of the intestate's parents, or – '

'Don't tell me!' said the Inspector. 'Or their issue!'

'Correct,' said Hugh, with a twinkle.

The Inspector eyed him respectfully. 'And that's your idea of perfectly clear?'

'Absolutely,' Hugh assured him.

'Well, if that's so I'm bound to admit that you gentlemen at the Bar earn every penny you get, which is a thing I've often doubted. Let me be sure I've got that right! If this aunt is very old, we can take it she hasn't got any parents or grandparents living, and I remember that Miss Cliffe said that she didn't know of any relations other than her, that Carter had. So if she and Carter were the last of the family, what happens next?'

'Oh, they'll dig up some remote cousin! Failing the male line, you can try the female line. Almost endless possibilities, you perceive.' He saw that the Inspector was frowning in an effort of concentration, and added: 'It might go to a descendant of the grandmother's family, her father being the intestate's great grandfather. Get the idea?'

'Yes, I get it,' replied Hemingway. 'What I'm thinking is, that I look like having started something, and no mistake! What was it you wanted to see me about, sir?'

They had reached Hugh's car by this time, and paused by it, in the shade of a great elm-tree. Hugh began to fill his pipe. 'Something my father said. I got him to attend the inquest yesterday, to see what he made of it. One circumstance rather puzzled him. It may have puzzled you.'

'And what might that have been, sir?'

Hugh struck a match, and guarded it in his cupped hand from the wind. Between puffs, he said: 'Fact of the rifle's having a hair-trigger pull. My father says he can't imagine what Fanshawe wanted with a hair-trigger. Says he would have found it dam' dangerous to use, and almost impossible to load.' He pressed the smouldering tobacco gently down into the bowl of his pipe, puffed again, and flicked the match away. 'He can't see the point. Occurred to you?'

'Yes, sir, it has, naturally. Might be several answers. Or whoever killed Carter with that rifle may have wanted a light pull.'

'Light, perhaps, but not hair-trigger, surely! It would only need a touch to set it off. Too risky.'

The Inspector's gaze was fixed meditatively on a large saloon car, approaching at a regal and stately pace down the village street. 'Very shrewd of your father, sir. I'm much obliged to him.' A grin suddenly spread over his face. 'Well, I wondered whether it was Royalty for the moment, but I see now that you won't be needing me any longer.'

Hugh looked round, as the Rolls Royce, taking up most of the available space in the street, drew up outside the little butcher's shop. In it, looking rather like the Tragic Muse, sat Vicky, swathed in black, and with her sunny curls smoothed into two demure wings that framed her face. A halo hat made an extremely becoming setting for this fair primness.

'*Now* what's she playing at?' said Hugh in an annoyed voice.

'Looks to me like Lady Jane Grey on her way to the block,' remarked the Inspector, following him down the street to the Rolls Royce.

By the time they had reached it, the chauffeur had opened the door, and received from one gloved and languid hand a scrap of paper bearing the order for the butcher. He went into the shop as Hugh came up. Hugh pulled the door open again, and demanded: 'What the devil do you think you're doing, got up like Queen Victoria?'

Vicky surveyed him in an aloof fashion. 'I feel like that,' she said simply.

Hugh looked grimly back at her. 'I thought I told you you were not to start any more of your antics?'

'Yes,' sighed Vicky, 'but my car died on me.'

'What's that got to do with it?'

'This,' said Vicky, waving a hand to indicate the opulence of her surroundings. 'It came over me in a wave. Such a lonely, sad-looking figure, lost in the cushions of the great, sombre car. I think I was left a widow frightfully young, and all my fabulous wealth is simply dust and ashes in my mouth. Though I rather like the idea of being a notorious woman with a shocking reputation, only no one guesses the tragedy that lies in my past, and made me what I am.'

'*Come* out!' said Hugh, leaning into the car, and grasping one slim wrist somewhat ungently.

'Oh, did you happen to think you'd got the *slightest* right to order me about?' inquired Vicky in silken accents.

'Don't you argue with me!' replied Hugh. 'Out you come!'

Vicky, dragged relentlessly out of the car, stamped her foot, and said: 'Let me go, you horrible beast! I loathe and detest you!'

'You'll have cause to, if you make any further public exhibition of yourself,' Hugh assured her.

Vicky was just about to retort in kind when she caught sight of Inspector Hemingway, an admiring spectator. She promptly recoiled, lifting her free hand to her throat, and uttering faintly: 'Ah! You! You've come to arrest me!'

'Well, I don't mind arresting you, just to oblige,' offered the Inspector. 'I'm never one to spoil another person's big scene, and I haven't anything particular on this morning.'

'For God's sake, don't encourage her!' said Hugh.

'Yes, I thought somehow you wouldn't be wanting me any longer,' said Hemingway. 'Intuition, they call it. I'll be saying good morning to you, sir. I dare say we'll meet again sometime or another.'

Hugh nodded to him, and turned back to Vicky. 'Come on, explain this act! What are you supposed to be doing?'

'I'm buying a saddle of mutton. And talking of mutton – '

'Yes, you can cut that bit. I know it. I remind you of a sheep. Your chauffeur seems to me to be buying the mutton. Did you swank into the village in that car just to play at being a wealthy widow?'

'Or a notorious woman,' said Vicky.

'Well, did you?'

'No,' said Vicky softly. 'I'm being driven to Fritton to pick up my car, *not* that it has anything to do with you, and I wasn't anybody but me until I suddenly caught sight of you looking like a lawyer, or something that's been stuffed, and *then* I thought I might just as well as not put on the sort of act you'd be bound to disapprove of.'

Hugh stood looking down at her, torn between a desire to laugh, and to box her ears. Finally, he laughed. 'Vicky, you abominable brat! Tell you chauffeur to finish the shopping, and go home. I'll run you into Fritton.'

'How lovely of you!' said Vicky, with wholly deceptive effusiveness. 'I expect if I had to choose between that and walking, I'd go with you.'

'Ha! a snub!' said Hugh.

Vicky met his quizzical gaze with one of her blandest stares. Lady Dering walking briskly down the street with a shopping basket on her arm, had ample opportunity to observe her only son's expression as he stood looking into the celestially blue eyes of the prettiest girl in the county. She came to a halt a few paces away from them, and said in her cheerful, matter of fact way. 'You look like two cats, trying to stare one another out of countenance. What's the matter?'

Hugh turned quickly. A tinge of colour stole into his cheeks; he said with a touch of awkwardness: 'Hullo, Mother! I didn't know you were coming into the village. I'd have given you a lift.'

'I hate men who neglect their mothers,' said Vicky, *sotto voce*.

'Walking,' said Ruth Dering, 'is good for my figure. How are you, Vicky?'

Vicky looked piteously at her. 'I *was* feeling quite extraordinarily well, but, if you don't mind my saying so,

I think your son is utterly loathsome, which makes me feel quite quite sick in my tummy.'

'Oh, I don't mind what you say about him!' said Lady Dering cordially. 'What's he been doing?'

'Exercising superhuman self-control,' said Hugh. 'Come on, Vicky, don't be stuffy! Are you going to let me drive you to Fritton, or are you not?'

Vicky glanced towards his car, and shook her head. 'Oh no! I dressed specially for a Rolls-Royce, and I wouldn't look right in an open tourer.'

Hugh grinned. 'All right, Shylock! have your pound of flesh! I apologize for having spoiled your act. If there were any mud about, I'd eat it. Will that do?'

Vicky looked at Lady Dering. There was a naïve question in her eyes. Lady Dering said: 'Really, you know, you couldn't expect him to say more. You'd better go with him.'

'Yes, but wouldn't you like him to drive you home instead?' asked Vicky.

'No,' said Lady Dering, wondering at the sound of her own voice. 'No, my dear. I like walking.'

She was left standing outside the butcher's shop, with her knees trembling a little under her. She went into the shop, and told the proprietor, to his bewilderment, that she wanted six pounds of granulated sugar. A jumble of thoughts seethed in her brain. What on earth have I done? she asked herself. What will William say? I quite thought it was going to be Mary Cliffe, but it's obvious he means to marry Vicky. Of course that mother is impossible, but Geoffrey Fanshawe was all right. She's an heiress, too, not that one ought to care tuppence about that, but in these days, what can one do? At any rate, William thinks she's a beauty, and she isn't any relation of that dreadful Wally Carter!

Rebuffed by the butcher, she had walked out of the

shop, and was suddenly recalled to a sense of her surroundings by a strident motor-horn that made her jump. She found that she was in the road, with Dr Chester's car swerving across the street to avoid her. 'Oh dear!' she said guiltily. 'I'm so sorry! Oh, it's you, Maurice!'

The doctor, pulling up with a jerk, leaned out to inquire with a note of considerable surprise in his voice whether she had joined a suicide club.

'Dreadfully sorry!' said Lady Dering. 'So stupid of me!'

'Can I give you a lift?' he asked. 'I saw Hugh going towards Fritton, a minute or two ago, with Vicky Fanshawe.'

'Yes, I know. No, I don't want a lift, thanks.'

He hesitated, and then said: 'Is there anything in that, do you think?'

The backward jerk of his head might have been taken to indicate almost anything in the street, but Lady Dering did not pretend to misunderstand him. 'My dear man, that's what bowled me over! Of course, I *had* begun to have a faint suspicion, but I wasn't sure till this morning. I used to think he was rather attracted by Mary, but there's no question of that now!'

'Do you mind?' he asked abruptly.

'I don't know. It isn't what I'd have chosen for him, though in some ways I quite see – well, never mind! But all this horrid scandal! I can't think what my husband will say!'

'I shouldn't worry about the scandal. Neither of the girls has anything to do with that.'

'Well, I wish it could be cleared up. Do you know if the police are any nearer to reaching a solution?'

'No, I'm afraid I know nothing. Hugh seems to be the one the Inspector from London has taken to his heart. Doesn't he know anything?'

'If he does, he hasn't told me. I shouldn't think the

Scotland Yard man would take him into his confidence. I haven't met him: is he any good?'

'It's hard to say. He doesn't give away much. We shall have to wait for results.'

This was what Inspector Hemingway was doing, somewhat to the surprise of the local Superintendent, who told Sergeant Wake that he couldn't for the life of him make out what kind of game his chief was playing.

'If you were to ask me,' he said severely, 'I should say you'd enough material to work on right under your nose here, without going off on any wild-goose chases. However, doubtless I'm wrong.'

Sergeant Wake did not consider it incumbent upon him to deliver any opinion on this point. After a great deal of painstaking research, he had succeeded in bringing to light one witness, in the shape of a twelve-year-old boy, who had seen a white sports-car, with black wings, upon the road to Kershaw on Sunday afternoon. The boy's notions of time were too vague to be trusted, nor had he observed the white car's driver; but he seemed to be quite sure that the car was travelling towards Kershaw, a circumstance which certainly tallied with Prince Varasashvili's story.

'What's more,' said Hemingway, when this was reported to him, 'it isn't likely there's more than one white sports-car with black wings in this district. I reckon that lets his Highness out. If he wants to go away, he can; but get his address, in case of accidents.'

'He told Inspector Cook he hadn't got one,' said Wake dubiously.

'Then he'd better think one up!' said Hemingway.

The Prince, however, discovered disconsolately flicking over the pages of a book in the doctor's pleasant library, was so relieved to hear that his presence in Stilhurst was no longer necessary, that he made no bones at all about divulging his address, but informed Sergeant Wake that he had a *pied-à-terre* in a private hotel in Bloomsbury. The Sergeant wrote it down, and the Prince said that for himself he would be very glad to be in London again. 'I find it does not suit me, this English country life,' he announced. 'One stifles, in fact! There is no conversation; it is not amusing.'

But when he informed his host of his imminent departure, nothing could have exceeded the grace with which he assured him that these days spent under his roof would remain in his memory as some of the most pleasant in his whole life.

The doctor said something conventionally civil; and, in answer to an anxious inquiry, advised the Prince most strongly not to adventure his person within the precincts of Palings.

'But it is absurd!' the Prince said. 'It is seen that I had nothing to do with Carter's death! Rather it is Mr Steel whom the police suspect, is it not so?'

'I really can't say,' replied Chester stiffly.

'I wash my hands of the affair!' said the Prince. 'But I must tell you, since you have been to me so extremely kind, that if it is Mr Steel whom the police suspect, I must be glad, for he is not, after all, *de nous autres*, and I have had some fears that you, my friend, might suffer a little unpleasantness.'

The doctor looked up quickly. 'I?'

'But, yes!' smiled the Prince. 'An absurdity, you say, but I find that your English police are very stupid, what you call thickheaded. Ah, pardon! It is ridiculous, without sense! Yet when one considers how I have been suspected, for no reason, except that I was out in Vicky's auto, one must be prepared for the police to suspect you, who were also not at home.'

'I was out on a case,' said Chester, his eyes stern under his frowning brows.

The Prince made a deprecatory gesture. 'But of course! Do I not know it? It is merely that these policemen – '

'Nor,' interrupted Chester, 'do I know what conceivable motive I could have had for murdering one of my patients!'

'My friend!' The Prince flung up his hands. 'I am sure you had none! I am sorry that I spoke of it, but indeed it seemed to me that you must have thought of it yourself. It is forgotten! Do not fear that I shall speak of it!'

'If you're wise, you won't,' said Chester grimly. 'I could hardly afford to let such a statement go unchallenged. We have a law of libel in this country.'

'Absurd!' murmured the Prince. 'You mistake me, I assure you! Without doubt, the police know you too well to concern themselves with your movements.'

He was not quite right, for Inspector Cook, pondering still over the case, had remembered that Chester had not been in his house at the time of the murder, and had thought fit to mention this circumstance, though reluctantly, to Hemingway. His own chief, Superintendent Small, snubbed him immediately. 'The doctor was called out on a case, as might happen to any doctor,' he said. 'What reason would he have to kill Carter, that's what I should like to know?'

'Only that he's very friendly with Mrs Carter – to put it no higher,' replied Cook. 'Mind you, sir, I'm not saying there's anything in it, for I'm sure I haven't anything against Dr Chester, and I know he's highly respected. But it just flashed across my mind, in a manner of speaking.'

'You'd better forget it,' said Small. 'Pack of rubbish!'

'Yes, sir,' said Cook, rather woodenly.

'That's all right,' interposed Hemingway. 'I'm always grateful for a bit of help. I wouldn't like you to think I haven't taken the doctor into account, because I have. But so far I haven't had so much as a smell of a motive. That isn't to say I won't have, of course.'

'Are you looking for one?' asked Small, staring at him.

'High and low,' responded the Inspector promptly. To his Sergeant, a moment or two later, when they were alone, he added: 'And that's truer than what old fat-face thinks. At least, when I say I'm hunting high and low, what I mean is that some other mug's going round Chipston making a fool of himself. I'm what you might call the brains behind the organization.'

'Do you mean you're expecting to find that Chester's the heir to the old mad woman's money?' demanded Wake, startled out of his customary stolidity.

'The secret of being a highly efficient officer,' said Hemingway, fixing him with a quelling look, 'is on the one hand never to expect anything, and on the other never to be surprised at anything either. You remember that, my lad, and you may do as well as I have. I don't say you will, because your psychology's bad and you haven't got vision, but you may. What's the time?'

'Going on for four o'clock,' replied Wake, swallowing these strictures with a visible effort.

The Inspector frowned, and lit a cigarette from the stub of his old one. 'If Aunt Clara isn't something Carter saw in an opium-dream, I ought to be hearing from the Chief pretty soon.'

The call from London came through five minutes later, and the Sergeant, informed that Superintendent Hannasyde wanted to speak to Inspector Hemingway, handed over the receiver to his superior, and tried to look as though he were not listening. He soon abandoned this detached attitude, for the half of the conversation which he could hardly have helped hearing was too maddeningly tantalizing to be ignored.

'That you, sir?' said Hemingway. 'I've been getting what you might call a bit jumpy. Did they find anything? . . . They did? . . . You don't say! . . . Oh no, I'm not surprised: I thought they would . . . They got what? . . . Oh, *trustee*! Yes, I get it. Was he able to tell us who the present heir is? . . . Nice work, sir! Let me have it!'

The Sergeant, stealing a glance at him, saw his face stiffen. He had been lying back at his ease in his chair, but he sat bolt upright all at once. 'Say that again, Chief!' he requested. '*What* name did you say? . . . You don't mean it? Well, I'll be – Good God! . . . Convey anything to me! Yes, it does! . . . What's that . . . He doesn't know what? . . . The address! Oh, he doesn't, doesn't he? Well, that's where I'm one up on him, because I do! . . . Yes, right here, under my nose! . . . No, it's got me gasping around like a landed fish . . . Not a breath! . . . Not so much as a whiff of suspicion! Right out of the picture! . . . Here, tell me this, sir! What's the sum total of this precious fortune . . . What, pounds? I'd do a murder myself for that . . . Finished? No, nor anything like it, but I will be, don't you fret, sir!'

He laid the instrument gently down on its rest, and drew a long breath. Across the table, his eyes met the Sergeant's avid gaze. 'I wouldn't have believed it!' he said, and shook his head. 'But a hundred thousand pounds! Is that a motive, or is it a motive? Do you know who's the heir to that little nest-egg, Wake?'

'No!' almost shouted the Sergeant. 'I do not, sir, but I'd like to!'

'White,' said Hemingway. 'Mr Harold White, my lad.'

There was a moment's astonished silence. The Sergeant broke it. 'But *he* couldn't have killed Carter, sir!'

'If he didn't, I'll resign from the Force,' said Hemingway.

'But, Inspector, you saw the spot where he was standing

when Carter was shot! It wasn't within sight of the bridge! It wasn't anywhere near where the gun was found!'

'He wasn't within forty yards of where the rifle was found,' agreed Hemingway. 'More like fifty, from what I remember. This bird is a pleasure to deal with!'

'Look here, sir!' besought the Sergeant. 'Setting that aside, isn't it a fact he was hoping to get money out of Carter for his little land-racket? Why, he'd even started negotiations to buy the land, let alone bringing Jones up to the house to talk business with Carter!'

The Inspector stabbed a forefinger at him. 'Bringing him up to the house to make a disinterested witness! All that shady stuff about the building estate was dust, my lad, dust to be thrown in our eyes!'

'But I don't see that you can say that, sir, honest I don't! I mean, the thing couldn't be done! Unless – why, do you suppose the son was in it, too?'

'That long-haired nincompoop?' said Hemingway. 'Not he!'

'Well, if you won't have him in it, how was it done, sir?'

'I don't know,' replied Hemingway, 'but if I didn't have a lot of yapping going on in my ear, I might be able to figure it out!'

The Sergeant relapsed into silence. Hemingway presently brought his gaze to bear on that offended countenance. 'That hair-trigger pull,' he said.

'Yes, sir, I know. I've been thinking about that, too. I've heard of guns being fired by the opening of a door, but this was out in the open, in full view of a couple of people who hadn't a thing to do with it – for you won't tell me Jones or Miss White were mixed up in the murder!'

'That's an idea,' said Hemingway. 'The opening of a door. Not bad, Wake, not at all bad! But you're wrong: it won't do. There couldn't have been any sort of string tied to that gate on to the bridge, because for one thing it would have been seen, and for another the rifle was about twenty yards off.'

'I didn't think there was anything tied to the gate,' said the Sergeant. 'I admit it looks queer, White being the heir to the old lady's money, but I've met some odd coincidences before, and it's possible he doesn't even know he's the heir.'

'If you've met any coincidences as odd as a chap getting himself bumped off when he's on his way to visit a relation of his, whose only hope of collecting a hundred thousand pounds is to see to it that the first chap hands in his checks before the present owner of that hundred thousand, you ought to write a book,' said Hemingway.

'Relation! He was so far removed that not even Carter knew what kind of a fortieth cousin he was!'

'That's all right,' replied Hemingway. 'Mr Dering was explaining the Law of Intestacy to me this morning. It would take too long to tell you about it now, but it's perfectly clear. Now, you just consider White's position, and stop making a lot of narrow-minded objections. The old lady's over eighty, by what the Chief just told me, so it's safe to say she isn't for this world much longer.'

'She might go on for another five years, or more,' said the Sergeant. 'They say mad people are often very healthy.'

'All the better for White if she did. You don't suppose he wants her to die until Carter's murder has been forgotten, do you? Oh no! He takes a long view, does Mr Harold White. By rights, we ought not to have known anything about mad Aunt Clara. If it hadn't been for Carter's way of lugging her into the conversation whenever he wanted money off his wife, I dare say we shouldn't. Maybe that was just one thing White didn't happen to know about. Now you answer me this! If Aunt

Clara had kicked the bucket before Carter did, who'd have come into her money? Not White, my lad! Oh no! Miss Cliffe would have got the lot, because Carter had made a will on a half-sheet of notepaper, and had it witnessed, too. Unless Carter died before his aunt, White hadn't a hope in hell of ever seeing a penny of that fortune.'

The Sergeant was slightly shaken. 'I grant you it looks black,' he admitted. 'But how could he have *done* it, sir?'

'That,' said the Inspector, 'is what we are going to find out.'

16

The Sergeant looked, if anything, more sceptical than ever, but Hemingway was paying very little heed to him. 'The man I want is Cook,' he said. 'I want to know every movement White made from the moment Carter was seen approaching the bridge. Cook took all those first depositions.'

'Yes, sir, but, as I remember, Jones and Miss White corroborated everything White said.'

'Of course they did! Don't you run off with the idea that I'm thinking White's movements weren't as advertised! The point is, that as soon as it was established that he was out of sight of the bridge, and within a few steps of Jones and Miss White, no one paid a lot of heed to his subsequent movements.'

'Subsequent movements?' repeated Wake slowly.

'You don't suppose the gun up and fired itself on its own, do you? If White's at the bottom of this, there must have been some kind of mechanism used, which, mark you, White disposed of before Cook reached the scene.'

'Maybe you're right, sir. But the more I think about it the more it seems to me that if White was responsible, then the mechanism used was nothing more nor less than his son's hands. Now, you just consider! Wasn't it young White who spilled that story about his father's plan to buy up part of Frith Field? Very unnatural thing for a man's own son to do. I thought so at the time.'

The Inspector accorded this suggestion his consideration. 'Yes,' he said. 'Yes, I'm bound to admit there may be something in that. All a put-up job between father and son. No, I don't think there's so much in it, after all. Young White doesn't get on with his father. We'll see what Cook has to say.'

Inspector Cook, delighted to be summoned to a conference, was much more impressed than Sergeant Wake had been by the disclosure that Harold White was now the heir to Clara Carter's fortune; and although, casting his mind back over all the circumstances of the murder, he said that he couldn't for the life of him see how White could have had any part in it, he was perfectly ready to work over every inch of the ground again.

'Though whether I'll be able to remember all that Miss White said, I doubt,' he warned Hemingway. 'There was precious little that seemed to have any bearing on the case, and you know how she talks!' He drew up a chair to the table, and sat down to refresh his memory with a glance through the folder that contained his own report. 'Taking it from when Miss White came out of the house, there was her, and Samuel Jones, and White sitting round the tea-table outside the drawing-room.'

'In full view of the bridge,' interpolated Hemingway.

'That's right. The garden's pretty overgrown with flowering shrubs, but there's a strip of lawn running down to the bridge which only has a bed of dahlias in it. Clear view of the bridge, and of the thicket on the Palings side, of course. I took note of that. You can catch a glimpse here and there of the paths they cut at Palings. And, of course, you can see the roof of Mrs Carter's house, through the trees. Now you'll have to let me think a moment. Yes, here it is.' His finger traced the typewritten words: 'Miss White was the one that called attention to Carter. She caught sight of him, coming down one of the paths, where the bushes aren't so thick, and she got up, and said she'd go and make the tea.'

'I remember that. The maid was out. White was sitting by the table all this time?'

'Yes, but according to Miss White, it was then that he asked her why she hadn't brought any cigarettes out.'

'It was, eh? After Carter had been seen?'

Cook raised his eyes from the folder, and gazed frowningly into space. 'Yes, after Carter had been seen. She said she'd go and get the cigarettes, but he told her not to bother, and walked over to his study window, which, as you know, Inspector, is hidden from the bridge by a bed full of flowering currant bushes, and the like.'

'Go on,' said Hemingway. 'What happened next?'

'Miss White said she was standing looking down to the bridge, when suddenly the shot sounded, and she saw Carter fall. I asked her particularly, at the time, if she'd noticed any movement in the shrubbery, and she said no, she hadn't noticed anything.'

Hemingway looked a little disappointed. 'No,' he said, scratching his chin, 'that won't do. Not as it stands. There must have been something else happened after White went to the study window, and before Miss White saw Carter fall. If there wasn't anything, then I'll have to own I don't see how White could have done it.'

'Well, nothing did happen,' said Cook. 'I remember Miss White saying that she was just standing there, not thinking of anything in particular – ' He stopped. 'Now, just a moment! The gate! She said she was thinking that the hinges on it ought to be oiled, or something of the sort. They certainly do creak badly. I wonder: would that sort of fit in?'

'It might. The creak of the gate being the signal, in a manner of speaking. Though it doesn't explain how White could have fired that shot. However, there's no sense in trying to rush things. What happened when Carter fell?'

'Miss White screamed,' replied Cook. 'White asked her

what the devil was the matter – he's a testy chap, you know – and she must have told him, I suppose, for he came over to her, to see for himself. Yes, and he had a box of cigarettes in his hand right enough, for he chucked it on to one of the chairs, and I saw it there myself, with the cigarettes spilled all round it. No hanky-panky about that. He said he was going to reach in through the study window for a box of cigarettes, and that's just exactly what he did do.'

'While his son shot Carter,' interjected Sergeant Wake.

Cook turned his head. 'What's that? Young White? I don't see him doing it myself.'

'Wake's got a notion it was a put-up job between the two Whites,' explained Hemingway.

'Well, that *would* surprise me!' said Cook. 'Why, it's common knowledge young Alan loathes his father! And as for him firing a rifle, I doubt it he'd know how. He's a regular wet, that chap: doesn't hold with bloodsports, and talks a lot of half-baked stuff about Bolshevik Russia, and that kind of thing.'

Hemingway lifted an eyebrow at his subordinate. Wake said obstinately: 'It's wonderful what a difference money can make to a man. Supposing that quarrel he and his father had at lunch-time, on the Sunday, was just a blind to make us think they weren't on good terms?'

'Then by all accounts they've been putting up those blinds ever since they came to the district,' said Cook dryly. 'No, I reckon that's straight enough: there's no love lost between White and his son.'

'Does White hate his son enough to send him out to murder Carter for him?' asked Hemingway.

'Good Lord, no, Inspector!' replied Cook, quite shocked. Why, that would be downright wicked! Things aren't as bad as that! Stands to reason they can't be, or they wouldn't live in the same house.'

'That's what I thought. Go back to the moment when White chucked the cigarettes into the chair, will you? What happened next?'

'He shouted to Jones and Miss White not to stand staring, but to come down to see what they could do for Carter, and set off for the bridge. They ran after him, of course, but Carter must have been dead before they got there.'

'In fact,' said Hemingway, 'White got his two witnesses out of the way, for it's not to be supposed they'd pay attention to anything except Carter's body, once they'd been set on to look after him.'

'You can put it that way if you like,' Cook said, staring. 'Seems to me a natural thing for them all to run down to the bridge.'

'It's too natural,' said Hemingway. 'The whole of it. There's something fishy about this chain of highly plausible circumstances. There was a very good reason for asking Carter over in the first place, and that same reason made it look as though White was the last person to want him dead.'

'Yes, but that's twisting things round, sir!' protested Wake.

'Maybe, and maybe it's doing exactly the opposite. You keep quiet! What about the fair Ermyntrude's instinct? Go on, Cook! What happened on the bridge?'

'White told Miss White to try and stop the bleeding, and ran back to the house to get hold of a doctor, and to ring us up.'

Hemingway nodded approvingly. 'And very right and proper, I'm sure! Where's the telephone?'

'In the hall. I saw it,' replied Cook.

'You don't say! So that it would be highly natural for Mr White to run round the corner of the house, so as to go in by the front-door, thus disappearing from sight of the bridge, behind those rhododendrons?'

'Yes,' Cook said. 'Yes, it would. You think he went into the shrubbery, once the other two couldn't see him? Well, now you put me in mind of it, Miss White said that it seemed ages before he got back to them. I didn't set much store by that, for no doubt it would seem ages, under the circumstances. But even supposing you're on the right track, I still don't see how he can have fired that rifle in the first place. Of course, I realize there would have had to have been a bit of mechanism used, which he'd got to get rid of quick. That's plain enough. What isn't plain at all, not to my way of thinking, is what actually fired the rifle. It can't have been the opening of the gate, now, can it?'

Hemingway looked at Sergeant Wake. 'Do you remember those scratches on that sapling?' he demanded. 'Do you remember I said we'd keep them in mind? They've got a bearing on the case! In fact, I've a strong notion I know what caused them. If that rifle wasn't fired by hand, it had to be rigged up somehow, and what's more, rigged up nice and securely, because if it wasn't held hard, the recoil would spoil the aim. What about one of those vices they use for cleaning guns? Clamp that to a handy young tree, get your rifle sighted along the bridge, and that's one problem solved.'

'Wait a bit, sir!' said Wake. 'I've seen those vices. You can tilt the rifle any way you please in them, so even allowing for the bridge's being a good way below the sapling, why would anyone fix the rifle up so close to the ground? For the grazes weren't but a foot or two up, were they?'

Hemingway was not in the least put out of countenance by this. He said briskly: 'We'll probably find there was a reason for that. As a matter of fact, I've found it already.

There's a drop of seven or eight feet to the level of the bridge, and it stands to reason our bird wanted to get as low a trajectory as possible.'

'There was something more than a vice there,' said Cook, thinking it over. 'The vice didn't fire the rifle. Why – why, now we begin to understand that hair-trigger pull!'

'You cast your mind back again, and see if there isn't another peculiar circumstance which you begin to understand,' recommended Hemingway.

'What's that?'

'Miss Fanshawe's dog didn't bark,' said Hemingway. 'And why not? Because there wasn't anyone there to bark at. Funny how simple things are as soon as you stop looking at them from the wrong angle!'

'I certainly think you're on to something,' admitted Cook. 'I suppose I ought to have been on to it myself.'

'You? Why, it's taken me long enough!' said Hemingway. 'I don't blame you for not spotting it. You got the gun, and there wasn't a ha'porth of reason why anyone should have tumbled to it that it wasn't fired by some bloke who dropped it, and made off.'

'Well, it's very kind of you to say so, I'm sure,' responded Cook, a little dubiously.

'I don't see that the case is solved, not by a long chalk,' remarked the Sergeant. 'It's all very well: and I grant you you've pieced it together a fair treat, sir, but what I want to know is, what is this mysterious gadget which set the rifle off just at the right moment?'

'What *I* want to know,' said Hemingway, 'isn't *what* is it, because we'll find that out all in good time, but *where* is it?'

There was a pause. Inspector Cook said in a disgruntled tone: 'Yes, and don't we hope we may find it! Ten to one, he took it up to the house with him. He's had plenty of time to get rid of it since Sunday.'

Hemingway tapped his teeth with a pencil, pondering. 'No,' he said presently. 'That's bad psychology. What you want to do is to put yourself in his place. To start with, you've got a vice to carry. On top of that, there must have been some bit of mechanism which actually fired the gun. Now, supposing you were to take a chance of getting them hidden away in the house: what happens if you go and run into someone on the way?'

'Well, he'd have to take some chances. The maid was out, anyway.'

'This bird takes chances?' said Hemingway scornfully. 'I fancy I see him! Supposing Miss White had come up to the house for brandy, or bandages, or something, and had run into him carrying that ironmongery? She might easily have done it.'

'Well, if it comes to that, how was he going to explain himself to Miss White, if he'd run into her *without* his gadgets?'

'Easy!' said the Sergeant promptly. 'He could have pitched a tale about hearing someone in the shrubbery, and running after him. You bet he had all that planned!'

'Then you say he hid the vice, and whatever else it was, down a rabbit-hole, or some such place?'

'What was wrong with that pool I saw?' inquired Hemingway. 'It seems to me that if he had to dispose of something in a hurry, the pool was the quickest and the safest place. All he had to do was to climb that sandy bank, heave his gadgets into the pool, and be off up to the house to put through those telephone-calls.'

'What about the splash?' suggested Cook. 'I grant you they might not have heard it on the bridge, seeing that it's round the bend, and a bit of a distance off, but wouldn't you have expected Miss Fanshawe, or that dog of hers, to have heard it?'

'That's where White was luckier than he knew,'

answered Hemingway. 'Five minutes earlier, Miss Fanshawe was down by the stream, and would have seen the whole thing. But she told me that after she heard the shot, she turned into one of the paths leading up the slope. Now, I reckon that between the firing of the rifle, and White's heaving the vice and what-not into the pool (if that's what he did do) must have been all of five minutes, and very likely more. Miss Fanshawe would be out of earshot by that time, or if not absolutely out of earshot, far enough away for a splash not to catch her attention.'

'Yes, and supposing all this did happen like you say, sir,' put in the Sergeant. 'White's had plenty of time to fish his gadgets out of that pool, and dispose of them for good and all.'

'Time, yes, if he'd thought it necessary, which he probably didn't. But there's one thing you're forgetting: it's muddy down by the water, and Mr White couldn't get anything out of the pool without leaving some nice, deep footprints. What's more, it 'ud be a pretty risky thing for him to go wading about in the pool when at any moment someone might have seen him from the Palings' side. No, if he threw his apparatus into the pool, it's there still, and that's where we'll find it.'

Half an hour later, two constables, with their trousers rolled well above their knees, were painfully stubbing their toes on all the foreign bodies sunk into the mud at the bottom of the pool. When the police-party had arrived at the Dower House, only Florence, the maid, had been in, and she had raised no objection to the Inspector's pursuing investigations in the shrubbery. As long as he didn't come getting in her way, she said, with a sniff, she was sure he could do as he pleased, for it was no concern of hers.

The first haul taken from the bed of the pool was

disappointing. It consisted of two glass jam jars, and something that looked like the handle of a saucepan. Then the younger of the two constables cut his foot on a broken plate, and swore loudly; and, a moment later, his companion bent, and plunged his arm into the water, and pulled out something that had been half sunk in the mud. 'I've got it, sir!' he exclaimed. 'It's a vice, sure enough!'

He waded to the bank, and handed his find to Hemingway. Hemingway betrayed not the smallest sign either of surprise or of gratification, but his Sergeant was visibly impressed, and regarded him with a good deal of awe. 'My word, sir, you were right all along!' he said. 'Well, I wouldn't have credited it!'

'I'm always right,' said Hemingway superbly. 'Keep going, Jupp! You'll find something more, or I'm a Dutchman.'

'It wouldn't be a sardine-tin, would it, sir?' inquired Jupp, with a grin. 'Fisher's just cut his toe on one.'

'You stop larking about, and get on with it!' ordered the Inspector, somewhat unfairly. 'Come on, Cook, we'll see how this fits those grazes on the sapling.'

Both Inspectors were recalled presently by the sound of tumult by the pool. They hurried up the sandy bank, and found that the cocker-spaniel, Prince, discovering strangers in a pool which he regarded as his own, had plunged into the water, not, indeed, to evict the interlopers, but to join them in aquatic sports. He bore with him a large stick, a circumstance which induced Hemingway to shout out: 'Never mind about playing with that dog! Get on with it!'

'We're not playing with the brute, sir!' called Fisher, stung into a retort. 'We're trying to shoo it off!'

'You leave it alone, and it won't do you any harm!' said Hemingway. 'You're only exciting it, waving your arms about like that. Here, come here! Good dog, bring it here, then!'

'Well, well, well!' said a voice from the farther bank. 'What's this? A regatta?'

'Oh, it's you, is it, sir?' said the Inspector, casting an unfavourable eye over Mr Hugh Dering. 'Well, perhaps you'll call your dog off, since you happen to be here.'

'Nothing,' said Hugh, visibly enjoying the sight of the constables wrestling with Prince's advances, 'would give me greater pleasure, if he were my dog. But he isn't.'

Vicky's Borzoi bounded into view at this moment, and at once began to bark at the strangers. The two constables showed a marked disposition to leave the pool in haste, but Hugh grasped the Borzoi by the collar, and told him to be quiet. The Inspector began to explain, as tactfully as he could, that neither Hugh's nor the dogs' presence was in any way necessary to him, but before he had succeeded in making this clear to Mr Hugh Dering, who was suddenly and unaccountably slow of understanding, Vicky had appeared upon the scene – a demure Vicky, in white organdie with black ribbons.

'Oh, I shouldn't paddle there!' Vicky said, quite distressed. 'It's a very muddy, dirty kind of a pond. My mother never used to let me go in it.'

'Miss, will you call your dog off?' begged Fisher, against whose legs the spaniel was thrusting his stick.

'Do you mind frightfully if I don't?' said Vicky. 'He's bound to shake himself all over me, you see, and I don't much want him to.'

Hugh, who had been interestedly surveying the treasures collected from the bosom of the pool, took pity on the police. 'All right, I'll rescue you,' he said. 'Stand clear, Vicky! Come here, Prince! Bring it!'

The spaniel, hopeful of finding a more willing playmate, left the pool, laid his stick at Hugh's feet, and shook himself generously over Hugh's trousers. Hugh knotted his handkerchief through the dog's collar, and bade Vicky remove him from the scene.

'Yes, but I want to watch what they're doing!' Vicky demurred.

'No, go up to the house,' Hugh said. 'I'll join you later – when I've discovered what all this is about.'

'Not even a fusty lawyer can just carelessly fling orders at me,' said Vicky, as one imparting valuable information.

'That's all right, ducky: you can play at being the child-wife married to a drunken bully,' suggested Hugh.

This immediately caught Vicky's ever-lively imagination. 'Yes, or a Roman slave.'

'Or a Roman slave,' agreed hugh, giving the end of the hankerchief into her hold.

From the opposite side of the pool, Inspector Hemingway watched Miss Fanshawe's departure with undisguised relief. When, however, he saw that Mr Hugh Dering, instead of accompanying her, was walking on towards a point where the stream could be jumped, his satisfaction waned swiftly. He called: 'Now, look here, sir, I'm busy, and I can't have you messing about here now!'

Hugh cleared the stream, and walked towards him. 'Can't you?' he said. 'Well, of course, if you won't have me on this side of the stream, I'll go back and watch you from the other side. I dare say Miss Fanshawe and her mother would like to come and watch, too, though of course I can't promise that they won't bring the dogs with them.'

Sergeant Wake bent a shocked stare upon him. Hemingway said: 'Oh! Nice state of affairs, I must say, if the police are to be blackmailed by gentlemen of your profession, sir! Now, you know very well you've no right to come meddling here!'

'Don't worry, I won't meddle. But all this earnest

search leads me to suppose that new and startling evidence has cropped up. Moreover, you are holding in your hand, Inspector, something that bears all the appearance of a vice. From which I deduce that, contrary to expectations, the rifle found here was not fired by hand. Correct me if I'm wrong, my dear Watson.'

Hemingway shook his head. 'Yes, you're wasted at the Chancery Bar: I can see that,' he said. 'All the same – '

'Hold!' said Hugh. 'These things being as they are, I am further led to suppose that you are about to lay bare evidence which will clear the fair name of the lady to whom I am shortly to be joined in holy matrimony. I contend that this gives me a right to be here.'

'Oh, so that's been fixed up, has it?' said Hemingway. 'Well, I'm sure I hope you'll be very happy, sir. I've been expecting to hear of it ever since I came down to these parts.'

'When you first came here I hadn't the slightest intention of getting married,' said Hugh. 'However, don't let me spoil your good story.'

'I won't,' said the Inspector. 'What you don't grasp, sir, is that if there is one thing I've got, it's intuition. Besides, it's been standing out a mile. But as for your having any right to be here, that's another matter. Still, I can see that Inspector Cook wants me to let you stay, so I suppose you'll have to.'

'I never!' Cook exclaimed, taken by surprise. 'Why, I never said a word!'

'Well, if you don't want me to let him stay rather than have a couple of women and two dogs getting in the way, I've been mistaken in you,' said Hemingway. 'What's more, he knows too much already.'

'Hair-trigger,' said Hugh. 'You might almost call me your good angel. Hallo, one of your henchmen has caught a fish!'

The Inspector turned, as Jupp came to the edge of the pool, holding an odd-looking object in his hand.

'Would this be what you're after, sir?'

The Inspector took it. 'Yes,' he said. 'Yes, it might be. At any rate, it didn't grow in the pool. Know anything about these things, sir?'

'About as much as the next man,' Hugh replied. 'I know it's an electro-magnet. I don't immediately see the connection between it and the rifle, though. Do you?'

Hemingway shook his head. 'I'm bound to say I haven't figured it out. You know a bit about electrical gadgets, Wake: could you fire a rifle with this?'

'No,' replied the Sergeant. 'I don't see any sense to it. Even when you pass current through it, it wouldn't have any effect on the rifle-trigger. Couldn't have.'

'Well, go on searching,' said Hemingway waving Jupp back to the pool. 'Maybe you'll find something more. Though I've got a hunch this did the trick.'

He stood for a few moments, silently, and rather abstractedly, watching the two constables, while his Sergeant frowned upon the electro-magnet.

'No,' said Wake at last. 'Look at it which way you will, you can't fit an electro-magnet into it. It wouldn't work, and that's all there is to it.'

Hemingway lifted his head quickly. 'Magnet!' he said.

'It sounds like "Eureka!"' remarked Hugh.

'It is Eureka,' said the Inspector. 'Now, don't you start asking me a whole lot of questions I can't possibly answer, sir! If I'm right, you'll know all in good time. All I want you to do now is to keep a still tongue in your head, which I'm sure you will do. All right, you two! That'll do!'

Twenty minutes later, in Fritton again, the Inspector produced from a drawer in his desk the magnet he had found in the shrubbery at the Dower House, and bade

Sergeant Wake tell him what effect on it an electro-magnet would have.

'It would attract it, of course,' Wake replied. 'Soon as you switched the current on. You mean, somehow or other it was fixed so that when it jumped to the electro-magnet, it caught the trigger?'

'Good Lord!' said Cook blankly. 'Could that have been done? I never heard of such a thing!'

'What we want to go in for now, is a bit of experiment,' said Hemingway. 'We'll rig that rifle up in the vice, and see how it could be made to work.'

By the time the rifle had been produced, and the vice clamped to the leg of a stout table, Hemingway had discovered an additional reason for the position of the grazes on the sapling. 'I get it!' he said. 'It had to be close to the ground, to get the trigger on the same level as the electro-magnet. Now, if the two arms of the horseshoe magnet had to point towards the electro-magnet, that must have been just behind the trigger, about like that. Come on, Wake! How would you manage to get the horseshoe magnet so that there's nothing to prevent its moving, and so that it's bound to pull that trigger as soon as it does move?'

'Well, it's got to rest on something. Couple of blocks of wood, perhaps.'

'That's it,' said Hemingway. 'Easily kicked away when finished with. Books will be good enough for us. Hand me down a few!'

Kneeling on the floor he carefully built up his two little platforms, one on each side of the trigger-guard of the rifle, and close enough together to allow of the horseshoe magnet's arms resting one on each platform. The magnet he placed so that the round end was within the trigger-guard, and in front of the trigger itself, and the magnet-ized ends pointing towards the electro-magnet placed under the stock of the rifle. While Sergeant Wake busied himself with a length of flex and a wall-plug, Hemingway tried to cock the rifle. After several abortive attempts, he sat back on his heels and eyed the rifle with dislike. 'It's no use: the damned thing won't cock!' he said. 'It goes off the moment you close the bolt. Now, how did he work that trick?'

'The bent's been filed down so fine that the searnose won't catch,' said Cook. 'I've got a brother in the gun-trade, and I've seen these things stripped. The bent was filed down to give it that light pull. He'd have had to load it with the trigger pulled back. Let me try it, will you, Inspector? I've got an idea how to cock it.'

Hemingway said: 'Go right ahead! If you can close the bolt without the blooming thing's going off, you're softer-handed than I am.'

'You don't need to touch the bolt to cock the rifle,' said Cook. 'I'll lay my life White didn't. You want to get hold of the cocking-piece, behind the bolt – this thing – and pull it gently back like this, until the nose of the sear – that's the piece which the top end of the trigger acts on – the bit that holds the firing-block back – catches in the bent. It won't do more than just catch, and you don't want to jog the gun, because it only needs a touch to set it off.'

Hemingway, who had been watching Cook suit his actions to his words, drew back as Cook cautiously released the cocking-pin. 'Jog it! I'm taking precious good care not to breathe on it. Why haven't I got a brother in the gun-trade? The silly fellow travels in some kind of patent baby-food. A lot of use that's ever been to me, or likely to be! You got that fixed up yet, Wake?'

Wake, who had been attaching one end of the flex to the electro-magnet, rose to his feet. 'All set, sir. Shall I switch on?'

'The sooner the better: the suspense is killing me,' said Hemingway.

Wake moved across to the wall-plug, and turned the switch on it. The horseshoe magnet shot forward, towards the electro-magnet, the closed end hitting the trigger, and so releasing the mainspring.

'And that,' said Hemingway, as the rifle clicked, 'is that, gentlemen! I said it was a pleasure to deal with Mr Harold White!'

'I'll have to say it's been a pleasure to *see* you deal with him, sir,' said Wake, making amends for past scepticism. 'I don't mind admitting I thought you were on to a wild-goose chase this time.'

Inspector Cook got up from the floor. 'Yes, but there's something that's bothering me,' he said. 'They're not wired for electricity at the Dower House.'

Hemingway looked at him in pardonable annoyance. 'I never met such a set of kill-joys! Are you sure of that?'

'Yes, I'm quite sure. They make their own electricity at Palings, but Mrs Carter never had the Dower House wired. They use oil-lamps.'

'Well, that has torn it!' said Wake. 'Surely to goodness they couldn't have run a flex to the electro-magnet all the way from Palings!'

'Talk sense!' snapped Hemingway. 'Run a flex from Palings! Yes, over the lawn, and down through the shrubbery, and across the stream, and up the other bank! I wonder if they laid it under ground, or had it fixed up on poles?'

'Well, I said surely they couldn't have!' protested the Sergeant.

'They couldn't have, and what's more there wasn't any point to it, even if it had been possible. What's the whole aim and object of firing a gun by means of a contraption like that?'

'To provide yourself with a water-tight alibi,' replied Wake.

'You're right. And what kind of an alibi had any of that Palings lot provided themselves with? Or Mr Silent Steel? Or his High and Mightiness Prince Tiddly-Push? Or young Baker? Who had the only alibi that was so good no one but me thought of trying to bust it?'

'Yes, it does look like White,' said Cook. 'Don't think it's any pleasure to me to have to say the Dower House isn't wired!'

'It not only looks like White; it was White,' said Hemingway. 'It couldn't have been anyone else.'

'No, but there's another point as well, though I dare say it doesn't mean so much,' said Wake. 'How did he get the rifle in the first place?'

'I don't know, but if you go and ask them up at Palings, they'll tell you anyone could have taken it.'

'Yes, that's what they say,' persisted Wake, 'but, come to think of it, it isn't quite as easy as that to walk off with a life-size rifle under your arm. Why, even supposing you had the run of the house, would you take a chance on it? Supposing someone was looking out of one of the windows? Supposing you ran into the butler, or a gardener, or someone? Of course, as soon as you started on White, I got to thinking about him returning Mr Carter's shot-gun in a case of his own, but that's no use, because the rifle wouldn't go into a shot-gun case.'

Hemingway turned his head to look at the rifle, still held in the vice. 'If I was to find that the fair Ermyntrude was right all along, I don't know that I could bear it,' he said slowly. '*Can* you break a rifle?'

'What, like you do a shot-gun?' said Cook. 'No, they're made differently. You can't break any I've ever handled.'

'Well, let's have a look at this one,' said Hemingway. 'Give it here, will you, Wake?'

The Sergeant loosened the vice, and handed over the rifle. Hemingway inspected it. 'I must say it doesn't look as though you could. What are these little eyebolts for?'

Cook peered over his shoulder. 'They're only to fix a sling on to, if you should want one, aren't they?'

'I can't say, but I believe in trying things out,' replied Hemingway, laying the gun on his desk, and beginning to loosen the bolts.

He removed them in a moment or two, and then, with the air of a conjurer sure of his trick, quietly lifted the barrel out of the stock. 'As easy as falling off a gate,' he said. 'Now we know why he chose the Mannlicher-Schönauer instead of that classy-looking Rigby. I dare say that doesn't come apart anything like as neatly, if at all. Measure that barrel, Wake – not that I doubt it could have got into the hambone-case.'

'Twenty-eight inches over all,' Wake announced, closing his foot-rule. 'My word, the evidence is piling up, isn't it? But we still haven't got round the main difficulty, sir – though it looks to me as though we will, the way things are shaping.'

Hemingway gave him the rifle to fit together again, and sat down at his desk. 'Some kind of a battery,' he said. 'Inside the study window, with a flex running from it to the electro-magnet.'

'Could it? Without being noticed?' asked Wake.

'Yes, easy, it could,' said Cook. 'There's a flower-bed running along the wall of the house, and creepers on the house, too. You'd never see the wire. He could have laid it along the bed till he got to the corner of the house, and then taken it across the bit of path lying between the house and the top end of the shrubbery. He might have sprinkled a bit of gravel over it just there, though I shouldn't think it would have been necessary myself. Then, all he had to do, once he'd got rid of the vice, and the electro-magnet, was to run back to the house, coiling up the wire as he went.'

Hemingway, who had not been paying much attention to this speech, suddenly said: 'Didn't you tell me White had got something to do with a coal-mine?'

'That's right,' said Cook. 'He's manager of the Copley group.'

'I thought so. What's that thing called that they use in mines when they want to blast? Electrical thing they touch off the dynamite with?'

'A shot-firer, do you mean?' asked Wake. 'But they don't blast in coal-mines, do they?'

'By gum, you've got it!' said Cook. 'They do do quite a bit of blasting here, because we're remarkably free from gas, as it happens! He could have got hold of one, too, without a bit of trouble, in his position.'

'Don't they check up on those kinds of stores?' asked Wake.

'Yes, but, don't you see? The murder was committed on a Sunday. White could have brought the shot-firer away with him on Saturday, and returned it to store on the Monday morning, and no one the wiser!'

'Would it work?' Hemingway demanded.

'Yes, work a fair treat. Ever seen 'em use one? All you do is push the handle down smartly, and the next thing you know is that half the rock-face has fallen off.'

The Sergeant bent, and picked up the horseshoe magnet. 'Funny he left this lying about for us to find,' he said. 'I must say, I can't understand him not slipping it in his pocket, so careful as he was about everything else.'

'Yes, but it wouldn't have been lying there like that,' Cook pointed out. 'You only turned the current off long after the recoil of the rifle. You've got to remember that White pushed down the handle of his shot-firer, and then released it. The jar of the rifle's going off must have hurled the magnet away, once there was no strong attraction to hold it in its position.'

'It did,' said Hemingway. 'I found it under some leaves, several feet from the sapling. White couldn't risk hanging about to hunt for it. I dare say he didn't even think it was so very necessary, either. Even if we did start hunting around, it wouldn't convey much to us. I'm bound to say it didn't.' He glanced at his watch. 'Who has charge of shot-firers, and the like? A storekeeper? Know who he is, and where he lives?'

'I can find out for you in less than no time,' said Cook.

'Thanks, if you'd do that, and let Wake know, he can go off and put in a bit of work interviewing the fellow,' said Hemingway. 'Not but what we've got enough on White, without that, to justify my applying for a warrant to arrest him. Still, we must tie up every end, if we can.'

Rather more than an hour later his Sergeant returned to him, in a mood of quiet triumph. 'We've tied the last end, sir,' he announced. 'They had one of the shot-firers repaired last week, and it came back from the repair-shop last thing on Saturday morning, after the storekeeper had gone off duty. He told me Mr White was the last off the premises, and that he'd put the shot-firer away somewhere in his office. Said he was sure of that, because White was a bit late on Monday morning, and the shot-firer couldn't be found.'

'And then White turned up, and said it was in his office?'

'That's right, sir. Turned up with a biggish sort of attaché-case, went straight into his office, and brought the shot-firer out. I reckon that settles it. You ought to feel proud of the way you've handled this case, sir. I know I would be. Because at one time it really did seem as though there wasn't what you'd call a good reason for suspecting anybody.'

The Inspector was secretly gratified by this tribute, but he replied with a mournful shake of his head: 'Yes, but there's always something to take the edge off for one. When I think about that silly widow sticking to it against all reason it was White that killed her husband, and being proved right, it quite makes me lose heart. And when I think of the way she'll pat herself on the back – ! Well, there! it doesn't bear thinking of, and that's all that there is to it. She's probably telling her family how her instinct shows her it must have been White, right at this moment.'

But, as it happened, Wally's murder was not just then paramount in Ermyntrude's mind. Her daughter's engagement had cast every other consideration into the background. It was, she said, the most delightful surprise of her life, and made up for everything. 'I couldn't have wished for better!' she told Mary. 'Of course, I don't say I haven't thought of an Earl, or at any rate a Viscount for her, but you can't absolutely bank on getting a peer, can you, dearie? And the Derings are county: there's no getting away from that! What's more, he's very nice, Hugh is, and not a bit up-stage with me, like an Earl might be. Fancy, though! I'd quite made up my mind it was you he was after! Well, I must say, you could have knocked me down with a feather! It's to be hoped I don't get any more shocks today, for really the excitement of this has made me feel quite exhausted!'

She was to have yet another. Shortly after dinner Dr Chester was announced, and came into the drawing-room looking rather grim.

'Well, and what little bird can have told you the news?' exclaimed Ermyntrude. 'If it isn't like you, Maurice, to be the first to come and congratulate. Well, I do think it's sweet of you!'

'Congratulate?' he repeated. 'What news are you talking about?'

'But, Maurice! Vicky and Hugh!' Ermyntrude said.

His brow seemed to lighten. 'Vicky and Hugh! No, really? Yes, of course I congratulate you both, most heartily!'

Hugh, who had stayed to dine at Palings, shook hands with him. 'Thanks. But I think you've got some rather different news, haven't you?'

'You know, then?' Chester said.

'No. I've an inkling, though, since I encountered Inspector Hemingway this afternoon.'

'They've arrested White,' Chester said.

'Arrested White?' Mary gasped. 'But why? On what conceivable grounds?'

'I don't know. Alan rang me up to come and attend to Janet, who was in hysterics. I came straight on here, to let you know.'

'I knew it!' Ermyntrude said, fulfilling the Inspector's prophecy. 'All along I said it was that White, though not one of you would listen to me! A woman's instinct is never wrong!'

'Oh, how awful for Janet and Alan!' Mary said. 'Is there anything we can do?'

'Not at the moment. I've given Janet a sedative, and told Alan not to let her get agitated. I hope – '

Ermyntrude arose suddenly from the sofa. 'Told Alan!' she said scornfully. 'Yes, I see him keeping himself quiet, let alone anyone else! The idea of your leaving the poor girl with only Alan and that blowsy, good-for-nothing maid of theirs! Well, I thought you'd have more sense, Maurice, I must say! Why didn't you bundle her into your car, and bring her straight up here, and that silly, feckless brother of hers as well, for heaven knows what he mayn't do, left to himself!'

'Bring them *here*?' repeated Chester, for once in his life startled.

'Where else are they to go?' demanded Ermyntrude. 'It seems to me you men never think of anything! Why, there'll be reporters swarming all over the Dower House by tomorrow, if not before! Enough to drive Janet out of her mind, for she hasn't any sense at the best of times. Vicky, love, go and ring up Johnson, and tell him to bring the big car round at once, will you?'

'But, Ermyntrude, wait!' said Chester. 'Are you quite sure you know what you're doing? The situation's rather difficult, isn't it? If White killed Wally – '

'Now, don't stand there talking far-fetched nonsense to me, Maurice!' said Ermyntrude. 'I never yet found any difficulty in doing my duty as a Christian, and I hope I never shall! What's more, I'm a mother, and leave even a tiresome, chattering girl like Janet alone at such a time I tell you plainly I couldn't reconcile it with my conscience to do! Now, that's quite enough arguing! Mary, you'll see to the bedrooms, won't you, dearie?'

'Yes, Aunt Ermy,' said Mary, meekly following her into the hall.

Ermyntrude sailed upstairs to put on a wrap for the journey to the Dower House, but Mary was overtaken, with her hand already on the baluster-rail, by Dr Chester. He put his hand over hers, and clasped it. 'Mary, that engagement!'

She found herself unable to meet his eyes. 'Yes, were you surprised? I was the only person who knew it was blowing up.'

'Mary, look at me! I thought – I could have sworn – ' He broke off, as though he did not know how to go on.

She did look up, but very fleetingly. 'That it was going to be me?'

'Yes,' he said bluntly.

'Well, so did I, at one time. Not that I had any real

reason to, and as a matter of fact it wouldn't have done at all. Hugh's a dear, but he's not my type, and I'm not his.'

His clasp on her hand tightened. 'Mary, is that the truth? I thought – And he's so much nearer you in age, that I made sure – '

'Maurice,' interrupted Mary, crimson-cheeked, 'wasn't it Aunt Ermy with you – ever?'

'Ermyntrude? Good God, no! Mary, this isn't the moment to ask you, but could you possibly – is there the slightest hope – '

'Oh, Maurice, I think I must always have – Oh, look out, here she is!'

'And a nice hot-water bottle in Janet's bed, Mary dear, don't forget!' said Ermyntrude, coming downstairs again. 'I always say there's nothing like a hot-water bottle for real comfort when you're in trouble.'